PRAISE FOR *THE DEVIL WEARS BLACK*

"A deliciously seductive second chance romance novel."

—*POPSUGAR*; selected as one of the
10 Best New Romance Books of March 2021

"Fake-fiancé tropes for the win!"

—*Marie Claire*; selected as one of the
Best New Romance Novels of 2021 (So Far)

"An expert at the dark and sexy antihero, Shen brings her seductive prose to an irresistible 'second chance romance.'"

—OprahMag.com

"[*The Devil Wears Black*] sparkles with wit and chemistry . . . This is a treat."

—*Publishers Weekly*

"Shen has created believable character arcs for her captivating protagonists, and the plot provides a terrifically smart twist on the fake-fiancé trope. Fans of Jennifer Weiner may enjoy this sexy contemporary romance."

—*Booklist*

PRAISE FOR *RUTHLESS RIVAL*

"This addictive enemies-to-lovers romance . . . captures both characters' intense emotions and undeniable chemistry. It's sure to have readers hooked."

—*Publishers Weekly*

BEAUTIFUL
GRAVES

OTHER TITLES BY L.J. SHEN

Sinners of Saint Series

Vicious
Defy
Ruckus
Scandalous
Bane

All Saints High Series

Pretty Reckless
Broken Knight
Angry God

Boston Belles Series

The Hunter
The Villain
The Monster
The Rake

Cruel Castaways

Ruthless Rivals

Stand-Alones

Tyed
Sparrow
Blood to Dust
Midnight Blue
Dirty Headlines
The Kiss Thief
In the Unlikely Event
Playing with Fire
The Devil Wears Black
Bad Cruz

BEAUTIFUL GRAVES

L.J. SHEN

Text copyright © 2022 by L.J. Shen
All rights reserved.

No part of this book may be reproduced, or stored in a retrieval system, or transmitted in any form or by any means, electronic, mechanical, photocopying, recording, or otherwise, without express written permission of the publisher.

Published by Montlake, Seattle

www.apub.com

Amazon, the Amazon logo, and Montlake are trademarks of Amazon.com, Inc., or its affiliates.

ISBN-13: 9781542036337
ISBN-10: 154203633X

Cover design by Caroline Teagle Johnson

The things that we love tell us what we are.
—*Saint Thomas Aquinas*

Hope is a waking dream.
—*Aristotle*

PLAYLIST

- Duran Duran—"Save a Prayer"
- Oasis—"Don't Look Back in Anger"
- Annie Lennox—"No More 'I Love You's'"
- Dubstar—"Stars"
- The Hollies—"The Air That I Breathe"
- Goldfinger—"Put the Knife Away"

PROLOGUE

This is not how I imagined I'd enter this church.

Wearing a black garment, my eyes sunken, my lips chapped.

The only thing roiling in my stomach right now is a lukewarm cup of coffee I gulped in one go to wash down the Valium.

Despite everyone I know being here, supporting me, I know it doesn't matter. The thing about tragedies is, you can never outrun the Big Alone. At some point, it catches up with you. In the middle of the night. When you're taking a hasty shower. When you roll in bed and the linen is pressed and smooth where your lover should be.

The big moments in your life are always experienced in solitude.

But I'm not ready to say goodbye.

"You don't have to stay for the burial," Dad, practical and to the point, tells me. We pass by people. I keep my gaze firmly on the church's doors, refusing eye contact. "They'll understand. You're going through hell right now."

Maybe it's wrong not to care what people think, but I genuinely don't. I'm not going to be here when the casket is lowered to the ground. I'll be long gone before everyone falls apart. Before it becomes real. Maybe it makes me a coward, but I just can't take it. Another premature goodbye.

"I bet he'll have a beautiful grave." I hear my own voice. It rises from the pit of my stomach, like bile. "Everything about him is beautiful."

"Was," a voice behind me corrects.

I don't need to turn around to know who it belongs to.

It's the man who holds the other piece of my heart.

And that's it—I can't take it anymore. Two feet from the church's doors, I sink to my knees, drop my head, and begin to cry. Mourners around me murmur in hushed voices. *Poor child* and *Not her first tragedy* and *What is she going to do now?*

They're not wrong. I have no idea what I'll do. Because even in the best of times, I've always been torn.

Between the man I am about to bury.

And the man standing behind my back.

PART 1

ONE

Eighteen.

It starts with a dare on La Rambla Street.

With my best friend's callous attempt to catch some guy's attention.

"You're killing yourself, bro."

Pippa reaches for a cigarette clasped inside his mouth. She withdraws it from his lips and snaps it in two.

It's our first hour in Barcelona, and already she is looking for creative ways to get us both killed.

"Here. You're welcome. Just saved you from cancer." With a toss of her ombré hair, she slips past the sliding doors of a pharmacy, leaving the guy to stand there.

"Sorry. We forgot to pack her manners." I yank my earphones out of my ears, muttering to the smoker on the curb.

This is what we do, Pippa and I. She starts fires; I put them out. She runs hot and messy; I'm as emotionless as an ice statue at a royal wedding. She could get it on with a lamppost, and I . . . well, I still suspect I might be asexual, despite (or maybe *because* of?) losing my virginity a couple of months ago.

Pippa and I go way back. We met on the first day of kindergarten and fought over the same sorting cube (which, legend says, she bashed my head with). We've been inseparable ever since.

I'm the macabre, army-booted goth girl to her shining, Technicolor Ariana Grande self.

We went to the same elementary school, same middle school, same high school, and same summer camps.

Now, Pippa and I are both enrolled in UC Berkeley.

It was Pippa's idea to go to Spain for two weeks. A last hurrah before we start school. She is half-Spanish from her mother's side, and one of her aunts, Alma, lives in Barcelona, which means a free place for us to crash.

"Let's make a new rule." I adjust my backpack over one shoulder as we dip below the green, glowing FARMACIA: 24 HORAS sign. "No more aggravating the locals. If your ass gets in a street fight, I'm going to walk past and pretend I don't know you."

That's a lie. I'd take a bullet for her. It's just that I would strongly prefer not to.

"Please." Pippa snorts, picking up a green basket on her way to the personal-hygiene section. "We have two weeks to let our crazy hang out before we get back to reality. College is serious business, Lawson. Now's *exactly* the time to get in a street fight. Especially with a hottie like that dude."

She tosses shampoo, conditioner, toothpaste, and two toothbrushes into our basket. I add Tylenol, sunscreen, and body lotion. Neither of us wanted to pack anything that could detonate in our suitcases.

Pippa stops in the middle of the aisle with shaving supplies. "Do you think they sell Plan B over the counter here?"

"Why? Are you planning on having unprotected sex with a rando?" I ask.

"Your girl is curious, okay? Nobody said anything about taking it." She shrugs, then grabs my hand and tugs me to the next aisle. I'm aware we're about five decibels louder than everyone else in the store. It's not empty either. There's an elderly couple talking to the pharmacist, a pregnant lady squinting at a laxative bottle, and a bunch of guys in soccer uniforms checking out jock itch creams.

She stops by what we refer to as the Sexy Time aisle. Pippa runs a flame-tipped stiletto fingernail over different products.

"Don't forget to buy condoms." I nibble on my black nail polish, desperate to get out of here. I want to throw myself into her aunt's shower and wash away the twelve-hour flight, then decompress. "You know, just in case you change your mind about bringing back chlamydia as a souvenir."

"Chlamydia is a lame souvenir." Pippa swings her gaze my way, grinning. "We need a *real* souvenir. We're getting tatted here."

"*You're* getting tatted here," I correct. "I'm not."

"Why? It's not like you have a fear of needles." She eyeballs my septum ring, popping an eyebrow.

I tuck it inside my nose. "Piercings are fine. Tattoos mean commitment, and I don't do that. Might I remind you, I can't even commit to a cereal?"

"You so *are* committed to a cereal," she huffs. "Reese's Puffs."

"As enamored as I am with Reese's Puffs, I'm always happy to destroy a bowl of Frosted Flakes and Apple Jacks."

"Apple Jacks." She shudders. "Sometimes I think you're beyond help. Anyway, you have to get a tat. Your mom's going to be hella proud if you take the plunge."

"I'll bear the burden of disappointing her."

Pippa is not wrong, though. Barbara "Barbie" Lawson would be totally down if I told her I was getting a full-fledged arm sleeve. She herself inked the majority of her back, calves, and wrists. Quotes that are dear to her heart. *Tattoos are like putting wallpaper on a generically painted house*, she always says.

Born in Liverpool, England, Mom ran away to San Francisco when she was sixteen. She is not your typical mother. It's why I love her not only as a parent but also as a human.

"Ever." Pippa stomps. Everlynne is my name. But let's be real: life's too short. "C'mon."

I use both my index fingers to do the sign of a cross, like she's a vampire.

"Ugh, fine!" Pippa throws her arms in the air before plucking a pack of condoms. "No tats, but I'm going to corrupt you. I'm staging an intervention. Everlynne Bellatrix Lawson, you've been a bad, bad girl. And by bad, I mean good. Super good. *Nauseatingly* good. We're Gen Z! Screwing up is in our DNA, okay? We grew up on social media and the Kardashians."

"I'm screwing up plenty without screwing anyone," I say, though we both know it's not true. As far as rebellious acts go, I'm aggressively boring.

"I'll drop the tattoo business if you promise you use one of these puppies during our two-week trip." She is waving the condoms. I'm about to combust into miniscule pieces of embarrassment. The only thing stopping me from doing so is I'd hate to make a mess here on top of causing a scene.

A chuckle comes from the aisle next to us. We have an audience. *Yippee ki-yay.*

"I'm *not* a virgin." I snatch the condoms, then shove them into the bowels of the basket under the tampons and toothpaste.

"Well, it was with Sean Dunham, so does it even count?" Pippa quips.

A snort comes drifting toward us, but I can't see who the person is because there's a wall of condom packs blocking the way. Talking in English really sucks. No matter where you are in the world, everyone knows what you're saying.

"Hey! We went all the way."

"More like crawled there. It was so underwhelming. And you broke up half a second after," Pippa counters.

Accurate. Disturbingly accurate. I can't argue with that.

"What if I don't like anybody?" I fold my arms over my chest.

"You never do," she sighs. "I'm not counting on you falling in love here. Just do it for the pleasure."

The person on the other side of the aisle is full-blown laughing now. The voice definitely belongs to a male. Low and gruff.

Would you like some butter on your popcorn, my dude?

"You need to learn how to be a team player, Ever. That's your exercise for this trip. Finding pleasure with a total stranger. No consequences. No relationship. Just a hookup in a foreign country."

Positive the person on the other side of the aisle has heard enough about my sex life (or lack of), I turn to Pippa with a death glare.

"I'm not having sex with a stranger."

"Yes, you are."

"No, I'm not."

"Then I'll just have to bug you to get a tattoo with me."

Tired with her antics, I groan. "Whatever. I'll use one. Go find us some snacks. I need to make a call."

"If it's Barbie you're calling for emotional support, don't bother. She'll side with me, and you know it." Pippa flutters away like a fairy, leaving stardust of giggles in her wake.

I produce my phone from my backpack and wait for the reception bars to appear.

I call Mom. She picks up on the first ring, even though it's gazillion o'clock or whatever in California.

"Ever!" she coos. "How's Barcelona?"

"Been here for a little less than an hour, and Pippa has already tried to pick a fight with a local, bought condoms, and tried to convince me to get a tattoo."

"And I'm guessing you're horrified by the entire thing?" There's a smile in Mom's voice.

"Gee, Mom, it's like we know each other."

"Well, then. All is normal in the land of Pipper." *Pippa and Ever.* I love that she gave us a shipping name. Barbie Lawson is a supremely cool mom.

"I already miss you." I dig my teeth into my lower lip.

"Actually." She chuckles. "The reason I'm awake is because I'm going through old photo albums of yours. I can't believe my baby is across the ocean, in Europe, on a girls' trip."

Ugh. I'm not going to cry in the Sexy Time aisle. I'm not.

"Yeah, neither can I. Gotta go now, Mom. I love you."

"Same, to the moon and back."

I end the call and am about to tuck my phone back into my back pocket.

A shadow looms over my frame, blocking the entrance to the passageway. I glance up. It's Smoker Dude from the street. Pippa is right. He *is* kind of hot. In a nonobvious way. He seems tailored to my taste. Drawn in sharp strokes of coal, like a manga character. He is tall, more than conventionally attractive, and lean. His posture mimics that of a wilted sunflower. Head tilted down, like he is struggling to hear normal-height people. He has dark-blue eyes and a square jaw and a nose that is a little too long and pointy. The averageness of his nose gives his otherwise-flawless features more room to shine. It's nature's final stroke of genius, making him both attractive and relatable.

"Water balloons," he deadpans, in an American accent.

"Um, what?"

He jerks his head toward the condom shelf. *Right.* Pippa's insane demand that I use at least one condom.

"Fill it up, smash it over her head."

"That's mean," I say.

"Mean? No. Fair? Yes."

"Can't do water balloons." I untuck my septum ring from my nose. "That's cheating."

I want him to see the ring. I'm not sure *why* I want him to see it. Maybe because he is wearing a faded pair of Levi's folded at the ankles and worn-out Chucks. Or maybe because his tousled dark hair and *Anti Social Social Club: Applicant Need Not Apply* tee call to me, the way a stranger reading your favorite book on the train calls to you.

"I didn't realize we were playing on high moral ground here." His face breaks into a haywire smile. Something inside me melts. It's warm and gooey and settles in my stomach. *Jesus.* No wonder Pippa is obsessed with guys. This feels like getting on a Six Flags roller coaster after stuffing your face with a superburrito.

I'm suddenly extremely aware of my arms. Were they always this long? This heavy? This clumsy?

"Were you eavesdropping?" I ask, trying to see myself through his eyes. With my kilt and ruthlessly orange hair. The color rivals that of a perfectly baked autumn leaf. But since redheads make up less than 2 percent of the entire world population, I don't have it in me to dye it.

He raises his arm, gesturing to a little pack in his hand. "I came to buy this."

"Lip pencil?" I cock an eyebrow. "To go with your fake lashes?"

There's a dark edge behind his smile, and it calls to me to come closer, peer in.

"Fine." He shrugs. "I came in to give your friend a piece of my mind but stayed for the entertainment. Sue me."

"Sorry about that." I chuckle. "Pippa's cool, you know. In a some-times-I-want-to-duct-tape-your-mouth-but-I'll-always-love-you kind of way."

"If you say."

"I do say. Of course I say. I'll say it again and again. She is my best friend."

Somewhere in the back of my head I recognize that I'm displaying extremely odd behavior here. But I want to keep the conversation going. "You two are different."

"Why? Because she's Miss Popular and I'm goth?"

"Yeah," he says flatly.

This guy is a real rebel. An OG. Not like me and my aesthetically cute septum piercing.

Then he says, "Mainstream people aren't revolutionary. Nothing good ever comes out of them. Average equals comfort."

"Is there a compliment hidden somewhere in this sentence?" I squint.

His lips hitch up slightly. I feel light all of a sudden. As if I could drift like a balloon if he continues giving me his drugging attention. "Do you want there to be?"

I think, despite his blank tone, that he is not as nonchalant as he wants me to believe he is. My heart roundhouse kicks my rib cage. But since hope is a great recipe for crashing and burning, I try to examine it from all angles. Maybe he is here for my glamorous, eccentric friend, and I'll soon be left with one of his wingmen while he woos her. I've spent countless nights in awkward conversation with random guys while Pippa was flirting up a storm. It doesn't normally faze me, but this time, I know it's going to sting if he wants her.

"What are you listening to?" He changes the subject, jerking his chin toward the earphones slung over my shoulders, just when I ask, "So, are you here on vacation, or . . . ?"

We both laugh. I answer first. "The best song to ever be recorded in the entire world."

"'Never Gonna Give You Up,' by Rick Astley?" His eyes widen comically.

More laughter. "No, but you're in the right decade."

"Challenge accepted." He rubs his palms together. I can tell his interest is piqued. "Let's see." He gives me a slow once-over, taking me in, like the answer is written across my shirt. "I'm going with 'Where Is My Mind?' by the Pixies."

"You would be wrong, my friend." I turn my phone around to show him the iTunes app still dancing on my screen. "'Save a Prayer,' by Duran Duran."

"Shit. That's a really good song."

"My mom's favorite." My smile feels like it's about to split my face.

"Your turn." He raises his phone in the air, then scrolls and picks a song. "What's on my iTunes right now?"

"Give me a decade."

"Nineties."

"That barely narrows it down." I lean against a row of lubricants. "I want to give you the credit for listening to something that's *not* 'Smells Like Teen Spirit.'"

"Why, thank you for indulging me. Think British." He grins.

I frown, thinking. "'Don't Look Back in Anger,' by Oasis."

"Final answer?"

Hesitantly, I nod. "Yes."

He turns his phone around, and I see that I was right. *Whoa.* Holy crap. Have I just met the male version of myself?

"How'd you do that?" he says, looking at me differently. Like I've passed some sort of test.

"By the power of deduction. In the war between Blur and Oasis, you are *definitely* for the working-class band. And also that guitar solo."

"I just think it's funny to find a fellow American Anglophile . . . in *Spain*."

"My mom's English. What's your excuse?"

"Don't have one." He shrugs. "Sometimes you're just born in the wrong place. And decade. And era."

"Too true," I hear myself say. "Now your turn to answer my question."

His face fascinates me. It's like I've never seen a human before. This is not normal Everlynne behavior. Typically, when I meet another person, I count back the minutes until I can say goodbye to them. It's not that I hate people. I even like some of them. But I prefer to spend my time with my carefully curated books, music, and pets. Those three have rarely let me down.

"I—" Smoker Dude starts, but Pippa barges into our conversation, waving two plastic bags in her hands.

"Here. I bought a crapload of chocolate. I'm PMS-ing. Are you PMS-ing? Ever since our cycles started to sync, I feel like I—" She stops when she notices Smoker Dude (what's his name, anyway?). I'm yet again mortified that now he not only knows my entire sexual history but also all about my menstruation cycle.

". . . Hi?" She cocks her head in confusion.

He reaches into her plastic bag, grabs a chocolate bar, tears the wrapper, and eats it in one clean bite. "Hello, cigarette snatcher."

Pippa's mouth is agape. "What *else* do you eat like that?"

"Wouldn't you like to know."

"I would, actually." She throws him a sultry smile.

He gives her a bored bad-boy stare of the type that convinces teenyboppers to buy posters.

I look between them, nervous that I'm witnessing an epic falling-in-love moment.

I suddenly realize that I really, *really* don't want to hear from her how he kisses. I don't want to *aww* and *ahh* and pretend that I'm happy for her after the inevitable happens and they sleep together. The more they stare at each other, the more cold sweat forms over my skin. Until it becomes unbearable. The silence. The prospect of Pippa and Smoker Dude locking lips in a dim corner of a Barcelonese nightclub to a slow Arctic Monkeys song while I engage in mindless conversation with one of his buddies.

Whatever happened to *Mainstream people aren't revolutionary?*

Pippa opens her mouth, no doubt to flirt with him. Something seizes me. I grab her by the wrist and pull her away. She is stumbling behind me, trying to yank herself free. But I'm propelled by fear and motivation.

"What are you doing?" she demands. "Ugh, he gave me big-dick energy! Let's go back."

"Nope." The air-conditioned pharmacy spits us out to the tree-lined avenue. "I'm not going to let you fall in lust and disrupt our entire girls' trip by planning your schedule around some guy."

Apparently, this is the reason for our early departure. I pulled it out of my ass, but now that it's here, it's my hill to die on.

"Oh my God, you nutcase. Is that why you did this?" She stops when we're on the corner of the street, then slaps my hand away. "You thought *I* was about to hit on him?"

We're a good yard away from the pharmacy. I come to a halt, glancing around me.

"Or he was about to hit on you. Whatever. Same stuff."

"Well, joke's on you, Lawson, because when I said he was cute, I meant for *you*. He looked like a reflection into your soul. I've never seen anything like it. You smiled like two idiots when you were talking. I was going to make sure you got each other's numbers. It's not every day my best friend shows signs of life."

Now it's my turn to be speechless. "That's why you did it?"

She smacks my arm with one of her shopping bags. "Yes, dufus!"

"But you two stared at each other."

"He was giving me make-yourself-scarce looks." She laughs. "He wasn't subtle about it either."

I want to throw up. In fact, I think I did, a little, in my mouth. Just now. "So why *didn't* you?"

"I was trying to make sure he didn't mess it up."

"Oh, Pippa."

"Don't *Oh, Pippa* me. Run back in there and give him your number!"

"Just like that?" I blink, still rooted to the ground.

She hitches one shoulder up. "You can flash him your boobs for dramatic impact, I guess."

I cut through the air like a bird of prey. I burst inside the pharmacy, whipping my head from side to side. If Smoker Dude asks why I'm here, I'm going to tell him I lost my wallet. I pace the aisles. I check the restrooms. Even the photo booth. Smoker Dude is nowhere to be seen.

Panic grows inside me. What if he left? It's not like he really came here to buy a lip pencil. What if I've missed him? What if this is it? I'll never find out his name. Where he lives. Whether he is Team Guns N' Roses or Nirvana (he'd better be Team Guns N' Roses, or he'll have a lot to answer for).

"He go after you," *tsks* the pharmacist over the counter in a thick Spanish accent.

I turn to him. "He did?"

"Yeah, he was fast." He smiles apologetically. "But you, faster."

TWO

For the next week and a half, we eat and drink and visit cathedrals and Camp Nou and Bershka. Pippa hooks up with guys in clubs, I shop till I drop, and Smoker Dude becomes almost a myth, someone I'm not sure even existed anywhere but in my head.

Four days before we're scheduled to go back to the States, we even find a good deal to Gran Canaria and hop on a plane. Pippa makes fast friends with a group of American girls on the plane, and this is how we find ourselves at a beach party the night before we'll board a flight back home.

The moon is fat and white. It hangs over my head like a lollipop. The sand, tan and cool between my toes, is different from the blond grains of San Francisco.

I sit in front of a bonfire, pop music blasting from the speakers. There are probably a hundred people here, all in different stages of undress, drinking and dancing.

Pippa is somewhere among them. She disappeared twenty minutes ago with three girls from Tallahassee for a game of flip cups.

I sip my bottled beer and think about Smoker Dude. More specifically, how brutally random life is. All that separates me from him in this day and age is his full name. I want to be Gwyneth Paltrow in

Sliding Doors. I want to make it to the train. I want a do-over. To choose right this time.

Beside me, I notice a black canvas backpack. There's a notebook spilling out of it. It looks abandoned. Thrown haphazardly, looking for a new owner. My fingers tingle to touch it. *The girl hasn't met a book she didn't want to read*, my mom often brags, and it's true.

I'm aware that reading this thing without permission is wrong. Still, temptation crawls over my limbs like ivy.

I mean, it *is* strewn here, on a beach full of people, with the bag open. If it were private, its owner would carry it with them.

I decide to give the owner of the notebook ten minutes before I read it. If they went to the bathroom, they'll have a chance to stop me. If they are somewhere else, well, then they don't care so much about anyone reading it.

Ten minutes pass, then fifteen. I pick it up and open it at a random page. My heart is racing in my chest. I feel like a thief. It looks like some kind of journal . . . an essay? The words bleed into one another, like they were written in a great hurry.

It's two in the morning and he thinks he is going to jump. Maybe jumping is all that's left to do. And is it pathetic that a part of him doesn't want to jump because he is afraid of what his boss would say when he doesn't show up at work tomorrow?

But that's exactly the problem. The reason why he is here, on this roof, in the first place. He worked so hard making a living, he forgot to live. Now this cliché that you can find on a cheap mug at a dollar store has brought him to the point of suicide.

He had his chance and he blew it.

He should've run after her faster.

And when he almost reached her, he should have yanked the back of her shirt without caring what it'd look like.

He should have told her she was perfect.

But he didn't, so now he needs to jump.

Jump . . . or do something else. Even more ambitious. Pack a bag and go to New Orleans. To look for her.

My eyes sting. It looks like a short story. Or the beginning of a novel. I flip the pages, eager for more, but an array of blank pages stare back at me.

A hand presses against my shoulder, making my head jerk up.

"No reading, missy!"

Pippa is all drunken, swaying limbs. I sag with relief because it's not the owner of the notebook. I also slump with disappointment—for the exact same reason.

"Come. Get shit faced. Live a little." Pippa tosses the notebook to the sand, then pulls me up and dances her way to a cluster of people. A ring of bronzed bodies moves around us, trapping me in. I shift my feet from side to side, awkward like the skin I'm in has been newly sewn onto me. I try to guess who the journal belongs to. The girl with the locs? The guy with the chest tats?

I drift away from Pippa. She is dancing with her new friends, shouting all the lyrics to the songs in their faces.

I make my way toward the sea. By the shore is the only slice of sand that's not populated. I stop. Take a closer look at the famous *Neptuno de Melenara*. It's a four-meter-tall sculpture of Neptune rising from the sea, not too far away from the coastline. The water is metallic blue. It glimmers under the stars. I dip a toe into it. The temperature isn't freezing. I could swim my way to the statue. I'm a strong swimmer. My brother and I grew up surfing. Renn (his name means "reborn" or "little prosperous one") has even made a career out of it.

A small voice inside me tells me I'm being a dumbass. That getting into an unfamiliar body of water in the pitch black is a rookie's mistake. But the sculpture is less than a hundred feet away, and there's a whole freaking party behind me. It'd be hard to lose sight of that.

I slip out of my bodice dress. I traipse into the sea. I swim toward Neptune in sharp strokes. The water is choppy, colder than I expected. I'm thrown off by the currents. I wasn't expecting them. The sea looked flat from the outside. Inside, I can feel it carrying me with it, no matter how I try to swim in a straight line. I lift my head to see how far I am from the statue and realize I'm about fifteen feet sideways.

Goose bumps roll over my skin. I'm in trouble, and I know it.

I turn around and make a U-turn. Just as I do, a huge wave thrashes me against a large rock. I push off it with my feet before I smash into it again. Salty water fills my mouth, and I swallow some of it. Fear morphs into panic.

Don't flail. Let the current take you, then recalculate.

I've known these things to be true—learned about them in summer camps. But now that I'm in the situation, I'm freaking out. I start calling for help.

What if I'm going to drown? What if I'm going to die? What if they never find my body? Would Pippa think it was her fault? Would I ruin her life too? Do I even care? She's the one who insisted I come here tonight.

Mom. Mom. Mom.

Dad and Renn would be devastated, but Mom wouldn't be able to survive.

I can't die. With that understanding, I begin to fight back, knowing I'm the underdog.

The currents are strong. Still, I push through, trying to keep my head above water and see where the shore is. Another wave rips through my body. It sends me a few feet away. I let it take me, crane my neck, and blink amid the blackness around me. It takes me a few seconds to realize the wave has brought me closer to the beach. I can see a thin golden necklace of lights twinkling back at me. An upsurge of relief rolls through me. I begin swimming. My muscles are burning, my body is shivering, but the adrenaline numbs the pain. I'm a mermaid, running away from pirates who want to gut me.

The closer I get, the more I feel hope gathering behind my rib cage. Suddenly, a pair of arms grabs me from above. The arms pull me up by the armpits. I become slack and heavy inside them as they sling me honeymoon-style, and I'm pressed against a warm, dry chest.

"You have her?" a Spanish, smoke-filled voice asks.

"Yeah."

"Is she . . . ?"

"I don't know." The other voice is American. "Help me get her to that tree, and we'll take a look."

A few moments later, I'm wrapped inside a warm blanket. I'm too exhausted to open my eyes. A flashlight illuminates my face behind my eyelids.

I wince. "Please stop."

"How long were you in the water?" Spanish Voice asks.

"Seven or eight minutes." I'm coughing out my words. My eyes are still closed. I feel arms wrap around me. Normally, I would recoil at the proximity to a stranger, but there's something about the arms that hold me that feels right. Like this is exactly the place I should be in.

"Did you swallow water?" Spanish Voice is speaking directly into my face. His breath, of chewed tobacco and beer, is warm against my flesh.

"Not too much." I cough some more.

"Are you hurt?"

"No, not hurt. Just . . . tired."

"Open your eyes for me, *chavala*."

My eyes flutter open. A tan man with a sheepskin-like white beard and a flashlight glares back at me.

"I'm okay," I say. I start to move my hands, my feet, rolling my neck from side to side. I'm breathless, and in shock, but everything seems to be intact. I just had a scare.

"Ah, no. I didn't save you." He shakes his head. "He did." He points a mud-caked fingernail to the human blanket that is holding me. I twist my neck so I can look at the person, but it's making me dizzy.

Not dizzy enough, though, to miss the important part.

The pinnacle of my trip.

The person who is holding me is Smoker Dude.

And he doesn't look like he is about to let go.

◆ ◆ ◆

Smoker Dude saved me.

He is here, on Gran Canaria. At the same beach party. What are the odds?

I pinch my forearm, in case I'm hallucinating. He is still here, and now I've given myself a bruise. He notices and bites down a grin. I shake my head. Maybe it's a concussion. But he looks so real, so alive, so warm, wrapped around me.

For a few moments, all we do is stare. No words seem adequate enough for what is happening here. We've beaten all statistical odds. Things like this only ever happen in movies.

Instinctively, I put a hand on his cheek. One last test to make sure he is not an illusion. His skin is rough and hot. I'm surprised I don't burst into flames. I don't know what it is, but I feel a hundred times more alive right now than I did a minute ago.

"You." Smoker Dude cups my hand in his. His voice is hoarse. Thick. He didn't know. Up until our eyes met, just now, he didn't know it was me in the water.

"*You,*" I murmur back. "What's your name?"

The suspense has been killing me. I've been obsessing about his name from the moment we met.

"Joe."

"Joe." I test his name in my mouth. *Joe!* Good ol' Joe. Such a simple, unassuming name. I'm a little disappointed at his parents. That's all they could come up with? Do they not know how rare and special their son is?

"Thank you for saving me, Joe."

The Spanish man, whom I've forgotten all about in the last few minutes, salutes him. He stands up and ambles toward the promenade, disappearing into a cloud of people. I look around us, finally remembering that we are a part of a larger universe. We're under a tree, somewhere secluded. The party is still in full swing. They're doing the limbo now.

"What's *your* name?" he asks.

"Ever." I drop my hand from his face, realizing that it's not cool to randomly grope strangers. "Everlynne."

"Thank you for saving me, Everlynne."

"I didn't save you . . . ?" I say.

"*Yet.*" His smile is slow and teasing and screams trouble. "But now you owe me one. And I always collect."

"I'm glad we've met again," I say, before I forget. "I've got an important question, and it's been bugging me ever since I saw you."

He blinks at me, waiting for more. I take a deep breath. "Guns N' Roses or Nirvana?"

He tips his head back and laughs. "What kind of question is that?"

"Not a tricky one if you have good taste." I grin.

"Nirvana had 'Lithium' and 'Smells Like Teen Spirit' and basically nothing else. Guns N' Roses are living legends."

I stare at him blankly. This is *exactly* how I feel. How can we be thinking the same things?

"How did I do?" Joe wiggles his eyebrows.

"Disturbingly good," I admit. "I'm sure we'll find some things to disagree about musically, but so far we're on the same wavelength."

There's a brief silence. We're just basking in the pleasure of staring at one another. We breathe in the same rhythm, huddled closely together.

"What were you doing out there, Everlynne? Besides the obvious, which is giving me a heart attack at age nineteen." Joe brushes wet hair away from my face gently.

He is a year older than me. My heart twirls like a belle getting ready for her first soiree. It doesn't care that my body is going through an adrenaline crash. It's happy and hopeful and dumb.

"I wanted to look at the statue up close." And then, realizing something is amiss, I add, "I'm still wearing nothing but my bra and panties, aren't I?"

"And the panties are see-through," he confirms, biting down on his lips to catch his smile.

Closing my eyes, I whisper, "When I imagined being in your arms naked, it looked pretty different."

My ears feel hot. I don't know where this honesty is coming from. I never say what's on my mind. Especially to strangers. *Especially* boy strangers. But Joe feels familiar.

"You imagined being in my arms, naked?" He raises an inquisitive eyebrow.

"Hmm, maybe once or twice."

"And you thought a good way of indicating that to me was by running for the hills the first time we met?"

I don't miss the irritation in his voice. Cinders of what must have been anger.

"I thought you and Pippa were hitting it off. I couldn't stand the idea of watching you two . . . I don't know, flirting. Because I liked you. And I never like anyone. I came back to look for you a few minutes later."

I'm still in his arms as we're having this conversation, wrapped in a fuzzy plaid orange-and-purple blanket.

24

"You thought I was hitting it off with *Mainstream*?" He sounds surprised . . . and a little smug.

"Well, yeah."

"Dare I ask if you were jealous?"

"I plead the Fifth."

"We're not in America right now," he points out.

I shrug.

I want him to tell me that he likes me, not Pippa. Instead, he says, "I went after you too."

"The pharmacist told me." I nod.

"And now you're here."

"And now *you're* here." I sit up and turn my body toward him so I can look at him properly. My butt hits something on the sand, and I pluck it from underneath me. It's the black canvas bag that was sitting by the fire earlier this evening. I pick it up. My fingers are shaking. My breath catches in my throat.

"Of course."

"Weird reaction to a bag." He frowns. "I'm going to need some context."

"I read some of your story." I pass him the backpack, feeling myself blushing. "Sorry, I couldn't resist. It was—"

"Terrible?"

"—exhilarating," I finish at the same time.

He studies me a little warily, drumming his long fingers on his knee.

"It needs some work, but the bones are there, I think. It's why I'm here, actually. In Europe. To write a novel."

"You can't write a novel in America?" My question comes out like an accusation. It sounds like he is going to be here for a while, and I'm flying back in less than twenty-four hours. Nice work, fate.

"Technically, I can." He drops the backpack by his side. "But I needed to get away. Home's been intense the last couple decades."

"You're nineteen," I point out.

"Good math." He winks. "I've had a pretty rough start."

So he has one of *those* families. One that doesn't have cute Christmas traditions and go surfing together. Where Mom and Dad don't slow dance in the middle of the kitchen. Nothing like mine.

I rub my thumb over my chin. "Define *rough start*."

"I will. When we have more time and run out of fun things to talk about. Let's leave our troubles at the door tonight." He tucks away another lock of wet hair from my forehead, and it's the most romantic and heartbreaking thing anyone has ever done to me. More than when Sean took me to prom and then to the Ritz-Carlton after. The night I lost my virginity and the little interest I still had in boys.

"Okay?" he asks.

"Okay."

"Don't go anywhere," Joe warns. "I'll go get your dress. Beige, right?"

He stands up and kicks the sand off his jeans. Some of it gets into my eyes, but I'm too stunned to care. "You noticed me? I mean, before?"

He tousles his hair, flashing his earth-shattering grin. "I was about to come over when you were by the fire. My friends told me not to bother. That I was imagining you. I may or may not have thought I saw you at least a dozen times the last couple weeks. Active imagination." He knocks on the side of his head.

Satisfaction floods me. I did the exact same thing. Imagined him in thick crowds.

"Then I heard you crying for help in the sea, and there was no doubt. You have a hot-girl voice. You should narrate books or something. Don't go," he says again as he goes to retrieve my dress, leaving me with all this information and my heart in my throat.

Basking in the compliment, I use my alone time to run my fingers through my tangled hair and wipe the runny mascara from my eyes. It's going to be hard to seduce him when I probably look like a swamp creature. When he comes back, he is holding my dress and my purse, where I keep my cash and phone. He disposes both of them next to his backpack.

"Thanks," I say.

"Are you feeling better?" He plops beside me.

"Eons better." I shove my arms through my sleeves, dressing quickly. My body is pale and slender, peppered with freckles everywhere the sun touches.

"Good. I met Mainstream by the fire and told her you were with me and that you were fine."

"What did she say?"

"That I'm fine too," he deadpans.

I laugh.

We catch up on these last couple of weeks. I tell him about Barcelona. He tells me about Sevilla and Madrid. He's here with three friends. All four of them are from Boston. The rest of his party is going back to their respective colleges at the end of the week. Joe is staying in Spain a little longer, then will go backpacking through Europe alone in hopes of finishing his book. "Romania, Poland, Hungary, Italy, and France." He uses his fingers to count the countries. "I mapped it all out, including the hostels and bed-and-breakfasts I'll be staying in. Shouldn't take me more than four months to write the entire thing."

Four months? He can't be on a different continent for four months. He can't be single and ridiculously attractive for four months. He can't just continue existing like we never happened.

Only he can, and there is nothing I can do about it.

Tucking my crazy in, I decide not to broach the subject of us. The conversation flows, despite my crushing disappointment. I tell him about growing up in San Francisco. About Renn and his surfing, and about Mom's gallery in the Castro. He tells me about his upbringing. Two Catholic parents, one sibling, and an ocean of unsolved issues.

I tell him about my art.

This is the part where I expect him to freak out. It's not every day you meet an eighteen-year-old who designs headstones as a hobby.

"It's less sinister than it sounds." I lick my lips, already on the defense.

"You design headstones, not kill babies for a living." His eyes sparkle with amusement. "But I'm sure there's a story behind it."

"When I was, like, eight, my cousin Shauna died in a boating accident. She was only fifteen. My mom wanted me to attend the funeral, but Dad thought I was too young. There was a lot of back-and-forth between them. In the end, they left it for me to decide. I wanted to go. Shauna and I had been close. It was the first time I'd visited a cemetery. I remember looking around and thinking, *All these headstones look the same. How is that possible? We're so different from each other when we're alive. Why are our personalities reduced to nothing when we're dead?*

"A few months later, Mom and I went back to freshen up the flowers on her grave. Shauna had the most beautiful gravestone. It was so her it took my breath away. Her mom splurged on a real piece of art. A granite angel embracing a heart. It made me think. Personalized gravestones are a great way to pay your last respects to someone, you know? We live in a world where everything is customized to us: our clothes, our mattresses, our cars. Why not design something that's unique? Something that represents the person who was laid to rest?"

"What do you do with your designs?" Joe isn't showing any signs of distress. I'm fairly sure his creep-o-meter is broken. But, more than likely, this is just another way we are alike.

"I mostly keep them to myself. You have to consider people's personalities to make gravestones for them, and thinking about the people you love passing away is . . . well, next-level psychotic. So I design them for late celebrities and stuff like that. A few people have heard about what I do through the grapevine and asked about pricing. I gave them the designs for free. I don't know if there's a market for what I do . . . I just know that it feels right to do it."

Joe tugs at the hem of my dress, just for the physical connection. "People are always in the market for fucking awesome."

"What if I'm not fucking awesome?"

"You are," he says, sure as the morning sun. "If you were mediocre, you wouldn't be running circles in my head."

I think about the words from his novel.

He should've run after her faster.

He should have told her she was perfect.

The dull beat of the music coming from the party makes the earth quake beneath us. My body feels in tune with his, and I can anticipate the next time he'll move. I feel his breaths in my own lungs.

"So." His knee brushes against mine.

"So." My elbow bumps against his.

"Did you ever use that condom?" he asks.

I bury my face in my hands. My skin is hot with mortification. I shake my head, peeking at him from between my fingers.

He tries to catch my gaze, tilting his head down. "Is that a no?"

"Why's it important?"

"Knowledge is power."

"It's a useless piece of information." I'm drunk on the idea that he cares but also embarrassed that I didn't go through with Pippa's dare.

"Don't limit my fields of interest, missy. I'll have you know it's a matter of great interest. Books will be written on the subject. *Books*, I tell ya." He shakes his fist in the air.

To this, I full-blown laugh. "This is not normal."

"What's not normal?"

"You. Me." I wave my finger between us. "This."

There's nothing much to say, really. Which leads me to my next question to fill in the silence.

"Did *you* use any condoms while in Spain?"

"Promise not to be disappointed?" He sighs. I nod, but I already am. It shouldn't feel like he's cheated on me. It does, anyway.

"No," he says. "I didn't use any condoms."

Punching his arm, I groan, "Then why did you tell me not to be disappointed?"

"To see if you were jealous, of course."

This time, there's no point denying that I was.

From the distance, "Boys of Summer" starts. It's the Ataris' cover, my favorite. People raise their arms in the air and sing. Dawn breaks above the surface. The waterline shimmers rose gold. Our time is almost up.

"Where were we?" I ask.

"Spain," Joe provides. "And on the subject of condoms, specifically."

"It's not too late to use one." I lick my lips. "A condom, I mean."

"Hmm." He leans back, bracing on his forearms. He is kind of ripped.

"Are you thinking what I'm thinking?" I bite down on my lower lip.

His throat bobs. "Yeah. And there's plenty of water to fill the condom with."

Before I have a chance to laugh, he leans forward and kisses me.

At first it's just a kiss. A sloppy exchange of saliva between two teenagers, greedy with unbridled passion. Our tongues meet and swirl together. Dancing, teasing, testing. He tastes like ocean spray, summer, and cigarettes.

Then his fingers wrap around the back of my neck, and the kiss stops being a kiss and becomes a war. Joe devours my mouth. It's ruinously raw. With teeth and moans and gasps. We're ivy, coiling around one another. I touch his hair, his corded arms, the rock-hard ridges of his abs under his shirt. He lowers me under the palm tree, cups the back of my thighs, and presses his erection against my center. It twitches between us. I'm breathless, and my heart is racing, and now I get it. *I get it, I get it, I get it.* The term *boy crazy.* Because Joe is a boy. And he drives me crazy.

My back hits the sand, and sweet oblivion, I want him inside me. To fill every inch of me. For us to fuse together. *This* is how I like to be touched. Sean pawed and squeezed my breasts like he was trying to milk me. Joe flicks my nipple through my bra with his thumb while his hot kisses lower to my neck, then my chest. He unclasps my bra. Sucks one of my nipples into his mouth, grazing it with his teeth teasingly.

"Ever."

I knot my legs over his waist. We ride each other through our clothes, enjoying the friction and the feeling of our teeth sinking into new skin. Our scents swirl together, creating a unique and heady combination. Then Joe produces a condom from his wallet and holds it between us in question.

"Don't feel pressured." His voice is raspy, strained. "This can stop right here, and I'm still going to end the night feeling like the luckiest bastard alive."

I know he means it. I know he won't be mad if I decide I don't want to. Unlike Sean, who booked the Ritz-Carlton with the expectation—the silent agreement—that sex was a part of the package. Probably why I broke it off a week later, citing long distance.

"I'm sure." I tear the condom wrapper open with shaky hands, hoping I haven't damaged the actual product.

I reach between us and roll it over him clumsily. He is bracing himself on top of me, his sculpted arms two columns bracketing my shoulders. We both watch my unsure fingers with fascination. It takes me four attempts, and even though we are both frustrated, neither of us says anything about it.

"Is it rolled all the way?" I ask.

"Feels good to me. Are you ready?" He catches my gaze. His eyes, dark blue with silvery dots, are his best feature.

"Yes." I'm already quivering. "I'm ready."

He presses home. For the first few seconds, we just hold each other, staring at one another. I think we're both stunned.

"Is it always like that?" I whisper.

He knows exactly what I'm asking, because he shakes his head and says, "No, Ever. It's never like that. This . . ." He dips his head, kissing the shell of my ear. "This is heaven. This is worthy of death."

Our bodies get in sync. We move to the same soundless song. I'm tingling everywhere. Joe's skin is a blanket of goose bumps. We're lost in each other in what feels like forever. A gust of wind sweeps my hair across my face, and he blows it away, kissing me again and again and again.

"I think I'm coming," I say. That's a first. With a guy, anyway. But the friction feels so good, and he is hitting just the right spot inside me.

"Oh, thank *fuck*." He drops his head to the crook of my neck, picking up speed. "So am I."

We collapse in each other's arms just as the sun peeks from the flat blue line of the Atlantic Ocean. Everything is pink, orange, and quiet.

That's when we realize that there are no more thumps of music and chatter coming from the distance.

The party is over.

And so is my time with Joe.

◆ ◆ ◆

"Sixteen-hour flight, huh?" Joe buttons his Levi's. "That's rough."

I hate this. The small talk. This is my first dose of reality since I've met him again. And the reality is that I just had sex with a total stranger who saved me from drowning. Someone who is about to become a stranger yet again, in five minutes, after we've said our goodbyes.

"No big deal. I have my Kindle and my earbuds." I shrug.

This is the part where I should suggest we exchange emails, or numbers, or Instagram handles. *Anything*. Have I learned nothing from the past two weeks? I've felt homesick toward this guy like he was a place, and now I'm going to let him walk away, just like that?

But something stops me. Pride? Fear? A combination of both?

I push my dress down my waist and collect the upper half of my hair into a messy bun.

"When's your flight?" Joe shoves his feet into his sand-filled Chuck Taylors.

"Two in the afternoon. We'll only have an hour once we get to El Prat Airport."

"That's plenty." He flings his backpack across his shoulder.

"Yeah. I'm not worried." I check my phone in my purse for missed calls. Sure enough, Pippa called me eleven times.

Mom sent a message. **Miss you! See you home soon. I'm making your favorite casserole. x**

I look up and smile at him tiredly. A part of me can't wait to leave so I can finally cry, and a part of me doesn't want to leave this spot. Ever.

"Well." I salute him. "It's been real."

"Wait." He tugs a Polaroid camera from his backpack, aims it at my face, and snaps a picture. It slides out of the camera's mouth, a white block of indistinguishable shadows.

"Okay, that was creepy."

"Oh, yeah. I forgot to tell you. I'm an axe murderer."

"Now that you mention it, you do have that look," I tease him.

He waves the picture back and forth, holding it by the edge. "I'll walk you."

Walk me? Why? Am I now incapable of walking a straight line by myself? My hackles hike up the more my mood goes down. I'm mad. Mad at my cowardice. Mad at the opportunistic Joe. Only I know he is not really opportunistic. He didn't take advantage of me tonight. We hit it off and enjoyed a night of no strings attached. Pippa is right. Why must there be more?

"Don't worry about it. I can see Pippa from here." I point to the cluster of girls standing on the edge of the promenade, laughing as they rub at their own arms, braving the morning chill.

"Sounds good," he says.

Sounds good? It sounds terrible. Stop me, dammit.

"So, uh, bye." I turn around quickly, before he can see the tears in my eyes.

"Bye." I hear his voice as I trudge my way to the boardwalk.

The first tear rolls on my neck, disappearing between the valley of my still-sore breasts. The second follows closely behind. I want to turn around. To run back to him. To lie and tell him I'd be okay if he wants to have his fun in Europe, as long as he comes back home to me in four months' time. I realize it's not even my pride I'm concerned about. It's the fear of rejection that stops me from telling him how I feel. It's pure unadulterated heartbreak. At least now, as I walk away toward the rest of my life, there's a tiny part of me that still believes we stand a chance. That maybe he'll look for me and somehow find me. I clutch onto this hope like a lifeline.

"Everlynne!" His voice booms behind me. I turn around so fast my head spins. He is not standing where I left him. In fact, we are less than fifteen feet apart. He followed me. I wipe my face quickly.

"This is stupid!" he yells, opening his arms, laughing incredulously. "I don't want to say goodbye. We don't have to."

"You're staying." The wind carries my voice like it's a ribbon. My heart feels like it wants to rip my chest open and jump its way to him.

"You're going," he replies softly, as if to say, *No one is to blame. It's all just crappy luck.*

"I don't want to go," I admit.

"I don't really want to stay." He ducks his head, hiding what's in his eyes, and I wish I could take a picture of him like that, all beautiful and raw and mine on the beach. My wilted sunflower.

"I'll give you my number?" I offer.

34

He looks back up and grins. "I'll call."

"Hey, Joe."

"Yes, Ever?"

"What's your favorite English invention of all time? *Don't* say Emilia Clarke."

He laughs. I'm going to miss this laugh so much. "The World Wide Web, also known as the internet. Tim Berners-Lee is the bomb dot-com. Yours?"

"The chocolate bar," I say without hesitation.

We run toward each other, exploding into one unit. He wraps his arms around me. His lips find mine, and we kiss, and we kiss, and we kiss. I want to hit roots in this sand. To become a tree of limbs and kisses with this guy.

Joe pulls away. He takes my phone and programs his number into it. He saves himself as *Joe Boyfriend*. I laugh and cry simultaneously. I don't even know his last name. I'm about to ask for it when he pats his front and back pockets.

"Shit. I left my phone in the hostel." He flings his backpack open, takes his notebook out, and rips a paper full of text out of it. Now *that's* the most romantic thing I've ever seen. "Give me your number. I'll write it down and save it as soon as I get back. I'll probably tattoo it on my arm. What's your favorite font? Don't say Times New Roman. It's the white bread of fonts, and we'll have to break up."

"Cambria," I assure him.

"Good choice, *girlfriend*."

I write down my number, then read it again and again to ensure that it's correct. It doesn't matter, though. I'll call him as soon as I get back home. I'll probably text him when I land, to tell him I'm okay. He *is* my boyfriend now.

Mother of pearl. I'm coming home with a boyfriend. Mom is going to freak out. Renn is going to tease me to death.

Joe shoves the note with my number into his front pocket, grabs the edge of my dress, and tugs me to him.

"Fuck, I'm gonna miss you," he murmurs into my mouth, devouring it again.

"I'm going to climb the walls while you're in Europe." I wrap my arms around his shoulders.

"I'll come visit as soon as I get back," he promises, kissing my nose, my forehead, the side of my jaw. "Butter up your folks for me in the meantime. A smoking college dropout with no job or prospects isn't exactly every parent's dream."

"You dropped out?"

"Never applied. But it sounds better, doesn't it? Like at least I gave it a shot."

There's more laughing and more kissing before I hear a familiar shriek.

"There she is! Ugh, I thought he murdered you!" Pippa's voice is getting closer to us. I remove myself from Joe. She is trekking barefoot on the sand, sinking a little with each step. "How was I supposed to explain this to your parents? They would have *killed* me."

Joe drapes an arm over my shoulder. Pippa stops and glances between us. Her Cheshire cat smile says she is over her momentary anger.

"I see what's going on here, rascals."

"Nothing's going on," I say impishly.

"If that's the case, I'll have two of these nothings. Wrap it up, love-birds. We have a flight to catch."

"Five minutes," Joe bargains.

"And who are you again?" Pippa arches an eyebrow. "We didn't get a chance to meet properly."

"Joe." I gesture toward him like Vanna White revealing an important vowel on *Wheel of Fortune*. "My boyfriend."

"Your *boyfriend*," Pippa echoes, grinning.

"Her *boyfriend*." Joe squeezes me close. "Keep her safe for me till I'm back, Mainstream."

"It's the twenty-first century. She can hold her own. But I will, asshat. You've got twenty minutes." She wiggles her finger at me. "And because I'm an amazing, understanding friend, whom you'd totally give a kidney to if I ever need one, and also because I'm sure you *did* use a condom tonight, and that's worth celebrating, I'll go back to our hotel, pack up both our stuff, and check out. I'll meet you back here in a bit."

"You're the best, Pip."

"I know." She flicks her hair. "But it's nice to be reminded."

Joe and I spend the next twenty minutes kissing, and hugging, and promising each other phone calls, and letters, and the entire sky, stars included. Then Pippa comes to collect me, and I steal a few more minutes with him, because if I'm about to maybe give her a kidney, I feel like I can milk a bit more time with Joe. Then, finally, we say goodbye.

As we stuff ourselves into a cab to the airport, I marvel at the last twenty-four hours.

It *is* too good to be true.

And Pippa is wrong. Joe and I didn't use a condom tonight.

We used two.

THREE

Six years later.

Loki is gone.

I come to this realization after looking for him everywhere. I searched both my and Nora's rooms, under the beds, in the closets, all the cabinets, and behind the couch.

I try to keep myself together, which is impossible enough even without a disaster looming over my head. I tell myself there are only so many places a fifteen-pound aging cat can hide in. Especially in a tiny two-bedroom apartment.

But Loki has never done this before. Disappeared on me like this. Not since I adopted him from a shelter my first (and last) week living in Boston.

Nora says my cat has the personality of a tyrannical king. Moody, vocal, and sporting three chins, Loki usually limits his cold war tactics to peeing in our shoes when we leave him alone for long periods of time. But he never gets out of the house.

Partly because we live in a certified crap hole. It's a converted single home that's been split into three apartments on Upham Street, Salem. Two of them are used as storage spaces for our landlord, probably because no one is crazy enough to live in them. Utility poles tangle the sky of my neighborhood like cobwebs. There are chain links and barking dogs everywhere, and a whole lot of nothing to explore. From his usual vantage point on the windowsill, Loki has no reason to believe the world is his oyster. If anything, the world probably appears to him as a very unappetizing broccoli flower.

"Try not to freak out, babe." Nora tornadoes from her bedroom to the hallway, collecting her silky blonde hair into a colorful scrunchie. She is wearing high-waisted baggy jeans and a cropped pink shirt. "I'm sure he's around somewhere. Maybe he got out and doesn't know the way back."

"Very comforting," I deadpan.

"Oh, you know what I mean. He's a cat. They always land on their feet."

I look at her doubtfully. Nora knows optimism is not my forte. In fact, it takes very little to make me crawl into bed and not leave unless I have work to go to.

She sighs. "Have you tried looking outside? In the hallway? By the park?"

She shoves her feet into her sneakers on her way to the door. She is already late to her movie date with her boyfriend, Colt. I should be getting ready for work too.

"Not yet. No. Not outside the house." I find myself crouching and looking for Loki in places I've already checked. I don't want to look for him outside. Something tells me that if he got outside, he is not alive anymore. And *that* makes me want to just cease to exist. Not actively die. Just . . . discontinue to be.

"You should post about him on Facebook and Craigslist. With a picture." Nora grabs her clutch from the stand next to our front door. I hear a horn honking. It's Colt. She throws me a guilty wince. "Sorry to bail on you like this. C's been dying to watch this movie. It's with Margot Robbie, you know."

I shake my head. "It's fine. You think if I post an ad, it'd help?"

"Can't hurt, and you know Lauren, who works the reception at Saint Mary's? She lost her French bulldog the other day. Posted about him on Craigslist and got a response a day later. The dog was found in a park near her house. It's worth trying."

"Okay," I say. "I'll do it."

Nora kisses the palm of her hand twice and waves at me. "Let me know if you need anything. And text me if you find Loki. Bye!"

If. My stomach churns.

After she is gone, I tromp my way up and down my street, looking in all the trash cans and front yards. When it is obvious he is not in the neighborhood, I go back home, power up my laptop, and get on Craigslist. It's not a super-active community page. Salem is pretty small. In fact, for all its rich history and reputation, Salem is the home of fewer than forty-five thousand residents.

I click on the Lost and Found section, then skim through it. Some of the featured pets have been found. Some are still missing. Nora is right. This is worth a shot. It's been a few hours since Loki went missing. Enough time for him to venture out of this zip code.

I open an account, then roam through my phone for a picture of Loki. Embarrassingly, most of the pictures on it are of him. That's what happens when you don't have a boyfriend/friends/family/life. You become a cat lady at age twenty-four.

I make sure I choose a good picture of him. One where he looks straight into the camera with the seriousness of a self-important duke. In the picture, he is sitting on our windowsill, showing off those furry chins. I upload it to the site, then write a quick post.

> REWARD. Missing since 10/20. Neutered male. Tuxedo black and white. May have a studded black leather collar. Answers to Loki or Lulu. Has a small piece missing on his left ear.

I sit back and read it. It reads fine. Clinical. Informative. But I want more. I want them to know Loki isn't just a cat. Pets are never just animals. They're family. So I add:

> Please let us know if you see him. We miss him so
> much. Thank you.

We is me. Loki is my cat. Nora just took him under her wing because he and I were a package deal. We are both strays under her mercy. Lost souls moving in this world without any rhyme or reason.

Nora, with her big smile and even bigger heart. We've been rooming together for almost five years now, and I know that she is ready to start her next chapter in life. She wants to move in with Colt.

Every week, I try to muster up the courage to tell her that she can. That I'll be fine. But the truth is, I might not be. The truth is, I'm not really fine. Most days, I feel like a flower cut from the stem, midwilt. Not dead yet, but unable to grow further.

I click on the mouse. My ad has been posted. I copy and paste it onto Facebook, just in case.

I can't believe I have to go to work now.

Whoa. Work. I forgot all about work. I look up at the overhead clock hanging in our tiny open-plan kitchen, and it's seven forty-five. *Shit.*

I run to my room, stumbling over one of Loki's squeaky toys in the process, and slip into a long black dress and a matching cape—black on the outside, burgundy on the inside. I pull on my lacy black gloves, screw on my witch hat, and lace my boots before unzipping my duffel bag to ensure I have everything I need.

I run out of the apartment like my ass is on fire, get into my car, and slam the accelerator all the way to work. Luckily, there's only one red traffic light on my way there. My phone, lying on the passenger seat, lights up with a message. I angle it to my face to see the text.

Pippa: Miss you mucho, bitch. Still haven't given up on you. Call me.

I hate when she does this.

When she pretends like I'm Old Ever.

Like nothing happened.

Like I could still have nice things for myself.

Friends, family, a social life.

I open the text, then delete the message.

You don't need to give up on me, Pip. I've given up on myself for both of us.

Fifteen minutes later, I step onto an imaginary soapbox on Essex Street, then clear my throat.

It's not that I'm good with crowds—I hate public speaking of any kind—it's that putting myself through something I absolutely loathe gives me a perverted sense of pleasure. As I said, I deserve any punishment I can get. Why not add frequent and stressful human interaction into the mix?

Tonight is packed. There are maybe fifty people waiting. The maximum we allow on a single tour. I adjust my cordless headset and smile a painful, wide smile that almost cracks my skin open. I know I've caught everyone's attention with my ghoulish attire and red, witchy hair.

"Good evening, everyone, and welcome to the Salem Night Tour. My name is Everlynne, and I will be your tour guide." Camera flashes blink back at me as people take pictures. I continue, feeling my soul drifting away from my body. I've always hated getting my picture taken. So this is a nightmare.

"We're going to cover some of Salem's history, including the witch hunt hysteria of 1692 and the exhumation of bodies of people who were believed to turn into vampires—yay, consumption!" I punch the air, making people laugh.

"We'll talk murders, ghosts, curses, civil war. You know, all the fun stuff!"

I draw another wave of giggles from my audience. A mishmash of tourists from out of state and teenagers looking for a way to burn time tonight. Originally, I'd moved from San Francisco to Boston looking for a library job. But a week into the hubbub of the big city, I realized it was all too much. Too big, too gray, too harsh. Everything was expensive, packed, and sold out. Boston felt like San Francisco, sans the rose-colored filter through which I viewed my hometown. After dropping out of Berkeley and running away, it felt redundant to return to California a few weeks post my escape. So I moved to Salem instead. It seemed like it was tailor made for me.

Morbid? Check.

History drenched? Check.

Cold? Gloomy? Full of witchery and cemeteries? Check, check, check.

"First things first." I grin at my audience conspiratorially. "I need to know who here still goes to school and wants to impress their history teacher?"

As expected, dozens of arms lift in the air.

"Did you know that slavery was partially abolished in Massachusetts on July eighth, 1783, nearly a century before the Civil War? And there's an interesting story behind it."

There are gasps and murmurs. This is the beginning of a ninety-minute tour I am going to give around the city.

I laugh, and I take questions, and I point at the things they should take photos of and tell them which filters work best for them. But I'm not really there. My mind is with Loki. With the traitorous cat who decided to leave me.

And with Pippa, over three thousand miles away, in California, who still doesn't understand why I disappeared one sunny day. Not long after I fell in love with Joe.

◆ ◆ ◆

When I get back home, Nora isn't there. She is probably spending the night at Colt's. She's been doing that more often than not lately. Normally, I snuggle with Loki and binge-watch whatever is trending on Netflix. But right now, there is no Loki in sight. The hollow pain in my chest reminds me I'm all alone. The phone burning a hole in my cape's pocket reminds me that I have to be.

I power up my laptop and check my email, then Facebook. No new notifications. My heart sinks. I check Craigslist anyway, a glutton for punishment. Nothing.

I pad to the kitchen, fill a glass with tap water, and lock the front door on my way to my room. I slip under the covers and flip my phone screen down on my nightstand. I overthink myself to sleep.

Four hours later, I'm awakened by my alarm. I have a shift today, selling witchery souvenirs at a local store. It's not ideal, working two jobs, but it's necessary if I want to save money and do something with my life at some point. I'm not sure what that something is going to be. Actually, I'm not sure I'll ever have the guts to pursue anything at all. But saving money toward something gives me the illusion that my life hasn't been flushed completely down the toilet. It feels like at least I have a plan, and all I have to do is figure out which fork in the road to take once I've saved enough.

The first thing I do after brushing my teeth is check my laptop to see if there are any answers on Craigslist. There is one. It's a private message. My heart flips like a fish out of water. I click on it.

DominicG: Hey. I'm pretty sure your cat is crashing on my balcony recliner.

Loki? Crashing somewhere else? Wouldn't he be scared? Then it occurs to me this guy could be a creeper trying to lure women into his apartment.

EverlynneL: Thanks for the message. Can I see a picture, please?

I stand up to do something with my body, then go to the kitchen and make myself some coffee. I'm restless. I'm anxious. I forget to put creamer and sugar in my coffee before making my way back to the laptop in my living room.

DominicG sent you an attachment. I open it. It's a picture of a picture. Of a frosted-over lake.

EverlynneL: Hilarious. I meant of the cat.

DominicG: Tough audience. Coming right up.

He sends another attachment. I open it, praying to God it isn't a dick pic, and sure enough, it *is* Loki, in the flesh (or rather, fur), sitting on an expensive-looking recliner in a balcony of what looks like a fairly upscale downtown apartment block. He stares into the camera defiantly. It must be him, because I can recognize those chins anywhere, and also because a part of his left ear is missing. The girl at the shelter told me an older cat ripped it out the day I adopted him. It was one of the reasons I chose him, in fact. I loved the fact Loki and I had something in common. We were both a little damaged.

Wait . . . he got all the way *downtown*?

EverlynneL: Do you live downtown?

DominicG: Yeah.

EverlynneL: And you just . . . woke up and found him there?

DominicG: Actually, I came back home late at night and heard scratches coming from the balcony. When I opened

the door, he was there. He looked healthy, but I still gave him milk (that's okay, right? I've never had a cat, but I know they like milk. From cartoons, mostly). He slept somewhere in my apartment. Then when I woke up today he scratched the balcony door again. I let him out. And that's where he's been chilling for the last couple hours. I think he likes it here. Great view and lots of sun.

I tend to believe this guy. What are the chances that he broke into my house to steal my cat and waited until I posted about it on Craigslist just so he could lure me into his place? If he had any weird ideas, he would have murdered me in my own apartment. Or kidnapped me instead of the cat. Or not have left an internet paper trail, corresponding with me here. Clearly, I need to stop listening to true-crime podcasts. My mind drifts to terrible places when unattended.

EverlynneL: Can I pick him up?

DominicG: You can and should.

EverlynneL: Can you do noon-ish? I need to wait for my roommate and her boyfriend to come with me (no offense, but I can't take any chances that you're an axe murderer).

I think about Joe's axe-murderer joke from six years ago and want to throw up, like it happened yesterday.

DominicG: I start a shift in a couple hours, so noon doesn't work (and none taken, although let the record show that if I were a murderer, an axe wouldn't be my first choice of weapon. Too messy. Poison, however . . .).

I find myself smiling, despite myself. It's the first time I've smiled in a very long time. This guy has jokes. And good punctuation. Both, my dark little heart can appreciate. I decide to take a chance. He sounds normal. If he opens the door and looks off, I'll run (sorry, Loki).

EverlynneL: Okay. Can I pick him up now, then?

DominicG: Give me twenty.

EverlynneL: Thanks.

DominicG: Pick up doughnuts on your way here.

EverlynneL: Excuse me?

DominicG forwards me a copy of my post.

DominicG: Says right here. REWARD. Doughnuts are my reward.

I'm encouraged by his odd request. No murderer I've ever heard of ever left a half-eaten box of Dunkies at the scene of the crime. And I listen to a *lot* of morbid podcasts.

EverlynneL: Cheap date. Noted.

DominicG: Glazed. The real stuff. No strawberry frost or chocolate. Any of those fake, pretentious doughnuts.

EverlynneL: Fine. Just don't be an axe murderer.

DominicG: No promises.

FOUR

Dominic lives on historic Chestnut Street, which confirms my suspicion that he is, as my dad likes to put it, doing well for himself.

He mentioned something about coming home in the middle of the night in our conversation. I bet he is the clubbing type. I buzz when I reach his building. It's a black multiapartment complex that looks luxurious and understated at the same time. It sticks out like a sore thumb in the middle of the redbrick street: a giant modern middle finger.

Dominic buzzes me up but doesn't answer when I hit the intercom. I cringe, balancing the box of doughnuts in my hand. If this is how I die, it's going to be a sad way to go. In the elevator on my way up, I shoot Nora a quick message, explaining that someone answered my Craigslist post, and that I'm picking Loki up at this address. The elevator dings. I tuck my phone into the back pocket of my jeans and pour myself out once I reach his floor, heading for apartment number 911, of all numbers.

I knock on the door. It swings open immediately, like the person behind it has been waiting.

And the person behind it is . . . well, obnoxiously, freakishly, *creepily* perfect.

Dominic stares back at me with eyes the color of marble. The gray and blue swirl together, fighting for dominance. His hair is cut short and neat. The geometry of his face is so precise, so sculpted, he almost looks like a different species. A better species, to be sure. He's the kind of beautiful that makes someone become a douchebag. A young Alain Delon doppelgänger, if I had to describe him.

He is also wearing green scrubs.

That's why he came back in the middle of the night, you Judgy Janet, you. Not because he went clubbing. Because he was busy saving lives.

"Hey, EverlynneL. No. Don't come in just yet." He grabs the box of doughnuts from my hand, flashing me a sweet, dimpled smile. "We have a hostage situation here. I need to check my demands have been met in full."

"It's all there," I say in a deadpan. "Bankrolled into wads of sugar."

He flips the box open and sees six glazed doughnuts and two chocolate-with-sprinkles doughnuts for me.

He looks up, frowning. "Your chocolate is touching my real doughnuts."

"Don't be such a purist."

"I don't like chocolate."

"Tell me you're a sociopath without telling me you're a sociopath." I roll my eyes.

"She's onto me." Dominic's flawless face breaks into a grin. "Time to lure her in before she calls the cops."

"See, you may want to think this and not actually say it out loud next time. Haven't you read *Serial Killing for Dummies?*"

"It's in my curriculum for next year. I'm just a freshman killer. Come on in."

After this exchange, I find that my anxiety and worry somewhat disappear. DominicG has a midwestern, all-around-good-guy vibe about him. I follow him inside, still clutching my phone in a death grip.

"This way. He is still on the balcony." Dominic motions to me with his hand. His apartment is small but neat. It smells like new paint and untouched books and the cleaning products they use in hotels.

I recognize some of the furniture as IKEA. The Lack side table and Klippan love seat. Every twentysomething's staples.

It's easy for me to admire Dominic, for the same reason I like his apartment. They're both gorgeous, clinical, and not my type. Not that I really have a type in men. I haven't dated anyone since Joe. But something about Dominic's perfectness puts me off. I'm sure he feels the same way about my averageness. Guys like him end up marrying women with endless legs and pronounced cheekbones and toenails that are always painted the right color for the season.

He pushes the balcony door open, still holding the doughnuts, and I come face-to-face with my traitorous cat. Loki offers me one slow, leisured blink. He is largely unmoved by my presence.

Took you long enough, his expression drawls villainously. *Were you too busy finishing the last season of* Bridgerton *without me?*

"Know what, pal? I'm not a huge fan of you right now either."

I detest him for this attitude. And, in fact, yes, I should have stayed home and finished watching a series instead of coming here to fetch him. I lower the pet carrier I brought with me to the floor and jerk my chin toward it.

"Party's over, pal. Get inside."

Loki continues staring at me, not moving one inch. I step toward him.

"I wouldn't do that," Dominic cautions from behind me. "If he found a way into my apartment through the balcony, he may try to find his way out and injure himself."

He has a point. Dominic lives on the ninth floor.

"Do you always think of everything?" I turn to him.

"Only ninety percent of the time." He turns around and starts walking in the opposite direction. "Wait here."

Dominic disappears inside his kitchen and reappears holding a can of tuna. He makes a show of cracking it open. I watch as Loki's eyes sharpen comically. Dominic tucks the tuna can into the pet carrier by his couch. "Make yourself comfortable, EverlynneL. I'll get you some coffee and we can annihilate that box of doughnuts. Once Loki breaks and gets inside, you can close it."

Genius move. I nod, thanking him quietly. He wastes no time flipping the switch on his coffee machine.

"How do you like yours?" His voice carries from the kitchen.

"Two sugars, infinite amount of cream, cinnamon if you have it. I basically like my cream with a little coffee in it."

"I knew I was getting heathen vibes from you." He laughs.

I take a seat on the edge of his couch and watch Loki, who is staring at his pet carrier, licking his lips. He is definitely tempted. Dominic comes back with two cups of coffee. He puts mine on a coaster. Wow. That's a grown-up move. How old is this guy, anyway?

He flips the doughnut box open, takes a glazed one, and stuffs the whole thing into his mouth.

"So!" he says brightly.

"So. How old are you?" I take a sip of my coffee. I don't mind prying about his age. Pippa and Nora have told me that I couldn't flirt my way out of a paper bag. Apparently, I'm hopeless when it comes to seduction.

"Just turned twenty-nine. How 'bout you?"

"Twenty-four." I lift my mug up in the air. "Happy belated birthday."

"Thanks for not saying what you're thinking."

I fight a smile. "And what exactly is it that I'm thinking?"

"That I'm an old fart."

"Don't know about the *fart* part."

That makes him laugh. He is easily entertained.

"What do you do in life, EverlynneL?" He sprawls back on the recliner I saw in the picture he sent me. He is far enough away from me to indicate that he is, indeed, not a creeper.

"Call me Ever. And I'm a guide for the Salem Night Tour and a part-time cashier at a witchcraft store. What do you do in life, DominicG?"

"Then you may refer to me as Dom. And I'm a nurse practitioner. I work for the local hospital. The pediatric oncology clinic, specifically."

"Wow, Dom," I say, actually smiling now.

"Thanks, *Lynne*." He winks. "I want to feel special."

I don't like the name Lynne for myself, but what does it matter? It's not like we'll ever meet again. He can call me Prudence for all I care.

All this time, I was worried he was a murderer, when he saves kids' lives for a living, while I tell bored tourists spooky tall tales. The one meaningful thing that used to define me—designing gravestones—I no longer do. Not since . . . well, never mind. I just don't. My contribution to this world is raising an ungrateful cat who apparently doesn't even want to be mine. I feel inadequate next to this dude.

"Now I feel guilty for giving you crap," I say. "Sorry for being an ass in our chat."

"Well, then you're in luck." He takes a sip of his coffee.

"Why?" I frown.

"Because I'm an ass man."

I burst out laughing, which never, *ever* happens anymore.

We talk a little more. I tell him I'm originally from San Francisco. He's never been. He tells me he was born and raised in Massachusetts and has lived here his whole life. That he wanted to find a job in Cambridge, but ultimately, Salem's general hospital had an opening, and he couldn't be picky after graduating.

Dom tells me that a doctor who works with him, a woman named Sarah, suggested he look on Craigslist to see if someone was looking for Loki in the Lost and Found section when my cat showed up on his patio. Otherwise he never would have thought about it. I thank my lucky stars Dr. Sarah is alive.

Every now and then, I sneak a glance at Loki. Each time, he is an inch or two closer to the pet carrier. The scent of the tuna becomes overwhelming. So much so that Dom and I stop eating the doughnuts because everything is starting to smell and taste like canned fish.

It's becoming pretty clear, just as I suspected, that Dom and I have nothing in common. We're comically different. He likes action films and blockbusters; my favorite movies are *Donnie Darko* and *Eternal Sunshine of the Spotless Mind*. He loves sushi and seafood; I swear by McDonald's and Taco Bell. He does CrossFit; I . . . get cross when people tell me to get fit. He is a regular at the gym, the library, the local book club, and a choir (a choir!), and I only leave my house to earn money or spend it on junk food.

"You really highlight my lack of ambition." I finish the coffee and put my cup down. "You're like . . . pep talk, personified."

Dom chuckles. "Can't help it. I want to grab life by the balls. Not to sound clichéd, but today is the first day of the rest of your life."

"Could be my last day too," I point out, the sunshine that I am.

He salutes me with his cup of coffee. "Yet more reason to seize the day."

"*Or* no reason at all." I get philosophical. It's liberating. To talk to someone who is so out of your league you don't even have to pretend to be charming. "Because if something is inevitably going to end—our lives, in this case—why even start it?"

Dom is about to answer me, but then he frowns and looks behind my back.

"Lynne?"

Boy, I'm not going to miss being called that. "Yeah?"

"Lucky just got into your carrier."

I don't correct him that it's Loki. I turn around, crouch down, and quickly flap the carrier door shut, locking it in place. Loki lets out a guttural meow in protest, but a few seconds later, I can hear him purring and gorging on the tuna. This cat is a real piece of work. He needs *Will sell principles and all future plans for a snack* embedded on his collar.

I hop up on my feet. Now that Loki is safely inside the pet carrier, and Dom's apartment is never going to smell un-tuna-y again, my job here is done. "Thanks so much, Dom. I owe you big time."

I flick my wrist to look at my Apple Watch. It's a hand-me-down from Nora, who thought it would encourage me to get in my ten thousand steps a day. In practice, it's only highlighted my 2,393-step lifestyle. I see that Dom and I have spent almost an hour together, which means his shift must be starting soon.

Dom stands up and walks me to the door. He opens it for me.

"Don't worry about it; you paid in doughnuts."

"Well, yeah, but I kind of worry the stench of the tuna is now inked into your walls." *And your soul.*

He laughs. "It'll remind me of the ocean."

"Ugh, Dom. You are obnoxiously optimistic. Have a good life."

I'm stepping away from his threshold when he blurts out, "Can I have your number?"

I turn around and stare at him, just to make sure I heard him right.

"Mine?" I stab my chest with a finger, looking around, like there are other people on his doorstep. Hasn't he listened to our conversation? We're polar opposites. In looks too. He is movie-star gorgeous, and I'm pitifully normal. Not ugly by any stretch of the imagination, but nothing to write home about.

"Yours." He ducks his head down . . . is he blushing? For real?

"But . . . why?" I ask, flabbergasted.

"Because I had fun?" He raises an eyebrow in confusion. "And because I made the deduction that if you had a boyfriend, you wouldn't have wanted to wait for your roommate and her man to come with you."

He's got me there. "I don't have a boyfriend," I admit.

"Great for me. Sucks for hypothetical him." His smile widens. It's a nice smile. And he's a great guy—gorgeous, funny, and way nicer than I deserve—but I'm not in the market for romance. For boyfriends. For *magic.*

It depresses me, because if a guy like Dom can't get under my skin, who could? He is perfect.

Perfect is boring, I hear Mom yawning in my head. *It's a state where there's no room to grow.*

"It's just that . . . ," I start, shifting Loki's carrier from one hand to the other. "I'm still kind of hung up on someone."

"An ex-boyfriend?"

"Yeah." None of this is a lie—I *am* still hung up on Joe, and he is technically my ex-boyfriend. But I can't help but feel a little stupid, talking about something that ended six years ago. "Sorry," I add awkwardly.

Dom shakes his head. "No hard feelings. Have a good life, EverlynneL."

"You, too, DominicG."

When I check my phone in the car, there are a few messages from Nora.

Nora: I just Google Earthed the address. I think Loki is looking for a new sugar daddy.

Nora: Okay, it's been twenty minutes. Answer me.

Nora: Thirty now. Did sugar daddy kidnap you???

Nora: Forty. I'm sending help.

Nora: FIFTY. And I really don't want to be that Karen who overreacts by calling the cops but OH MY GOD, SHOULD I?

I laugh and text her back.

Ever: It's me. I'm fine. Loki is fine. Everything is fine.

Nora: I don't believe you. Say something Ever would say so I know that it's you and not your sadistic capturer trying to throw me off scent because really he killed you and got rid of your body and wants it to decompose before I send out a search party.

Have I mentioned that I got Nora into true-crime podcasts? We sometimes spend weekends binge-listening to them in our pajamas, working on fifteen-hundred-piece jigsaws.

Ever: Cakes that look like burgers or poop or soccer fields aren't cute. They're disturbing. The dissonance between the visual and the taste buds makes the whole eating experience chaotic and unpleasant. I want my cake to look like a cake. Not like a Doritos bag. This is my truth. Thanks for coming to my TED talk.

Her answer comes promptly.

Nora: Okay, weirdo. See you at home.

FIVE

Later that day, when I get back home from a shift at the witchcraft store, Nora is there, sans Colt. It shouldn't make me happy. There is nothing wrong with Colt. He's a great guy. But I still find myself giddy that we have some alone time.

"Well!" Nora is perched on our threadbare sofa, feet propped on the coffee table, Loki in her lap. She scratches his lower back, by his tail. His butt is arched right in her face. "Tell me all about the guy you picked up Sir Meows-a-Lot from."

I drop my backpack by the door and make my way to her, then throw myself on the couch. "He is twenty-nine. A nurse. Super nice, super hot, super the opposite of me in every way . . . which made the fact he asked me out pretty shocking."

"Shut up!" Nora sits upright, shrieking. The sudden movement makes Loki jump from her lap to the floor. "When are you going? What are you wearing? Do you have his last name so we can cyberstalk him?"

Shaking my head, I laugh. "I said he asked me out. I didn't say I said yes."

"Of course you didn't." Her shoulders sag in disappointment. "Why, I ask? Why!"

Nora is in the same vein of Pippa—funny, eccentric, cup-half-full kind of girl—only not as crazy, impulsive, and daring as my former best friend. I can see the two of them hitting it off, and it makes me sad they'll never know each other. Despite Nora's bubbly, outgoing nature, what she does for a living is pretty intense. She is a mortuary makeup artist. She works for Saint Mary's Funeral Home. I once asked her what made her choose this line of work. I needed to know if she had a Cousin Shauna story that had turned her life upside down too.

But she just shrugged and said, *Nothing really happened. Originally, I wanted to go to beauty school. Then my mom told me she knows a cosmetologist and that she makes good money, works few hours, and is basically helping people and making a change. This was exactly what I wanted for myself. Not many people are drawn to this profession, but someone's gotta do it. It's an honor to prepare people for their last journey. Make sure the last time their loved ones see them, they don't see the horrors they've been through.*

It surprised me. I couldn't shake the feeling that death chased me, even when I tried to run away from it.

"Well?" Nora demands. "You still haven't answered me."

I'm trying to remember what we were talking about. Oh. Dom. *Right.*

I shrug. "You know I don't date."

"No, what I know is you're still hung up on this random fuckboy you met on vacation six years ago. It's nuts, Ever. Even with everything that happened. It's time to move on. I feel like I need to stage an intervention or something."

She is only half joking as she stands up and makes her way to our kitchen, soon returning with our healthy, nutritious dinner, a.k.a. Snyder's pretzels and two cans of Diet Coke. She passes me a can and slops beside me. I don't know many things about life, but I do know that nothing tastes better than extra-salty pretzels and an ice-cold can of Diet Coke.

"It's not that simple." I break a pretzel in two, sucking on the salt until it becomes soft. "You can't just forget."

"Sure you can, if you try."

But I have. For six years.

The more I tried to forget, the deeper the Seed of Joe had been planted into my heart, hitting roots. Growing, flourishing, conquering more and more space. It spread out to my limbs, to my lungs, to my brain.

The more days, and months, and years that passed, the more Joe grew into a mammoth, mythological figure in my head. Powerful and immortal. He had no beginning, middle, or end. He was nothing, and yet everything. He was the reason for the biggest tragedy in my life, the one that led me here, and yet I knew, deep down, I couldn't really blame him for what happened.

And the sad part is that I still haven't given up on finding him. To this day, I wander into bookstores, flipping through softcovers, looking for his name. But Joe is such a generic name. I curse myself every day for not asking for his last name.

"Till when, Ever? How long do you intend on pining for a guy you will never see again?" Nora asks seriously. She isn't touching the pretzels anymore. Instead, she leans forward, desperate to catch my gaze. I know she isn't just talking about my love life. She is talking about hers too. She wants me to find someone so she won't feel so bad about moving out when she does. Her departure looms over our heads like a green, slobbery monster that wants to tear me limb from limb.

I put the soft pretzel on the coffee table after sucking the salt off it, then pop another one into my mouth. Then I take a sip of my Coke. "Sorry, I reject the narrative that you need a knight in shining armor to save you from yourself. You act like I have to jump on every guy who looks my way. Maybe if I found someone who is more my style—"

"Why is Loki's sugar daddy not your style?" Nora asks, cutting into my speech. She is not letting it go.

I sit back. "Well, for one thing, he is too gorgeous."

"Always a terrible thing in a sexual partner." Nora folds her arms over her chest. "What else?"

"We don't have the same taste in movies, music, and art."

"Good thing you are not starting a band, then. Hit me with your next one." She rolls her eyes.

I give it some genuine thought. I may be difficult about dating, but I genuinely don't think Dom and I would make a good couple.

"He is an extrovert. He likes doing stuff. I'm a homebody. I'm pretty sure I'm allergic to fun."

"You mean he'll pull you out of your comfort zone? How dare he!" She clutches the fabric of her shirt next to her heart. I have a feeling even if I told her that Dom murders puppies in his spare time, she'd tell me it's probably to make warm fur coats for orphans. There is no point continuing this debate. Nora wanted to make her point, and she did. I'm wasting my life away, shying away from a chance at happiness, and I will probably die alone in this apartment and have my face eaten by Loki until someone finds me.

"It's done now, Nora. Let it go. I'm not going to go out with Dom." I stand up and make my way to the kitchen, where I tidy up just to do something with my hands.

"Yeah. I gathered. All I'm saying is that next time—and there will be a next time, because you're beautiful, funny, smart, and giving— make sure your heart is open. It's a terrible existence. To feel like you're not worthy of good things happening in your life."

That might be the case, but that's exactly how I feel.

◆ ◆ ◆

A week later, I think about the death of Virginia Woolf.

More specifically, how she filled her overcoat pockets with rocks and marched into the river behind her house. I remember how hard I fought the tide on the night Joe saved me in Gran Canaria . . . and wonder if I'd do the same today. So much has changed since then. I can relate more to Virginia than to the Ever of six years ago. And that scares me.

I'm giving a bunch of teenagers and history buffs the Salem tour again. It's a tough crowd this time. There are a few families with children under twelve. Three of them nag their parents about wanting to go potty, and when is the tour over, and why am I so boring, and who even cares about what Thomas Jefferson thought about the witch hunt trials.

I manage to push through, just barely. At the First Church in Salem, while telling the group about the legend of the Lady in Blue, I snap at a teenager who's not-so-discreetly stepped on another kid's foot to make her cry. Practically yelling at the teenager, I tell him that there won't be a second strike and he will be banned from all tours for good. Which I have absolutely no authority to do.

When the tour is over and the last of the tourists trickle away, I lock myself inside my rusty Chevrolet Malibu, which is the same age as me. I close my eyes and draw a few deep breaths. I wish I had some water with me, or maybe something sweet to wake me up. For all my love for junk food, I forget to eat pretty often. Nora always tells me she hates people who say they forget to eat. That unlike doing the laundry or paying a bill, eating is the one thing she *never* forgets to do. But I don't think it's a good thing, the fact that I forget to fuel my own body. It shows my complete lack of self-care.

I pick up my backpack and check my phone, something I haven't done all day. There are some missed calls from my dad. That's weird. Dad doesn't really call me all that much anymore. When he does, he treats me like one of his clients. All businesslike and formal.

My heart instantly kicks into high gear. Has something happened?

I call him, grateful that it's not outrageously late yet on the West Coast. He picks up on the first ring.

"Everlynne." His voice is paper dry, cold.

"Hey, Dad." I don't know why, but I still want to cry every time I hear his voice ever since That Day.

There's a pause. I think he didn't expect me to call him back. It makes me nauseous with shame. Has it really been this long since I last checked on him? I should get better about this. I should call my family every week. And send more postcards and gifts. Christmas and birthdays aren't enough. But I can't help but think I'm doing them a huge favor by distancing myself from them.

"Is everything okay? I saw a few missed calls."

"Excuse me?" He sounds puzzled, and also like I'm bothering him. Then he lets out an awkward chuckle. "Oh, right. My reception is awful. Doesn't matter which carrier I switch to, I always have to call a few times before I get a line. If I lived in the sticks, maybe that would make sense. But these companies keep telling me it's just the opposite. That because I live in the city, there's more competition over the network. Something about data priority. Can you believe they want me to pay premium just to be able to get a decent signal?" he rages. Because that's what's important right now. His reception. Not the fact that we don't have any kind of relationship.

"Outrageous," I agree. "We should all just stick to landlines. Show them where to stick their premium plans." I'm repeating the stuff he used to lecture us about at dinnertime.

"No need to be sarcastic." He sobers all at once.

I can't win with this man. "You're right. Sorry. You wanted to talk to me?"

Dad clears his throat. "Yes, there's something I want to talk to you about."

"Now's a good time," I say, trying to sound cheery.

"See, I was thinking we'd do it face-to-face. But you haven't been home in a long time."

"Not that long."

"Three years is long in my books, Ever."

Shame floods me again. I miss my family every day. Lots of people live far away from their families. I know that. People find work and go to colleges in different places. Or they meet someone worth moving for, or maybe it's their dream to live elsewhere. On golden beaches or in big cities that swallow you whole. But my story is different. I didn't move. I *ran*.

Dad hasn't invited me over in years, so I wonder what's made him change his mind. Is he . . . terminally ill?

"I hope everything is okay," I say cautiously.

"Everything's fine," Dad says curtly. "If what you mean by that is that we're healthy."

"Okay . . ." I'm buying time, because I really don't want to go back home. I'm pretty sure once I do, Dad will inform me he removed me from his will and would like me to change my last name not to cause them embarrassment. "In that case, why don't you—"

"Come for Thanksgiving." He cuts into my words. My dad is not huge on feelings. He's always been more comfortable with numbers and spreadsheets than with words. So I know if he summons me home, there's something explosive waiting just around the corner.

"Are you sure everything is okay, Dad?" I ask softly. "Because if not . . ."

"I already said we were okay," he says, a little impatiently. He is a mild man, and I know I'm the reason he becomes exasperated. "I just want you to be here for Thanksgiving dinner. I'll pay for your tickets."

"It's not about the tickets." I let out a sigh. I hate this, and I hate myself, and I hate that this is what my family has crumbled into. "I don't think I can take time off work. Spooky Season is our busiest time of the year. I'll need to find a replacement for both my jobs . . . I just don't see it happening at such short notice."

Even though this is not a lie, it's not the entire truth either. It's not work that's keeping me away. Dad is quiet. I hear Renn in the background, playing video games and laughing with his friends. My heart folds into itself, a tiny origami butterfly. I miss lazy Sunday afternoons with him, playing *Halo* and arguing about meaningless things, like which is better, *How I Met Your Mother* or *The Big Bang Theory* (*How I Met Your Mother*). Or are people who eat hot dogs horizontally sociopaths (yes).

"I see," Dad grunts, finally. "I can't change your mind, I suppose."

"We'll do Christmas together," I hurry to promise. This time, I intend on keeping that promise.

"I'll believe it when I see it," he says.

Taking a deep breath, I ignore his snark. "I love you, Dad."

The words feel so hollow, so sour in my mouth. This is not what love looks like. This is not what love feels like. It did, six years ago. Six years ago, we had weekly dates at a favorite diner and family Scrabble evenings every Wednesday and Taco Tuesdays.

He hangs up on me without saying it back.

Your own family doesn't love you. Let that sink in for a moment.

I bash my head against the steering wheel softly. The thumps are rhythmic. *Thud. Thud. Thud.* I do that for about ten minutes before using the remainder of my energy to rev up the engine and start driving. I put "Unfinished Symphony," by Massive Attack, on Bluetooth. The streets are littered with people. Laughing and kissing and hugging and living. I drive without direction or purpose. I drive because I know what's waiting for me at home. Nora and Colt, cuddled together on the couch like a human yin and yang, watching a movie, cooing at each other. I drive until the red line on my dash informs me I'd better get my ass to a gas station before my car dies.

I stop at the nearest station and pump gas. I glance at my watch. It's close to two in the morning. I haven't eaten all day. I need something sweet and comforting. With the gas pump still inside the tank, I amble into the 7-Eleven and head straight to the candy aisle. A tall dark-haired man is standing on the other side of it. Our bodies are positioned exactly as Joe and I were in that pharmacy, six years ago. My heart skips a beat. For a moment, I'm tempted to sidestep, see if it's Joe. But then

Nora's words reverberate in my head. It's not him. It *can't* be him. I'll never see him again. It's time to move on.

After grabbing a bag of Skittles, a pack of Oreos, and a Big Gulp blueberry slushie, I make my way to the register. I nod at the cashier.

"That it?" The guy pops his gum in my face.

"Yeah."

"Hey, man, you ran out of sandwiches." I hear a male voice coming from one of the beverage fridges, and I know it belongs to the tall dark-haired guy. There's no one else here.

"Shit happens, bro." Cashier Guy snaps his gum again as he hands me a plastic bag and my change. "There's some frozen meals if you're desperate. Or you can eat chips like the rest of the modern world."

"Shit happens? That's your answer? And I don't want junk, I want a fucking sandwich." When the guy materializes from behind the aisles, my heart does a one-eighty. It's Dom. The nurse guy who saved Loki. He is wearing his green scrubs. He also looks like *shit*. And by shit, I mean, still stunning, but like he hasn't slept in months. His hair curls messily around his ears and forehead, and his eyes are bloodshot, the skin around them dark and sunken.

"Dom?" I ask.

He stops, cocks his head, until the penny drops. "Oh. Lynne. Hey."

I cringe at the name he gave me. Now's not the time to tell him I despise the nickname, though.

We stand in front of each other, me with my plastic bag dangling from my fingertips, him with his soul bleeding all over the floor between us.

"Everything all right?" I peer into his face.

"Yeah, I'm . . ." He looks around us, pushing his fingers through rich strands of chestnut locks. "I *will* be all right. I'm having a night. That's all."

"What happened?"

65

I'm aware that we have an audience in the form of Cashier Guy, but I don't care. Dom looks off.

"Oh, it's nothing." He grabs a bag of chips, then slams it on the checkout counter. "Normal life stuff. Here. I'm getting fucking chips. Happy?" he asks the cashier.

"No, tell me." I stay rooted in place. I'm not going to be an asshole twice tonight. I let Dad down. I'm not failing this guy too. Especially after the solid he did for me.

Not when I was thinking earlier how we all have a Virginia Woolf inside us. Someone who wants to fill their pockets with rocks and disappear into a lake.

Dom gives me a once-over. His smile hangs on his face like a half moon. Sad and incomplete. "I lost a patient today. She was nine." The last word is barely audible as Dom's voice breaks. I feel my heart ballooning to a monstrous size, then popping right there in my chest. I grab his hand and pull him from the cashier and from the pitiful bag of chips and from the convenience store. Far away from this place, with the static lights and stained linoleum floor.

"Come with me."

"Who's the axe murderer now?" he asks tiredly, but he doesn't resist. For all his strength and muscles, his hand is limp and cold in mine. He follows me.

"I'm going to feed you something that's not chips, and then I want you to tell me everything about your shift." I stop for a beat, then add, "And *then* I am going to kill you. Don't worry, I'll dump your body somewhere exotic."

He laughs weakly, because he has to, but he still laughs, which is what I was aiming for.

I shove him into my Chevy. I untuck the gas pump and start driving. We split a sleeve of Oreos, and I engage him in light small talk. Where did he go to college? (Northeastern for undergrad, Boston College for his nursing degree.) What's his favorite color? (Purple.) If he could date one celebrity, who would it be? (Probably Kendall Jenner, though he reserves the right to switch to Zendaya.)

He answers my questions, subdued. I head to Wendy's, where I buy him a Baconator burger with a side of fries, a Frosty, and chili. Okay, the chili is actually so I can have the crackers that come with it. I park in the joint's parking lot and take the food out, then lean against the hood of my car. Dom joins me. I pass him his food.

"How long had she been there?" I ask.

He knows exactly who I'm talking about. The nine-year-old. He hangs his head, shaking it. I can't see his face, but I know that he is crying. "Three months. It was horrible, Lynne. There was nothing we could do. Nothing I could say to her. And she was such a trooper. Strong, courageous, engaging. She tried to fight it with all she had. You should've seen her."

"Dom." I'm surprised by how deeply sad I feel for him, for her. Both of them are practically strangers to me. "I'm so sorry. Please eat. Tell me everything, but eat too."

Dom takes a tentative bite of a french fry, just to appease me. His dim eyes zing when the salty fried potato hits his taste buds. He grabs two more and shoves them into his mouth. I think he is starting to succumb to his hunger, which is a good thing. It would make me very unhappy to know Dom, like me, is used to forgetting to eat. Though I cannot imagine it to be the case, based on how buff and healthy he looks.

"Was it . . . did she . . . ?" I don't know how to ask the question. Thankfully, Dom knows exactly what I'm trying to say. He takes a pull of the milkshake before passing it to me. I put the straw in my mouth and suck, like it's normal. Like sharing drinks, saliva, and secrets with beautiful men is something I do on a regular basis.

"No. She couldn't really feel anything. She was in a medically induced coma. Her systems started shutting down in the afternoon, one after the other. It was the worst shift I've ever had. It was like watching a church being burned down, section by section. The fire consuming everything—the Bibles, the pews, Jesus on a cross."

I close my eyes, picturing it. A chill runs down my spine. You don't have to be religious to want to throw up.

Leaning back against the hood of my car, Dom grabs his burger and takes an enormous bite. I rub at his arm, knowing words are meaningless right now.

He rips another piece of his burger with his teeth. His jaw ticks sharply each time he takes a bite. "And all I was thinking as I watched her losing the battle to this disease was that . . . there's so much *bullshit* in the world, you know? Right now, at this very moment, there's a tabloid columnist writing a nasty piece about a pop star just because they can. Because it's *cool* to hate on celebrities. A politician plotting to ruin a colleague standing in their way to the presidency. A girl crying into her pillow because she cannot afford a fucking Gucci bag. When all the while, people are losing their lives and would happily sign on for a Gucci-less existence. I know there's this whole thing about not minimizing people's problems, but fuck it, I feel like some things should be minimized, you know? Yeah, being an Afghan refugee trying to escape a horrible fate is a bigger problem than not getting asked by your crush to prom, and I'm tired of pretending all troubles were born equal when obviously that's not the goddamn *truth*!"

Proportions. Dom's got them in spades. I now understand why he is in a choir and a book club and does CrossFit and goes to the movies twice a week. He knows better than anyone how fragile life is.

"Don't expect the world to be fair. It's a lost battle. What you're doing is amazing. The way you help those kids . . . I mean, I don't know why anyone would put themselves through this, but I'm glad the world has Doms in it," I say.

He finishes the burger in three bites before washing it down with the milkshake. The color is back to his cheeks. He still looks sad, but not sickly anymore.

"Yeah, well, I didn't really have a choice." He grimaces.

"What do you mean?"

He grabs the wrappers and disposes of them in a nearby trash can. It gives me time to admire his body in the scrubs. I know I shouldn't. I know it's not the time. But I can't help but feel a pang of desire when I think about what's under his uniform. Then he's back next to me, ready to tell his story.

"When I was five years old, I was diagnosed with acute lympho-blastic leukemia. The most common blood cancer among children."

I feel like he's punched me in the gut. I actually fold over a little. Dom, beautiful and big and tall and sturdy Dom, had leukemia? How could it be?

"I'm sorry," I say dumbly. *Humbly.* What else can you say in this situation?

He nods. "It was actually a pretty by-the-book case. A story with a happy ending, as you can guess. I got chemotherapy right away. Went into induction. Four weeks later, I started going into remission. We weren't out of the woods for a few years, though. It was a whole process. The interim maintenance, the checkups, the wait for the results to come back each time. Sleepless nights. Hearing my parents cry in their room when they thought I was asleep. Knowing my baby brother was sitting there, waiting for someone to throw him a crumb of attention because everyone was too busy taking care of me. It was . . . I don't think there's even a word for what it was."

"I can imagine. No child should go through this." My hand is on his arm again, and I realize clichés exist because they're true. No child *should* go through this.

"The one thing I remember more than anything else was the nurses. The doctors. The people around me," Dom continues. "I felt like they truly cared. They would call my mom after hours to see how I was doing. They would give me gifts, and tell me stories, and play with me. And the few people on staff who weren't so nice stood out too. So I

69

decided being a nurse was what I wanted to do pretty early on. I wanted to make a difference. I wanted the next Dom to know I had their back. That's why I chose the oncology department."

We talk about his childhood a little more. How it was overshadowed by the constant reminder of his mortality. How his brother was discarded at their grandparents' house, sometimes for weeks at a time. How Dom is still guilt ridden about what he put his family through. Then Dom takes a deep breath and says, "And what brought you to 7-Eleven at two in the morning, young lady? I'm assuming your night has been as shitty as mine."

"Not anymore." I let out a soft chuckle.

He poured his heart out to me. Now I owe him at least a fraction of my truth.

"Family stuff." I wave my hand. "My dad wanted me to come home to San Francisco for Thanksgiving. I dodged it."

"Why?"

Deciding I don't want to tell Dom too much, I explain: "I can't look at my family again after I broke it into a million pieces."

"So I'm not the only one with a guilt trip. Interesting. How did you break your family into a million pieces?" he asks patiently. I get the feeling that he truly wants to know. That I'm the center of his attention.

It feels new . . . and not unwelcome.

I wiggle my toes in my boots, frowning at them. "I . . . my mom died."

Silence engulfs us from all angles. Finally, Dom says, "I'm so sorry, Lynne. How is it your fault, though?"

"It is. Trust me. It's a long story, but it is." I'm not exaggerating. It's not me being melodramatic. I really did cause it. And I know Dad and Renn think so too. It's something I'll have to live with for the rest of my life.

"Let me get this straight." He rubs at his jaw. "You think you caused your mom's death, yet you're not in prison, so I'm going to go ahead and assume it was an accident. Your solution is to deny the rest of your family a daughter and a sister too?"

I know he has a point, but it's not that simple. I can't look at Dad's and Renn's faces without feeling like the Grim Reaper, who slunk through the crack of their door and stole their joy. Plus, it's not like they're so hot on getting back in touch with me either. Renn is cordial at most with me. Mostly, he ignores my existence. Dad treats me like a long-distance cousin he feels obliged to text every now and then.

Shaking my head, I push away from the hood and round the car back to the driver's seat. Dom takes my cue and does the same. The drive back to the 7-Eleven, where he left his car, is silent but not uncomfortable. It feels like we're both processing what was said tonight.

I park behind his red convertible Mazda MX-5 Miata. It's such a Dom car I want to laugh. He likes big shiny things in bold colors. A part of him must always be that five-year-old kid who almost died.

The sun begins to rise, bruising the historical town in bluish-orange hues. Dom unfastens his seat belt and turns to me. "Thanks for the company. And the burger."

"First doughnuts, now a burger. Perhaps my calling in life is to feed you." I wink, trying to keep it light. "Hope you feel better today."

"Even if I don't, I have two fitness classes to attend, and my brother said he wants me to come over for a few beers and to watch the game. At the very least, I'll have a distraction."

I reach to squeeze his hand. I don't want to let go, but I don't want anything romantic with Dom either. I just want us to coexist in the same sphere. To be there for each other. I've missed having someone who listens. So I brave the rejection this time. I put myself out there, so to speak.

"Hey, Dom, do you want to maybe . . . exchange numbers? I would really like to be your friend."

Dom smiles, squeezing my hand back. "Thank you for the offer, Lynne, but I can't be your friend. I'd be constantly pining for you, and that would be a very miserable existence indeed."

And then, before I can say anything more, before I can tell him Nora is going to kill me if I tell her we met again and I didn't get his number, he reaches over, kisses my cheek softly, and leaves.

SIX

Two weeks pass.

I never tell Nora I ran into Dom at the gas station. I have a feeling this would just inspire another you-have-to-get-over-Joe conversation. As it turns out, Nora doesn't need Dom as an excuse. One day, when we are perched on a picnic blanket at the park, a semicute guy glances my way. He is reading a book. A book I happen to like a lot. *Infinite Jest*, by David Foster Wallace.

"You should go over there and talk to him," Nora urges, rolling from her back to her stomach, thirstily drinking in the measly rays of sunshine slipping through the fat clouds.

"That's a hard no." I bury my face in my own paperback—Stephen King's newest.

"Why? Because of Joe?" She pushes her sunglasses up her nose.

"No," I say, but the real answer is *among other reasons*. "Because I'm not that person who goes up to a guy and asks for his number."

"Do you need to be a certain type of girl to do that?" Nora blinks. "It's always a risk to ask someone out. Do you think your feelings are more precious than those of a girl who *would* ask this guy out?"

"I'm not saying that at all. Kudos to girls who have the guts to hit on men. I think they make the world a better place. But in the risk-management hierarchy, I scale pretty low. I'm not a risk-taker. I don't . . . I don't put myself out there." I use Pippa's words. It makes me miss her again. I wonder if one day I'll stop missing her like she was a part of my body. I wish for that day, but I also dread it.

Nora groans as she drops her face into a patch of grass. "You're going to die an old, lonely hag."

"Thanks," I murmur as I get back to my book. Relief washes over me when I spot the guy who looked at me tuck his book under his arm, lift his picnic blanket, and carry it back to his car.

"You'll see, Ever. It's going to be so sad. And don't think I'll be there to change your diapers or buy your groceries."

"We are the same age. Who told you I'm going to be in need of a nurse while you live your best athletic life?" I pop an eyebrow up.

"Even Loki is not going to stick around. He is not getting any younger, your cat," she continues, ignoring my words.

"He'll live forever in my heart." I tear the bag of Skittles I bought at the 7-Eleven two weeks ago and empty its contents into my mouth.

But Nora is on a roll. She is still talking, her words muffled by blades of grass. "And Joe? He is probably married right now. Or at least has a serious girlfriend or something. She is lovely. An artist. They met in New York. Fuck three times a day, even though they've been together for three years now."

I smile bitterly, relishing the pain that comes with this statement. Because pain, after all, is a feeling, too, and I haven't felt for so long. She's probably right. Joe would be twenty-five now. This guy, filled with magnetism, sarcasm, and talent, is a catch. Anyone could see that.

"Good talk, Nor."

We collect our blanket and head to my car. I drop her off at the funeral home for work, then drive to the post office and send Renn a huge package for his twentieth birthday. I got him funky new socks, ankle length—his favorite—a special Australian wax for his surfboards, and a gift card for Billabong. I add a heartfelt handwritten note. Then I go back home.

I push the door open and head to my room, where I toe off my boots and drop off my backpack. That's where I usually find the lord of the manor sitting on the far corner of my bed, a look of deep exhaustion on his face. I don't know what makes cats always look like they are fed up with your shit, but it's one of the things I admire about them the most.

Only Loki is not here. I stroll to the living room. "Loki Lucifer Lawson, where art thou?" I call out. Normally, he'd meow something that translates to *You're not my real mom* at his full name. Not this time.

Has he gone to his sugar daddy again?

I head over to the kitchen and crack a can of Fancy Feast open. I lower it to the floor and make all the noises people make when they want their kitties to show themselves. Nothing happens.

Not again. Have some self-respect, dude.

My pulse kicking up now, I grab my laptop. I power it up and pull up Dom's email.

I feel like a world-class idiot, coming to him with this for the second time in a month. But maybe Nora is right. Maybe Loki got tired of slumming it up with Two Broke Girls over here and adopted Dom, who lives at the Waldorf Astoria in comparison.

> Ever: Hey, Dom, it's Ever. Loki is missing again. I checked everywhere. I know it sounds bizarre, but is he at your place by any chance?
>
> (I swear I don't abuse him or anything. I wish I could attribute it to a rebellious phase. But he is ten years old, which is sixty in cat years. Let me ask you— have you ever met a sixty-year-old who is such a pain in the ass?)

P.S. I've been wanting to ask how you're doing since we last spoke, so here I am asking—are you okay?

E.

I'm about to go look for my cat outside. But first, I need to pee. I shut the laptop and amble to the bathroom. After pushing the door open, I'm surprised to feel something solid and fluffy looping around my leg. I look down, and it's Loki. The bastard.

"Where do you think you're going, young man?" I'm at his heels. He was in the bathroom all along? What for? It's not like he can use it. No, he has his own litter box. He takes immense pleasure in watching me clean it every day.

Loki whacks his tail irritably before finding the open can of Fancy Feast and helping himself to an early dinner. I sag against the hallway wall, closing my eyes. I think I'm losing it. I'm too lonely. Too deep in my own head. A ping from my phone alerts me that I have a new email. I take it out of my pocket and swipe the screen. Pulse pounding, I open my email, but the connection is slow, and I find myself pacing from side to side.

Dom: Hey. Nope, sorry. No sign of Loki. But I'll keep an eye out. P.S. feeling better. Hope you are, too.

My heart sinks. Nothing Dom said is wrong, per se, but it is not very personal either. Another email pops up immediately after.

Dom: But I'm happy to help you look for him if you need me to.

I realize maybe my default was to message Dom because I *wanted* to message him. Not because of Loki. Nora is right—I have to move on at some point. Dom may not be a mirror image of my soul like Joe was—no man is probably going to be—but he is kind, nice, smart, and hot.

> Ever: False alarm. He barricaded himself in the bathroom.

> Dom: Grumpiest sixty-year-old in Salem. Glad you found him.

> Ever: But . . . I'd still like to meet.

> Ever: Do you wanna grab coffee this week?

A beat passes before he answers. I brace myself for another rejection.

> Dom: Already told you, Lynne. I like you too much to do friendship.

> Ever: Yes, but . . .

But it's been so long, and I've been so lonely, and you are kind, and sweet, and funny . . .

> Ever: Maybe I want more than friendship.

> Dom: Maybe or definitely?

> Ever: Honestly? That depends on your answer.

The world stops on its axis. I'm sure of it. Nothing exists other than this moment, this conversation between two people who live across town. I've missed being nervous about things. I've missed caring.

Dom: The answer is yes and no.

Ever: ?

Dom: Yes, I want to hang out. No, I don't want coffee. Ready to be wowed?

I type always, but I inwardly say *Rarely*.

Dom: Meet tonight after your tour.

SEVEN

"Pottery studio," I say, looking around me.

When Nora said Dom was going to get me out of my comfort zone, I thought he would at least let me stay in its general zip code. Alas, that's not the case. It's ten thirty at night. I thought Dom for sure was going to take me for a romantic walk or a restaurant. But no. We're at All Clay Long Pottery Studio—open twenty-four hours; that's its shtick—just on the outskirts of Salem.

Despite the late hour, the place is buzzing with people. It's a small, crowded space, with a long oval table at the center, individual pottery wheels around it, and purple bowls full of clay next to each one. On the shelves is a display of bowls and sculptures.

There's no specific type of people who comes here. I spot two more couples who I bet are here on a first or second date, a group of elderly women, and what I bizarrely (yet probably correctly) assume is a bachelorette party. I bite down on a smile, because if Pippa were here, she'd have gone on a rant. I can almost hear her. *A bachelorette party at a pottery studio is exactly the kind of thing I expect you to arrange, Lawson. So I'm telling you right now, I want a stripper, and a cake, and some degree of debauchery that would make us not speak of the night ever again unless we get really hammered and the husbands are not around. You feelin' me?*

"I know it's unorthodox, but I wanted to think outside the box." Dom grins down at me. He looks fantastic, in a pale-blue dress shirt, elegant jeans, and loafers. I, on the other hand, am in a gothic black dress, my septum piercing visible to all. I'm pretty sure if my mom ever met him, she'd find him a little *too* perfect, but she is not here, is she?

"I'm digging it." I smile big to show my enthusiasm. Nora knows I'm on a date tonight, and I suspect that if I don't come home pregnant or at the very least engaged, she is not going to let me in.

A woman named Maria approaches us and introduces herself as our teacher. She is wearing an apron stained with clay and passes us two aprons. We wrap them around our waists and follow her to our stations. After that ensues an explanation about what we're going to do tonight. Then we start pottering. It's not exactly the Demi Moore and Patrick Swayze experience in *Ghost*. It's awkward and sticky and a little frustrating.

In the end, Dom and I both get out of the place, leaving our mugs behind to pick up tomorrow.

Well, *I* made a mug. I'm not sure what Dom created, exactly. His clay cup looked like it was trying to consume itself from within.

"I thought you loved pottery." I shove one fist into the pocket of my dress—because it's that kind of awesome dress.

"Never tried it before. I do things for the fun of it. Even if I suck."

He's a walking, talking self-help book, I think. It's *exactly* what I need.

"You can take mine, then. Tomorrow, I mean."

Since there's no way I'm coming back to pick it up, and all.

"Why, thank you." Dom tips an imaginary hat. "I shall drink my morning coffee with it from tomorrow until the end of my days. Or at least until one of our children breaks it. Darn Dominic Jr. Always up to no good."

Okay. Hold up. What?

I stop in front of his car. He turns around, then walks back to face me as he speaks. "I'm kidding, Lynne. You should see your face."

"Whatever," I say, and it feels good to smile again. It reminds me how rarely I do it these days. "You don't scare me."

"We men don't think that far ahead. I, for instance, am still stuck on our wedding invitation, the future Mrs. G."

I laugh harder, then ask, "What does G stand for, anyway, DominicG?"

"Graves," he says. "Dominic Ansel Graves. What's your full name, EverlynneL?"

"Everlynne Bellatrix Lawson."

"Bellatrix?" His eyebrows jump to his hairline. He looks pleased and infinitely amused.

"Bellatrix," I confirm with a nod. "It means *female warrior* in Latin. My mom was a 'go big or go home' kind of lady when it came to naming her kids."

"Don't sell yourself short, Everlynne Bellatrix Soon-to-Be-Graves. I'm sure you'll come up with interesting names for our kids too."

"You know, statistically speaking, there's a ninety-nine-point-nine-nine percent chance that won't happen." I slip into the passenger seat of his car. I feel lighter than I've felt in six years.

Dom shrugs. "But point oh one percent is more than zero chance, and that's good news for me."

"Where to now?" I ask. I have a feeling tonight is not over yet. It won't be over until he kisses me. Dom is the kind of man who knows what he wants, and he's been staring at my lips all night. I'm ready to kiss him back, just to try to see if I'm not broken. If I can still feel something.

He kicks his car into drive. "You'll see."

His smile tells me what his mouth doesn't. That the best is yet to come.

We get to the Pickering Wharf Marina. Dom parks, rounds the car, pops the trunk open, and produces an elaborate, beautifully wrapped charcuterie. My initial reaction is that it is yet another sign he is so much more mature than me. I don't necessarily dislike it. It would actually be nice to have a responsible adult in my life, since it doesn't look like my dad and I are on our way to reconciliation. He takes out individually boxed wine and saunters to a picnic table of a clam shack.

When we get to the benches, he wipes the condensation off so our butts won't be cold, which is an epic boyfriend-material move.

The cold is more pronounced near the ocean. There's something about the scent of brine and salt that brings me back to San Francisco.

To Mom.

Dom must pick up on it, because his next question stuns me.

"So. How did she die?" He pops a grape into his mouth as he sits across from me.

I don't want to talk about it. To be fair, this has nothing to do with him. I never share details about what happened. Even Nora doesn't know the details. The only person who might know, other than Dad and Renn, is Pippa. But that's because of what she saw in the local news.

"Is it okay if I don't want to talk about it?" I smile weakly and take a sip of my wine. It's red and subtle.

He gives me a thumbs-up. "Of course. Only share what you are comfortable sharing."

So I tell him how Mom had a gallery. How the theme was gothic, and how much I loved it. I tell him she was a free spirit, a great dancer. How she didn't know how to cook but still made the best pancakes ever. How my life changed after she died. I dropped out of college before starting the year, before I even set foot on campus at Berkeley, and moved to Boston to get away.

"It's not too late to go back," Dom says. Maybe he is right. Maybe he is wrong. I don't have the guts to go back there and face the damage I did.

I pop a piece of cheddar into my mouth. "What about you? Any screwed-up family situations you want to brag about?"

"Afraid not. The majority of drama in my family surrounded my illness. My mom is a retired elementary school teacher, and my dad owned a construction company, which he later sold for a nice profit since neither I nor my brother wanted to take over. They live in the burbs. My brother and I visit them often."

"And he lives nearby?" I ask, remembering they were supposed to watch a game together a couple of weeks ago.

Dom nods. "In the same building, actually. On the second floor. We leased our places at the same time. Seph is a longshoreman. He works at the docks, loading and unloading ships. It's crazy hours, but the pay is great and he is built like a Transformer, so manual labor doesn't faze him. What about Renn?"

I like that he remembered my brother's name. "Renn just turned twenty. He goes to college, but his real passion is surfing and taking big, juicy bites of this thing called life. Traveling, partying, stuff like that. I bet he's still what teenage girls' dreams are made of."

At least from what I can remember. Renn and I haven't spoken about anything personal in six years. It's all "Happy birthday" and "Merry Christmas" these days, usually delivered by laconic text messages.

We polish off the charcuterie and most of the wine, then go for a walk. My hand slides along the banisters as we stroll. There's a thin layer of ice on them.

"Are you cold?" Dom asks.

"No," I say, which is a lie. I don't know why I'm lying to him. I guess my default is to say what I think should be said in a specific moment. It's not like with Joe, where I said whatever was on my mind.

Stop thinking about Joe.

"Your lips are blue. Here, take my jacket." Dom slips out of his stylish pilot jacket and drapes it on my shoulders. He smells of an expensive aftershave and male. I notice he doesn't remove his hand from my back after putting it on me. *Smooth.*

"Thanks."

"Sure thing. I like to keep my victims nice and cozy."

"So you *are* an axe murderer."

"Depends on how tonight progresses. So be nice." He winks.

Dom is right for me. Even if I don't feel this insane, overpowering need to pounce on him. And who wants to be consumed by the man they date, anyway? My problem is lack of motivation and direction. He has enough of both to fuel an entire army.

"Do you know"—Dom leans against the banisters, letting go of my back and staring onto the black vastness of the water—"the Atlantic Ocean makes up roughly twenty percent of the entire world? It kisses Morocco, Brazil, Iceland, London, and Florida. But no matter how big it is, I cannot help but think it makes the world seem so small. You are always a ship's journey away from anywhere."

Licking my lips, which are starting to crack from the cold, I add, "My geography teacher once told us that the deepest part of the Atlantic is near Puerto Rico. It's over twenty-seven thousand feet deep over there."

"Have you ever been?" he asks.

I shake my head. "It's on my bucket list, though. You?"

"No. But it's on my bucket list to take you, as of two seconds ago."

And then, before I can answer him, he leans forward and kisses me. It's a surprising kiss. Ardent without being too aggressive. I feel that a wall has been broken between us. Just like when I fed Dom the other night, and he realized how hungry he was. I find myself surprisingly ravenous. For this kiss. For his touch. I've *missed* this. The skin, the heat, the scent of someone else's body pressing against mine. And so, for the first time in six years, I forget about Joe.

I forget about Joe as Dom plunges his tongue deep into my mouth, grabs me by the waist, and pulls me into him.

I forget about Joe when I realize that I like Dom's roughness. When I moan into Dom's mouth, clutching the lapels of his dress shirt, tasting the bitterness of his cologne when my lips drag across his neck.

I forget all about Joe when Dom rolls his groin against mine with a grunt, letting me feel what I do to him, then grabs the back of my neck and kisses me even more passionately. When our teeth crash together and there's an explosion of fireworks in the back of my eyelids.

I forget about Joe when Dom and I quiver in each other's arms. When desire ripples through me, like the ocean, deep and vast and everywhere. When I'm suddenly hungry for things whose taste I fail to recall.

I forget about Joe, even when I'm desperate to remember.

Because what's one night in an ocean of days in your life?

EIGHT

I get back to the apartment looking like I've just performed an epic walk of shame. My dress is askew, and my lips are raw and puffy. My hair is tangled in rough knots. The only thing that stopped me from going all the way with Dom was the sliver of common sense I had left.

When I flip the switch and turn on the light in the living room, I find Nora and Colt on the couch. Nora is straddling Colt and wearing nothing but his crimson MIT shirt, and I can see that his belt is unbuckled.

"Ahhh!" I toss my backpack in the air between us, like it's an electric fence. "Get a room."

Better yet, go to the one Nora is renting here.

I'm glad I didn't eat much, because I'm pretty sure I accidentally got a glimpse of my roommate's boyfriend's penis. There was a pink, long thing between them while I processed everything that was happening.

"How was I supposed to know you were coming home?" Nora laughs lightly while I give her my back. By the sound of it, they're both making themselves decent while I stare hard at the overhead clock in our kitchen.

"How was your date?" Colt asks.

"Awesome," Nora answers for me. "Otherwise, she wouldn't come back so late, and her lips wouldn't look like two inflatable mattresses."

They both cackle. I feel my cheeks warming up. Why am I blushing? They were having *sex* on my couch not even a minute ago. Okay, fine, *our* couch. But I think everyone can agree that once a couch doesn't belong exclusively to a couple, it is not okay to consecrate it with bodily fluids.

"It was actually great." And it was. Even if there's a small part of me that's sad to let go of my emotional crutches.

"That's what I like to hear," Colt says. I bet. He's been asking Nora to move in with him for two years now. I know I'm in the way. He can't move here—it's a dumpster, and he is an aerospace engineer. He legitimately designs aircraft. He has a nice condo downtown, with a claw-foot bath and heated flooring, just ready for Nora to move into.

"Brings you a step closer to your goal, huh?" I grin.

"I'm rooting for Mr. Perfect," Colt admits, laughing. "If he were a stock, I'd invest in the dude."

I roll my eyes, kicking my boots off on my way to my room. Colt can be a little forward sometimes, but he means well, and it's just our banter. When push comes to shove, he's a great guy who's always happy to help.

This time, I don't have to worry if Loki is here. He is sitting on top of the dining table, staring at the wall.

"Your girlfriend is welcome to move out anytime she wants," I inform him.

"She wants to make sure you're settled first," Colt says.

"Sorry my life is not to your satisfaction. I'll get out of your hair soon enough."

"Soon enough has already passed!" Colt hollers back at me, buttoning his jeans. "You're deep in overdue territory, missy."

Nora swats his chest, laughing. "Shh. You animal."

"I know you are, but what am I?"

"Your little cheetah." She giggles.

I'm going to vomit all over my feet, aren't I? They're leaving me no choice in the matter.

Ambling down the hallway toward my room, I hear them kissing and moaning again in the living room. I close the door, fall into the sea of fabric of my sheets, and close my eyes.

Expecting to see Mom on the other side of my eyelids.

Maybe Renn, maybe Dad, maybe Joe.

But looking back at me is my new obsession, marble eyes and dripping masculinity.

Dom.

◆ ◆ ◆

The next morning, Renn calls. It's eight a.m. eastern time, which makes it five a.m. on the West Coast. Renn is used to waking up at butt-crack o'clock to catch waves. What he is not used to is calling me, so I'm guessing Dad strong-armed him into this call.

"Hey," I answer on the first ring. I'm so happy to see his name on my screen that it actually takes an effort not to weep. "Did you get my package?"

"Uh . . ." The sound of a yawn and a female moan pierces through the air. She says, "Renn? Are you already up? Should I get my surfboard?"

He is losing himself in a girl. Dad's been saying he's been doing that a lot. I sometimes wonder if Renn always needs a woman by his side to tell him how loved he is because of me. Because of what I did to our family.

"Renn?" I ask when his "uh" is not supplemented with any other words.

"Sorry. Yeah, got your package. That was some rad-ass shit. Thanks, sis."

He always calls me *sis*. Even when things are bad. I love him so much for it. For his ability to act civil with people he loathes.

"Happy birthday." I hope he can hear the smile in my voice, because it hurts my face. "How've you been, anyway?"

"Good. Yeah. Listen, so, we need to talk."

There's commotion in the background. The girl next to him got up too. "I'll go get my car," she says, and she sounds so much older than his twenty years, and what the hell is going on? I am suddenly freaked out that I have no idea what's happening at home. Or whatever is left of it, anyway.

"What's up?" I ask.

"Things are changing. You need to come here."

I'm silent for a moment. Dad said the same thing, more or less, but he insisted that they were both healthy. Now I'm starting to think he lied.

"Are you guys okay?"

"Physically? Yeah. Top condition."

"Money problems?" I ask. Unlikely. Dad is the most fiscally conservative man I know. He has a great job. Mom was the one who made uncalculated money moves, and he still loved her.

Renn snorts. "No."

"Mentally . . . is there . . . I mean, are there . . . ?" This is a hard one to articulate.

"It's nothing like that. Nothing apocalyptic." He sounds short, annoyed.

"Then what's going on?" I press.

"It's not for the phone. Just come home. You've been gone for years. I know you're pissed with yourself, and honestly? Dad and I are pissed with you too." It hurts to hear, even though I already knew that. "But now there's shit to deal with, so it's time to drag ass back home before it's too late."

Late for what? I've already lost you.

"I'm coming," I say defensively, sitting up straighter in my bed. "At Christmas. I already told Dad."

"Christmas is too far away. It's not even Thanksgiving yet."

"I can't help that I have a job, Renn."

"Don't bullshit a bullshitter. Your job's the last reason you're staying away. We both know that."

A loud, lengthy honk pierces my ear through the other end of the line, followed by, "Are you coming, or what?" It's the woman he's seeing. I already hate her. Can't she see he's busy?

"Yeah, yeah," Renn mutters, sounding completely bored with her existence. To me, he drawls, "Thanks for the gifts. Just remember next time that material stuff means jack shit. When we need you, you aren't here."

The line goes dead.

A storm rolls over Salem that day to complement my shitty mood. I have a shift at Witch Way Out, and I'm working on autopilot. Whenever the shop's empty—and it's mostly empty, seeing as nobody in their right mind is strolling the streets in this weather—I use the time to call Renn. I get his voice mail again and again. Something stops me from leaving a message. I don't know what it is. Or maybe I do—I have no good excuse. He is right. They need me to be there for whatever reason, and I'm not ready to face the wreckage I left behind. I'm so much better at sending birthday gifts and cards and letters.

Dom texts me throughout the day to make sure I'm okay. I don't bring him up to speed on my family drama. He has a day off today, but we can't meet. I have to go and give a tour right after my shift. When I close the shop for the day and prepare the register for tomorrow, I hear a knock on the glass. At first, I think it's hail.

But when I look up at the display window, I find Dom plastered against it, holding soaked flowers and a clichéd heart-shaped box of chocolate.

Rain pours down on him, rolling along his nose, stroking his cheekbones. His hair is drenched and jet black. I'm worried he'll catch a cold. I think I'll always be a little freaked out about Dom's health, knowing what I know. I bolt to the door, then unlock it as I pull him inside.

"Jesus, Dom. What are you doing?" I usher him inside.

"Wooing you with a romantic gesture, I'm hoping." He shakes the raindrops away like a dog after a bath. "Is it working?"

I laugh. "Not if you end up catching pneumonia. If I have to visit you at the hospital, I'll be pissed. Hospitals aren't my favorite."

"Ha!" He raises his fist skyward. "She cares. I knew it."

I grab a quilt from behind the register, the one Jenine, my boss, usually lets her dog sleep on, and wrap it around his shoulders.

"Hope you're not allergic, but this quilt is the equivalent of seven big-size dogs."

"You're smothering me with all your love. I can't take this anymore." Dom leans down and drops urgent, desperate kisses all over my face. His lips are cold and wet. I giggle as I stumble backward, trying to hold his face and pull away. But he stalks me across the room until my back is pressed against the wall, and we are tucked far away from the display window view, between crystals and the tarot section. He drops the flowers and chocolate to the floor with a thud. His rapid-fire kisses continue down my neck. My willpower to take care of this crazy man is diminishing, replaced with white-hot need for him.

He grabs my ass and hoists me to wrap my legs around his waist, then rolls his pelvis against mine. I groan into our kiss, yanking at his hair to bring him closer. Then I remember that he could truly get a lung infection, and I pull myself together.

"Come on. Let me see you," I say breathlessly, finally managing to hold his face still. He looks a little pale and cold but otherwise fine.

He wiggles his eyebrows mischievously, pretending to bite the tip of my nose. "Hello. Hi. This is me. Dom. Let's make out."

I burst out laughing. "You're a nutcase, you know that?"

"Well, it's your fault for being so pretty." He kisses the edge of my jaw. "And interesting." He kisses my chin. "And, uh, let me see . . . talented." This time he travels south, down my throat.

"Wait a sec." I roam my hands over his chest. "Your clothes are soaking wet. You need to go home and draw yourself a hot bath. I'll come nurse you back to health as soon as I'm done with my tour."

"Haven't you heard? Work's canceled. There's a thunderstorm." He points to the storm brewing outside. "Call your boss and ask them if you're working today. We both know what they're going to answer."

"I can't bail on work, Dom."

"No one's asking you. I'm sure you're the best tour guide in the world, but no one is going to show up, and we both know that."

Hesitantly, I pick up my phone and call Jenine. She owns both the witchcraft store and the night tour. She answers with a thick smoker's cough.

"Crazy storm, huh? Haven't seen one like that since the eighties. We'd better not see a power outage. I'm too old for this shit." She has this habit of starting a conversation from the middle.

"That's what I was calling you about." Just as I answer her, a tree collapses over a power line outside. On the street is a heap of wires and wood. "Crap. I think I need to call 911 and report that," I say.

"I'm on it." Dom dials up the emergency number and wanders to the little kitchenette at the back of the shop, leaving wet shoe prints everywhere.

"So, I'm guessing you know the answer to your question." I hear Jenine lighting up a cigarette.

"Yes, ma'am."

"No one in their right mind is going to get out of the house in this weather. Not to mention, if you catch something, you'll be missing much more than a couple days' work. I'll handle the cancellation."

I'm hanging up the phone just as Dom reappears beside me. "Help's on the way."

"Thanks. I'm off for the rest of the day." I grab the flowers and the chocolate box from the floor, then press them to my chest. "That was sweet."

Dom grins. He is so wholesome. So vibrant. "I *am* sweet."

"Right. And it will take me time to get used to it."

Dom takes a step forward and tucks a lock of my hair behind my ear. "I have all the time in the world," he says slowly, meaningfully. "Or at least, I hope I do."

"Let's draw you a bath. Race you to the car," I suggest, snapping us out of the moment. Things got heavy for a second there.

"*Which* car?" He tugs me by the collar of my shirt, frowning. "Mine or yours?"

I think about it. "Yours. You can drive me back here later. Because, you know, we're *not* going to have sex." Just putting it out there, in case he gets any ideas. I like Dom a lot, but I also don't feel ready yet. Not only do I still not believe I deserve good things, but I'm also not 100 percent over Joe.

"None whatsoever. No sex." Dom raises his fingers in a scout's honor.

We race it to his car, giggling and shoving at each other and ducking our heads like we can escape the rain. We both accept the unspoken truth of it.

That I'm not going to go back to get my car tonight.

I'm going to stay at his place. We'll cuddle, and watch movies, and make food, and make *out*. Pretending for one perfect day that I'm a normal girl. Just like Nora.

Because somewhere deep down, I think I still am.

NINE

Dom and I cover a lot in the four weeks that follow the storm.

We go to Boston—twice—once to the zoo, and another time for a ferry ride by the harbor (or *harbah*, as he calls it). We visit the New Bedford Whaling Museum, check out the Isabella Stewart Gardner Museum, and take a day trip to New York when both our schedules permit. We eat one-dollar oysters in Lynn and hit up an old record store in Ipswich. We ride bikes, smell flowers, run to the balcony, and dance every time it rains. Staying true to his promise, he drinks his morning coffee from my clay mug. At least when he doesn't work night shifts.

I haven't done so many things since my trip to Barcelona with Pippa, but Dominic insists I have the full Massachusetts experience. "You've spent enough time in New England purgatory. You're one of us now." He hooks his arm around my shoulder and pulls me close when we leave an axe-throwing joint. "Time for an early *suppah*."

Indeed, we cover a lot in the four weeks we date. Other than one serious milestone—we haven't had sex yet.

We've cuddled, we've spooned, we've fallen asleep holding each other, and we make out all the time, but we haven't gone all the way yet. I still fear taking the final step. Maybe because having sex is admitting the girl I created six years ago is no longer there. It's not like I'm not attracted to him. I truly am. And I don't know many men on the cusp of thirty who would wait around for a woman to have sex with him. But so far Dom has been understanding and hasn't pushed the subject.

The weekend before Thanksgiving, Dom picks me up for a dinner date. It's the first time we've gone out to a restaurant in Salem, and it feels like we're officializing our relationship. Christening our hometown, so to speak.

Loki is sitting on the windowsill, watching us with a malicious expression while snapping his tail here and there. Holding the passenger door, I wiggle my finger at my cat. "Be good to Auntie Nora, and don't you dare pee in my new boots."

He huffs and gives me his back.

"They grow up so fast," Dom sighs from inside the car.

I slide into the passenger seat and kiss him on the lips. He looks amazing. Freshly shaven and sporting a new haircut. There's a duffel bag strewn in his back seat, which I recognize not to be the same one he takes to the gym every day.

"Are the Feds after you? Are we fleeing?" I arch an eyebrow.

"Yup. Axe-murdering operation gone wrong. It's a whole mess." He leans in to give me a deeper, more passionate kiss. It lasts for a while, so I've almost forgotten what we were talking about when he continues, "I got you a fake passport too. Run with me to Argentina? I hear their dulce de leche is crazy good."

I smooth the collar of his shirt. "No, really. Where are you going?"

We are still parked in front of my dilapidated excuse for an apartment. Dom glances toward my front door, and I see that it is half-open. Weird. I remember locking it behind me.

"What's going on?" I turn to him.

His face pinks. *Uh-huh.* I don't like secrets. Don't like them one bit.

"About our dinner plans . . ." He rubs at the back of his neck. "How would you feel if we extend the evening, to, say . . ."

"The night?" I help him out. A sleepover would be nice. Warranted, even. We've been dating for a long time now.

"More like the entire weekend."

"You want to take me on a *weekend*?" I echo.

"Very much," Dom admits with a shy smile. "Very, *very* much."

My front door opens all the way, and Nora skips toward Dom's car, holding my suitcase. She *packed* for me. I don't know what's more disturbing. The fact that she did that without telling me, or the idea that she and Dom have apparently been talking to each other. They've met a couple of times, when he arrived to pick me up for our dates, and hit it off really well. I hadn't realized they'd exchanged numbers, though.

Nora swings the back door of Dom's car open and stuffs my small suitcase into it. She shoves half her body into the car through my window and smacks my cheek with a loud kiss. "Here you go, kiddos. Enjoy the Cape!"

Dom is doing the international *nope-nope-nope* sign with his hand to his neck.

Nora slaps a hand over her mouth. "I just ruined your surprise, haven't I?"

"In a spectacular fashion." Dom hangs his head, shaking it. He is so adorable my breath catches.

"You perfect asshole!" I grab his cheeks and pull him to me, kissing him frantically. I'm overwhelmed by his consideration. "That's so thoughtful."

"Not bad for an axe murderer, huh?" He winks at me. This joke never gets old. I imagine us bantering about it two, three, four years from now. And that's good. It means that I see Dom in my future.

"Not at all." I grin.

"So if I'm ever in need of help to get rid of a body . . ." Dom trails off.

"I'm your girl. Just a phone call away. No questions asked."

He leans to kiss me again before revving up the engine. I turn my head to the window and spear my roommate with a look. "*You.* Nice work. I didn't suspect a thing."

"Save your thank-yous for when you open your suitcase." Nora laughs as she skips back to our apartment.

What's in the suitcase? Now I'm curious.

Dom and I hit the road. He tells me he's made a playlist for the drive. He hooks his USB into his stereo and plays Nickelback and Dave Matthews Band throwbacks. It's not my jam, but I don't tell him that, since he's made such an effort to surprise me with this romantic weekend. Throughout the drive, our hands are rested on the center console, our fingers laced together. Sometimes he sings the lyrics to the songs. Sometimes we talk about his work or mine, or how awesome Nora is for going along with his plan. Apparently, he slid into her DMs on Instagram a week ago and asked for her help.

I've never been out on the Cape. I've never been anywhere. Actually, I *hadn't* been anywhere. Dominic is changing that, quickly. This couple-retreat experience feels so mature. Especially when, two and a half hours later, he pulls up at a charming bed-and-breakfast. It's a white Cape Cod colonial with black shingles and overflowing flowerpots. It is beautifully restored and offers an outdoor restaurant in a gazebo overlooking the ocean. I grab Dom's hand and squeeze.

"What are you thinking?" he asks.

"That I'm *so* going to put out tonight." I'm only half joking.

He laughs, then gets out and pulls out our bags. He gives the valet the keys to his car. Then he opens the door for me, bowing chivalrously. "Wait till you eat the scones here. This is the OG Mrs. G's favorite spot."

"Mrs. G?"

"Mrs. Graves. Mom. Gemma. My parents used to take us here for a traditional summer holiday, every year without fail. Well, save for one or two, you know."

When he was sick.

I feel even more overjoyed when we walk inside and the innkeeper, a woman named Dana, shows us to our room. Dom and I follow her, holding hands. I'm pretty sure I'm grinning like an idiot when I notice how she looks at us. With quiet approval. He tells her he's been here many times, and she shares that this is her first year running the place. Before she leaves, she hands us a brochure. Dom takes it and promises to try at least two of the things she suggests we do. He pushes the door open. The room is small but gorgeous. With crown moldings, oriental carpets, and nautical art. The balcony overlooks a golf course.

Dom walks over to the nightstand and picks up a small wooden ship. A smile touches his lips. I wrap my arms around him from behind, resting my head against his back.

"Hey," I say.

"Hello."

"What's up, the World's Most Perfect Guy?"

"Please stop calling me that. You make me sound like Chris Evans, and he looks like a douche." He puts the small woodwork down, turning around to gather me in his arms. "See that little ship I was holding?"

"Yeah." I peek behind his shoulder to take a better look at it. It's handcrafted, made from rosewood, with a long mast and yellow linen.

"When Seph and I were small and we used to come here, we would play with that ship all the time. In this specific room, actually. That's why I asked for it. We had this thing where we always tried to steal the ship when it was time to leave, and my mom always caught us and made us put it back. It was exasperating." He lets out a little laugh.

"And adorable," I add.

"Sure. The first decade. We did it until I was a junior in *college*."

Laughing, I kiss his chin. "And you couldn't find a replica?"

He shakes his head. "Apparently, hundreds of hours are required to complete one model, and the design belongs to this woodturner who died decades ago. I found models that came close, but never an identical. And anyway, it's about the nostalgia. This ship symbolizes cartwheels on the beach, lobster rolls, and Mom and Dad making out when they thought we weren't looking." He shudders comically.

Jealousy sinks its claws into me when I picture his family. They sound like a normal happy family. I remind myself that they've had their fair share of disasters. That I, too, have precious memories with my family. Even if they're now tainted by what I've done.

"So what do you wanna do tonight?" I ask, giving Dom my back so I can unpack, but also because I don't want him to see whatever's on my face.

"You," he deadpans. "Kidding. There's a place down the road. You're going to love it. They have the best stuffed quahog. And then we'll have lobster ice cream."

I can't unhear Dom's joke. It's not like it hasn't occurred to me. That he brought us here so he could seal the deal. A Sean Dunham move, only with more finesse. This is not the Ritz-Carlton after a couple of weeks of fooling around but a charming, nostalgic inn after four weeks. Still . . . I don't know if I like that the decision for us to have sex was one sided.

"Lobster ice cream?" I gag. "Is that a thing?"

"It's a thing, and it's the best idea since sliced bread," he assures me, then falls on the mattress and makes a snow angel on it.

"Just don't get bummed if I puke publicly when I taste it." I unzip my suitcase, only to find out that Nora stuffed it with an unholy amount of lingerie that does not belong to me. The tags are still attached. Some of these items have holes in places no one has business touching in the human body. I feel my ears pinking. I quickly zip the suitcase before Dom sees it. Subtlety is definitely not my roommate's forte.

"You won't," Dom reassures me. "We get each other."

"Do you think we get each other?" I turn to him.

He tilts his head from his position on the bed to look at me. "Of course. Mark my words, lobster ice cream is going to be your favorite thing in the world by the end of tonight."

◆ ◆ ◆

The lobster ice cream tastes awful.

Like cookie dough ice cream, but with fishy parts instead of Oreos. It reminds me of football field–frosted cakes. Exactly the kind of dessert debauchery that inspires trust issues between humans and food.

The stuffed quahog wasn't anything to write home about either. This is more than a simple culinary disappointment. It's a thumb-in-nose moment for our entire relationship. Dom and I are supposed to get each other. No soulmate of mine can ever accept a travesty such as lobster ice cream as a legitimate dessert. I'm still trying to get over Nickelback.

Listen to yourself, Ever. Does this sound like a sane person to you?

So I focus on the good parts. There *is* magic. As we walk back to the inn from Main Street, holding hands, I notice that the air is extra crisp. That the ocean twinkles in the dark like tiny black diamonds. That the man nuzzling my neck looks like a Disney prince. And I'm not talking Kristoff or Prince Ferdinand. Dom is Prince Eric or Prince Naveen hot.

I remind myself that Dom is giving me an introduction to his childhood, to his family, to the DNA of his soul. Of course he loves seafood and questionable ice cream flavors and Nickelback. Each of these things has a nostalgic weight attached to it. I try to think what it would feel like if Dom told me he hated the Painted Ladies of San Francisco, or Oasis, or Apple Jacks. I would wrestle him to the floor until he took it back.

And it's not like everything about our dinner date sucked. There was a live band, and Dom convinced me to dance on the table, which was the most liberating thing I'd done since I pierced my septum. At one point, his brother called him, and Dom answered the phone and put him on speaker and said, "Seph, tell this girl how crazy I am about her!" The man on the other line chuckled sardonically and refused to cooperate, but it did draw a few claps and whistles from other people in the restaurant. Including one: "Marry him now, girl, or I will!"

On our way back to the inn, Dom tugs me suddenly, and we cross the road to the beach. I stumble, trying to catch up.

"What are we doing?" I ask.

"Skinny-dipping," he says. "This is the most secluded spot in all of Cape Cod, and I'll be damned if we don't make a new memory here."

My heart picks up speed. The setting and the scent remind me of Joe. My emotions feel soggy, heavy. But I go along with Dom's plan. Just because this love feels different doesn't necessarily mean it is less than what I had with Joe, right?

We strip down to our underwear and run into the ocean holding hands. I shriek, braving the ice-cold water of the Cape in November. I don't slow down, even when Dom dives right into the deep end, taking me with him.

My head breaks the surface of the water first. Dom follows closely.

"Oh my God. It's freezing!" I wail. I don't usually wail. But I imagine that Dom goes for girls who do. Delicate girls, who are more sugar than spice.

Since when are we adhering to what guys want us to be? I hear Pippa in my head. Or maybe it's Mom. Either way, they aren't happy about the wail.

"Poor baby Lynne," Dom tuts, his body latching against mine. We swim close to the shore. I learned my lesson the hard way the last time I went into a large body of water in the middle of the night. Dom curls his strong fingers around my ass. I instinctively lace my legs around his torso. Our teeth chatter when we kiss. My nipples are puckered against his hard chest. He's seen me naked before, but this feels different. *More.*

I no longer feel the achy, unexplained longing to be Virginia Woolf. To fill my pockets with stones before getting in the water. And that's a huge win.

"Confession time." He captures my lower lip between his teeth. The contrast between the cold water on our lips and our hot mouths gives me shivers.

"Hit me with it."

"When I first opened the door for you all those weeks ago, you were so cool, so funny, so pretty, I *was*, in fact, ready to propose."

"But . . . why?" I can't shake the feeling I am not what he usually goes for. It's not that I think little of myself. It's just that on first glance, we don't fit.

"Because you're gorgeous." He kisses my chin, my neck, the tip of my nose. "And inspiring. And sweet. And caring. That day in my apartment, I didn't want you to leave. I kept thinking it was a good thing you couldn't read my mind, because then you *would* think I was a creeper. Then when we met again, the night I lost my patient . . . sweet Anna . . . it felt like God had sent me a sign. I just knew. Knew our hearts were made out of the same material. Cracked in the same places. That they beat to the same rhythm."

My forehead falls against his. I close my eyes, trembling. His words are so beautiful. I want to believe each and every one of them. I realize a part of me does. I can't deny how much my life has changed since Dom entered it. Nora is right. So what if we don't like the same music or movies, or have the same hobbies? Dom is quickly becoming my best friend. My *hot* best friend.

"What did you think?" he asks me, his fingers caressing the sensitive spot behind my knee in the water. "The first time we met."

I decide to tell him the truth. "I felt painfully average looking, you know, in comparison." That makes him chuckle. "You were hot, put together, and super intimidating. I also thought we had nothing in common."

He slants his head, studying me. His eyelashes—dark and long and unfairly wasted on a boy—have little drops of water clinging on them, like fallen stars. "I hope that's changed."

I kiss him hard in response. We grind against each other in the ocean. The friction and waves lapping on my skin bring me close to the edge. My breasts feel heavy and tender against his body. He lowers his head, takes a nipple between his lips, and sucks on it. His hot tongue is on my ice-cold nipple. I moan, watching my fingers disappear inside his thick hair.

"I need to be inside you." He drags his teeth along my nipple, making it even more sensitive.

I grab his hand, and we both make our way back to shore. I shimmy out of my soaked underwear and walk backward, hooking a finger and motioning for him to follow. He does, but he no longer looks like Prince Charming. Now he looks like the big bad wolf.

"Lynne." Dom's voice has an edge to it now. He is moving toward me, cornering me against a wooden fence. I feel so alive. Oxygen scorches its way to my lungs.

"Yeah?"

"I need a condom."

"Not necessarily," I say. "I got on the pill a year ago to control my cramps and breakout situation."

"So you're into dirty talk, huh?" He narrows his eyes. "You're good at it."

I let out a surprised laugh. "Oops. That's the definition of TMI, isn't it?"

He steps forward. I stumble back, liking this game. The chase.

"*Nothing* you say to me would be considered TMI. I want to know you better than you know yourself."

Dom takes another step. My lower back bumps against the wooden fence. I'm breathless from giggling and swimming and kissing. Positively buzzed.

He boxes me in place, resting his hands on either side of me against the fence with surgical precision. His face is so close to mine I can taste his breath on my tongue. There's nothing I want in this world more than to have sex with this man right now.

"I'm clean," he croaks.

"Me too."

"Are you . . . ?"

"A virgin?" I resist the urge to smile. "Sorry to disappoint, but no."

"Just wanted to make sure. I'm not completely confident in my ability to be gentle right now." He smiles sweetly. I reach for him between us, running my index finger along his shaft, stopping at the tip teasingly.

"Hmm, what do you know? Turns out you like me back." I revisit our conversation in the witchery store all those weeks ago.

"Guilty as charged. I like you too much for my own good, Everlynne."

Dom lowers me to a dune of sand, his mouth moving over my jaw, drifting lower. His tongue trails a hot line between my breasts and toward my navel. My fingers sink into his hair. We're grainy and cold and drowning in this perfect moment.

He pries me open with his tongue, kissing me where I'm the neediest, where I ache for him. My legs fall open. I buck my hips forward, wanting more. He takes his time, licking leisurely, until I come undone, physically and emotionally, clutching his shoulders.

"Please, Dom."

He lifts his body and slides into me without warning. Bare. Several seconds pass, but he doesn't move inside me. I'm guessing he is giving me time to adjust. But then he starts kissing my face, and I realize to my horror that I'm crying.

"Sweet Lynne," he whispers, capturing another tear between his lips. "I'm sorry the last few years have been hard for you. I'm here to change that. Trust me?"

Nodding yes in response, I kiss him back.

Maybe Dom does get me, because he knows I don't want to stop. Instead of retreating, he starts driving into me harder and faster. It takes me a few moments to gather myself, but after a couple of thrusts, I begin to loosen up. To enjoy it.

I writhe beneath him and clutch onto his forearms as a second wave of pleasure crashes against my body. Dom climaxes too.

He collapses on top of me. I sink deeper into the sand, hugging him.

He kisses the crown of my head. "Thank you. I know this hasn't been easy for you. But I'm here to stay. You won't regret this decision." Then, after a pause. "By the way, *I'm* the decision."

I smile. I've spent years thinking it would never be okay, wasting days and months angry at the world, and Joe, and cell phones, and myself.

At the same time, I can't help but draw parallels between the last time I had sex and this one.

Both times were with a guy from Massachusetts.

Both were at the beach.

In both, we danced around the subject of a condom awkwardly before doing the deed.

But not everything is similar. Because no matter how much I like Dom, he does not consume me. I'm not desperate for him. I don't feel like the world would end if *we* end.

Dom feels safe.

And that's exactly what I need.

The next morning, we go whale watching, play mini golf, and take a scuba diving class in a shallow pool. By the time we get back to our room, I'm exhausted. Tomorrow, we'll drive back home and return to our reality. But we still have tonight, and I'm afraid my overdriven boyfriend (he *is* my boyfriend, right?) will want to bungee jump, go to the rail trail, and adopt a village during this time.

As if reading my mind, Dom gets out of the bathroom, steam trailing behind him. His torso is sun soaked and glistening. A small towel is wrapped around his waist.

"Babe. Do you want to go out? Grab a few beers, maybe catch a late-night show?"

I want to say yes. After all, this is his place. His passion. But the truth is, I miss being Ever. I want to veg in front of a good book and eat things with more artificial colors than actual food.

"Would you mind very much if we stay in tonight?" I ask from my position on the mattress.

Dom sits on the edge of the bed, rubbing at his forehead. "I wore you out, didn't I?"

"A little." I smile.

He squeezes my foot, and it wants to scream in relief. All my muscles are bunched up from walking all day. I'm not as athletic as he is. "I'm sorry. Sometimes I get carried away. Let's have an Everlynne Lawson evening."

"Really?" I light up.

He nods. "What's on the menu?"

We order room service and have sex while we wait for the food. The sex is great, and the generic burger with fries is divine. Then I send Dom downstairs to bring us the most uninspiring, common snacks he can find while I browse the pay-per-view movies the inn has to offer. When he comes back, we tumble into bed *again*, because there's nothing sexier than a guy who brings you junk food. For a movie, I suggest we settle on a classic, but Dom insists we watch what *I* would watch if I were all by myself. I choose *Parasite*, since it won a bunch of awards, and because I love watching foreign films. It's like winning a free trip somewhere.

The movie is great. Real and raw. But I can see Dom in my periphery dozing on and off. When the movie is over, Dom tries to sound excited about it, to show me he was into it too. "Holy crap, that was a ride, huh?" He rips a bag of M&M'S open and pours some into my hand. "The ending was . . . whoa."

"Yup. It was a doozy. I liked it."

His smile drops, and his eyes snap to my lips. "I like *you*, Lynne."

I stretch in bed next to him, kissing his shoulder. "You're not too bad yourself, mister."

"Actually . . ." He hesitates. "I'm lying. I don't like you."

I sit up straighter, confused. We stare at each other. He looks sad. A little pale.

"You . . . don't?" I ask.

"No." He swallows, looking me in the eye. "I love you."

"Oh."

"Oh." He grins.

Panic flares in my chest. It spreads to the rest of my organs. My heart is beating like crazy. The silence is too vast and too big and too loud, and the only way to fix it is to fill it with something equally as powerful as Dom's declaration. But I can't. I can't lie to this man, who has been nothing but amazing to me. He deserves more than lip service. And I don't love him. I'm *almost* there, but not quite.

"You make me feel like no one else does, Dom," I say. Each word rings true. "You're hope, personified."

I can tell Dom is not satisfied with my answer. It's not what I said that is wrong. It's what I *didn't* say. That I love him back. He draws me in, tousling my hair like a big brother.

"Thanks, babe. Now excuse me while I go chew some tobacco and do some lumbering to restore my masculinity."

Desperate to make it right for Dom, and for Nora, and even a little bit for myself, I take his hands in mine. "When I was in second grade, all I wanted was to be Luke Kim's girlfriend."

Dom's eyebrows scrunch in confusion. "Okay . . . ?"

"I wrote him a note, but I never gave it to him. I didn't have the guts."

I can see Dom is not following me, so I jump from the bed and tell him to wait there. There are no notepads or pens anywhere in the room. This is a place that doesn't pretend to think you come here to work. I put my slippers on and go down to the lobby and ask for a piece of paper and a pen. Before I leave, I tell the receptionist I need to talk to Dana tomorrow morning.

"She'll be here around six."

Not wanting to forget, I pull my phone out of my pocket and set my alarm for five forty-five.

I write the note in the lobby before I go back to the room. When I push the door open, I spot Dom exactly where I left him, looking puzzled. I shove the piece of paper into his hand, then run into the bathroom to hide.

Hi Dom,

It's Everlynne. I don't know how to tell you this, but I really like you. I would really like for you to be my boyfriend. I promise to be a good girlfriend and always be nice to you and not bug you about your friends. Please let me know and please do not tell your friends. Thank you.

PS, I'll share my Fruity Loops with you if you say yes.

Everlynne Lawson

It's a replica of the note I wrote to Luke, only with Dom's name. A minute passes. My back is glued against the bathroom door. Anxiety begins trickling in. What if Dom thinks it's weird, not cute? What if he doesn't want to be with someone who doesn't love him back? What if he is so put off by my idea of a perfect night that he is reconsidering our entire relationship?

But then there's a soft knock on the door. I feel the ricochets of the raps across my back. Dom's body glides down the door. He is sitting on the other side, both our backs pressed against the wood.

"Fruity Loops, huh?"

I close my eyes and smile, embarrassed. "They're negotiable, if you are partial to Dunkies."

"I definitely am," he responds.

"Then I'll feed you one perfectly glazed Dunkie every day. To be sent to your doorstep, rain or shine." I intend to keep this crazy promise somehow. It's high time I start something and stick to it. And since the gym is not an option . . .

"I have other conditions," he warns. "Before I accept your offer."

"Playing hardball," I note. "Let's hear it."

"I'm not down with the whole not-telling-my-friends part. I want to shout it from the rooftops. Would that be okay?"

"Ah, let me see . . ." I pretend to think. I'm glad to hear he sounds like he is chuckling. "Yeah. I guess that works for me."

"And I have another condition."

"Ballbuster."

"Don't promise to be a perfect girlfriend. Just promise to be yourself. Because I think I caught a glimpse of the real you tonight . . . and I want more of her."

Hope blossoms in my chest. I feel grateful that I found Dom, that he found me, that he is so patient.

"Deal?" he asks.

"Deal."

"Should we make it official?" he asks.

"Sure."

We stand up at the same time, open the door at the same time, and fall into each other's arms at the same time. It is the first time we're in sync.

And it feels *almost* perfect.

It's dawn. Dom sleeps like the dead, deep in slumber. I watch his chest rise and dip to the rhythm of his breaths. His face is flawless, save for the shadows under his eyes, which tell the tale of too much work and too little sleep.

I go down to the reception area and ask for Dana. I tell her that I would like to purchase the small ship on our nightstand. She tells me that it is not for sale, which I already know. She adds that a local artist commissioned for the inn specially made the ship. "I'm sure the interior designer who worked on the room wouldn't appreciate it."

"I'll pay anything," I say, and mean it. I care so deeply about Dom, and I want him to know that. It's also deeper than that—I want to do good by someone. And since I don't know where to start with my own family, Dom seems like a more reasonable goal to conquer.

Dana says she is sorry, but she can't help me. I reduce myself to begging. I tell her the story Dom told me. About his brother, and their vacations here, and how this ship means more to him than it does to the next customer who'd see it. How Dom and Seph tried to steal it.

Finally, Dana sighs. "Fine. I don't even know what to charge for this. Each piece is handcrafted, you know? How does five hundred sound?"

It sounds about four hundred bucks more than I am willing to pay, I want to retort, but instead, I reach to shake her hand. "You've got yourself a deal."

TEN

It is Thanksgiving Eve, and—surprise, surprise—I'm all by myself.

Nora invited me to spend the day with her family. *You know Colt is coming too,* she said. *Mom is a sucker for huge Thanksgivings.* I gave her a half-assed excuse about a stomachache, and now I'm off the hook.

Celebrations are another big fat no for me. There's something about putting myself in a positive situation that seems wrong ever since Mom died.

I called Dad and Renn to wish them a happy holiday. Renn didn't answer but sent a terse text message. Dad did answer, and he sounded like he'd rather talk with an IRS agent than with me.

With Loki in my lap, a half-empty bowl of popcorn under my arm, and *RuPaul's Drag Race* on the TV, I tell myself that I'm not the only one who is not celebrating this evening. Take Dom, for instance. He skipped going to his parents' in Dover and is working a double shift at the hospital.

I think about all the nurses, doctors, truck drivers, police officers, and firefighters, of all the essential workers, then take a deep breath and get over myself.

Still, I can't seem to concentrate on the show. Even when Loki stands up and headbutts me, demanding to be adored.

Rubbing at his nose with one finger, I pick up my phone and scroll through the last few text messages I've received.

Pippa: Happy Thanksgiving, bitch (yup, still here, waiting for you to get over yourself. Call me).

Dad: Say Hi to Nora's parents from us.

About that. I couldn't tell him I was going to sit around moping all by myself today. So I may have told him a teeny-tiny white lie.

Dom: Work's good. There's a potluck and some restaurants dropped treats for the patients, which is nice. How's it going for you?

Dom: Needless to say, there is one thing I'm particularly grateful for this year . . .

Ever: Is that so . . . ?

Dom: Your daily glazed doughnuts, of course.

I DoorDash him one doughnut every day, even though the treat costs less than the delivery fee. There's something very uplifting about doing something nice for someone else. I can see how doing charity could be addicting.

I'm rising from the couch to put the popcorn bowl into the sink when there's a knock on the door. Since Nora and I don't have a buzzer, delivery people usually leave our mail at the door. But I don't think anyone is delivering anything at eleven at night on Thanksgiving Eve, and my mind starts to fill with gory scenarios starring a serial killer. Preying on lonely women on Thanksgiving is low, even for psychopaths. A line should be drawn somewhere, right?

Before I figure out what I want to do, there's another knock on the door. I rush to the kitchen, drop the bowl, take out a kitchen knife, and tuck it in the waistband of my sweatpants.

Tiptoeing to the door, I ask, "Who is it?"

There's a beat of silence.

"An axe murderer. Open up."

I smile, my whole body sagging with relief. "Sorry, Mr. Slayer, no one's home."

"Bummer. In that case, I'll just . . ." I hear the shuffling of paper bags and realize he may need help. I swing the door open to find my boyfriend standing at my threshold with an unholy number of tin-foil-wrapped dishes. He is still in his scrubs, looking tired and gorgeous and all mine. My heart swells.

"Surprise." He leans to kiss me. "I brought food and my horny self. Let's get this party started."

"Dom, this could feed an army." I grab two of the dishes as I usher him inside. That's when he drops everything on the floor. He reaches for my waist. I think he's going to pull me to him and kiss me, but then he carefully slips out the knife I shoved into my sweatpants and holds it between us.

"Babe." His shoulders are shaking with laughter. "Your mind works in mysterious, disturbing ways."

"I wasn't expecting company!" I give him a light shove.

"Who's running from the Feds now, huh?"

"Not me." I grab the knife and toss it into the kitchen sink. "You'd have to be next-level dumb to attack federal agents with a butter knife."

We tuck into the food—roast turkey, green bean casserole, candied yams, and mashed potatoes. Local restaurants dropped off some; other food was brought over by patients' relatives. The gravy is flawless and the stuffing is celestial. We crack open a bottle of cheap wine and drink it from plastic cups, the ones that squish unless you hold them extra carefully.

When we're both in a state of a food coma, we drag ourselves to the couch and continue watching RuPaul. I'm pleasantly surprised when Dom tells me he actually watches it every now and then. I guess we *do* have one thing in common.

"This is nice," I say.

"Of course." He hooks an arm around my shoulder, pulls me close, and kisses my head. "Why wouldn't it be?"

"Because I'm not used to being happy. To celebrating holidays. To . . ."

"Living?" he finishes for me softly. "It's okay, Lynne. I'm here to teach you. And I have all the time in the world."

No one has all the time in the world, I think.

When Dom gets comfortable on the couch, I warn him that it is deeply contaminated with Colt's and Nora's bodily fluids.

"That's nasty," Dom says, lowering me against the cushions and kissing a path down my neck. "That all the memories on this sofa belong to Nora and Colt. How about we make new ones?" he suggests, pulling down my sweatpants, his grin lopsided, drowsy-eyed, and absolutely beautiful.

"Please. I have the belly of a six-month-pregnant woman." I pat said stomach.

"So do I." He does the same, his palm against his flat abs.

Minutes later, we are writhing on the couch, panting and grinding, seeking our release. Now I get it. Why Nora and Colt did it on the couch.

When you like someone, you want to leave footprints of your time together.

A few days later, when I sleep at Dom's place, I wake up to a note. It's stuck to the ship I bought for him, which he keeps on his nightstand.

> Have an early shift.
> Made you coffee. Seph texted that he has fresh scones.
> Second floor. Apartment 294.
> (you're off doughnut duty today)
> Love, D x.

I like that Dom is not afraid to remind me that he loves me, even though I haven't said it back yet. I like that he puts me first. That he wants me to have fresh scones.

After plucking the note from the ship, I make my way to his bathroom and use the toothbrush he bought me. He keeps it in a drawer when I'm not here. I'm still wearing Dom's white dress shirt. It reaches to the edge of my knees. I grab a mug from the row hanging by his sink and pour myself a cup. I open the fridge to get some cream and stop to check the magnet pictures on it, from hospital events. Dom looks happy in all of them. In one, he hugs a gorgeous blonde woman. It looks completely innocent, but it's a reminder that Dom is not just my boyfriend; he is also a red-blooded, gorgeous man who is out and about in the world.

I decide that now would be a great time to meet the mysterious Seph.

Dom and I have been going out for a few weeks now, and other than my introducing him to Nora and Colt, we've been keeping our lives completely separate. Well, with me, it's not really a choice. Nora and Colt are the only people I know in Salem. But Dom has an entire universe—a brother, parents, friends, aunts, uncles, college buddies, and a CrossFit team he meets every week. I tell myself that the fact I haven't met them yet is a testament that he wants to spend alone time with me more than anything else. But sometimes I wonder.

I slip into my boots and take the elevator down to the second floor. Despite myself, I find that I'm a little nervous when I knock on Seph's door. All I know of him is through Dom's stories, and it's all pretty intimidating. He is a dockworker. Sarcastic, wry, and not very social. I once asked Dom if Seph had a girlfriend, and his reply was: "He has many. But he doesn't always remember their names."

So, a real charmer, as you can see.

There's no answer from the other side. I knock again, because, let's be real here—fresh scones.

The door cracks open, whining as it slides an inch. I hear thuds of socked feet hitting a wooden floor behind it.

"Help yourself. I'm hopping in the shower," a gruff voice instructs callously.

Okay, then. Feeling like an intruder, but not wanting to flee the scene, I push the door open and head for the kitchen. If apartments had personalities, Dom's would be Mother Teresa and Seph's would be . . . I don't know, Genghis Khan?

Dom's place is neat, minimal, organized, and clean. Seph lives in chaos. Cigarette butts overflow an ashtray on the wonky coffee table, and there's an open can of baked beans with the spoon still inside. The few paintings in the apartment are resting *against* the walls, rather than hanging on them. There's a mountain of laundry near the closed bathroom.

When I arrive at the kitchen, I spot another pile—this time of unwashed dishes. There's also a basketful of scones. Pristine and inviting, like it has been photoshopped into this horror scene. I pick two, wrap them in a kitchen towel, and stand there, feeling like a useless piece of furniture.

I'm waiting for Seph to come out so I can introduce myself. With each ticking moment, my resolve breaks. After six minutes, I call out, "Can I make you some coffee?"

The reply comes after a tense beat. "You're still here? Leave."

Leave? What kind of jerk talks like that to his brother's girlfriend? Whom HE DOESN'T EVEN KNOW.

I swallow down my hurt, mumble *Asshole*, and close the door behind me.

On my way back to Dom's apartment, I try to shake the feeling of disappointment. Seph is nothing like Dom. He is rude, brash, and hostile. I don't get how he can be this big Casanova with an attitude the size of Kansas. But I shouldn't even care, I remind myself. It's not him I'm dating.

A text message snaps me out of my thoughts.

Dom: Did you get the scones? Were they everything you hoped for and more?

Ever: Got 'em. They were worthy of every love poem ever written. Thank you. ☺

Dom: And Seph didn't give you any trouble, right? He can be a little on the grumpy side, especially in the mornings.

It doesn't even occur to me to tell him the truth. I don't want to create any tension between the brothers. I know how close they are. Plus, I haven't had the chance to win Seph over. It could still happen, though the chances are looking slim right now.

Ever: Everything went smoothly.

Vague, but passable as the truth.

Dom: Good. Have an amazing day, babe.

Ever: You too.

◆ ◆ ◆

It's double date night with Nora and Colt.

Dom booked us a place at a tavern out in Beverly. He said it's supposed to give you the full Irish experience. We bum a ride in Colt's Range Rover. On the way there, Nora wonders aloud if an Irish experience includes drinking yourself into a stupor after Sunday Mass and changing our names to Mary and Desmond. Colt tells her it is deeply stereotypical. He points out that Dom is Irish. Dom chuckles and says, "Half-Irish, half-English. Besides, we're also known for being fantastic poets and generous lovers."

Nora makes kissing sounds from the passenger seat, squeaking in delight. Colt pretends to be embarrassed by her while casually hiking his hand up her skirt. In the back seat, Dom hooks an arm around my shoulder and pulls me into an embrace. He kisses the tip of my nose.

"Care to confirm that, Everlynne?" Nora teases.

"Unfortunately, I've yet to read Dom's poetry." I dodge the question.

"For you, I'll actually write some." Dom starts peppering kisses down my neck. I squirm free and press a finger to his mouth. He wiggles his brows, pretending to bite it.

"That's not fair," he says, my finger still pressed against his lips. "What if I have something important to say?"

"You've already said plenty this car ride."

Another round of giggles erupts from the front seats.

"And that's before I've even had a drink." Dom sighs.

Nora cackles. "He's a keeper, Ev. I hope you know that."

I think if Colt and I weren't in the picture, she'd be the one dating Dom in a heartbeat. The way she looks at him, like he is the only guy in the room, I sometimes wonder.

"I have a question for you," Dom murmurs through my fingers.

I remove my hand from his mouth. "What is it, Mr. Graves?"

"Would you do me the honor of accompanying me to Christmas celebrations with my family, Miss Lawson?" He flashes me a sincere, honest-to-God good smile. "It is high time my parents get to know the woman in my life. Someone needs to tell me that I'm punching above my weight, and Brad Graves is just the man for the job."

My knee-jerk reaction is to tell him that it is too soon. That it's too big. Dom and I have been dating for barely a few weeks.

Then again, these weeks have been great. I've felt more during them than I had in the six years before them. And I'd been skimming the line of depression for a very long time.

I'm about to decline the offer politely, to tell him that I promised my dad I'd come home this Christmas—this is actually true—when Nora cuts in.

"She would *love* to! Wouldn't you, Ever?"

"For sure," I agree. "The thing is, I told my dad . . ."

"Crap!" Dom smacks his forehead. "Of course. Your dad. Hadn't thought of that. You promised to go home for Christmas. Say no more." He takes my hand and pats it. We spend the rest of the drive in silence.

In the tavern, I decide that something is definitely off. Dom barely looks at me. He doesn't drape his arm along the back of my chair like he usually does, and he refrains from gushing about my outfit and meal choice and general existence. I eat my shepherd's pie and try to pretend this isn't acutely awkward. I ask myself if maybe I'm not being grateful enough for Dom. He fits himself so seamlessly into my life. He is great with my friends and showers me with gifts, attention, and orgasms. Yes, the plan was to spend Christmas in San Francisco, but I told Dom about it weeks ago; how was he to remember?

Besides, Dad hasn't mentioned it since. We haven't even had a decent conversation since I offered to make the trip there. It's not like he'd care.

And it's not like Dom overstepped. He knew I'd planned to spend Thanksgiving by myself, before he came to save the day.

In other words, Dom tried to do something nice, and not only did I reject his offer, but he'll also have to tell his parents I'm not coming.

At some point, Nora goes to the restroom and Colt takes a call outside. I turn to Dom and put a hand on his knee. "I'm getting weird vibes. Are we okay?"

He gives me a lopsided *Are you crazy?* grin. "Of course. Why?"

"I don't know. Ever since that conversation in the car . . ." I shift uncomfortably. "I feel like I did something wrong."

"Nah. You're right. I didn't think before I spoke. I'm the one who made a boo-boo."

There's silence before he exhales. "Well, actually, yeah, there is something. But it's not your fault, and I don't want to involve you in this, so just forget it."

"No, tell me."

He looks left and right, like he doesn't want to be heard. "I forgot to give you the entire story about my cancer situation. When I was twenty-two, I had another scare. Some tests had come back with atrocious results. Bad stats. I had to retake them and also get an MRI."

My heart is already in my throat. I nod.

"At the time, I was with a girl named Emily. She wasn't just a girl. She was *my* girl. First girlfriend, prom date, hand job . . ."

"Yup. I get it. Your point has been made." I close my eyes, waving a hand around frantically.

Dom chuckles. "We'd been together since junior high. When she heard about the tests . . . that it didn't look good for me . . . that I might have to start chemo again . . ." He rubs at the back of his neck. "Let's just say she canceled the Christmas plans she'd had with my family and broke up with me on the same day. Said it was too much for her. That she couldn't live with this fear, this cloud hanging over our heads. Mom didn't take kindly to it. Now, as I said, this has *nothing* to do with you, but Mrs. G has been touchy about the subject of Christmas ever since. Especially when it comes to my partners. I haven't brought a girl over for a holiday since. So when I told Mom I wanted to invite you, she got her hopes up. That was my fault, though, Lynne. Not yours."

Even though he is assuring me that I can go to San Francisco, I understand the predicament we're both in. There's no doubt his mother's reaction if I don't go with him will be unwarranted, but someone once told me that people are merely a collection of their experiences. It's not my place to judge her if she gets upset.

I grab his hand and press his knuckles to my lips. "I'll come."

"Lynne, please." He gives me an embarrassed smile. Like maybe he shouldn't have said anything.

"No, really. My dad . . . he'll understand." Just as I say that, a rush of relief rolls through me. I realize to my shame that it didn't take a lot for me to neglect my San Francisco plans. Hearing about Dom's distress was the final push, but I would prefer to spend my holiday with total strangers than with the family I single-handedly destroyed. As for Dad and Renn, they're better off without me. I'd just spoil their Christmas and make things awkward for everyone. "I'll deal with it. Don't worry. Dom?"

"Yeah?"

"I'm not Emily," I say.

"I know."

"I'm here to stay."

"Sounds like your ninety-nine-point-nine-nine-percent nonmarriage prediction is more like a ninety-one percent now." He tucks a lock of hair behind my ear.

I lean over, grab his face, and kiss him. "And you know what else?"

"Hmm?"

Taking the plunge, I close my eyes and Band-Aid it. "I love you too."

In the end, I use the coward's way out.

I call Dad when I know he is at work. Specifically, when he is in his weekly partners meeting, and I leave him a voice message, pretending like I tried to get ahold of him.

Hey, Dad, it's me, Ever. Look . . . I don't know how to say this. I'm really sorry, but I don't think I can make it home this Christmas. Something came up. A friend invited me over, and I think it's really important that I go. I really am very sorry. Let's get on the phone and pencil a date and I'll come soon. January soon. I . . . I hope you'll have fun without me. More like *know* that you will. I know Dad's and Renn's invitations are purely out of guilt. They made their feelings about me known after what happened. *I . . . well . . . call me back. Bye.*

A day passes. Then another two. By the third day, I know I'm not going to get a call back. A part of me understands him. Another part wants to lash out, to explain that I was never made welcome after what happened to Mom. That the accusation was written plainly on his and Renn's faces every time they looked at me, which wasn't very often. After I dropped out, after I left, they didn't call. They didn't text. They didn't want my company. It is only now, a few years later, that they're starting to show signs of interest in me. But what if it's too late?

Dad is ghosting me like I'm an underwhelming Tinder date, I text Renn.

He doesn't respond. Not even with an LOL.

I think about texting Pippa to ask if she could check on them for me. But I haven't responded to her messages in so long; it seems like a deeply selfish move.

Throughout all this heartache and turmoil, Dom spins golden stories and makes plans around our upcoming Christmas. About decorated trees, epic ugly sweaters, mistletoe, and an old-school door-to-door carol.

I eat it all up, ready to devote myself to my new instant family.

ELEVEN

I wake up to a knock on the door before the alarm goes off.

It's morning enough and weekday enough that I don't instinctively think an axe murderer has come to kill me. I drag myself to the front door, knocking into Loki's water bowl by accident in the process.

"Whoever you are, you'd better be bearing pastries."

I unlock the door, and no one is there. I peer around the peeling wallpaper and wonky floorboards and notice a small square box at my feet. I recognize it, even though it's covered with shipping labels. I don't need to see the return address to know it came from my childhood home.

To: Everlynne Lawson
From: Martin Lawson
OPEN

It is the ultimate fuck-you from Dad. He knows it. I know it. His guess is I won't open the box. That I don't have the guts to face what's inside it. He would be right. But the fact that he is trying to hurt me is new. Well, mission accomplished, Dad. I am hurt. A stab-to-the-heart hurt.

Why would he do this to me?

Begrudgingly, I pick up the cursed thing and carry it into my room, putting as much space as I can between us. Loki is at my feet, sensing my looming distress and wanting a front-row seat in case this develops into a full-blown meltdown.

The box is heavy. Heavier than it probably should be. Heavy with memories. With regrets. With all the things I didn't say and should've. Heavy with one moment of recklessness that turned my life on its axis. I tuck it into my closet, between old boots and balled-up dresses I'm too lazy to hang.

My hands linger on the box's surface. It's an engraved wooden thing. My fingertips tingle. A part of me wants to open the box. Another part knows how badly it is going to affect me. I'm currently bottling up a lot of things in order to survive, and opening this box would unleash my demons all at once.

I hear the flick of the button of the coffee machine outside my room. Colt roars out a yawn. I can see him from my ajar bedroom door, stretching. The door to my room is halfway closed, so he can't see me.

Nora appears next to him in the hallway. She snakes her arms around his torso, pressing her head to his chest. He pats her ass, then pushes her hair to one side with his free hand.

"Well?" he says. "There you have it. Morticia has finally found her Gomez, and he doesn't even seem like a sociopath or anything."

Wait, is he talking about me? Nora quickly rushes to my defense. She swats her boyfriend's chest. "Stop calling her that, you big meanie."

"C'mon, Nor. You know I like her." He pats her ass again as he moves toward the kitchen. She follows him. I press myself against my door so I can still hear them. "She's a great girl. Funny. Smart. Kinda hot, if you take out all the weird black shit she wears. I'm just not down with how you're so overprotective of her."

Colt throws our fridge open. I don't need to be there to know he is chugging our milk straight from the carton.

"I'm not overprotective of her," Nora objects.

"That so? Great. Move in with me, then."

"You know I can't do that."

"Right. Remind me why again?"

"Ugh." Nora stomps her foot. "You don't understand, do you? She doesn't have any friends here. She barely leaves the house when it's not for work. She's lonely. She's sad. She's lost. And . . . look." She takes a breath. I hold mine. I don't care that I'm eavesdropping. It is *me* they are talking about. I need to hear it. What they say about me when they don't know that I'm listening. The hard truth they keep at bay.

"I pity her, okay?" Nora admits quietly. I close my eyes. Humiliation sinks its pointy teeth so deeply into me that I'm surprised it doesn't break my skin. "She doesn't have anyone. She works one solitary job at the shop, and another one dealing with tourists. I'm a big chunk of her world right now."

"You're a big chunk of *my* world," Colt reminds her, his voice softer now. "What does this mean for me? Are you going to live with her for eternity?"

"No. Don't be ridiculous." Nora lets out a nervous laugh. "Things are moving fast between her and Dominic. I bet he'll ask her to move in with him in the next few months. He's almost thirty, you know. He wants to settle down."

"So my wanting to settle down with my girlfriend depends on Dominic's desire to settle down with his?" Colt asks edgily, his tone slightly mocking. I hate that he has a point. I hate that everything he says makes sense.

"Yup," Nora says simply. In this moment, I don't know if I want to hug her or shake her. I'm standing in her way to happiness with her boyfriend, but she is doing what she thinks is the right thing. "Pretty much."

"Let's just hope she doesn't miss out on this opportunity. This Dom guy seems neat." Colt sighs, knowing that he's lost the battle this time around.

"They'll get married. Mark my words," Nora purrs.

"We'll go first."

"Aww. Colty!"

The machine shrieks, announcing the coffee is ready. The sound of wet kisses and sweet nothings fills the kitchen. It's another day in the world.

Another day my mom won't get to see.

TWELVE

On the drive to Dover on Christmas Eve morning, Dom tells me that he bought us a cooking-class pass for the next six months, and that he signed me up for a calligraphy course as an early Christmas present.

"You know, because you said you used to do art." A shy smile touches his lips.

Art is such a big, wide field, and calligraphy is definitely not my thing.

I am grateful for his thoughtfulness, but I also feel a little suffocated. I get that he lives in high gear, but I live at a turtle's pace. I always feel like I need to catch up.

"That's a lot of extracurricular activity," I note lightly.

"Well, you can't be doing what you're doing forever. For one thing, you hate it. For another, art is more fun, more fulfilling, will offer you better prospects."

I haven't told Dom about designing gravestones. I'm pretty sure it would make him run for the hills. I kept it vague, so I can't exactly get upset that he got it wrong.

"Yeah," I say. "Guess I could try and see. Maybe it's my thing."

"Have you talked to your dad recently?" Dom asks.

"We spoke on the phone before you picked me up."

Honestly, I wouldn't qualify what we had as a conversation. We shared empty miss-yous, hollow inside out. But we didn't address the fact that I'm not in California right now, or that he sent me the box, or that the gap between us is widening every minute of every day.

"I hope you figure it out. If you go in January, maybe I can tag along. I have a lot of vacation saved up," Dom offers. Just thinking about it makes me want to heave. I haven't mentioned Dom to Dad. I'm too ashamed to admit I might be happy.

"What should I expect of your family?" I ask, to change the topic. "Prep me."

"Well, Mom's just the best. No preparation needed here. She is warm, sweet, and enjoys company. She will love you instantly because you love her son." He lets the statement hang in the air for a beat before continuing. "As for Dad, he keeps to himself most of the time. He and Seph have the same personality. Dark, broody, skimming the verge of rude. As long as you stay away from politics and the Red Sox, I'm pretty sure you'll have no trouble winning him over. And then Seph, you've met."

"Actually, I haven't," I say. Dom and I haven't discussed Scone-gate, but since I'm going to meet Seph in about an hour, it's time to fess up. Dom arches an eyebrow, surprised.

"I thought you did?"

"No, he was in the shower. I just picked up some scones and left."

"Seph's a real gem once you get to know him. Hard exterior, but inside he's a kitten. He's a wiseass but makes up for it with a heart as big as his trap. I don't know what I'd have done without him."

"Why didn't we drive to Dover with him?"

Dom shakes his head. "He doesn't do lovey-dovey couples. Can't stand them. He probably wanted to make sure he wouldn't get stuck in a make-out-fest."

"Isn't he happy for you?"

"He is, but it's complicated," Dom says. His phone rings. He puts it on silent. I wonder what's so complicated about being happy for your older brother and his new girlfriend.

"He sounds like a character."

"He is, but . . ." He smiles. "Don't write him off just yet, all right? He's a good guy."

An hour and a half after we hit the road, Dom pulls up at a gray shingle-styled house in a picturesque cul-de-sac. With three garage spaces, big bay windows, and tended rosebushes.

Dom turns off the ignition and rounds the car. He opens the door for me. I get out and smooth out my oversize black sweater, which serves as a dress over my black leggings. I put on a white dress shirt with a Peter Pan collar underneath, to look more preppy than goth. I also tamed my fire-engine hair into a braid and tucked my septum piercing into my nose so it's not visible. If Pippa saw me right now, she'd call me a sellout. A fraud. She wouldn't be off base. I feel strange in my own skin.

Dom hauls both our suitcases out of his trunk. The front door opens.

A petite woman with sharp yet pleasant features hurries toward the car. Her hair is naturally gray and cut short. Her smile makes her entire face open up. She is wearing a red turtleneck dress.

She flings herself over Dom and cries, "Oh, honey. How I've missed you."

Something inside me breaks. Because there is nothing I want more in this world than to hug *my* mom, but she is six feet under.

Dom kisses his mother, cups her cheeks, and takes a step back to observe her. I love seeing men being affectionate with their mothers. I love seeing them tenderly clasp the women who made them, especially when they're over two heads taller than them.

"You look amazing, Mom."

"You look tired. And stunning. But mostly tired." She laughs. I realize that she is spot on. Dom looks *exhausted*. I normally don't pay attention to it because . . . well, because he is a nurse, and maybe that's just the way they are.

"Let me introduce you to my girlfriend, Lynne."

I don't correct him that my name is Everlynne. It seems redundant at this point. He likes the name Lynne—so what?

Smiling big, I reach a hand out to her. "Hi, Mrs. Graves. Thank you so much for having me."

"Call me Gemma, honey. Thank you so much for coming! Dom speaks so highly of you. I'm glad to finally meet." She grabs my suitcase and wheels it in. I try to protest, but she shakes her head vehemently. "No, no, you're a guest. Now, come inside. There are refreshments and some warm-up pies before dinner. Dad and Seph are already arguing over the Red Sox. Your interference would be most welcome."

"Shocker," Dom snorts out. "Don't worry, I'll make them behave."

The inside of the Graveses' home is just as impressive and grand as the outside. All wooden floors, chandeliers, plush carpets, and upholstered sofas. As if sensing my insecurity, Dom presses a hand to the small of my back and drops a kiss to the crown of my head. "You're doing great, babe," he whispers as we follow his mother. "She loves you."

When we walk into the informal living room, we find that it is empty. Gemma parks her balled fists against her waist and frowns. "Why, they were here just a second ago. Now, where in the heck did those two disappear to?"

She peers behind Dom and me, and her face breaks into another huge smile. "Oh, there they are."

And then I feel it. A brewing storm. The small hairs on my arms stand on end, like lightning is about to strike. I want to fall to my knees and bend forward, dodge being electrocuted.

But I know it's too late. That thunder has already struck me.

All it takes is for me to turn around.

I swivel on my heel. And then I see him.

Seph Graves is standing in front of me; only I don't know him as Seph Graves at all.

I know him as Joe. My *Joe*.

My lost love and my downfall is my boyfriend's younger brother.

The limb I've been missing these past six years.

He is here. In the flesh.

And he looks *gutted* to see me.

◆ ◆ ◆

Every single one of the Graves family members is staring at me right now, but I can't get a word out of my mouth. I'm thunderstruck, my face probably whiter than a sheet.

All I can do is stare at Joe/Seph. His face is all bricked up. A cold, icy demeanor I've never seen on him before. It makes him look unlike Joe, which I understand is an idiotic thing to think. I don't even *know* him. Maybe that's his usual face. Maybe he always looks like he wants to punch his way through a crowd.

Oh, God. I need to throw up.

"Babe? Are you okay?" Dom rubs soothing circles over my back, frowning.

I nod weakly, forcing myself to snap out of it.

"Yes . . . yes! Sorry, I'm Everlynne." I reach to shake Mr. Graves's hand first. I cannot process what he looks like. Tall, I assume, since I have to extend my neck to smile up at him. There's a mustache and a cardigan, too, behind the blurry cloud of panic forming in front of my eyes. The only thing that seems to be on portrait mode, sharp as a razor, is Joe's face.

"Hello." Mr. Graves is curt. Nothing like his human ball of sunshine of a wife. "I'm Brad. Nice of you to join us."

Nice of you to create my entire dating history.

Next, I turn to Joe. He is still looking at me with something between sheer indifference and confusion. I'm weak at the knees. Of all the scenarios I've run in my head about what would happen if we ever met again, this situation has never come up. Rightly so. This is torture. The stuff nightmares are made of.

I tentatively reach for his hand. I'm shaking. My palm is clammy. I feel like a prisoner who's been caught trying to escape their cell. Our skins touch. I nearly jolt. His hand is warm and dry. Big. His eyes are on mine. Blue and cool and utterly unreadable.

"*Lynne*, right?" Joe/Seph drawls. The first words to come out of his mouth. His voice cracks through me like whiplash. *He remembers. Oh my God.*

"And you are *Seph*?" I ask pointedly, gathering my wits.

"That's what my family calls me." He is polite, but he's by no means the same guy who kissed me six years ago like the world was ending. "Drive was good?"

"Sure."

He turns to his dad, seemingly done with our conversation. "I'm getting a Guinness."

"Make it two, punk." Brad chuckles.

"Anything for you, D?" Joe/Seph asks, jerking his chin toward his older brother. Dom shakes his head, watching the two of us alertly. He must've picked up on the off vibes between us. "I'm saving myself for the eggnog. I'm trying to convince Lynne to have some."

"Not in this lifetime, buddy." I smile. My cheeks feel as stiff as clay.

"Why don't we all get a drink? I'm sure Lynne could use a glass of something too." Gemma herds us all into the kitchen.

I can't stop myself this time. "It's Everlynne. Or Ever. Dom's the only one who calls me Lynne, really." I don't know why I'm telling them this. It's not like this would win Joe over. And it's not like there's anything to win over. I'm with his brother now. Case closed.

And then it hits me. I *slept* with his brother. I slept with two brothers, six years apart. They make up 66.67 percent of my sexual partners. Since the only other partner I've slept with was Sean.

I guess you could say you're a Graves digger, I hear Pippa cackling in my head. *Pippa*. I want to call and tell her what I've just found out. I need her advice.

It doesn't help that Joe and I could have technically been together right now. That I cut it off suddenly, viciously. After I came back from Spain, we texted every day, all day. The last text exchange we had was unassuming. I still remember it by heart.

Joe: Thinking of cutting my trip short.

Ever: Interesting.

Joe: Is it?

Ever: I mean, I'm sure your family misses you.

Joe: And they'll have me, for a day and some change. Then I'm heading west.

Ever: Goldrush?

Joe: Better than gold. See, there's this girl.

Ever: There's always a girl. Tell me more.

Joe: She is hot, she is into rad music, and she gets me.

Ever: Does she have a name?

Joe: Yes.

Joe: Mainstream.

Ever: LOL. I hate you.

Joe: While we're on the subject of feelings, well, hold onto your butt cheeks, because I have a confession to make.

He started typing more, but I never saw what he wrote. I never replied.

Now the device I used to talk to him with is sitting at the bottom of the Pacific Ocean, collecting rust and seaweed.

And I'm sitting right here, with a strange family, celebrating Mom's absolute favorite holiday away from home.

Back in reality, we settle at the table. It is laden with sweet potato and fruitcake pies as well as wine and beer. "Just to nudge your appetite in the right direction before dinner." Gemma's church bells laughter rings through the warm, decorated room. I opt for wine and drain the first glass before the pies are cut. Dom silently pours me another one, throwing me a worried look. I have to keep myself together. But every time I glance Joe's way, he is staring at me with what I'm beginning to recognize as awe and confusion, nursing his bottle of Guinness.

The memories must be rushing back to him now. How I ghosted him for no reason at all and disappeared from the face of the earth.

Dom, Gemma, and Brad are all engaged in small talk. About the bad traffic on our way here, and things to do in Dover during Christmas, and *Oh, do you remember that time Mrs. Pavel's house caught on fire when the kids lit up the chimney because they were scared of Santa?* Tuning them out is no trouble at all.

The more I stare at Joe, the more I realize how my memory hasn't done him any justice. He is not half as gorgeous as Dominic, yet I am drawn to him more. To his too-sharp nose, and the ears that poke out a little, and the curve of his lips that are always tilted in a slightly mocking grin. He is built like a quarterback. Muscular and sturdy and sun kissed, golden everywhere.

I can't believe this is the *third* time we've met like this. Through kismet. Without meaning to. And that every single time we do, something gets in the way of our togetherness.

There are so many things I want to say to him, so many things I want to ask, to *explain*, but now is not the time. I doubt there will ever be a time.

Side note: I have to tell Dom. Immediately. Crap. What a mess.

"So what do *your* parents do, Everlynne?" Gemma asks. The words *teacher* and *construction-company owner* flew around while I was ogling Joe.

"My dad is a CPA. He has his own firm. And my mom . . . she owned an art gallery."

I hold my breath, hoping they don't pick up on the past tense. Opening my family tragedy for discussion is not something I'm keen on doing. Especially not in front of Joe. Luckily, Gemma and Brad don't dwell on it. "I've been to San Francisco twice, and both times I was amazed by how foggy it is. This is not how one imagines the Golden State, you know?" Gemma says.

Smiling, I force myself to concentrate on the conversation, which requires ignoring the loud voices in my head that shout IT'S JOE and DOM IS GOING TO BE FREAKED OUT and YOU HAVE TO TALK TO BOTH OF THEM.

"Yeah. All coastal cities are breezy. San Diego's the same. It's when you go inland where it gets the-depths-of-hell hot."

"*Wicked* hot." Dom taps my nose, grinning. "You're a New Englander now, remember?"

I force out a laugh, but all I want is for this portion of the evening to be over so I can finally be alone with Dom and bring him up to speed. Christ-MESS indeed.

The evening stretches across minutes, and hours, then days, and finally years. At some point, I struggle to remember myself *before* entering this house. After hopping into the shower and getting ready for dinner, Dom and I are subjected to a seven-course meal. Then we drink homemade cocktails by the fire and open the door to the Christmas carolers (Dom is right: they *are* good). Then we all bundle up and go to see the Christmas lights downtown. We go by foot, and Dom holds my hand so I won't slip on the melting snow. Gemma insists on taking pictures of Dom and me hugging in front of a massive Christmas tree, blinding us with the camera flash.

Even though people surround me, I've never felt more alone. I wonder what Dad and Renn are doing right now. Are they by themselves? Did they go to Aunt Mimi's for the holiday?

I marvel at the fact that every family has its own DNA. Its unique traditions, inside jokes, its inborn oddness. The Lawsons, for instance, are big on eating a quick early Christmas meal, opening *all* the presents before midnight, and then completing, through a team effort, a two-thousand-piece puzzle by morning. The Graveses, apparently, like to cram every single Christmas tradition known to mankind into one day.

Joe and I carefully ignore one another throughout the entire never-ending ordeal.

By the time we get back home, it is close to midnight. Gemma leads us to Dom's old room, babbling energetically. It's a beautiful room, with a queen-size bed, one blue accent wall, and navy gingham curtains.

I don't let myself wonder what Joe's room looks like.

Dom closes the door, but not before kissing his mom good night. I sit on the edge of his bed and brace myself for the most awkward conversation in my life.

So, funny story. Do you know your brother? Yeah, the only one you got. Well, turns out, we used to date slash sleep together slash I was kind of, sort of, crazy in love with him.

Yeah, no. The announcement can definitely use a few tweaks before I make it.

When Dom starts getting undressed and slides into his pajamas, I wonder if I should tell him without consulting Joe first. It's his secret to tell too. Causing sibling issues is the last thing I want to do here. That would be the second family for me to break apart. That's one hidden talent I did not want to discover about myself.

"So? What'd you think?" Dom slips under the covers. It's my turn to stand up and prepare for bed.

"It was great. Your family is lovely."

"Told you." Dom props his chin on his hand as he watches me take off my bra. His gaze glides along my upper body, lingering on my chest. He kicks off his blanket, and I catch his erection twitching behind his pajama bottoms. He wants to have sex. I throw my bra on his face, pretending to laugh. "Get your mind out of the gutter. Your parents are two doors down."

"Three," he corrects, nuzzling his nose against my neck. "It's all bathrooms and guest rooms. Seph's room is the closest, and I've heard him banging girls through this wall enough times to mistake this place for a brothel. Dude had prolific adolescent years. It's payback time. What do you say? Help me even out the score."

Nausea washes over me. It feels like he's punched me in the gut. Thinking about Joe with other women hurts like we are still together. Like the last six years didn't happen. Of course, there's no way my current boyfriend can know that.

I change into a black hoodie and matching sweatpants, then get into bed. Dom wraps his arms around me instantly. He thrusts his cock between us. "He wants to say hi."

I force out a hollow laugh, kissing his lips. "Manners dictate I say hi back. But I'm tired, and just trying to process today. In a *good* way." It's my first lie to him since we met. Up until now, I've only ever just selected what pieces of truth to tell him. "Rain check?"

He scans my face for a fraction of a second, but it's enough to show me that he knows something is up. I hold my breath, waiting for him to say something.

"Always. Good night, babe. I love you."

He hasn't called me out on it. *Phew.*

"Love you too."

For the next five hours I toss and turn, sleepless and tortured, waiting for a sign, for a clue, for a *breath* from Joe. Something to tell me what he is thinking, feeling.

Like all my prayers, this, too, remains unanswered.

THIRTEEN

Dawn breaks through the gray Massachusetts fog at about quarter past seven in the morning, washing Dom's childhood room in cool hues of blue and pink. The moon slinks behind naked winter trees. I've been watching it retreating for long minutes through the window. Knowing sleep is not on the menu, I shove my feet into Dom's slippers and tiptoe to the bay window overlooking the Graveses' garden.

It's largely pebbled, with flowerpots and wooden vegetable beds. There's one round wrought-iron table by the fence, accompanied by two chairs, and next to it stands Joe, smoking a cigarette.

I gasp a little at the sight of him. The dark circles under his eyes tell me he hasn't slept either. It makes me feel validated. Like I'm not overreacting to what's happening here. As if sensing my eyes on him, Joe lifts his gaze and meets my stare head-on, billowing a thick ribbon of smoke sideways. I swallow, waiting for his next move.

He *doesn't* move.

He is daring me. I can see it in his eyes.

What are you going to do about our little problem, Ever?

One of us needs to move the next piece on the chessboard. And since it was me who disappeared on him, I might as well bite the bullet. Gingerly, I make my way out of Dom's room and to the backyard.

A wave of frost hits my face as I slide the backyard door open. I stand at a safe distance from him, like he could bite me. Joe opens his soft pack of cigarettes, tilting it in my direction.

I shake my head. "I don't smoke."

And you know that, I don't add.

He shrugs, taking a drag of his cigarette as he stares at the last traces of the moon before it evaporates behind the trees.

"So. Seph, huh?" I ask. This is not the strongest way to start clearing the air, but I'm not known for my eloquence in times of crisis.

"My family insists on shortening Joseph to Seph." He is matter of fact. Not too friendly, but not short with me.

"That's weird."

"Blame my granddad. This was his nickname. I'm Joe to everyone else. What's your excuse?" He refers to my new nickname.

"I'm Ever to everyone, but I'm guessing when Dom mentioned me, he said my name was Lynne."

"You're guessing correctly," Joe says, still looking at the spot beyond the pine trees. I decide to call him Joe. I know what it feels like to be called by a name you're not particularly fond of.

"Uh." I rub at my forehead, looking around us. "I have to say, I'm low-key freaking out about what's happening here."

"Join the fucking club. We've got beer."

I wish he'd just turn around and look at me. He is trying to keep his distance, and I'm guessing it is out of respect for his brother.

Silence rings between us. "What happened to the writing?" I ask, finally.

"I grew up, that's what happened." A sardonic smile touches his lips. His eyes sweep over me quickly, stealing one glance before he shifts his gaze back to the brown fence. "It was time to earn a paycheck."

"Getting a paycheck and writing are not mutually exclusive. You can work and still be a published author," I say.

Joe whips his head my way, flicking his cigarette into a puddle of muddy melted ice. Smoke fans from both his nostrils, and his eyes are narrowed into dangerous slits. "Tell me more about chasing your dream, Miss Giving Random Tours in Salem to Bored Teenagers. Glass house, baby." He raps the glass door behind my shoulder.

I stumble back from the impact of his words. I'm not used to this version of him. The callous one. Then again, I'm not used to him at all.

"How do you know?"

"Dom told me. What are you doing in Salem, anyway?"

"I didn't go to Berkeley." I offer this piece of information as concession. To show I'm not here to argue. That I want to explain.

"Why?" he asks.

"My mom died. A few days after I came back from Spain, actually."

Finally, he drops the mask of indifference and looks at me. *Really* looks at me. His eyes are full. Full of things I want to dissect and drown in. For a second, I think he might hug me. But then he shoves his fists deep into his back pockets to stop himself, and my heart drops in my chest.

"Oh, shit. I'm really sorry, Ever."

Ever. To hear my name on his lips again makes me want to shatter into rubble. It is the first time I feel like he is who I remember him to be. A boy who made me feel as bright and magnificent as the sun.

"Thank you."

"How'd it happen?"

"She fell under a train at the BART." I swallow hard. "To save me."

Joe closes his eyes. "Double *shit.*"

Tears sting the back of my eyes. I haven't told Dom how it happened. Or Nora. I haven't told anyone. It's so intimate . . . so violent . . .

Joe's resolve breaks. Mine does too. Our bodies explode together in a desperate hug. It's of the bone-crushing variety. Fingers clawing, bodies meshing together. So fierce and protective I never want to leave his arms. I shudder at his touch. I feel him shaking too. He strokes the back of my head. I weep until I run out of tears. Time evaporates into the atmosphere. Then I remember his shoulder is not mine to cry on.

Pulling away, I drink him in. I now know why I was drawn to Dom the first time we met. Both brothers have the same eyes. Marble blue, with gray dots.

Neither of us mentions that I stopped answering his texts and calls. That I disappeared from the face of the earth. I imagine he puts two and two together.

"I'm just glad you're okay. Alive and safe. I wondered about that, you know," I croak. His face turns steely again when he remembers how abruptly we parted ways. He takes a step back, putting space between us. "I'm sorry I—"

"Don't," he says, cutting me off. "You had a lot on your plate. And it's for the best. We were kids. We rode the hormone train together. You got off first. Not your fault. It sucked at the time, but I got over it. I'm a big boy."

It rips me open when he says that, even though I know it shouldn't. Guilt consumes me. I feel horrible that Joe has to see his brother and me together. But I also feel terrible that Dom, unbeknownst to him, inserted himself into this messy situation.

"I'm happy with Dom," I say quietly. Maybe *happy* is not the right word. I haven't been happy in a long time. But existing hurts less when Dom's around.

"Great," he says matter-of-factly. "That's great. Dom's a stand-up guy. He is kindhearted and responsible and, well, the better-looking one, if I'm honest."

My nostrils flare. Why is he like that?

Like what? Loyal to his big brother and refusing to throw himself at you?

"Look, it's no one's fault it happened this way." I don't know why I'm saying this. He knows. He knows this is all a terrible coincidence.

"No. Now that I know why you disappeared, I can't fault you for it. But even if you didn't have a good reason, I'm hardly crushed." An amused, crooked smirk touches his lips. I want to die. Perish. "It's a surprise, is all. But we're going to be grown-ups about it, so no harm done."

"Well. We should probably tell him about what happened . . . ," I say.

"Oh, Ever. Please." Joe throws his head back and laughs. "I appreciate your overactive moral compass, but there's nothing to tell. We *fucked*."

The way he says the word *fucked* makes me want to slap him. I don't believe that's all we shared. I don't believe *he* believes this was all we shared. But what are my options here? To convince him that what we had was good and real? What for? It's not like we can go back. There will be no do-over for us. No chance to explain. To mend. To heal.

"Wouldn't you want to know if you were in his shoes?" I ask.

Joe makes an *Are you kidding me?* face. The good news is, finally something has penetrated his indifference.

"No. I would be pissed if he told me. If I were in love with someone Dom screwed once under a full moon, and he shoved it in my face, I'd break his nose. Twice. Ignorance is bliss."

Ignorance is bliss is the Antichrist of *knowledge is power*, which was what he told me the night we were together. Joe obviously did a one-eighty in the time we were apart.

Hearing him say that is pure agony. Not only because it highlights how deeply Dom cares about me, but also because it reminds me that Joe feels *nothing* toward me anymore.

"This is morally dicey." I fold my arms over my chest.

"*Everything* about this situation is morally fucked. I know it, you know it. Let's just keep our distance and pretend like Spain never happened," he says bitterly. "I still need to wrap my head around this. Promise you won't say anything."

My back is against the wall. I can tell Joe wants to protect his brother. I want that too. But the lie sits heavy on my chest.

Joe's eyes scan me, never leaving my face, begging for confirmation.

I cave in and nod. This is the least I can do. "All right. Yeah. I promise."

He leans forward and presses his cold lips against my forehead. I close my eyes. "Thank you," he breathes.

Before I can answer, Joe thunders toward the door, pushes it open, and disappears, leaving me in a cloud of cigarette smoke.

For the first time in six years, my heart cracks open.

And all the tar-like, gooey grief pours out.

FOURTEEN

Christmas Day comes and goes without a hitch. Joe and I perfect the art of ignoring one another yet glaring at each other throughout. We've come up with a few looks so far. The *This is so crazy, right?* look, as well as the *What did we ever do to deserve this?* glare. When he gives me the *I know he is not the one; I can see it on your face* glance, I am almost tempted to repay him with a *By the way, your brother is great in bed* stare.

I'm surprised no one mentions how much we glare at each other. Neither of us is making an effort to conceal what's happening. And when Gemma asks if Joe and I can help tidy up the kitchen together while everyone else is on dining room duty, I wash the dishes and he dries them, and all we do is whisper-shout.

"You're being obvious," I hiss at him.

"That's not the greatest sin to commit. I could be mean, bitter, short tempered . . ."

"I hate that this is happening," I groan, handing him a dripping plate.

"You know." He runs a towel over it. "Strangely enough, I hated it more when *this* wasn't happening."

Does this mean he is glad to see me? That he still cares? I daren't ask. It's an unfair question to ask him, and one of devastating consequences to me.

The next morning, Dom and I pack our bags, say our goodbyes, and leave. During the ride home, I think about my conversation with Joe and decide that he is not wrong. Telling Dom what happened between us would achieve nothing but heartache. It is likely Dom wouldn't end things with me, but he would always know, and it would *always* haunt him.

He'd imagine us kissing, writhing, groaning, gripping.

When I get back home, the apartment is empty. It's better that way. I still have to digest Nora and Colt's conversation about me. I have an urge to tell them that I'm fine. That they can move in together. That she can *leave*. I'm not lonely at all. But the truth is, all I have is Dom, and even that looks like a big fat question mark right now.

Time stutters throughout the day. Dom has a shift at the hospital, and I find myself pacing my room, back and forth. My thoughts revolve around Joe, but I tell myself it's natural. It's just the shock. It'll wear off. Dom is my reality. He is the man I'm in love with.

I want to prove Joe wrong about me, and I don't even know why.

Struck by an unexplainable desire to do something with my hands, I take out the fuck-you box Dad sent me and pour its contents onto my comforter. There's an old camera Mom gave me when I was a preteen and dabbled in amateur photography, and the sketches of the graves I drew. There are also Polaroid pictures of Mom and me in her gallery. Pictures from our Alcatraz tour and eating ice cream in Union Square, crossing the Golden Gate Bridge on our bikes, and riding the back of the cable car. Mom always said it was a travesty that big-city people never saw their home through tourists' eyes. We loved to do the corny stuff on our free weekends, when Renn and Dad were busy hitting the waves.

I miss her so much I can't breathe. I collapse on my comforter, next to all the memories of her, and weep. Once my tears start flooding, so do the memories. But in all this pain there is also a seed of hope. I am reminded of who I am, and more importantly—who I can become.

"I'm going to do you proud, Barbie Lawson," I whisper, jamming my feet into my boots. I run downstairs and out the door in the pouring rain to the nearest hobby shop and slap the door open, a woman possessed. I buy a sketch pad, drawing pencils—I splurge on a thirty-five-piece set, with charcoals and pastels—and a pinboard with some pins. Then I make a beeline back home, brew myself a cup of green tea, like Mom and I used to drink, and for the first time in six years, do something that makes me happy.

I draw a gravestone.

For Mom.

◆ ◆ ◆

When Nora comes home a day later, I tell her about the whole Joe-is-Seph debacle.

"Wait. Wait, wait, wait, wait, wait." Nora waves her hands frantically in front of my face. We're on the couch. Loki is in my lap, purring like a broken laundry machine. I am 55 percent sure my roommate is either drunk or completely hungover and not in a state to digest all the information I've just thrown at her. She is currently holding her head, presumably to keep it from exploding.

"You're telling me that the mysterious Graves brother, Seph, is actually Joe? *Your* Joe? And that he's been living in Salem all along?"

I nod, watching her closely for a reaction.

"Damn, Ever! You are so unlucky!"

I don't like her reaction. Which is okay. Nora is entitled to say whatever is on her mind. I'm the one who volunteered this information. But I cannot help but miss Pippa. Pippa has a knack for always knowing what to say. She'd know what to do. She'd take charge and give me an in-depth analysis, followed by step-by-step instructions on what to do. But I cut all ties with her after Mom died. Not that she had anything to do with it. I was too ashamed, too embarrassed, too unworthy to keep in touch with her.

"Okay, sorry, that was totally insensitive." Nora pats my shoulder. "What I mean is, as much as I'm impressed by how you found each other after all these years, I'm sure you know you can't be with him, right? With Joe, I mean."

She looks me in the eye to make sure I don't get any crazy ideas.

I look sideways and chuckle. "Of course not. What am I, insane?"

"*Phew.*" Nora wipes imaginary sweat from her forehead. "Because you *need* to stay with Dom. I mean, any girl would be lucky to have Dom, but you two seem especially good together. He gets you. You complete one another."

The problem with listening to Nora's advice is that I'm no longer sure if she is giving it to better my life or her own. I know how convenient it would be if Dom asked me to move in with him tomorrow morning. Which he might, by the looks of things.

"I mean . . . sometimes I wonder, you know." I put it out there, in the universe.

"Wonder about what?" She angles her head.

"About Dom and me. If we're really that good together, or if it's just because we're so . . ." Desperate to love someone. *Anyone.* I need Dom because he fills my life, so loving him is easy. He is my lifeline. As for why he picked me—I'm still not completely sure about that.

"Of *course* you're good together. Do you think I don't wonder about other guys every now and then? Because I do. All the time. But ultimately, Colt is the entire package for me."

Yes, I want to say. *But that's the thing about relationships. Experience may vary.*

"I don't know if he's the one," I say, because it's the honest-to-God truth. Especially now.

"Well, do you love him?" Nora asks.

"Yeah, of course."

"And is the sex good?"

"The sex is *great*."

"Do you think he'll be a good dad?" Nora fires her questions in dazzling speed.

"Dom? He's going to be perfect. A T-ball-coach type of dad."

"Then there you have it. He's the one. Final verdict."

I don't think it's that simple, but I have a feeling Nora and I will be going in circles for eternity if I continue questioning my feelings. She is firmly on Team Dover (Dom and Ever). Loki jumps from my lap, heading for his bowl. Nora sighs dreamily.

"What?" I look at her more closely now, noticing for the first time that she is not drunk nor hungover. She is *glowing*. Her smile is big enough to fit a banana into. Horizontally.

"Nothing. Nothing at all." She waves her hand in my face again—for the sixth time since she got in the door, actually—and I finally see it. The big, glaring, shiny diamond ring twinkling on her engagement finger.

I let out an ear-piercing shriek, and we both jump on the couch in unison, holding hands. Words fly in the air like confetti. *Oh my God* and *Show me the ring again* and *You're going to be a perfect bride* and *How did he do it?*

It takes us ten minutes to stop crying and hugging and gasping at the huge diamond Colt chose for her. She tells me that it happened over the Christmas holiday. That she had begun unwrapping all her gifts, and Colt made her open the smallest one last. Her parents recorded the entire thing. And she and Colt are now trending on TikTok as a result. Then she shows me the video of Colt getting down on one knee while her mom shouts in the background, "Back straight, Nora!" and I cry and laugh all over again, because I'm happy—so happy for her—and because I want that kind of stability in my life too.

A little voice reminds me that I can, in fact, have it. I can choose perfect. All I have to do is turn my back on one night in Spain.

Hashtag Best Couple Ever.

FIFTEEN

Two days later, I cook Dom a meal at his place. I stick to my winning (and only) recipe. Pasta with a premade supermarket sauce and fried drumsticks coated with breadcrumbs. Dom has pulled numerous double shifts this week, covering for some people who took extended Christmas vacations. Since we didn't do the deed at his parents' house over Christmas, it has now been a week since we've had sex. Honestly, I'm not sure I *want* to have sex with him right now. I'm still tangled up in my feelings.

I hate that I'm hiding a secret from him. Which is why I try to compensate by being the girlfriend he deserves. Also, I'm aware that the clock is ticking and that Nora is a breath away from telling me she is moving out. She *should* move out. I've ruined enough lives in my short lifetime.

I've already done the calculations, and I can rent the place on my own. It's probably for the best that I stay there for at least one more year. I can't see myself taking big steps with Dom, with everything that's going on.

"Food's amazing, babe," Dom moans as he tears into a drumstick. My mother always said you can tell a lot about a man by the way he eats his fried chicken, and Dom's a savage when it comes to his meal. He licks his fingers and separates the meat from the bone, crushing the semihard parts with his teeth. Oil drips down his chin. He is like that during sex too. Hungry and raw and *real*. Yet in just about any other area in life, he is sweet, agreeable, almost placid; the two versions of him coexist, but I cannot help but suspect that he is one more than the other. What bothers me is I don't know which part of him is real and which part is for show.

After Dom is done eating, I clear the table, wash the dishes, and massage his feet while we're watching a movie adaptation of a book he forgot to read for his book club. We're in his bed. At some point my earring disappears, and I crouch down and look for it on his floor. Dom puts the movie on pause and helps me. He shakes the blanket and the pillows. Pads along the hallway, squinting at the floor. He is at the edge of the hallway when my fingers touch a thin gold necklace under his bed. I grab it. It spills between my fingers, shimmering. It has the letter *S* on it.

Sally?

Sonya?

Slutbag?

"Dom?" I call out, angling the necklace here and there, watching as it glimmers under the streaks of sunlight pouring through the venetian blinds.

He strides over to his room. "Yeah, babe?"

Silently, I raise the golden necklace between us, waiting for an explanation. He reaches and plucks it from between my fingers, frowning.

"Whoops."

"Indeed," I say. "Care to explain?"

My heart is in my throat. I realize this is my out. If Dom has cheated on me, I can turn my back. Walk away. Not feel guilty about it . . . then what? Hit Joe up? *Oh, hey, so your brother and I are over, and I was wondering if you wanna catch up?*

What am I even thinking right now? I don't *want* to break up with Dom. I love him. He is my safe haven.

Dom hands me back the necklace, ruffling his perfect hair. "It was before we got together. Way before. Her name was Sierra. It was one date. Tinder. I don't usually do those, but I'd just lost a patient and was feeling really raw. Needless to say, I went and got checked afterward. Washed the linens five hundred times. *Boiled* them. The cleaner must've not reached under the bed. I'll talk to her tomorrow."

Even though Dom has done nothing wrong (officially, anyway), I'm still a little put off by both the necklace and his explanation. I also feel a weird sense of disappointment to know there was no foul play. That means that he is perfect, after all. And perfect, as we all know, is where nothing grows.

"What, you don't believe me?" He sounds shocked and hurt.

"No, I do. Of course I do!" I find myself apologizing. Now I feel bad. "It's just . . . jarring."

Dom takes the necklace from me, then makes a show of dumping it into the trash can. He claps his hands clean in a good riddance motion. "There. Done. Now let's move on, please. This was before I knew you were in existence. Before I became your seventy-six-percent chance to marry. You're a game changer, Lynne."

"Speaking of game changers." I muster a smile, chanting in my head *It's fine, it's fine, everything is fine.* "It's supposed to be chances we *don't* get married. You changed the rules."

He hooks his finger around the collar of my shirt and pulls me into him in a savage kiss. "Maybe I play dirty."

"I like dirty."

I forget all about my missing earring, and the movie, and suddenly his teeth are skimming the side of my jaw, nibbling and biting softly as he makes his way to my breasts. Then he stops, remembering something.

"Have you called the people about the calligraphy class?"

My old friend, dread, pops in for a visit. It feels like I have a chore list, and that I'm failing miserably at tackling it.

"Nope. But I will, in February. January is always a busy month for me. Tours every day. Inventory in the shop. I couldn't even find a time to jump on a plane and see my family." That's my version of the truth, and it's a murky one. Technically, I haven't been invited there since Christmas. "And I'm taking more shifts at the shop, now that Nora's engaged and could move out on me any minute."

And the kitchen sink, I hear Mom's voice chuckling in my head. *You've given him every excuse on planet earth why you don't want to go to this course, other than the truth—that you're not bloody interested in it!*

"You know you can always move in here," he says. "I mean, Loki already hinted he'd be down for it."

"Thanks for offering. I don't want either of us to feel pressured, though."

"I don't feel pressured. Do *you* feel pressured?" Dom asks.

I don't know how to answer that. I mean . . . yes? No? Sometimes?

"No," I say, finally, because it's not his fault that I'm completely messed up and obsessed with his baby brother.

"It's settled, then. When Nora moves out, you're moving in with me."

"Let's pin this conversation," I suggest.

Dom presses his thumb against an imaginary pinboard between us with his hand. "All right, but I'm not going to forget. You don't have to be alone anymore. I'm here to help, babe."

Something between appreciation and anxiety stirs in my chest. I lean to kiss him. With his hand pressed against the small of my back, he pulls me down on top of him. He splays my thighs on either side of his waist and pushes me down, taking charge. I can no longer postpone the inevitable. He reaches between us, under my skirt, and nudges my underwear to the side, his thumb rubbing against my entrance. I'm soaking wet. Even when my brain is unsure of Dom, my body has no doubts. I'm embarrassed and annoyed and, above all, confused.

He stares at me lazily, through hooded eyes. "I want to make love to you," he says. And I can't deny him. This is what we should be doing.

153

A young, happy couple in our prime. I'll get over Joe. Now that he is no longer a faded, romantic memory but a real person, always within reach, the glow of his greatness will diminish.

"I . . . ," I start, but he is already inside me. Still fully clothed, after tugging his sweatpants down.

I gasp in surprise, digging my fingers into his shoulders and pulling back. Dom grabs my ass and pushes me over his erection, filling my insides until I feel my lips hitting the root of him.

"Ahhhh." I throw my head back, the pleasure too intense, too addictive.

It is good, but it is also different. The entire time we have sex, I feel disconnected. Like I'm floating, hovering, not present in the situation. It almost feels like masturbation. We both come. When Dom collapses by my side, spent and sweaty, I realize we didn't kiss the entire time we were having sex.

He picks up a lock of my hair and twirls it around his forefinger. "Oh, I almost forgot."

"Hmm?" I smile up at him, feeling like a china doll. Precious and fragile and incredibly empty. I can feel the echo of each of my heartbeats.

"Seph suggested we all grab lunch sometime this week. Apparently, he's feeling bad for not giving you enough attention during Christmas."

I forget how to breathe. Or, at the very least, do it incorrectly. I'm heaving.

"What do you think?" he asks.

Dom can't possibly know what I'm thinking. *I* don't even know what I'm thinking. Yet his shoulder tenses against mine, his whole body bracing itself for some kind of a blow.

I can't stop thinking about your brother. I never stopped thinking about him. I hate that I do. I hate that I can never make a good choice in my life.

I lean down to catch his lower lip between my teeth, sucking it into my mouth. "He doesn't have to do that. I'm not grilled cheese. Not everyone has to like me."

"You are so grilled cheese, Lynne." Dom pulls away from our kiss, looking serious and determined and . . . sad, I think? But why? "In fact, you are a perfectly glazed doughnut. Just like the one you give me every morning."

Almost every morning. I still keep my Girlfriend Promise to him.

"So what should I tell him?" Dom eyes me curiously.

Is he catching up on things? No way. He'd say something, surely.

The answer, of course, is *Hell to the no*. I don't trust myself around Joe. I especially don't want to be alone with the two brothers, tucked between my almost-forever and my maybe-future. I don't know what business Joe has suggesting this in the first place. His last words to me were *Stay the hell away from me*. Not exactly what I call a heartwarming invitation. Maybe he wants to prove a point. To show me that he is committed to his supportive-brother act.

Or maybe it's not an act. Maybe he *is* doing this for Dom. In which case, he is certainly more honorable than me, because I'm not willing to subject myself to this kind of emotional inferno.

Either way, I'm not sure what the correct answer is. I don't know if Dom wants me to make an effort or not. Right now, he looks a little iffy about the whole thing. So I try to play it by ear.

"Let me look at my schedule this week, and I'll get back to you, okay?" I run a hand over his pecs.

He looks at me a moment longer before he clasps my hand, kissing it. "I can tell him what you just told me. That you're having a busy month. He'll understand."

It looks like Dom isn't eager for us to do a three-way meetup either. It suddenly occurs to me that he might know more than he is letting on. He might've even seen Joe and me in the backyard. When we fell into each other's arms and the entire world melted around us. The idea that he knows makes my chest hurt.

"You're a pal." I offer him my pinkie finger. "I'll let you know when my schedule clears up a little. Deal?"

He curls his pinkie through mine. "Deal."

"I love you, Dom."

"Love you, too, babe."

And he must, because even though we can't find my earring, the very next day, he surprises me at work with a new set of earrings. Solitaire diamonds.

The real deal. Just like him.

◆ ◆ ◆

It's been a week since I last saw Joe at his parents' house. New Year's Eve came and went in a flurry of a house party, a hasty kiss at midnight, an empty promise for what's to come this year.

Joe's presence lingers, soaked into the sidewalks, drenched into the air. Salem is suddenly exclusively Joe's territory. It's like knowing you're at the same hotel with a celebrity.

I find myself catching a waft of his scent in the elevator on the way to Dom's apartment. I spot tall dark-haired men all the time again, wondering if it's him. He fills my days, when I cannot stop thinking about him. And my nights, too, when he slips into my dreams.

I go about my life. I smile, I shop for groceries, I give Loki belly rubs, and I step on invisible soapboxes on Essex Street on star-filled, frosty nights.

Nights like this one.

"Good evening, everyone, and welcome to the Salem Night Tour. My name is Everlynne, and I will be your tour guide. I know I look like a witch. And, well . . . that's because I am." I bow deeply in my black cape, spewing out my usual rehearsed text.

Phone cameras flash. Teenagers giggle. It's depressing. How routine sucks the magic out of everything. Even a cool job like mine.

I straighten my spine, and that's when I see him. I freeze. The words shrivel and roll back into my mouth.

Joe is standing right in front of me, the throng of tourists his backdrop.

Dirty Levi's. Tattered peacoat that screams mysterious British rocker. Celestial eyes that peer past my clothes and skin and bullshit. And that face. The face that feels like home.

His gaze is like a poisonous arrow straight to my heart. All eyes are on me. Waiting. Gauging. Studying.

What is he doing? More specifically, what is he doing *here*? Haven't we decided not to seek each other out? I've fulfilled my end of the bargain. Why can't he? And why is there a part of me—and not a small one—that is happy and relieved to see him?

I step toward him. My knees are weak. I don't trust my ability to complete a simple three-word sentence. Yet I somehow do. "It's tickets only."

I don't want him here. In my sphere, in my world, in my *bones*.

Joe raises a wrinkled ticket, which I recognize as a legitimate one. He must've purchased it online. His face is unreadable, impassive. I thought he wanted to stay away.

"Y-you bought a ticket?"

"Crashing without one would've been rude," he confirms.

"Why?"

"Because you shouldn't be working for free?"

"You know what I mean," I snap.

His nostrils flare, and his eyes dart down, to his sneakers. "Because I think we were too shell shocked to deal with things over Christmas, and there are more words to be said."

That's a valid reason, but I don't buy it. I just *know* he is here for the same reason that I can't bear the idea of spending time with him. The connection between us is unreal.

"You could've tried reaching out without showing up unannounced," I say testily. I don't trust myself to have a one-on-one conversation with him.

"You'd have dodged," he says matter-of-factly. "I frighten you, and we both know that."

"Screw you, Joe." He has no right calling me out.

His lips pull in a bitter smile. "Been there, done that. That's what got us into this whole mess."

I twist my wrist and check the time. Only five minutes have passed since the beginning of the tour. Eighty-five more to go.

"Are you all right?" One woman steps forward, resting a hand on my shoulder. "You look pale."

I shoot her a smile. "Yes. Of course. So!" I clap my hands, returning to the center of the group, determined to survive tonight. "Well, my dear morbid friends. We're going to cover some of Salem's history, including the witch hunt hysteria of 1692. We'll talk murders, ghosts, curses, civil war. All the fun stuff!"

Everyone giggles.

Everyone but *him*.

◆ ◆ ◆

The next hour and a half is pure torture. I pretend that Joe doesn't exist, even though the world seems like it's resized itself around him. I'm acutely aware of everything coming out of my mouth. I don't veer off script or crack a joke. I'm in a minefield, tiptoeing my way to safety.

Eventually, the hour and a half passes, albeit six days later. I sum the tour up as I always do. "Two misbehaving young girls who got misdiagnosed by a doctor as under the devil's hand started a craze. Divided a community. Planted seeds of hatred in every heart in the colonies. But make no mistake—this wasn't the girls' fault. We still have a long way to go in terms of unity, and the best way to start? With ourselves and our own prejudice."

People clap. I stay behind to answer some questions. Joe hangs back, leaning under a lamppost, the light from his phone screen illuminating the chiseled planes of his face. He is waiting for me, and a mixture of excited nausea and dread fills me.

He is so gorgeous, so alive, so *real*, that his mere presence here throws me off kilter.

Once the last of the tourists have trickled away, I walk toward him. We stand in front of each other like two drunk fools getting ready for a duel.

I cross my arms over my chest. "What happened to staying away from each other?"

Joe flicks the back of his Lucky Strike soft pack. One cigarette pops from its opening. He raises the pack and clasps the cigarette between his teeth, then lights it nonchalantly. "This is not a social call."

I inwardly laugh at my young self. The one who fell in love with him. He is such a bad-boy cliché. Only I know in Joe's case, he's the real deal. There are no hidden personality traits, no fine print. If I had to guess how he eats his fried chicken, I'd say he annihilates it, just like everything else he touches. He is a storm, and I'm lightning, and whenever we meet, there is chaos.

"Yeah. I gathered. What do you want to talk about?"

"Not here." He shakes his head. "Your place?"

"Ha! For you to even suggest that . . ."

"Well, what's the alternative?" He elevates one eyebrow. "If we go to mine, Dom might catch us."

"I'm not going to yours either."

I grab my backpack and start for my car. He falls into step with me. In fact, his stride is so fast, his legs so long, it looks like I'm slowing him down. "If this is about the whole getting-together thing, I can't do a three-way lunch, Joe. I have a lot of work this month. Consider us over, done, and dealt with. And I'll respect your wish and won't say anything to Dom about us. But please don't make me play BFFs with you." *It hurts too much*, I don't add.

Every word feels like a bullet in my mouth. I can feel the metallic taste of it rubbing on my gums. I fling the driver's door open. He reaches behind me and slams it shut. His body is so close to mine it radiates heat. I turn around, narrowing my eyes at him. "Step away or I'll kick you in the balls."

Slowly—teasingly—Joe takes a small step back, still close enough that I can feel him everywhere.

"Ever," he rasps.

I close my eyes. God, I'm so screwed. My name on his lips alone makes my insides liquefy. I'm trying the best I can here, but I'm helpless.

"No," I respond, without hearing the rest. I can't do this to Dom. I can't do this to myself. I've reached my guilt quota for this lifetime.

Joe's fingers curl around my collarbone. I resist the urge to collapse onto his chest and sob. It feels so good. So right to be touched by him. I try to think if it's appropriate or not. His touch. It is somewhere between a shoulder clasp and a tender caress. But I'm so confused, I can't tell.

"Open your eyes. Look at me."

I do. We stare at each other.

"Relax. I'm not going to kiss you," he reassures me, a good amount of satisfaction in his voice, probably because he knows that he can. He knows I wouldn't be able to push him away.

"I'm not scared of you." I narrow my eyes.

"That so?" He looks entertained, in the same deadpan, dark way of his. "Maybe you should be, based on your reaction to me."

"Why *are* you here?" I ask, for the millionth time.

He tosses his cigarette to the curb. "After Christmas . . . I don't know what happened. Or, I'm not sure *how* it happened. But suddenly, for the first time in six years, I started—"

"Writing," I finish the sentence for him. His eyes widen slightly, but he keeps himself in check. It is beneath the great Joe Graves to show emotions.

I nod, feeling even more depressed than I was before. "I started sketching after I saw you. For the first time, also."

It sounds like we stopped creating at around the same time. Like when we said our goodbyes, we took each other's muse and held it hostage. I understand what this is now. A barter situation. *Give me my talent back, and I'll grant you yours.* Joe doesn't want me. He just wants what I'm able to give him. His muse back.

"What do you think it means?" he grunts, looking annoyed.

I shrug, trying to ignore the fact his hand is *still* on my collarbone. "I don't know. That we inspire each other?"

"It's more than that," he says tersely.

"That we're each other's muses," I correct.

"Yes." He nods, half-relieved, half-furious. "Which is fucked up."

"That doesn't make it any less true." I prop one foot against my car. "But it doesn't matter. We have Dom to think about."

Sweet, beautiful Dom. Who asked me to move in with him. My biggest cheerleader. The man who liked me before I learned how to like myself.

"So what are you suggesting? Give up on our art? Turn our backs on our chance to create?" Joe looks appalled. Like we both have some huge duty that requires sacrifice. Maybe we do. When did I stop believing in myself?

On the day Mom died. On the day you caused it.

"Art?" I snort out. "You mean my doodles?"

He pinches the bridge of his nose, exasperated. I can tell he is struggling with a hundred emotions right now. His loyalty to Dom, his desire to create. We're messy. Not fiends, nor friends. I can tell Joe doesn't hold a grudge against me anymore for what happened between us, and at the same time, he is mad. Mad like I'm mad. At the world. At this situation.

He reaches for his front pocket and pulls something out. A crumpled pack of tissues. He tugs one sheet and waves it between us.

"Let's start over."

"I don't want to start over." Maybe if I keep repeating this, it'll be true.

"You have to. I raised a white flag. There are rules in this world, Ever. A white flag symbolizes an approaching unarmed negotiator."

Too bad his presence is the very weapon I fear the most.

"Look, I don't know why things happened the way they did." He rakes his fingers through his dark hair. "I thought about it all week. Maybe I did something really fucked up in my previous life, and this is all karmic retribution."

That's what I thought too. No surprises there. He and I are too much alike.

"Or maybe you and I weren't meant to be," he continues. "*Or maybe this is just a part of life's randomness.* Whatever it is, it doesn't change one fact—I didn't manage to write one goddamn word since the day you left Spain, and in this past week, I wrote four pages." He takes a deep breath and adds, "Front *and* back."

"It felt good," I admit, biting down on my lip. "To create again."

His gaze drops to my lips. "I can make you feel even better."

My senses heighten and my temperature hikes up when he takes another step forward. He leans forward, his lips touching the shell of my ear. "By making you *draw*, not come."

I push him away, almost violently.

He chuckles in response. "C'mon, Ever. I'm just trying to break the ice!"

"What are you suggesting?" I ask impatiently.

"We meet up. Hang out. Bounce ideas off each other. Talk books, music, general life stuff. We'll keep it platonic. You spark something in me, Ever. We don't have to give each other everything. We can just . . . be there for one another. The spark is there."

"Don't you see?" I fling my arms in the air, ignoring the verbal jab. "This is *exactly* why we can't hang out. You know what happens to sparks?"

"They turn into flames." Resigned, he hangs his head between his shoulders, shaking it. "You feel it, too, huh?"

"Bone deep," I admit.

"So what? Lots of people want to fuck each other but can't. We're not animals. We can shoot the shit without exchanging bodily fluids. We can be . . ."

He doesn't say *friends*, because we can't be friends.

I smile sadly. "Be what? Whatever it's gonna be, it'll be betraying Dom. Emotional cheating is still cheating."

He frowns, looking thunderous. "Dom won't mind. I can be friendly with his girlfriend."

"Do you guys have a good relationship?" I ask, remembering in Spain how resentful Joe had felt about his family. Now it all makes sense. Dom hogged all the attention, and Joe stayed on the outskirts of his parents' conscience. There, but not really.

"Sure." Joe shrugs. "Peachy."

"Doesn't look it."

"We have baggage. All siblings do. And I have some disagreements with him, which I'm not going to talk about with you. But I love him. Too damn much. Too much to do something we'll both regret, I think."

Not sure what to say, I let myself digest what he's just said silently.

"Well?" He frowns. "What do you say we help each other out?"

"I'm sorry, Joe. I can't."

His look, of defiance and anger, sears me. My walls are falling one by one. I want to drop to my knees and collect the invisible bricks. Put them between us again.

"Ever," he says quietly. It's a plea. *Please, help me.*

I shake my head, pressing my lips together to muffle a sob.

He closes his eyes. "I fucking hate this."

With a knot in my throat and the world's weight on my shoulders, I turn my back on him, slide into my car, and drive off.

Leaving my imaginary bricks and very real heart behind.

SIXTEEN

Two weeks after Joe cornered me, Dom surprises me with two tickets to Puerto Rico for a long weekend. It's sudden but not unwelcome. I've worked myself to the bone lately, no doubt to forget the cluster I sometimes affectionately refer to as my life.

With fully estranged father and baby brother, no family to speak of (without casting blame here), a roommate who is a flight risk, and a ghost from the past with the potential to ruin my life, I have a *lot* to run from.

The universe, naturally, decides to give me a long middle finger in the form of Joe driving us to Logan International Airport. Joe appears comfortable with driving his brother and ex-girlfriend to a romantic getaway. Slunk back lazily in his seat, one arm draped over the steering wheel like Michelangelo's Nile river god.

Dom is in the passenger's seat of the truck. I'm sitting in the back. The brothers seem in good spirits. They talk about their mutual hatred for the Yankees—there's a specific game they're referring to—and I can tell, in this moment, that they are heartbreakingly close. More than Renn and I ever were. They have this easy camaraderie, these inside jokes. This confuses me, seeing as Joe seemed determined to get what he wanted from me only weeks ago with little regard for his brother. But I guess relationships are complex, and Joe can both hate his childhood and love the brother who made it unbearable. Just like Dominic can adore Joe and still envy him for being the "healthy" brother.

"Babe Ruth killed my soul before I was even born. How is that fair?" Dom jokes.

"An eighty-six-year championship drought, man. Should've been born in New York."

They both look at each other and grin. *"Nah,"* they say in unison.

"So . . . were the Yankees to blame for the Red Sox drought?" I ask from the back seat, offering my important contribution to this conversation.

Joe shakes his head. "Not really. But Bostonians never forget."

"Also, I would like to note that we invented the wave. Legend has it the wave owes its existence to Fenway Park—because the seats are so close together, whenever a fan has to stand up, everyone else in the row has to stand too. And then the people behind them get pissed because they can't see anything, so they get up too. And that creates the human wave," Dom explains, eyes sparkling.

"Fun fact," Joe notes.

"From a not-so-fun stadium," Dom delivers the punch line, and they both burst out laughing again.

This is my important reminder that they are attached at the hip, that they moved to the same town together, the same *building*. I'm the outsider here.

The conversation bleeds into what Dom and I are going to do in Puerto Rico.

"Eat, dance, take pictures . . . and, *you know*." Dom lets out a chuckle, and my stomach rolls with nausea. "What about you? Are you still seeing that chick? Stacey? Tracy?"

Crap. Crap, crap, crap, crap, crap. I was not expecting this gut-wrenching reaction to hearing that Joe is seeing someone. Now I cannot help but envision him having hot, sweaty sex with a faceless woman. In my bedroom, for a reason beyond my grasp. Slowly smiling at me, his half-moon smirk, while pounding into her. It is so his style.

"Presley," Joe corrects in his easy, dispassionate tone.

"I was close, wasn't I, Lynne?" Dom meets my stare in the rearview mirror.

"Hmm-mmm."

"How's she doing?" Dom asks.

Joe shrugs. "Dunno. Ask her."

Now *our* gazes meet in the rearview mirror. I know what he thinks.

I'm not giving you the pleasure of knowing what's going on in my love life. Choke on the unknown, baby. We both know it hurts more than any naked truth.

"She sounds like a great girl," Dom marvels. "Funny, nice, into you, got a great job." There's a comical beat before he adds, "*Hot.* Sorry, babe, it had to be said. The girl looks like a fashion model or something."

Knife, meet heart.

Joe smiles idly but doesn't say anything. I wonder if it would hurt as much if I heard something similar about Dom, but then I remember that I found a necklace in his bedroom, and although I was a little annoyed, it didn't feel like I'd been chopped to tiny pieces and fed to the gators.

I know I have no business being jealous. Not when Dom all but stated we'd be spending our weekend rolling in bed together. But the thing about feelings is, they care little about logic.

"Give it a chance, bro. Seriously. Just . . . take her out." Dom beams, all positive energy. *So* much positive energy. Must he always be so optimistic?

"Yeah. Maybe." Joe throws his old Jeep Cherokee into park. I realize we're at our gate at the airport. Joe slides out of the driver's seat and pulls out our suitcases for us. I watch his arm muscles bunching under his tee and remember what they felt like when I clutched them while he drove into me. When we had sex on the beach. He and Dom give each other a brotherly hug, slapping each other's backs.

"Safe travels, bro," Joe says.

"Thanks for the ride, man."

Then Joe moves toward me while Dom fumbles with his backpack for our passports. He presses his hand to the small of my back in a quiet yet possessive half hug. His lips disappear in my mane of ginger hair.

"Offer still stands," he whispers. "No funny business. Just art."

"Enjoy Presley," I hiss back, unable to help myself.

"You're a sweetheart for caring." He kisses my cheek quickly, feigning innocence. "And I fully intend to."

Before I can say anything, before I can kick and scream *How dare he*, he drives off into the distance.

Dom wraps an arm over my shoulder. "Shall we, babe?"

Manufactured bliss.

That was what my mother called the suburban lifestyle. That is why she insisted that we stay in San Francisco, even when all my parents' friends had drifted to the small towns that bracketed it. Lafayette and Orinda and Tiburon. Even Sunnyvale. She called it the happiness lie. People think their life will be better if they live in a bigger house, drive a bigger car, grow a vegetable garden. But wealth doesn't equal happiness, necessarily. The city offers you struggle, and struggle keeps you hungry and in survival mode.

Right now, I am feeling pretty suburban.

"Doesn't this tree look like Chewbacca?" I point at a tree in Old San Juan the day after Joe dropped us off, leaving with my soul in his pocket.

Dom and I have just finished eating the most delicious coconut candy and crab empanada, and now we're taking a romantic stroll among the narrow cobbled streets. The historic buildings are a kaleidoscope of pastel colors, and my boyfriend has never been more gorgeous and attentive.

"A what?" Dom slants his head sideways, staring at the Spanish moss tree.

"Chewbacca!" I exclaim.

"Don't laugh, but this cultural reference just flew past me at the speed of light." Dom chuckles.

"You've never watched *Star Wars*? You know, *The Phantom Menace*? *The Clone Wars*?"

"Nope."

"Oh, my God, Dom! How?"

"I don't know!" He throws his arms in the air, laughing. "I just . . . I think I was busy doing chemo when it was big with all the kids my age?"

My smile immediately falls, and I feel like an idiot for not thinking about it. Dom notices and rushes to hug me.

"No, babe. Don't feel bad about it. Change it. Change *me*." He kisses my lips. I melt in his arms. He smells so good. He *feels* so good. *What's wrong with suburbia?* I think. It is so popular for a reason. "Show me your ways. Teach me the magic of Chewbanka."

"Chewbacca."

"Yup. Her."

"*Him.*" I laugh, pulling him back to the hotel. "Come on, we have a history lesson to teach you."

"While we're at it, I also failed anatomy in school. Just saying . . ."

I swat his chest, feeling light and happy all of a sudden. Nora is right. He is the one. He makes me laugh. He gives me joy. He is not hard and callous and difficult like his baby brother. He is not San Francisco. Filthy and hilly, with a subway—one of the worst inventions in human history (there is absolutely no freaking way I'm ever getting on a subway).

"I'll teach you biology too," I promise.

"Thanks, Teach."

◆ ◆ ◆

For the next couple of days, Dom and I eat mofongo, hit the casinos, and have lots and lots of sex. By the time we get on the plane home, I feel more connected to him. More sure of our relationship. Yes, Joe was a plot twist. A bitter reminder of what could have been. Of the past. I'd lost my footing when we reconnected, but I'm back on the horse. I'm not going to let Joe mess with my happiness again. Next time we talk, I'll be the one encouraging him to date Presley. Maybe we could even double date. Nip all the doubts in the bud.

The universe provides, and after we land back home, we catch a cab instead of having Joe pick us up. I don't ask why Joe hasn't arrived to collect us. Dom explains, anyway.

"It's Mom's birthday tomorrow. The big six-oh. Joe's in Dover for the long weekend. I know I'm springing this on you last minute, but would you mind very much if we head over there tomorrow evening for dinner? I know it'll mean a lot to her."

"Of course!" I beam at him.

"Thanks." He picks up my hand and kisses my knuckles.

When we get to Salem, I ask the driver to drop me off first. I need to make sure Loki is okay. In the apartment, I find a note on the fridge from Nora.

> Sleeping @ Colt's
> Hope you had fun in PR.
> Love you xoxo

I pluck it and throw it in the trash on my way to find Loki. Nora has been feeling a lot less guilty about spending time with Colt. I'm happy for them. To be honest, I no longer feel like I'm drowning. It would probably be okay if she moved out at the end of the month. I make a mental note to actively encourage her to do so.

I find Loki sprawled in my bed. He stares at me with great enthusiasm, which for a cat means he blinks at me once, to acknowledge my presence in the room. When I reach to stroke him, he gives me his belly and tilts his chins up so I can rub his throat the way he likes.

"Missed me?" I ask tiredly. He rolls his eyes, stands up, and exits the room.

I grab a shower, do my laundry, try to call Dad (and get his voice mail. *Again*), and enjoy a balanced meal of Reese's Puffs. There are still grave sketches hanging on my pinboard from the week after I met Joe. I glance at them, and something inside me wilts, because Joe was right. When we don't see each other, we don't create. And when I don't create, I feel underwater.

It is only when I go back to the living room to turn off all the lights before I slip into bed that I see there is something I missed all along. A batch of A4 papers that's been shoved through the crack under the door. One of them is even stamped with my boot print. I fall to my knees and collect them. I don't need to guess what they are. What they mean. I *know*.

I grab the scattered pages. They're out of order. Of course Joe wouldn't bother with a stapler. It's all handwritten, a violent cyclone of blue and black ink. He must've gone through several pens.

After picking up the pages with shaky hands, I start reading snippets.

. . . it was Kerouac's fault, of course. He was the one who said that writers needed new experiences like flowers need the sun. He was the one who made young Jack hit the road and drive past state limits, past cornfields and skyscrapers. Past horizons. And so, inevitably, he was the one who pushed Jack to meet her.

. . . some nights, after Jack lost his car and had to hitchhike his way, he'd lay on a patch of grass, staring into the sky. He dreamed of ripping a hole in it. Slipping through it. Disappearing into another, better universe. One where people who should be together stay together. He'd bathed in dirty ponds and ate from trash cans. And yet, his most desperate moment had occurred under the night sky. So clear and pure and full of stars. He closed his eyes and saw her. A girl. Or maybe she was a woman at this point. Whoever she was, he belonged to her. But she no longer belonged to him.

And then I find it. The first page. It has a yellow Post-it Note attached to it. There is only one word on it, written in a red Sharpie.

PLEASE.

The word feels like a sword has been dipped in my chest. I want to pick up the phone and fight with him, but I don't have his number. I want to find his social media accounts and message him, but he doesn't have any—I checked. I want to . . . I want to go to his building, to his apartment, and give him a piece of my mind, but he is in Dover right now, at his parents'.

A part of me wants to help Joe, but a bigger part of me is scared of what it would mean.

I flip over the Post-it Note and notice that Joe scribbled his phone number on the back of it. Once again, he anticipated my reaction. I type him a message.

Ever: What would it look like? Us helping each other.

His response is immediate.

Joe: I don't know yet.

Ever: It's going to hurt.

Joe: We're no strangers to pain.

I'm lying on the cold floor, staring up at the screen. This feels wrong. Like cheating. But also right. Like maybe Joe is the one I've been cheating on. I'm just so confused.

Ever: It's not fair. I thought I'd never meet you again. I couldn't have known you're so close by.

A few seconds pass before he answers.

Joe: Why are you here, Ever? In my state. In my territory.

Ever: I don't know.

Joe: What do you know?

Ever: That I don't want you to be with Presley.

He types, then deletes. Types, then deletes. My heart is in my throat.

Joe: I don't want to be with Presley, either.

Ever: We should delete this conversation.

Joe: You can do whatever you want. I've got nothing to hide.

I notice he doesn't tell me he doesn't want me to be with Dom.

Ever: How can you say that, when you were the one who told me not to tell Dom?

Joe: This is not hiding. It's omitting. I'll own up to it if he finds out.

Joe: Look, I love my brother. But that doesn't mean I can't have you. He can have your outside. I can have your inside.

Ever: Do you think that'd be enough for him?

Joe: I think he doesn't get you, so it's not going to matter to him, no.

Ever: And you do?

Joe: You know I do.

I close my eyes, taking a breath. I do. I do, I do, I do.

Ever: And what would I be left with? If he takes my body and you take my . . . everything else?

Joe: Simple. You'll get both of us.

Joe: It's all you want in the first place, isn't it? Both brothers.

He's hit too close to home, and he knows it. Dom is the smart choice. The *safe* choice. He is also, at present, my only choice. Joe . . . he is not even up for offer. Even if he were, it would be too messy, too painful . . .

Ever: Dom gets all. You get hang-outs. Last offer.

I cave. Because I can. Because, at least on paper, it is innocent. Because I radiate, and I never radiate, and I *want* to radiate whenever Joe and I talk. I want to exist in color. I want to listen to old Smiths records on Joe's floor while I draw, while he writes. I want the city's filth, then to come back to the suburbs for the night. Even though I know this arrangement won't have a happy ending.

Joe: Lucky Dom.

Ever: This is strictly work.

Joe: In that case, I'll set up a workroom for us.

Ever: I'll make playlists.

Joe: No Blur.

Ever: I'm no heathen.

Joe: ☺

My heart hiccups, because Joe is not an emoji person. I can tell without even texting him much.

Ever: Oh, and we're telling Dom.

There's a beat before he answers this time.

Joe: Your funeral.

Ever: God. I'm already regretting this.

Joe: Regrets make good stories.

SEVENTEEN

On the drive to Dover, Dom is fidgety and out of focus. When I ask him about it, he tells me that he's been pulling double shifts to make up for the long weekend he took off, but that he's still keeping up with all his other commitments.

"When was the last time you slept?" I demand. "Like, really slept. Not just catnaps."

Now that I'm taking a better look at him, he looks shattered. Like he hasn't slept the better half of this century.

Dom frowns, giving it some thought. "Two days ago. And on the flight back too. From San Juan."

"Sleep is not Pilates. Doing it three times a week is not sufficient," I chide him.

"I'll get better about it," he soothes, rubbing at my back. It's all empty words. I know he won't. Dom is incapable of slowing down. He wants to make sure he takes big, juicy bites of the world. Every day is a greasy burger. He doesn't have salad days in between.

"No, you won't." I shake my head. "You need to clear your schedule a little. CrossFit. Book club. The movies. Something's gotta go."

"It's easy for you to say. You don't know what it feels like. To look your mortality in the eye every day. I do. It's hard for me to pass on things."

This time, I don't take the bait. "First of all, you don't own exclusivity rights on death, mister. I'm going to expire one day too. Second, you still have a lot of time to do them."

He flashes me a look. "You don't know that, babe. I'm sorry, you just don't."

"You're being weird." I nibble on the side of my thumbnail.

"Sorry. I don't want to fight. It's just . . . I've got it under control." Dom darts his gaze from the road, throwing me a reassuring smile. Our car drifts into the opposite lane, causing the truck in front of us to honk loudly and veer to the side. Dom screams *Shit*, then takes a sharp turn back to our lane. I let out a gasp, clutching the edge of the passenger door.

"Sorry, sorry," Dom mutters, sounding genuinely sincere. "Oh, hell. That was close."

"What the hell, dude?" My voice is shrill. My hands are balled into fists. I'm shaking all over.

"I wasn't paying attention. I said I'm sorry."

"And that makes it okay?"

"Get off my back, all right?"

Something is up with him, and I don't know what it is.

If we move in together, I could monitor him more closely. I don't actually feel ready to make this step with Dom. Especially with the entire Joe mess. But I'm desperate to save him the way he saved me. And right now . . . he looks like he could use a helping hand.

We pull up in front of his parents' house a few minutes later. Dom opens the door and bows a little. "Hey."

"Hi," I say stiffly.

He takes my hand and kisses the back of it. "This is me. Your ninety-nine-percent-chance-to-marry guy. I'm sorry about what happened. You're right. I won't get behind the wheel before I get more sleep. Crack a smile, will ya?"

He is back to being playful, sweet Dom. But I'm still worried. I'm going to be the one driving on our way back. The thought of having him behind the wheel scares me now.

I muster a smile. He thanks me quietly.

Laughter and the sound of a football game roll in from the living room. We follow the noise. Soon, I come face-to-face with Gemma, Brad, and Joe. The latter looks casual, in worn jeans and workman's boots. Not like a man who could devastate a girl's entire universe. Who could make her lose her mom, and maybe her boyfriend, and definitely her sanity.

The city always corrupts you, Mom used to say. *But corruption is bloody fun!*

We stare at each other like two people with big fat secrets in their pockets. Dynamite that could detonate the entire room.

"Hey," I say, staring at Joe.

"What's up?" he asks.

"You look tan! Had a nice vacay?" Gemma jumps up, stepping between us, almost like she can pick up the tangible tension.

A tornado of air-kisses and pleasantries follows. I hand Gemma the flowers and present I got for her—an assortment of handmade soaps and candles—and she puts it aside, next to a pile of wrapped gifts. We all retire to the dining room for dinner. Dom and Joe heatedly discuss the new gym equipment that was installed in their building. Brad has ordered pizzas and chicken wings so Gemma doesn't have to cook. He makes the obligatory dad joke about how he worked hard to prepare this meal. We all say grace on Gemma's request and dig in.

Joe and I exchange glances as Gemma tells us about her sixtieth-birthday surprise. Brad took her to watch ballet, which he hates, and to a yacht club restaurant—which he also hates because "no one should pay ninety bucks for a lobster in Massachusetts, goddammit."

Joe laughs. "No one should pay a dollar for a lobster."

"But maybe love is simply putting up with the other person's bad judgment and questionable taste in order to keep them," Brad contemplates aloud. Joe's foot brushes mine under the table. I don't know if it's accidental or not, but I do know I *definitely* shouldn't have felt that shiver.

Dom reaches for my hand. "What does it say about me that I think Lynne's taste complements mine?"

"That you're pussywhipped?" Joe asks flippantly.

"Language in this house!" Gemma roars, but she is laughing.

"Happy wife, happy life." Dom wiggles his eyebrows.

"Putting the cart before the horse, I see." Joe tears into his chicken wing. Like a savage. Just as I suspected. Mom's never wrong. Which is why I'm weirded out by how Dom eats chicken. It doesn't go with his mild, sweet nature.

"I'm a horse now. Awesome," I mumble, feeling the tension building at the dinner table and trying to diffuse it.

"Listen, man, I love you. I will die for you if need be. *But.*" Dom salutes Joe with his beer bottle graciously. "You're just jealous because I'm out of the game and don't have to go on Tinder anymore."

"You're right on one account." Joe takes a pull of his Guinness. I cough out my drink, mutter a weak apology, and lock myself in the bathroom for a quick session of clutching the sink and hyperventilating. I stare at myself in the mirror, shaking my head.

"Of course it'd happen to you, Ev. Of course."

By the time I come back, Dom and Joe are laughing, reminiscing about the time they both wrapped themselves in bubble roll and jumped from their tree house, resulting in a broken arm for each of them. Their relationship is so bipolar. I'm picking up on intense protectiveness vibes, and a lot of love, but also an underlying competition and bitterness. This doesn't look like something born out of a girl. I think it is deeper. Older than my relationship with both Graves brothers.

After dinner, we spill back to the living room. Gemma starts opening her presents, which is a whole ceremony. First, she opens mine. She seems to be genuinely delighted. "Everlynne, it's fantastic. Thank you so much. I've been wanting new candles for a while now!"

Then it's Joe's turn. His gift is swimming in fancy tissue paper. I crane my neck to peer into the box and see what it is. When she picks it up, tears prickle her eyes.

"Oh, Seph, honey." She grabs the item, clutching it to her chest. It's a peach-colored dress, sixties style. Gemma looks up at Joe. "But . . . *how*?"

He is sprawled on a recliner, peeling the label off his beer bottle.

"I'd been thinking about it the entire year. Where it could've gone. Last month, I started making some calls. One of them was to the woman who bought our old house on Church Creek. I asked her if I could take a look in her attic. She said yes. I spent a good portion of my last weekend on the project. Now her attic is organized and clean, and you have your favorite dress."

Dom leans toward me, squeezing my knee. "It's the dress Mom wore for her first date with Dad. She thought she'd lost it forever."

A knot forms in my throat. What a terrific gesture. Gemma almost falls over when she reaches to hug her younger son. Dom passes her a small green box. His smile is apologetic. "So, this is definitely not a punch-you-in-the-heart kind of gift . . ."

"Shush. Not everything is a competition," she says.

The words slide smoothly out of her throat. Like she's said them hundreds of times before. *Called it.* These two have a layered, complex relationship, and I'm best to stay out of it.

She unwraps the white satin bow, grinning at her elder son. Dom blushes, ducking his head down. Gemma pops the box open and picks up a pearl lock bracelet. It is gorgeous. Elegant and understated. But it doesn't hit as close or as personal as the dress you wore the day you fell in love, and Dom knows it.

"Sorry it's not more . . ." He scrubs his overnight stubble awkwardly.

"Dominic!" Gemma gasps, securing the bracelet on her wrist. "What's the matter with you? It's wonderful. You work so hard, such long hours, I'm surprised you brought me anything at all."

She hurries to hug him. As they embrace, Joe's eyes catch mine. He gives me a conspiratorial smirk. Suddenly, I ache to spend some time with him. One-on-one. Even if it hurts. Even if it kills me.

"But, I think I might be able to top off Joe's gift, after all." Dom throws his baby brother a wink. "Because I have another gift."

"Well, well, well." Brad sits back. He crosses his ankles over the coffee table. "Just remember I took you to the ballet, Gem. Because these boys are trying to up the ante, and all you'll find in my envelope to you is a Nordstrom gift card."

"Actually, this present is not for Mom." Dom stands up. "Although . . . some would argue that it is."

My heart speeds up. I suddenly forget how to breathe. *No. No. No.* What's worse is that I understand what's happening before everyone else does. Can anticipate Dom's next move. I speak his body language fluently.

He lowers himself to one knee before me in his parents' living room.

I want to die.

I close my eyes, thinking about how Dad is going to respond when I tell him I'm engaged. How Mom is not going to be at the wedding. How Pippa is going to hear about it, eventually, in passing one day and say, *She ended up marrying a Ken? Maybe I didn't know her after all.* I think about our future lives, in suburbia. About Honda SUVs designed to contain three baby car seats. I think about double dates with Joe and his flavor of the week. Cooking and calligraphy and claying classes.

Then I remember that I don't have to say yes.

But I *do*. I have to say yes because Dom chose me, in a time when no one else had. I have to because Dom makes things right. Because he took a look at my underbelly, at my darkness and insecurities, and stayed. And because Dom is not okay, not really. He needs my help in letting go of what happened to him. He is on self-destruction mode. I can't turn my back on that.

But all of those things don't hold a candle to the real reason why I can't say no—because the proposal is so public. I simply cannot turn him down in front of his family.

"Lynne." He clears his throat. "I know we've known each other for only a few months, but in those months, I've felt more than I ever have before. I fell in love, I gained a friend, I found out who Chewbacca was, made memories even more precious than my childhood nostalgia on the Cape—all with you."

Gemma coos. I force myself to open my eyes. All I see is Dom, and the hope marked on his face.

Be honest, Mom says in my head.

Be fierce, Pippa adds.

But their voices are so faded that I can barely hear them anymore.

"Everlynne Bellatrix Lawson—God, I love that name! So unique." Dom laughs. "Would you do me the honor and do the thing you warned me is ninety-nine point nine nine percent not going to happen and marry me? Because, baby, I've always believed in miracles, and you are my favorite point oh one percent."

Silence stretches for a few moments before I finally choke out, "Yes."

It is small, it is unsure, it is pained—but it is there.

I have no choice. He is putting me on the spot here. How could I have said no, in front of his entire family?

Everything happens fast afterward. Dom swoops me from the floor, spinning me in the air as if I weigh nothing. Our kiss is tender and brief. Gemma and Brad hurry to congratulate us.

"Welcome to the family." She holds my cheeks and smacks a wet kiss on either side of them.

"Been meaning to find an excuse to buy a new suit for a while now." Brad winks.

I search for Joe. I find him in the exact spot he was earlier, on the recliner. He hasn't moved an inch. His jaw is locked. He appears calm, but underneath the surface, I can feel that he is shattered. I'm shattered too. But I'm also happy. And there's a selfish, horrible part of me that is happy Joe can never escape my proximity now. We'll be bound forever soon.

"Seph, come congratulate your brother," Gemma urges. She grabs Joe's hand and tugs him to us. He doesn't budge. Dom tucks me under his arm, cocking his head sideways.

"All good, bro?" he asks.

Joe flicks his lighter back and forth, his thumb running over the flame. "Congratulations."

"Thank you."

"Treat her well." He says that in a way that implies Dom hasn't so far, which is completely untrue. Dom has been great. "I *mean* it."

Dom bows his head a little. I don't understand this exchange, and it unsettles me.

Joe's gaze drifts to me. There is something inside his eyes. Something I can't read, but it tells me that he's had enough. That he loves his brother dearly but that this charade needs to stop.

For a moment, I think it is all going to be over. That Joe is going to uncover what happened between us. That they'll kick me out of their home, and I'll have to walk my way back to Salem. But then Joe stands up, grabs his beer, and leaves.

"I'm going out for a smoke."

An hour later, Dom and his father go into the kitchen to tidy up while Gemma takes a phone call on the patio. Dom asks if I can bring him his tennis equipment from the closet in his bedroom. Apparently, he has a game next week. I want to tell him he has no business picking up tennis when he barely has time to sleep, but I stop myself. I'm going to argue with him to death, but not in front of his family. The weight of the diamond ring on my engagement finger comes with newfound authority. I intend to sit Dom down when we get back to Salem, look at his schedule, and make him trim the fat. I get that he wants to eat the world, but right now, the world is eating him.

I also intend to make it clear that we are not getting married this year. It would be unfair on both of us.

When I get to the hallway on the second floor, I pass by Joe's room. The door is ajar. I can see him lying on his bed. I can't help myself. I push the door open and peek inside.

I've dreamed of this moment daily. At some points in my life—hourly. To step into Joe's domain. Now that I'm finally here, bittersweet satisfaction washes over me. It is exactly how I've imagined it. The black-accented wall, the band posters (the Kinks, Oasis, Duran Duran). The bookshelves (Kerouac, Ginsberg, Burroughs, Bukowski).

"Joe?"

No answer.

"Are you ignoring me?"

Clearly, he is, because all I can see are his socked feet moving to a soundless rhythm on his bed. I push the door open all the way, frustrated. "Very mature, asshole. We were literally in front of your parents. What did you expect me to—"

That's when I see that he has his earbuds tucked into his ears. He plucks one out. His eyes hood into dangerously angry slits. Wrath in the air. But he is not the only one who is angry. I'm pissed. Pissed that I said yes because of peer pressure. Pissed that Dom got his way somehow again. Pissed that if I only felt toward Dom a fraction of what I feel toward his baby brother, none of this would be an issue.

Pissed at Dad and Renn, who are MIA again.

And at myself, for taking advantage of Nora's good heart and not telling her to just *move* already.

"Wrong brother. The bed you're looking for is next door down."

"Stop." I storm into his bedroom without permission.

"Stop what?" His tone is cold. "You didn't come here for me, did you? Because . . ." He hops off the bed, then plucks his keys from his study desk and shoves them into his pocket. "I have a date to go on. Decided to give it another go with Presley. She *does* give good head."

My tears fall before I can stop them. I would punch him if he deserved it. But he doesn't.

"Joe," I croak, reminded of the way he tried to appeal to me the night he came to visit me at my tour. *Ever.*

"Don't *Joe* me. What the fuck are you doing? Tell me." He gets into my face, tilting his chin up defiantly. "You barely know this person. You have no idea who he is. You've been with him for . . . what, three, four months?"

I don't necessarily disagree with him. The progression of my relationship with Dom has been . . . well, *unusual,* some would say. Also, is Mercury in retrograde? Since when is surly, angry, unbearable Joe the voice of reason in my life?

"Look, I was put on the spot here." I run a hand over my face. "Don't be unfair."

"Oh, *I'm* the one who is being unfair?" He arches an eyebrow diabolically. "That's interesting. We make promises to each other. I change my plans for you. I rearrange my goddamn *life* around you. You disappear one day without as much as a 'See you later.' Fine. You told me why; not gonna hold it against you. You had a crisis, not that I knew that. Then you come back in the form of my brother's fiancée. Please, tell me more about your fucking woes, Ever."

"Don't be an asshole. It's not like I used your heart as a squishy toy. And back downstairs, we had an audience," I hiss. "What was I supposed to say back there?"

"No," he drawls blandly, looking at me like I'm a complete idiot. "Know that word? Starts with an *N*, ends with an *O*. People use it from time to time. No."

"I use it. I used it on Dom before we started dating, because I still wasn't over *you!*" I ball my hands into fists, slamming them against his chest. "You self-righteous asshole!"

But Joe soldiers on, not even acknowledging my words, and not budging an inch at the physical contact.

". . . though I'll be honest, you seem to have a weakness when it comes to a Graves dick. You do know Dad is taken, right?"

I slap his right cheek. The sound of my palm against his flesh rings in my ears. When he looks back at me, deadly calm, a terrible smirk smears over his face. It is the first time I've seen Joe ugly. He reminds me of Rhett Butler in that scene when he leaves Scarlett O'Hara with a stolen, half-dead horse and a carriage full of people to fend for herself. This is the trouble with Joe. I never know if he loves me or hates me. If he is indifferent to me, or if he is just playing a game because he doesn't want to get his feelings destroyed.

"You shouldn't have done that." He licks his lips, grinning devilishly. "Slap me."

I swallow hard. "Why?"

"Because now I know how deep I've gotten under your skin. Just like the tattoo you were so scared of getting. Inked permanently. Not to be removed or lasered off."

He grabs me by the throat with scary selfishness and kisses me. *Hard.*

My body is a series of volcanoes, blowing off one after the other. My spine, an endless row of dominos that fall piece by piece until my legs buck. Everything is hot and desperate and raw. His fingers curl around my neck, drawing me closer. My lips slam against his with a pained grunt. His tongue pries them open, not asking—demanding—to get inside. The fool that I am, I yield. His body is flushed with mine. I feel him everywhere. Down to my toes. He scrapes the inside of my mouth with his teeth, skimming the line between pleasure and pain. Marking me, making my lips deliberately swollen.

We kiss with such passion I feel like we're both about to combust. But he tastes wrong. Not like that night in Spain. Like anger and vengeance and hate. Like everything I feel toward myself for not being proactive about starting to fix the mess also known as my so-called life.

I push him away. "No!"

Even though I did the pushing, I'm also the one who stumbles backward from the impact. I clap my hand over my mouth. "Holy shit, what have we done?"

Joe drops his head back, face tilted at the ceiling. He looks fed up, and I can't blame him.

"Kissed. I'm sure you're familiar with the concept."

"Stop being a smart-ass. But I—"

"Let me guess, regret it? I'm noticing a theme here."

"How can you be so blasé?"

He drags a hand through his hair, pacing the room. "Don't worry. I won't tell your precious boyfriend. Sorry, *fiancé*. Just another secret to toss into Pandora's box. Well, well. This marriage is going to have quite the turbulent start. *I'll save you all my prayers.*"

Another reference I don't miss. He remembers my favorite song in the whole wide world. Dom doesn't. In fact, Dom and I never discuss music.

"Don't be a hypocrite. It wasn't me who said we shouldn't tell him about what happened six years ago." I hate myself for continuously making mistakes when it comes to this man. My self-control is in the toilet where he is concerned.

Joe chuckles darkly. "Whatever you say, *Lynne*."

"Don't *Lynne* me. What we did to Dom right now was horrible."

"Drop the guilt-fest." Joe shoves his feet into his sneakers. He is going to see Presley. There's nothing I can do to stop him. "No one's buying it. And even if I did—*I* don't feel guilty about kissing you."

"Why are you so angry?" I ask. He's not always angry. Most of the time, he is resigned to our fate.

"Because," he says, calm, collected, and bored. "We never broke up. Technically, Ever, you're still my girlfriend."

It's like a punch in the face, and as such, I stagger back. "You can't be for real right now."

"I can, and I fucking am. No breakup talk—no breakup." He shoves his shoelaces into his sneakers, as opposed to tying them.

"How we broke up was terrible, but we *did* break up. I'm sorry I hurt you."

"You hurt yourself too. You chose mainstream."

His words hit me. I remember them from all those years ago.

Mainstream people aren't revolutionary. Nothing good ever comes out of them. Average equals comfort.

But I need comfort. I need safe.

"You stopped being a choice the day I kissed your brother," I rasp. "We can't do this to him, and you know that."

"God, you're like a broken record. Your morals *bore* me." He lets out a short breath. I see his frustration. All the things he's given up over the years for Dominic. The attention. The sleepless nights. The worrying. Always low on the totem pole. Even now, Dom is the golden child. The one who went to college, who got a good job, who is getting married. "And the worst part is, I am the only aspect in your life where you do the good thing, even if it's not the *right* thing. Everything else about your relationships, including Dom, is fucked up because you always take the easy way out."

He is right. He is right, and it's time I own up to all my mistakes. Especially the one I left in California.

Joe's shoulder brushes mine. He stalks out of the room. And then I hear the words that undo me. They pull at me like a frayed old sweater. Until I'm nothing but a long string of pain.

"I loved you, Ever Lawson. But I want you to know, you're the worst thing that's ever fucking happened to me."

EIGHTEEN

I drive us back to Salem, not allowing Dom to get behind the wheel. Now we're both leaning on the car, the silence between us so palpable I can taste it on my tongue. Since I don't trust him with a vehicle right now—or a coffee machine, for that matter—I tell him I'll take his car to my apartment to pick up Loki, and then I'll bring it back. Dom doesn't argue. Like with everything else, he is understanding and cooperative. *Perfect.* He kisses my neck, pressing me against his sports car, his hands on my waist.

"Did you have a good time at Mom's birthday?" he murmurs into my neck.

"Of course." My mind involuntarily drifts to Joe. I think about his words. About *that* kiss. It still lingers on my lips, an unspoken secret.

I need to tell Dom. I can't plan a wedding with this man without coming clean about everything.

I need to tell him that this is too soon, too much. That we don't have to tell people, but the engagement needs to be on hold. Otherwise, we're just going to hurt more people. And ourselves.

When I try to pull away, Dom hugs me tighter and says, "Put Loki in his carrier, grab a few clothes, and hurry up. I need to be inside you."

The proof of his desire for me is nestled between my legs, through our clothes. It twitches against my groin, demanding to be taken care of.

"We need to talk first," I say.

"About what?" He pulls away, scanning me. "You're not getting cold feet, are you?"

I chuckle, feeling extra dead inside. "We just need to smooth some things over."

I can tell he is unhappy about this, but he nods. "All right. I'll wait."

"I might take a second. I need to get some tampons."

Actually, I don't. I don't have my period. But there is no way I can have sex with Dom, even on the off chance that he's okay with what happened with Joe.

Dom kisses my forehead. "I'll buy 'em. You go pack for the night."

"It's just on the way," I protest.

"The Walgreens is right across the street." He laughs. "And you're taking my car, remember? So it's not like I'm at risk of driving into a wall or something."

I roll my eyes. "Don't even joke about that." And then, before I forget, I say, "I love you."

"Love you too."

He sends me off with a pat on my ass. In the car, once it's quiet, I replay tonight's scene with Joe in my head over and over.

I loved you.

Joe used past tense, while I'm still here in the present, pining for him.

It occurs to me that after I tell Dom about my kiss with his brother today, he'll almost certainly break off the engagement. What frightens me even more is the feeling that's tethered to it. Of relief. Not because I don't love Dom, but because I'm in love with his brother too.

Maybe taking a step back from the entire Graves family would be a good thing. I could tell Nora to move in with Colt, anyway. Living by myself for a while would do me good.

When I walk into my apartment half an hour later, Nora is not there. I can't remember the last time she's slept at home. At this point she's just paying half my rent. I grab a quick shower, push Loki into his carrier, and pack a light bag.

I've picked up the sticky note pad by the fridge, about to write Nora a message, when my phone rings in my back pocket. I pull it out and see Joe's name across the screen. My heart skips a beat. For a second, I contemplate not answering. Or at least, I pretend to contemplate this, because there's no way I can resist the urge.

I swipe the screen, sighing.

"Look, I know there's still stuff to talk about—"

He cuts me off. "You need to go to the hospital."

"What?" I ask.

"Salem's general hospital. You need to go there. Right. *Now*. Dom's in critical condition."

I drop the sticky notes and the pen on the floor. My legs are shaking. I try to breathe, but the air gets stuck in my throat. "What do you mean? How? Why?"

"Ever. Ever. Ever." Joe's voice is husky, like he's been screaming. The lack of his casual indifference throws me into the depths of hysteria. "It happened about half an hour ago. He crossed the street back from Walgreens. Got hit by a truck."

"Oh my God!" I yelp. "What happened? Was the driver drunk?"

I need something, or someone, to be mad at. The roaring engine and the rain hitting Joe's car tell me he is on his way too. I kick into high gear, running around the apartment, putting my shoes on.

"They don't know," Joe says, finally. "They don't know shit, Ever. I only got the call ten minutes ago. A couple witnesses who were there said that he fell right into incoming traffic. On a red light."

"Like . . . collapsed?" I choke out.

Another beat of silence. This time, I realize, Joe is trying to control his emotions. "Yeah."

"But why? Why would someone just collapse like that? It doesn't make any sense."

He doesn't answer.

"People don't just fall into traffic. Something must have happened," I continue arguing with no one in particular.

I can't think straight. I run out the door before remembering I don't have my keys.

"Cab it," Joe says. "Don't get behind the wheel. It's pissing rain and you're in no condition."

I don't have the mental capacity to argue with him right now, so I just ignore his words. "Where are Gemma and Brad?"

"On their way. I shouldn't take more than twenty minutes. I just left Pres—"

Presley's apartment. Or bedroom, more specifically. He doesn't have to say it. Not so surprisingly, though, I don't give a damn right now.

"It'll take me ten minutes," I hear myself say. "Call me when you get there."

I don't know how I do it. The mundane small things that usually require no special effort from me. Buckling my safety belt. Maneuvering the steering wheel. Waiting on traffic lights. Especially as I slide into the designated parking spot in front of the emergency room. I kill the engine, curl my fingers around the steering wheel, and let out a scream so shrill it makes me nauseous.

Then I wipe my tears, get out of the car, and walk over to the emergency room's reception. The receptionist directs me to another wing. Apparently, Dom is in surgery. I'm in some kind of a waiting room, with depressing blue chairs, a smaller reception area, and big windows overlooking the parking lot.

I'm standing in front of a set of doors leading to a hallway with *another* set of doors. Dom is somewhere back there, though I'm not sure what kind of surgery they're performing on him. I don't know anything, and it is driving me mad.

I don't allow myself to think about the fact that his last visit was to Walgreens, to get me tampons. For my *fake* period. I don't dwell on how stupid it is. How meaningless. I can't do this to myself right now. Instead, I pace from corner to corner, playing with my diamond ring on my finger. He can't just die. People don't get engaged and die on the same day. This is not how the world works.

A petite blonde woman in blue scrubs dashes across the hallway toward the waiting room. She's out of breath. Is she one of the doctors who is performing the surgery? Can she tell me anything? I'm about to ask her, but she bypasses me, slapping her hands over the reception desk.

"Belinda?"

"Dr. Nelson!" The receptionist stands up and reaches over the counter to give her a brief hug. "I'm so sorry. What a nightmare."

The blonde lets out a low moan, leaning into Belinda's shoulder. "I called Dr. Hansley. He's performing the surgery right now. It's a penetrating brain injury."

"Did he say how it's going?"

The blonde shakes her head no.

I tell myself that they might not be talking about Dom. It's juvenile to think there's only one surgery going on in this hospital at this moment. I stop pacing, listening to their conversation nonetheless. It's the only thing I can do right now.

The blonde notices my presence for the first time. She turns to me, her face open and friendly despite her obvious distress. "Sorry, are you waiting for someone?"

"Yes." I find my voice—barely. "Ah . . . Dominic Graves."

"Are you a friend of his? A patient?" The blonde woman strides over to me. Up close, she is beautiful, in a cool, swanlike way. Then, before I can answer, she offers me her hand. "I'm Dr. Sarah Nelson."

"Sarah!" I take her hand, squeezing. Relief washes over me. She is the woman from the fridge magnet, of course. From the charity event Dom attended earlier this year. "Dom told me about you."

I think about the time he mentioned that a doctor named Sarah had told him to check on Craigslist for missing posts when Loki disappeared.

Sarah gives me a sad smile. "Oh. Thank you."

"Do you know anything about his . . . situation?" I lick my lips. It is so nice of her to be here, to make sure that he is okay. I'm not surprised, though. Dominic is an amazing guy who digs his way through a lot of hearts and stays there.

Sarah blows out a breath. "Well, I called the neurosurgeon who's operating on him as soon as they told me he's here. They're performing a delicate brain surgery. He only said that Dom fractured his skull, that there is bleeding in multiple areas, and some tearing of brain tissue."

I drop my face into my hands and weep. I hate that I'm so powerless. That things are out of my control. I hate how unnecessary this situation is. How random.

Sarah reaches over, rubbing my arm. "I know. It's terrible."

Instead of answering her with words, I just bawl harder. She clasps me into a hug. I don't know why everyone I love ends up dying or seriously injured. Mom. Dom. Maybe I'm cursed. Maybe the best thing I can do for Dad and Renn is stay the hell away from them. Maybe they know that, which is why they never call anymore.

No wonder you are obsessed with gravestones. You have the tendency to put people under them.

"I should call his family . . . ," I hear Sarah murmur in my ear, thinking aloud. "See if Gemma and Brad are aware."

I pull away from her, sniffing. Finally, I feel like I'm not totally useless. "They know. They're on their way here."

Sarah frowns. "They are?"

"Yeah. I spoke to Joe . . . I mean, Seph, about twenty minutes ago. Everyone's coming."

For the first time since we met, Sarah takes a step back, drawing an invisible line between us. She looks at me like I'm a different person. "Who did you say you were again?"

"I didn't," I hiccup, offering her my hand. "I'm Everlynne."

"Everlynne . . . ?" She wants credentials. Doesn't take my offered hand.

"His fiancée." I turn my empty hand just so, revealing a sparkling diamond ring.

"His fiancée?" she repeats.

"Yes."

"Interesting."

"Why?"

Dr. Sarah doesn't look so friendly anymore. "Because I'm his girlfriend."

NINETEEN

The floor doesn't shatter beneath my feet. The world doesn't explode into miniscule pieces. And still, something breaks inside me. It is so fundamental, I know I will never, *ever* be the same person I was two minutes ago.

Dom has a girlfriend.

Dom is two-timing me.

The clues start *ding-ding-dinging* in my head. Oh, how small they looked, separated from one another, seemingly unrelated and innocent.

How Dom never, ever took me out on a date in Salem.

How he worked way too many hours—even for a nurse—and didn't come home for three and four nights in a row sometimes.

How Joe said he didn't feel guilty for kissing me. The way he would always allude to Dom not being the saint I'd pegged him to be.

The disgust he felt about my and Dom's relationship—does he know Dom is cheating on me? Of course he does. If Sarah knows Gemma and Brad, she knows Joe too. And then it hits me . . .

The necklace.

The necklace.

The necklace.

The letter *S. Sarah.*

She and I occupied the same bed, rolled in the same sheets, kissed the same skin of the same man all these weeks and months. Now that I think about it, she is everywhere in his apartment. On magnets on his fridge. In the way the mugs are always coordinated by color neatly in the cupboard. The women's deodorant he'd let me use once and said belonged to his mother . . .

"I'm not sure how you expect me to respond to what you're saying." Sarah speaks, and although her voice is curt, I can see her chin is wobbling. "Dom and I have been together for three years."

"I'm sorry," I say, feeling sorry for *me*, not for her. "It's the truth. He asked me to marry him tonight. At his mother's sixtieth birthday dinner."

Sarah closes her eyes. I can tell it's sunk in. That she believes me. Me, I'm still struggling to come to terms with this new reality. Dom can't be a cheating dirtbag. This is not who he is. He is the Savior of Lost Girls. The sweet, dimpled, mild man who stormed into the picture and made it all better.

"How long have you been together?" She wipes her eyes.

"Three months." It feels inadequate in comparison to her three years. *I* feel inadequate. She is a gorgeous doctor. I'm a . . . I'm *me*. What was Dom thinking? Why did he start things with me?

"I guess that's why he stopped inviting me over to his parents'." A brittle laugh bubbles up her throat. "I thought it was because of my night shifts and his schedule. Wow."

The double doors between us slap open. Joe appears like a mirage, oozing dark energy. He sees Sarah and me standing in front of one another and makes a face. It is something between *Shit* and *Dom, you dumb fuck*. It is an exceedingly Joe-like expression.

"Seph," Sarah moans. Her shoulders sag. "Oh my God."

I don't know if she is saying this about the accident, or about the acuteness of Dom's situation, or about the cheating, or about all of it.

"Sar. How're you holding up?"

Seph and Sar. This is all the confirmation I need that these two know each other.

"Terrible," she says.

Joe's eyes travel to me. He is checking the temperature. Trying to gauge how angry I am.

Because it is easy—and because he deserves it—as soon as he reaches for me, to give me a hug, I slap him. This time I get his left cheek. Two slaps in one day is some kind of record, I'm sure.

He rubs at his cheek. "I deserve that."

"You bastard," I hiss.

"Guilty as charged. We'll revisit the subject later." He turns to Sarah. "Any news on him?"

Sarah is hugging herself. I can tell that she is watching our interaction closely, and that she finds it very odd. She shakes her head. "Not yet, but I was going to try to get into the operating room."

"You should do that," he says firmly. *"Now."*

After looking between us helplessly, Sarah stalks off down the corridor. Joe and I are left alone. It seems stupid to talk about Dom's infidelity when he might not even make it. Then again, there is nothing else to talk about. We don't know anything. As screwed up as it is, Dr. Sarah Nelson is exactly the distraction I need to forget that my fiancé is currently fighting for his life.

"He is two-timing me," I say matter-of-factly once Sarah is gone and it's just the two of us between the mint-green walls. I notice that Belinda the receptionist is showing a healthy interest in what's going on in her waiting room. She's been reading the same page in her novel for ten minutes now.

Joe scratches his jaw, looking away. "He's my brother, Ever. What was I supposed to do? Rat him out?" His jaw hardens. "I tried to indicate to you in numerous ways that it wasn't the end of the world if we kissed."

"Two wrongs don't make a right!" I snap.

"In my book, if you're stupid enough to cheat on two perfectly good women, you're not good enough for either of them."

"Why didn't you talk sense into him?"

"You think I haven't tried!" Joe thunders, flinging his arms in the air, exasperated. "I did my best drilling logic into that thick skull of his. Hundreds of times. You think I liked seeing this mess unfolding? Especially when you were a part of it?"

"Yes," I hear myself saying, even though I'm not sure I think that at all. "I think you drew some sort of nasty satisfaction from knowing my relationship was screwed. Doomed. That I'm being made a fool—"

"You don't know me." His voice is razor sharp as it cuts into my words. "I would never sign up for this shit. You know why?"

I flinch in response, noticing that he is wearing an ugly, bitter smile. One of a man marred by pain. "Because I know what it feels like to have your heart broken."

And it's horrible. How, despite how angry and scared I am, I still want to collapse to my knees and ask him for . . . what? His love? His acceptance? His forgiveness? What do I want from this man?

"Why did Dom ask me to marry him?" I change the subject. "Why did he ask me to move in when he has a steady girlfriend? Wh—"

"Sarah and Dom haven't been steady this past year," Joe interrupts me again. "They broke up a ton of times. She went on a Doctors without Borders mission for a while, came back, almost took a job in Portland . . . they've been on and off for a while. That's why my parents welcomed you with open arms. They were sure that things with Sarah were done."

"When was the last time he brought her over?" I ask.

Joe runs a hand over his hair. "I don't know, Easter?"

Dom is so lucky he is in the operating room right now, because I am liable to punch him no matter his physical state right now.

"He said he hadn't brought a girl over for Christmas since Emily," I point out pettily. How is this important right now? I don't know.

Maybe I'm trying to villainize Dom now that his existence in my life is in question. So far, it isn't working.

Joe looks at me like I'm crazy. "Who is Emily?"

I frown. "Emily. His ex-girlfriend."

"He never dated an Emily."

My whole body is shaking. I feel like I'm about to burst. Emily was a lie. He gaslighted me. The manipulative son of a . . .

"So he and Sarah weren't serious." I try to keep my voice calm. "But he still asked me to marry him when he has another girlfriend."

"He was . . . *is*," Joe corrects; "look, Dom is a hard person to read. I don't know what he is thinking. Half the time I don't think he knows what *he* is thinking."

"Why didn't he break up with her right away?" I demand, like Joe is the source of my pain right now, and not Dom. Like he is to blame for all this mess.

He gives me a bone-tired look, rubbing his knuckles over his jaw. "You want the truth?"

"Please."

"Because Dom has been used to getting away with whatever the fuck he's done from a young age, and he thought he could have it both ways until the very last minute. You weren't a sure thing until you had his ring on your finger, and he wanted to keep his options open. I think a part of him will always love Sarah. She had detonated his life when she moved to Yemen. He just needed . . ."

"Someone without a career and a busy schedule and a huge life. Someone he could mold into the woman he needs," I finish for him, bitterness exploding in my mouth. Because that's exactly who I've been to Dom. From the get-go, I was this detached girl he'd met in weird circumstances. No family, no friends, no direction. I was not in danger of fleeing. Of doing something big and not including him.

He took you to a pottery class, I internally taunt myself. *Because he knew he was going to mold and shape you into who he wanted you to be.*

There is not enough air in the room. In this town. In the universe.

"As soon as he bent the knee in Mom and Dad's living room, I knew he'd made a decision." Joe's Adam's apple bobs with a swallow. He looks so shattered right now, and I don't have it in me to keep fighting with him. Actually, he is right. He is not to blame. So what if he knew? I wouldn't rat Renn out, no matter what he's done.

Sarah and I were in competition. The old versus the new. And now it hits me why Sarah told Dom to get on Craigslist all those months ago when Loki showed up at his balcony. Because she was right there, in his apartment, when it happened.

Joe turns to Belinda. "When are we going to get some news about my brother?"

Belinda shoves a bookmark into her hardcover. "We will have new information when one of the doctors performing the surgery comes out, Mr. Graves."

"Thanks for nothing," Joe mutters.

"No news is good news." I rub at my forehead. "There's nothing to work on if he's dead."

The last word explodes between us, and we both stare at each other, wide eyed.

Sarah storms back to the waiting room wearing fresh scrubs, a face shield, and all the other stuff surgeons wear. She passes the double doors leading to the surgery room, not sparing us a look.

"He is going to be okay, right?" I ask Joe.

He takes my hand and squeezes it wordlessly. The answer is in his touch.

Gemma and Brad arrive at the hospital in their pajamas and matching UGG slippers. Two police officers show up as well. The policemen tell us that the truck driver who hit Dominic, a forty-year-old father of three from the Boston area, was tested sober and was not driving over the limit. That, according to witnesses, Dom collapsed from the sidewalk onto the curb just as the truck was making a right turn. Unfortunately, he not only suffered the impact of the hit but was also dragged across the pavement while the truck completed its turn.

Sarah is not out of the operating room yet. There's no word from the other doctors working on him. It feels like we're stuck in one of Dante's circles of hell. Maybe in the treachery circle.

"I'm going to get everyone some coffee," I say to the Graveses before retiring to the small cafeteria on the other side of the floor. I'm jittery and out of focus. I also want to call Dad and Renn and tell them that I love them. That I don't take them for granted. That I'm sorry that I suck. That I'm going to suck less from now on, because it's true. There's no guarantee any of us are going to be here tomorrow. We have to make the best of today.

While I wait for four cups of coffee and some pastries no one is going to eat, I shoot Nora a quick message about what happened to Dom. I tell her I left Loki in his carrier in my haste. I ask if she can get him out of there and make sure his litter box is clean and that he has water and food.

She messages me right away that she is extremely sorry and horrified for me, that she and Colt are on their way to the apartment, and to keep her posted.

The woman who works at the cafeteria gives me a tray to carry the coffee and pastries. I make my way back to the waiting room slowly. There is no point in rushing. It feels like the surgeons will never get out of that room. It's five in the morning, and we still haven't heard anything. It scares me that I'm getting comfortable in the state of not knowing. That the limbo of being in the dark is, to me, preferable to knowing he is not going to make it.

The closer I get to the waiting room, the more it is apparent that a commotion is going on there. If it's Sarah causing a scene about the engagement, I am going to scream. The Graveses don't deserve this kind of chaos right now. But when I push the doors open with my shoulder and see two exhausted-looking doctors, a devastated Sarah, and a lifeless Joe and Brad, I know.

Gemma is on the floor in a heap of limbs, sobbing her eyes out.

The tray slips from my hands. Hot liquid splashes on my shins, but I don't feel it. Brad and Joe turn to face me. They are talking to me, but I can't hear them. Everything goes white and dotty. I stumble backward. Away.

No. No. No.

Everything sounds like I'm underwater. I cannot hear them, which is for the best.

I turn around and start running. Or try to run. I'm like a baby giraffe taking its first steps. My legs tangle. I fall on the floor. Another body launches itself atop of me from behind. The weight feels tragically familiar. His arms engulf my whole frame.

His lips brush my ears. "Shhh. I got you. Let it all go."

I fall apart on the floor. I kick, I cry, I scream. I make a scene. I claw at my own face. I don't know how long I do this for. But after a while, I run out of energy. I become limp in his arms. He is still holding me in his grip.

"We should be there for Gemma," I mumble, congested with tears and snot.

It's always the mother who hurts the most.

Joe stands up and offers me his hand. I take it, sniffling.

Together, we walk to our new, Dom-less reality.

TWENTY

We decide to stick together for the next few hours in a postapocalyptic daze.

We consisting of Joe, Brad, Gemma, Sarah, and me.

Sarah and I don't talk much, but when we do, it's not hostile. We're both exhausted and reek of despair. Even cheating and infidelity is small in the grand scheme of life. And what does it matter that Dom made both of us look like fools if he is not even here so we can properly yell at him? The anger is so redundant, and duller in comparison to the pain of losing him.

Joe drives us to Dom's apartment, where I make everyone tea, moving on autopilot. Sarah cuts a Valium pill with a butter knife, then gives one half to Gemma and the other to Brad. She offers Joe and me something to take the edge off, but we both decline.

Joe locks himself in Dom's bedroom and makes some calls. I don't know what to feel. I don't know what to think. I'm scared of processing everything that's happening here.

Gemma, Sarah, and I are in the living room, sipping tea. Apparently, Dom just collapsed onto the street, right into incoming traffic. My guess is he was too exhausted to stay up on his feet. I'd always worried about him not getting many hours of sleep.

Sarah feels the need to fill the silence, because she is a doctor and because she was there during his last hour.

"He didn't feel it." She puts the mug to her lips, letting the steam create a condensation mustache above her lip. "Any of it. He suffered from a penetration injury. The impact forced a part of his skull into his brain. He was very much out of it. Didn't know what was happening. I know it's little comfort, but I thought you should know."

"So why did it take hours? The surgery?" I ask.

She looks up at me, surprised that I'm talking to her. Her eyes drop to my engagement ring, and tears fill them again. I tuck my hand under my thigh, embarrassed.

She clears her throat. "He didn't die immediately. They tried to stop the bleeding and to assess the damage of the ruptured brain tissue."

"So even if he survived . . ." Gemma presses a mangled tissue to her nose. Some of it is stuck to her cheeks and lips, but no one says anything.

"Yes," Sarah says gently, reaching to touch Gemma's knee. "The recovery would have been extremely long, and although this is not my field of expertise, I would say the damage to his brain would have been substantial. He wouldn't have been able to lead the life he'd had before."

"Thank you . . . for explaining all this," I say. Because in a way, it is a little comforting. To know Dom was spared the destiny of being in a long coma.

Gemma completely breaks and takes both our hands and says, "I'm so sorry, girls. I know how hard it must be for you to sit together in the same room. But can I just say, seeing how the two of you are dealing with this complex situation just shows me why Dom was struggling to make a choice."

Sarah and I exchange horrified looks. I'm sure she doesn't like being talked about like she is a pair of flattering jeans either. My acceptance of Sarah has nothing to do with my love for Dom and everything to do with the fact that *she*, personally, didn't know of my existence and therefore didn't do anything bad to me.

"This is fine," Sarah says curtly. "It doesn't matter. We all loved Dominic."

Eventually, Joe gets out of Dom's room and fills his parents in about all kinds of bureaucratic stuff. He puts a hand on my shoulder. "You should call someone. I'm not letting you out of here until I know there's someone to take care of you."

Though I dread this phone call, I also know that it is necessary. I take my phone and lock myself in Dom's room. A fresh wave of tears hits me at the scent of him. Of his bed, his aftershave, his laundry, his *life*. It seems so surreal that I'm not going to have him anymore. That his scent will fade, and his possessions will be tucked away or donated. That his body will no longer be warm and strong and vital.

I call Dad before Nora, thinking he is for sure not going to pick up. Why would he? I've been nothing but a shit kid to him over the past six years. But maybe parents have a sixth sense, because this time not only does he answer, but he does so on the second ring. Before I can tell myself that it's okay to hang up. That I've tried.

"Everlynne," he clips out.

At the sound of his voice, I break. With reckless abandon. I moan in pain, not even recognizing my own voice. I sound like an animal.

His tenor immediately changes. It is soft now. "Oh . . . don't . . . don't cry. I . . . um . . . Everlynne, please, tell me what's going on. I hate to hear you like this."

This, of course, only makes me cry harder. Because I've given up on this amazing father. Who read me stories and learned how to dance from watching YouTube videos with me, and always maintained that I was talented and beautiful and could do whatever I wanted if I put my mind to it.

"What happened? Tell me." I hear the door to his office click shut.

"Dad, I'm so sorry. So sorry for the way I've behaved . . ."

I can't seem to finish the sentence. He clears his throat, soothing me again. "I'm your father. I can be here for you, even if I don't necessarily agree with your behavior at certain times. Now, tell me what happened so I can help you."

But he can't help me. No one can. I lost Dominic and no one can bring him back.

"I-I-I had a fiancé," I hiccup.

"A fiancé?" He sounds stunned.

"Y-yes."

"And . . . you broke up with him?" He sounds confused. Cautious. Put off.

"N-n-no." Each word falls out of my lips like it's a hot potato. "H-he—he—he *died*."

Putting this as a statement makes me lose it all over again. As if there is anything left to lose.

"Your fiancé died?" Dad asks. I can tell he is lost and shocked.

"Yes."

There's a pause while he digests the information. Finally, he speaks. "How did he die? When?"

"C-c-car accident. Yesterday. A few hours after we got engaged. I don't know what to do."

This is the truest thing I've ever said. I do not, in fact, know what to do. Not in the next ten minutes, next hour, next week. I have no idea how I'm supposed to behave right now. There is no protocol to what happens next.

There's silence on the other side of the line. For a moment, I think maybe Dad has hung up. I don't know if I can blame him, after everything that's happened.

"I'm getting on a plane, Ever. Wait right there. I'm coming to see you. Today."

"Oh. You don't need to do that . . ."

"I love you." The words hit me with the force of a semi. He says them in a low growl. With heat. "You hear that, Everlynne? I love you."

I cry hysterically all over again, this time in relief. He loves me. He still loves me. After everything that's happened—he still wants to be there for me.

"Th-thank you."

"Stay strong. I'm coming."

The line goes dead.

For the first time since Joe called to tell me about Dom, I remember how to breathe.

◆ ◆ ◆

The funeral is an open-casket event.

In true Dominic Graves form, and despite his head injury, his face has remained flawless and scarless.

Nora was in charge of the makeup. She asked beforehand if it would be weird for me. I told her that it wouldn't, even though I had no idea how I was feeling about it.

This past week, I felt extremely disconnected from reality. Life seems to be happening in my periphery.

I don't sleep, but I occasionally pass out in random spots in my apartment. Dad and Renn have been here for a week now. They're staying at a nice hotel downtown and show up at my doorstep first thing in the morning with coffee. They brought Dunkies the first morning, but it reminded me of the Girlfriend Promise and I sobbed into the box, making a whole stink about it, like they were supposed to know.

Dad and Renn get along great with Nora and Colt. It's all very cordial on the outside. We look like just another family. But we're not, and all the things we don't say to each other pile up between us in an invisible mountain of sorrow.

Renn looks so different now. So tall and strong. So lost and mother-less. Dad looks different too. But not necessarily in a bad way. He looks like he's lost a few pounds and like he actually gets his hair profession-ally cut, now that Mom is not there to shave it for him.

Dad and Renn arrived the day I called Dad, just like he promised. Even though the funeral is taking place a full week later, neither of them have complained about the time they're missing from school and work.

I opt to not see Dom's body in the casket. Ironic, considering I'm obsessed with graves. Maybe I'm a fraud. Maybe that's why Dom and I got along so well. After all, he turned out to be a fraud too. Although, weirdly enough, I barely think about his betrayal and focus more on his loss.

As we sit and listen to the sermon from the front pew of a Dover church, I hold Dad's hand for dear life. Renn shoves his shoulder against mine lovingly.

I don't allow myself to ask Dad if he is mad at me, or what it was that he wanted to tell me all those months ago. I don't broach the sub-ject of how our relationship is going to look after this is all over. I also don't dare ask Nora what Dom looked like when she worked on him. I find myself incapable of making conversation with anyone. Everything feels swollen and raw. Things that bothered me—Dom's hectic sched-ule, *Lynne* and *Babe* and his awful—*awful*—taste in music—now seem so small and insignificant. I would pay in weeks and months and years from my own life just to be able to kiss and touch him again. To tell him that I love him. To explain that I really didn't need the tampons.

I didn't. Need. The. Tampons.

I marvel at the cruelness of the world. How it let Dom survive can-cer but ended up taking his life prematurely anyway. And I wonder how many losses one person can experience before they give up on the idea of happiness. I don't know where I land on the loss-meter. Happiness seems like a mythical thing right now.

After the ceremony, people peer inside the casket. I slip out of church and pass by Sarah and Gemma and Brad, who are standing by the door like one family unit. I try to muster the strength to feel jealous, but I'm so mentally exhausted I can't even do that.

As I round the churchyard, I notice Joe by a duck-filled pond, leaning against a tree trunk, smoking. The sun dances around him like a halo, and my heart squeezes despite myself at how beautiful he is. He looks tired too. It suddenly dawns on me. Why he is smoking. It's not to look cool or to live the tortured-writer way. It is because he feels guilty—has always felt guilty—that he is the healthy one. The cancer-less brother.

I approach him, wobbling a little on my fancy shoes.

"Can I bum one?" I ask when I get to him.

He doesn't make a big stink about it and offers me his soft pack, even though he knows I don't smoke. I pluck one cigarette out and clasp it between my lips. He lights it up for me and tucks the lighter back into his front pocket.

"Thanks," I say.

"Is it over?" He nods toward the church behind me, squinting.

"Yeah."

"And you didn't stay?"

"They're looking at him now. Inside his casket. It seems really barbaric. Why would anyone want to do that?" I ask. "It doesn't seem respectful. It seems . . . the *opposite*."

"You have a bone to pick with Christianity now?" He looks slightly amused. I would've suspected he was not shattered by it if I didn't know better. But I do know better, and this is Joe's go-to behavior. He wears sarcasm like armor. The opposite of his sweet late brother.

"No," I say. "I just don't understand the idea of looking at a dead person."

"Better thee than me." Joe flicks his cigarette sideways, blowing smoke in the opposite direction. "Humans have a weird fascination with death. You should know that better than anyone."

He is referring to my tombstone sketches. To my job as a tour guide in Salem. Now that I think about it, I surround myself with death a lot.

I haven't touched the drawing pad since our kiss, and I'm sure he hasn't written a word either. Whatever flame ran between Joe and me has been doused since the night Dom died.

"How are you dealing with all this?" he asks.

I take a drag of my cigarette and cough out the smoke. This is horrible. Why would anyone do this willingly? A few times a day too? It feels like french-kissing an ashtray.

"I don't," I admit. "I . . . I don't even feel human. I just exist. You?"

"I have Mom and Dad to take care of. Keeps me busy and going. When you feel like people depend on you, you have a reason to push through."

I pretend to take a few more drags of the cigarette, just to save face. He looks at me, amusement dancing in his eyes. "You're doing it wrong."

"Are you referring to life, or . . . ?"

"Smoking. But both, really. You have to let it hit the bottom of your lungs. If you keep it in your mouth, you might get mouth cancer."

"Because lung cancer is preferable?" I cough out some more.

"That's it." He plucks the cigarette from my lips and snaps it in two. *"You're killing yourself, bro."*

The way he mimics Pippa so perfectly, getting her Valley Girl drawl just right, makes me ache both for my best friend and for the time Before. Before Dom. Before Joe. When Mom was alive and Pippa and I were attached at the hip and my biggest worry was whether I was asexual or not.

"What are you going to do now?" Joe asks. He feels it's goodbye because it *is* goodbye. There is nothing to keep us in touch now. Dom is gone. Our one excuse to see each other has been taken from us.

"I don't know," I say. "You?"

He shrugs. "I go back to work next Monday. The world doesn't care that you lost your best friend. Your brother. Your fiancé. It's a blessing and a curse. You're forced to get back on the hamster wheel, whether you're ready or not."

"I'm not ready to human again," I say.

"You will be." He swallows hard, his eyes glittering with unshed tears as he reaches to move a lock of red hair from my forehead. "Eventually. And when you do, I hope you find what you are looking for, Ever."

And then I realize I forgot something. I pull the engagement ring from my finger and hand it over to him. It comes off easily, since I've barely eaten all week. "Can you give this to Gemma? Please? I'm sure she'd want this, and she is busy—"

"With Sarah." Joe pushes off the tree trunk and starts to make his way back to the church. I follow him. "Don't read too much into that. Right now you're deep in your feelings. Sarah is a doctor. She is clinical and pragmatic. She is exactly what Mom and Dad need."

"I'm not mad." But I am; I just know it's ungracious to be. "Take the engagement ring," I reiterate.

"As much as I'd love to be your errand boy, I think you should give it to Gemma yourself." He tromps past the church. Where is he going?

"I'm leaving," he says, as if reading my thoughts. "I can't do this."

"Can't do what?" I follow him, running after him.

Joe unlocks his car and slides into the driver's seat. "Can't watch them lower him to the ground. It's fucked up. And knowing Dom—he wouldn't want either of us to see it. Come with me, Ever."

He stops. Stares at me expectantly.

I'm standing in front of the driver's side of his car. The door is wide open.

I look back at the church. People are starting to trickle out.

"My dad and my brother are there."

"They'll understand," he says with conviction.

"Where to?" I ask, stunned.

"My apartment."

"I don't trust myself with you." God, how awful am I that I admit this out loud to the brother of the man I was supposed to marry while he is being *buried*? Does human selfishness know any bounds?

A grim smile touches his lips. "That makes both of us."

I take a step back. I don't want to do something I'll regret, and I think I might regret this very much if I get into the car with Joe right now. I feel myself shaking my head.

Joe hangs his head down. His signature wilted-flower move.

"I hate this." Fresh tears sting my eyes.

"Saying goodbye again?"

I nod. How many times can he and I lose each other?

"Hug me?" I shrug.

"Too painful. Have a good life, Ever." Joe slams his door shut behind him, in the car.

He drives away, taking whatever was left of my happiness with him.

PART 2

TWENTY-ONE

It's been three weeks since Dom's funeral, and I'm still in my bed.

Three weeks since I drove Dad and Renn to the airport. Before they boarded their plane, Dad hugged me and told me, "My door's always open, kiddo. I think you need some time off from Massachusetts."

Three weeks since my heart soared, because I knew he meant it.

Three weeks since Nora started living in our apartment full-time because she is worried for me.

Three weeks since Colt had a fit about it, then apologized to both of us.

Three weeks since I changed my sheets and went grocery shopping and took a shower.

I'm not always in my bed. Sometimes I get up to answer the DoorDash delivery person, as indicated from the mountains of takeout dishes littered around me. I sometimes go to the bathroom. I feed and water Loki religiously. But mostly, I'm in my bed.

The day after the funeral, I quit both my jobs without notice. Jenine, my boss, seemed understanding. Then again, the option not to be understanding was taken away from her. I lost my fiancé. I deserve a free pass.

Nothing really anchors me to Salem anymore. I don't have a job, or friends, or an affiliation with this place. Salem is soaked with Dom's presence. The city, in itself, is an open wound for me. Case in point—I don't leave the house anymore.

But then San Francisco is a reminder that my mom died. I can't stand either of these places right now. But I have to exist *somewhere*. Currently, though, the easiest thing to do is . . . well, to *not*-do anything.

Since I'm too distracted to watch TV and read books, I mainly spend my time going over Dom's social media accounts, holding on to the remainders of him. There's not much there. Dom wasn't big on social media. I keep staring at his three Instagram pictures over and over again. I get into the comments section. Check the profiles of all the people who liked them. That's how I find Sarah's Instagram profile. It's public but scanty. There's one photo there of her and Dom smiling at each other in a nightclub. I notice that Dom liked and commented on her photos until his very last day alive.

Two days before he died, he liked a picture of her and commented with a string of hearts. Presumably, he already knew he was going to propose to me.

I'm so mad at him; sometimes I wish I could resurrect him just so I could bitch-slap him. Other times I promise God that if he brings him back to me, I won't complain. I'd forgive him. Pretend it never happened.

Now, I hear Colt and Nora arguing in the living room.

". . . said we're moving in together. I'm tired of this shit, Nor. It's been years. Not months—years!" Colt groans. I wonder if he knows just how thin our walls are as I stare at the ceiling from my bed.

"What am I supposed to do, Colt? She just lost her fiancé!"

"Of four hours!" Colt hits back.

"Don't be gross." Nora sounds appalled more than anything else. "What an insensitive thing to say."

"Now who knows when she's going to feel better? You'll be stuck here forever. I can't do this anymore. I just can't."

I agree with Colt. Nora should move in with her fiancé. She can't keep being my crutch. I muster the energy, fling the blanket off, and hobble to the living room. I rap on the wall three times to indicate my presence.

Nora and Colt both turn to look at me, surprised.

"You left your bed." Nora's eyes widen in disbelief.

"Yup." I'm smiling. It hurts my cheeks so bad I'm surprised I'm not bleeding. "Just thought you guys should know I have plans for this evening."

"You *do*?" Nora's eyebrows reach her hairline.

"Yes."

"Who with?" she demands.

"Joe," I say naturally. He is the only person I know in this town other than them, so it's a no-brainer.

"Nice." Colt folds his arms over his chest. "Need a ride?"

"No. I just wanted you guys to know, so if you want to go out or anything, you can. I'm totally okay. And while we're on the subject." I turn to Nora, taking a deep breath. "I really appreciate everything you've done and are still doing for me. But please don't let it screw up your life. I promise I'm okay. Move out. Live your life. I'm still going to have you as a friend. You can keep an eye on me. You are welcome here anytime you want to check on me. I'll even let you have our spare keys. I've ruined enough lives, Nor. I don't want yours to be added to the list. Go live with Colt."

"Thank you, Jesus." Colt rolls his eyes up to the ceiling, pressing his hands together in a praying motion. "FYI, Ever, I think you're great. I just . . . I don't want us to get stuck. All of us. Me. Her. *You.*"

"Yeah, Colt. Sure." I smile sweetly at him. "The fact that you keep saying that I'm great totally excuses you from behaving like a world-class dick. Keep up the good work."

"Don't be like that!" Colt cries out.

Nora looks between us. Pain is marring her face.

"We'll give you a ride," she says.

"There's no need—"

"There is," she insists. "I don't want you to go by yourself. Plus, it'll be nice to check in on Joe."

"I'm not a kid, Nora."

"I know that," she says brightly, pretending like all is dandy and Colt and I didn't just have a standoff. "But I'm a helicopter parent in the making, so *deal*."

Begrudgingly, I call Joe to let him know that I somehow roped him into my lie and now we have to at least pretend that we're meeting. He answers after the third ring, sounding both surprised and worried.

"Is this your way of inviting yourself over?" he grunts, although I can hear that he's happy to hear from me. Why wouldn't he be? He wasn't the one who didn't want to hang out. I did.

Wincing, I explain, "I told Nora I have plans so she could finally leave the apartment and do something with Colt, and since you're the only person I know in this town . . ."

"You *do* know how to make a guy feel special."

I let out a rusty chuckle. "That's me. Ever the smooth talker."

"Might as well make it real if she drives you here, right?"

"Oh, I'm sure you have plans . . ." I trail off.

"What makes you so sure? You've very little idea of what my life looks like these days." Then, after an awkward pause, he asks, "Have you eaten anything today?"

I put my head on the pillow, surprisingly comforted by Joe's voice.

"Not really. Nora thinks I've lost fifteen pounds."

"What's left of you, anyway?"

"Mostly attitude and self-pity." I'm joking about it, but I don't actually think I have anything left in me. I feel so drained. "What do you want to eat?" I ask. "I can bring us something."

"Nah. Give me an hour and I'll go get some steaks and potatoes. And broccoli. You need broccoli."

"You sound like someone's sensible mom."

"And Ever?" He ignores me.

"Yes?"

"Bring comfortable shoes and a coat. We're going somewhere."

◆ ◆ ◆

An hour and a half later, I'm at Joe's building's doorstep. Colt and Nora peer at me from their Range Rover across the street. I feel like a kid who's been dropped at a classmate's birthday party. I'm so disoriented by the fresh air and general otherness of leaving the house that I don't dwell on the fact that this is Dom's building too.

I wait for Joe to buzz me up, but he surprises me by coming downstairs. He ignores me at first, instead crossing the street to say hi to Nora. My breath catches when he jogs across the asphalt. For a second, I trust the universe so little that I expect him to get hit by a car too. But Joe looks safe as he perches his elbows against the window of Nora's passenger seat. Exhausted, and not as muscular as he was a month ago, but still safe.

After a quick chat with my friend, he appears by my side. "You got a curfew, kiddo?"

"I'm only a year younger than you," I protest.

"That doesn't answer my question."

Damn him.

"Eleven. Nora is coming to pick me up. She is the overbearing mother I've never had."

Joe chuckles and opens the door for me. Instead of taking the elevator up to his apartment, we take it down to the garage. Even though we don't talk about it, I know the small, confined place reminds both of us of Dom.

Joe says, "Good thing you're all bundled up."

And I blink at him, still dazed. "Where are we going?"

"You'll see."

It's weird to get into Joe's truck without Dom sitting there, with his Red Sox commentary and friendly jokes. We drive out of Salem, going past little New England towns I don't know and a whole lot of darkness. There are no stars in the sky.

"Are you an axe murderer?" I ask, just to fill out the silence.

"Yes," Joe says deadpan, eyes hard on the road.

I chuckle and yawn at the same time.

"No, really. Check the back seat," he tells me.

I turn my head around, and sure enough, there's an actual axe lying on his back seat. It looks old, the wooden handle splattered with white paint. I look back at Joe, my heart picking up speed. "Please tell me you're shitting me."

He chuckles. "I'm not going to hurt you."

"Are we murdering someone?"

Now he is full-blown laughing, and I realize I've missed his voice terribly. The sound of it rolls in my chest. "Not at present."

"Then what—"

"Just trust me, will you?"

I decide that I should. That I *am*. Joe's never done me wrong. Even after all the crap I've put him through, he's always been amazing to me, even when he's done it in his own surly way.

Finally, we reach our destination. A junkyard outside Manchester-by-the-Sea. Joe parks, gets out of the car, and takes out the axe. I follow him silently. He stops by the fence to the junkyard, throwing me an expectant look.

"Give you a leg up?" He hoists the axe over his muscular shoulder.

"Are we breaking into a *junkyard*?" I ask the question extra slowly, so he can fully appreciate how crazy this sounds.

"Looks it." He shrugs.

"All right, then." I make my way to him. He drops the axe, then crouches down and laces his fingers together, a human step. I look at him underneath me, and God, I wish I wouldn't . . . couldn't . . . feel all those things I feel right now.

"I'm heavy," I say.

"You're full of shit." He smiles tiredly. "But not heavy at all. Now, hop."

I do. I hop across the fence and fall on my ass on the other side a little clumsily. It draws a breathless grunt out of me. This is the first time in three weeks that I have moved my body. Joe hops across the fence easily, but not before dropping the axe to the other side. Together, we amble deeper into the junkyard, our path illuminated by dimly lit lampposts.

We stop by a dirty, wheelless piece of junked red car. Joe throws me a look.

"This has been my favorite spot ever since I moved to Salem. I came here the night I found out about you and Dom. And the night after Dom died. I come here . . . a lot more often than I should."

"What do you do here?" I ask.

He raises the axe and smashes the backseat window of the car. "This is for all the Red Sox games I won't see with my brother anymore."

The glass shatters noisily. I jump back, yelping.

"And this is for all the things I won't be able to say to him anymore." He smashes the roof of the car, creating a huge dent in it.

"Your turn." He passes me the axe. I let it hover between us for a beat. Finally, I take it. It is heavy in my hand. I smile to myself. This was an ongoing joke for months between Dominic and me. Finally, I have an axe in my hand . . . and he will never know about it.

I close my eyes and take a deep breath. "This is for all the kisses I will not kiss you again, Dom."

I smash the axe against the front window. It cracks but doesn't shatter. Joe is standing behind me, taking it all in. He is nodding, somber.

"And this is for all the kisses you gave *her*."

This time I do break the window. And it feels good. Powerful. It feels . . . *right*.

"And this is for Mom dying." I aim at the back door and dent it.

"And for my fucked-up relationship with Dad and Renn." I break the beam lights.

"And for all!" *Slam.* "The time." *Crash.* "I felt less and weird and not enough and too much!" *Bang.*

It is only after I break apart the entire car, breathless and sweating like a maniac, that I notice Joe is clapping. The winter chill licks at my bones under my peacoat. I swivel toward him and hand him the axe. "Your turn."

I can barely speak I'm so out of breath. This is a great cardio. Axe murderers must be in excellent shape.

Joe shakes his head. "I think I'm done."

"Come on. One more." I smile. Yes, actually smile. And maybe it's because I make an effort—because I try to be normal—that he humors me and takes the axe.

He swings the axe and smashes it against the hood, making the entire car collapse flatly on the ground, demolishing it.

"This is for falling in love with the right girl at the wrong time, and still fucking paying for it," he says quietly, looking at me.

I turn my face to look the other way. "Let's go home."

After a quiet drive back, we take the elevator up to his apartment. I ask Joe if it hurts to still live here.

"In some ways, yes. In others, it makes me feel more connected to him. So I don't want to make any sudden moves right now."

We walk into the apartment. It looks much better than it did the day of Scone-gate. Tidier, even kind of nice. I realize he got himself together in the months since he found out Dom and I were together.

Joe starts working on dinner in the kitchen while I perch on the couch and stare at the ceiling. The scent of grilled steaks, steamed broccoli, and herbed potatoes hits my nostrils. He plates the food, then brings it over to the coffee table, where we both sit on the floor in front of the TV.

"Romantic," I joke.

Joe walks past me straight to the table. "Be as sarcastic as you want. You'll be singing a different tune when you see what we're watching."

What we're watching is *Dumb and Dumber*. It's an oldie but goodie. It is also exactly what we need. It is funny, it doesn't require us to follow a plotline, and it gives us something to talk about as we dig into the food. Joe insists I eat at least three florets of broccoli, and I make a show of squirming and moaning as I do. When we're done, I collect and wash the dishes. This is the most normal I've felt in a while.

"Do you have anything to drink?" I ask him as I run a kitchen towel over the plates, drying them before putting them back in their place.

Joe throws the fridge open and peers inside. "Water, orange juice, Coke. I can make you some coffee if you want. No sugar, though. That shit's toxic."

Said the smoker. Watch out, Dr. Oz. You have some competition.

"I was thinking something stronger."

He looks up, tilting an eyebrow up. "Bad idea."

"I haven't drunk anything alcoholic in weeks." Actually, since Gemma's sixtieth birthday dinner. "And I think we have a lot to talk about. I need liquid courage."

"What you need is a nice long shower. No offense." His eyes skim over my rat's nest of a hairdo. It is greasy and tangled and so oily it is actually heavy on my skull.

"None taken." I shrug. "I might muster a little more energy if I have a stiff drink."

Joe closes the fridge. He leans a hip against it, folding his arms over his chest. "Let's cut a deal."

I look at him expectantly.

"I'll give you alcohol if you have a shower."

I realize I'm wearing a pair of sweatpants and a hoodie that haven't been washed in a month. I probably smell. I still brush my teeth regularly, but my body hasn't met a deodorant or body lotion in three weeks. And, in what I think is an encouraging sign, I finally have the awareness to feel embarrassed about it.

"You mean with soap and everything?" I pout, trying to lighten up the mood.

"And everything," Joe confirms. "You're lucky my shampoo also moonlights as a conditioner, body wash, and a shower microphone. It's about to become your best friend."

"Ugh. Boys have such a basic hygiene routine."

"With all due respect, now's not the time to pass judgment, kiddo."

I feel a smile curling over my face. He stares at me, waiting for confirmation that I'll do it. That I'll have a shower. I roll my eyes. "Fine. But no peeking."

"Scout's honor." He reaches for one of his kitchen cabinets and takes out a bottle of tequila and two shot glasses. "Now let's get fucking smashed."

We take the first shot in the kitchen. It burns through my throat. The second and third one run smoother. Joe grabs the tequila bottle by the neck and walks over to the balcony. I follow. We sit on two plastic chairs with a round table between us, watching the busy night street as winter morphs into spring. The trees don't look so naked anymore. I can't believe Dom won't be here for the cherry blossoms. For the ice cream on the beach. For Cape Cod vacations. Which reminds me . . .

"I hope you took the ship," I tell Joe. "The one I got Dom from the inn. I know how much you two liked it."

"I find it hard to want anything Dom had these days." Joe lights himself a cigarette, and I wonder if he includes me in Dom's belongings, before reminding myself that it shouldn't matter. "And don't feel entitled to any of it. Losing him after everything we've been through seems . . . extra cruel."

We drink another shot. "So tell me how it happened. How you decided to drop my ass? I get that you didn't have time for romance when you were grieving your mother, but maybe a tiny 'Hey, by the way, I have bigger fish to fry. Good luck with your life' would've been nice." He tosses his lighter on the table.

The alcohol loosens my tongue. So does the unexpected pleasant company. Not to mention, today was the first day in weeks I've consumed actual food.

I squint at the cobbled street. "Do you remember when it happened?"

"When what happened?"

"The time I stopped answering."

He thinks about it for a moment.

"We were texting about my coming to see you in San Francisco."

I munch on my lower lip. "That day, just when you'd started messaging me, I had been waiting for the BART train to arrive. Standing on the edge of the platform with my mom. I wasn't paying her much attention. You have to understand that at that time, when I'd just gotten back home, all I wanted to do was sit in front of my phone and wait for you to text me. It was really pathetic. My mom had basically dragged me out the door to come help her at the gallery that day." I chuckle. Mom was so adamant I leave the house.

I understand that you fell in love and that the world is now so dull in comparison, but Joe is not going to show up at your doorstep in the next eight hours, so you might as well come with me.

Joe takes a drag of his cigarette. Smoke skulks from his mouth and nostrils, making him look diabolic. "I'm following."

"You had just started texting me, and I got all hyped up. I was twirling on the edge of the platform, waiting for you to write me a message. I was so wrapped up in you I forgot where I was. And . . . well, I fell to the tracks."

Joe closes his eyes. He shakes his head, ridding himself of the mental image.

"Were you hurt?" He swallows.

"I sprained my ankle and got hit in the head. A train was approaching. Mom tried to pull me up. She was a petite woman. Very petite, actually. She tried, but with my bad ankle and dizziness, I was dead weight. No one wanted to insert themselves into the situation and help her."

I take a deep breath, feeling shaky. Joe leans forward and pours me another shot of tequila. I down it in one go, wincing as I continue with my story.

"Finally, she managed to hurl me up back to the platform, but she fell onto the tracks in the process. Five seconds later, she was gone. The train approached. I tried to reach for her, I did. But she . . ." I draw a breath, feeling tears rolling down my cheeks. "She said, 'Don't you dare.' *Don't you dare.*"

And so I didn't. Didn't dare to live, to move on, to forgive myself for what happened.

It's all coming back to me now. The moment I've tried so hard not to think about these past six years. The looks. The horror. The shame. The guilt. The screams. The odd silence that followed. The police. The paramedics. The insurance people. Nice, but firm. Renn and Dad crying. Pippa asking too many questions, *so* many questions. The police officers asking me, again and again and again, in their softest, nicest voices, to relay the last few minutes. And me, being honest, and dumb, and scared, telling them that I danced over the edge of the platform because some boy I liked had texted me.

I knew they were judging me. *I* judged me.

"I've never gone into the subway ever again," I hear myself say. I don't feel the words coming out of my mouth. Rather, I listen to them. "And I never will. I cannot see a train without . . . without . . ."

Without thinking about it. Smelling it. Replaying the whole scene in my head.

"Ever," Joe says softly. "It wasn't your fault. It could've happened to anyone."

"But it happened to me." I smile sadly. I can barely see him behind the curtain of tears. It's happened to me twice, in fact. Dom was the second death I was responsible for. "I remember, as the policemen talked to me, as Dad and Renn frantically tried to understand what had happened, you kept on sending me message after message. The screen kept flashing with a green light. Until one of the police officers asked me to put it aside. I was still holding it in my hand. I didn't let it go, even when I fell to the tracks and hit my head."

There are tears in his eyes. I don't remember Joe ever crying. Not even when Dom passed away. But he is crying now, and when I reach over to hold his hand, he clasps my fingers like I'm made out of sugar. Carefully. As if I could melt away.

"So you blamed yourself for your mother's death, and me for causing you to act that way." Joe stubs out his cigarette in an ashtray with his free hand.

I run my thumb over his knuckles. "I let the phone run out of battery and threw it in the ocean a few days later. I wanted to throw myself inside, too, but didn't have the guts. I thought we shouldn't be together after what happened. I felt so guilty. Our relationship was the reason she died. It sickened me to think I'd just continue as usual after she was gone. Go on dates, have sex, laugh, live . . . all those things. They seemed too trivial after what happened. And, yeah, school was a part of it. Going to college was a way to better my future. I didn't deserve that. I deserved to be stuck in place, just like Mom was going to forever be stuck at age forty-three. So I dropped out. Cut all ties with Pippa and all my other friends."

"Punishing yourself," Joe comments.

I down another shot of tequila. The edges of my vision begin to blur.

"I decided to move to Boston. In retrospect, it's easy to see why. I wanted to run into you, even if subconsciously. I fed myself some crappy story. That Boston was a great market for jobs. That if I ever decided to go back to school, there were lots of colleges in the area. It was also far enough from home that Dad and Renn couldn't bulldoze their way into an intervention. I was free to destroy myself without interruption."

Joe doesn't say anything. He just listens. And God, it is so good to talk to him again. His gaze is like the sun. It gives me warmth and strength.

"But quickly, I realized that the city was too big, too gray, too rough. More than anything, it reminded me of you. And the pain of losing you, on top of losing my mom, was just too much. I couldn't take it. I moved to Salem. It seemed like a good place to get my artistic mojo back. Spoiler alert: even Salem didn't help. My art died with my mom."

"I don't think your art died," Joe says cautiously. "I think it's still inside of you, pounding on the door, waiting to get out. You're locking it in, because your art is a way to get ahead. To achieve things."

We hold each other's gaze before I pour him another shot. "Your turn to tell me what went on with you these last six years."

A ghost of a smile touches his lips. "Well, as you probably pieced together, I went to Europe because Dom had just received his all-clear after another cancer scare."

I give him a thumbs-up. After what happened with Sarah, it is hard to tell which of the things Dom told me were lies and which were truths. In the past month, I have questioned every single aspect in my relationship with Dominic Graves. Ultimately, even the anger and the pain can't make up for the fact that I genuinely loved him. And that with his death, he took any sense of closure I may have had to his grave.

"I wanted to get away from the Dom-fest. Not because I didn't care—because I cared too much and didn't know when the next opportunity to live for myself was going to present itself. I wanted to live for me. Write, drink, fuck. Live a detached, lonely life. Get lost inside myself, find out who I was." Joe strokes his chin, deep in thought. "Then I met you, and you went and crapped all over my plans. I couldn't escape you, no matter how hard I tried. You were the only thing I thought about. I wrote Dom and my parents letters about you. I told them I met the one. I wasn't happy about it. It was more like: 'Can you believe I met her before I slept with fifteen girls? Before I signed a book deal? Before I rented my own place?' That was to Dom, obviously. Not Mom and Dad."

His confession is ripping me apart. I feel like he is prying all my wounds open. I had no idea he was in just as deep.

"I bought a ticket back before I even talked to you," Joe admits, looking away so I won't see the color rising in his cheeks. "The plan was to go home, pack my shit, move to California, and hope to hell you wouldn't get your head out of your ass quickly enough to realize you were dating a loser. I was hoping being next to you would help me put a dent in my manuscript."

I clutch his hand in mine, closing my eyes. The past is so painful, because we were a breath away from a happily ever after. From my mom being alive and well. From Joe coming for me.

"But then I stopped answering you," I finish for him softly.

"That didn't mean I stopped trying, though." He rubs the back of his neck, frowning. "I kept sending you messages. Then emails to variations of your name. I couldn't believe I was dumb enough not to ask for your last name. Everlynne is such a unique name. I'd have found you in a heartbeat."

I sigh, because I felt the same way.

"And then I decided to go ahead and travel to San Francisco anyway." Joe smiles grimly, staring at an invisible spot on the floor.

"You did?" My heart jumps to my throat.

He grabs the tequila bottle by the neck and walks inside. I follow him. His back is to me when he speaks. "I went there for two weeks. Loitered around places I thought I might bump into you. The Beat Museum, coffee shops, places you said you liked. I was desperate. My mother was worried for me. She wanted me to see a therapist."

"Did you?"

He shakes his head as he shoves the tequila back into the cupboard. "There was no point. After San Francisco, I realized there was nothing I could do to win you back. I stopped writing. Started taking odd jobs. A year and a half later, Dom got an offer for a position in Salem and dragged me along. Said a change of scenery would do me good. And here we are."

He turns to me, smiling humorlessly.

"Here we are," I echo.

For a moment, we just drink each other in.

He snaps out of it first. "Time to hop into the shower, Stinky Face. I'll get you a towel."

Joe brushes past me on his way to the hallway. My hand reaches to grip his wrist. He stops. The air between us is charged. Buzzing with danger, desperation, and angst.

He shakes my hand off him. Gentle, but firm.

"No, thank you. I'm not going down in your history book as another reckless mistake."

He's making his way to what I presume is his bedroom when I snatch his hand again. In this moment, I'm so desperate for him I am not above begging.

"Come on," I coax, feeling particularly destructive. The world is fucked, and unfair, and full of injustices. It is random, it is cruel, and it's screwed us both over. Nothing matters anymore. Joe is not an author, and I'm not an artist, and Dom is not alive. All our dreams have gone up in flames, and there is nothing left to fight for.

Joe turns to me, looking annoyed. "What are you doing, Ever? I just told you how fucked I was after we broke up. Do I look like a game to you?"

He doesn't. He looks like the boy I never stopped loving. That boy turned into a man, and I love him too. So I rise on my toes tentatively and press a soft, dry kiss on his lips.

His eyelids fall shut, and he lets out a sigh. "Don't do this."

"Don't do what?"

"Don't give me unwarranted hope."

But hope is the only thing that's keeping me from not taking the next breath. I rise again, this time kissing the tip of his chin.

Joe's head drops to his chest. "Ever, *please.*"

I kiss his neck, running my hot tongue over his Adam's apple.

"Fuck. Here we go," he moans.

I know it's wrong. I know it's disastrous. Most of all, I know I'm going to regret it. And still, I kiss the spot where his neck meets his chest, scraping it with my teeth. Then I wait for a beat before rolling my tongue over that sliver of flesh and sucking it into my mouth, applying pressure.

"I—"

I cup him through his pants and feel his swollen, huge erection pulsating against my palm. Twitching. Daring me to squeeze. I look up at him and blink innocently. "You were saying?"

That's when he lets go of whatever is left of his tattered self-control. He grabs the back of my hair and walks me backward until my back slams against the wall. He kisses me so hungrily I think he is going to tear a chunk off my face. We're all teeth and tongues as we frantically push each other's pants and underwear down in the hallway. We kick them aside. Neither of us makes a move to the bedroom. We both know how fragile this is. How easily one of us can pull away.

I reek, and my legs are unshaven. I know Joe doesn't care. We're naked from the waist down but still wearing our sweaters. His hand finds my center as I grip his cock. I start pumping while he plays with my juices. I am so wet I should be embarrassed, but I'm too drunk to care.

"Shit," he hisses into my mouth, devouring me. "You're so wet." He drives two fingers into me, stretching me, preparing me.

I rub my thumb against the head of his penis, moving a pearl of precum over it. "Look who's talking."

"Ever?" He stops, pulling away from me as he looks into my eyes seriously.

"Yes?" I ask, panting.

"This is very important."

"Okay."

"Can I fuck you?"

"Yes," I say, relieved. I grab his face and kiss him. "Yes, please. Please fuck me."

He pins me against the wall and drives into me in one go. He is bare. He nails me against the wall, pounding into me like an animal. It is drunk. It is raw. And there are tears *everywhere*. We both cry silently as I hold on to him. His head is in the crook of my neck. There is nothing sexy about what we're doing. We're two broken people trying to be whole together, knowing it is doomed. That we'll fail.

"Presley," I pant, digging my fingernails into the flesh of his neck. "Are you still seeing her?"

He grunts, pushing deeper and harder into me. Shame floods me. My pleasure is so tangible I can taste it in my mouth. The dark tang of him. I'm about to come, and I know exactly what I'm doing.

Yes, I'm drunk. But not drunk enough to forget I'm fucking my dead fiancé's baby brother while I still wear his ring on my finger.

"Answer me," I demand.

"You goddamn know Presley was never in the race." Joe shuts me up with a dirty, violent kiss. "As long as you have breath in you, no one else stands a chance."

I fall apart in his arms. Wave after wave of pleasure is crashing into me. I clench around him. Then he comes too. I smile to myself, a twisted smile. The smile of a woman who's just done something horrible she can never take back.

We both tumble to the floor, limbs tangled. We're sweaty and smelly. He slides away from me. We stare at the ceiling. I wonder if we are both wondering the same thing. If Dom is somewhere up there, in the sky, watching us. If he is currently shaking his head, telling his new roommates, *See these two assholes? They're my fiancée and my brother.*

"I'm the worst human in the world." I close my eyes.

"You wish. That title is saved for me."

"No."

"I'm his *brother*."

"I'm still wearing his ring."

He groans, rubbing his face with one hand. "Good point. I'll kill a puppy or something and take the Worst Human cake."

"It's not funny."

"I wasn't the one who thought this is a good idea," he reminds me as he reaches for his jeans and takes out a pack of cigarettes.

I check my watch. It is half past eleven. From a distance, I hear my phone ringing. It's where I left it, in the living room. I bet it is Nora. I bet she is mad. I'm not going to be able to take a shower here after all.

"Do you think he'd have forgiven us for this?" I ask.

"Do you think he deserves an apology after what he did to you?" Joe counters, lighting up his cigarette. He is trying to be bold, but I can see the slight shake in his fingers. He is not completely okay with what just happened.

I consider his question. "I don't know."

"That's the thing, Ev. I'm not sure you are burdened with the same expectations and responsibilities an ordinary fiancée must go through."

Instead of answering, I try to envision Dom walking in on us doing what we just did. It doesn't end well in any scenario.

"What are you thinking?" Joe asks.

"I'm going to buy a one-way ticket to San Francisco," I hear myself say. Suddenly, it seems like the best idea I've had in years. "Yeah. I think it's time."

"You're *leaving*?" He sits upright, braced on his elbows, staring at me with thunder in his eyes.

"I have nothing here," I say helplessly, sitting up too.

It's only after the words have left my mouth that I realize how wrong they sound. Like Joe is nothing. Like he is not worthy of my time, and compassion, and friendship. And that's not all. He explicitly asked me a few minutes ago not to play with his heart, and I did just that. I coaxed him into sex, and now I'm leaving. I'm a terrible person. Double-terrible. Triple-terrible. The worst there is.

Joe stands up and walks into his room. He slams the door shut.

"Joe!" I call out. "Oh, come on!"

There is no answer.

It's my cue to leave.

I collect my things and get the elevator down, sweeping a hand over my face. The diamond on the engagement ring scratches my cheek. I bleed.

TWENTY-TWO

Every city has its best angle. For San Francisco, it's the eagle eye.

It looks beautiful from above. The ocean. The Golden Gate Bridge. The house-filled hills. The thick cloak of fog that blankets every part of it. I can understand why Mom was so fascinated with it when she was alive.

The captain announces that we will be landing in ten minutes. Loki meows in his carrier in response, fed up with sitting in the small enclosed space. He hasn't been a happy camper during the flight. No surprises here.

I shove another snack into his carrier numbly. "Sit tight. We'll be home in a few minutes, bud."

A part of me is frightened of what I'm going to find when I finally get home. I've been away for over half a decade. Dad and Renn said they had something to tell me. That was *months* ago. Whatever it was, I guess they didn't want to broach the subject when they were in Salem, which means I'm supposed to be upset about it.

Then there's another part of me. The part that is proud of myself for finally taking this step and going home. I know Mom would want me to do this. And I know that Nora is relieved, even if she'd never admit it. My roommate said she will keep the lease on the apartment until I decide what to do with my life, but I'll bet both my kidneys that after she and Colt dropped me at the airport (six hours after I'd exited Joe's door), she was already starting to pack her stuff to move into her fiancé's apartment.

Dad and Renn wait for me at the airport. They're holding balloons and a **WALLCOME HOME** sign to purposely embarrass me. They draw giggles from other people in the waiting area. I wheel my suitcase and my cat past them, pretending I don't know them. Renn jogs my way and wraps his arms around my shoulders. "You guys, this is my sister. My flesh and blood! We are blood related and everything!" he announces to the entire terminal.

He is about four heads taller than me, and I'm just noticing that.

"You know how deeply offended I am by bad grammar." I push him away, hiding my smile, still deeply ashamed that it took a full-blown tragedy to make me come back here.

"All right, I guess the sign was too much. But you have to admit it was funny," Renn cackles. I turn around and hug him, suddenly feeling very exhausted and very happy to be back. California is my home.

Dad pats my shoulder in a friendly manner. He is much more reserved than Renn. He is still guarding his heart, unsure of how this whole thing is going to pan out. Renn pries Loki's carrier from my fingers. He peers inside. "Hey there, furball. How are you with mice? No free meals in the Lawson household."

I can only imagine the *go fuck yourself* look Loki is currently awarding my brother.

"It's good to have you back," Dad says quietly.

"I'm so sorry I've been gone for so long." I shiver, inhaling his familiar aftershave scent. The one Mom used to buy him for both Christmas and his birthday, so he would never run out.

We hobble to Dad's car, but Renn is the one who gets behind the steering wheel. It reminds me that he drives now. I have been so wrapped up in my own misery these last few years that I've failed to witness the amazing blossoming of Renn Lawson from a kid to a very handsome, very goofy man.

The secret they've been keeping from me is hanging over our heads like a guillotine. Or maybe it's just me. I want to ask about it, but I don't want to ruin the mood, which is currently friendly.

"So, am I going to find out you turned the house into a brothel? Just wanna know what I'm dealing with when I open the door."

"She found out about the surprise, Dad," Renn says seriously. "Told you it was obvious. We should've gone with a circus theme."

Dad elbows Renn. "The house is exactly how you left it. We'll discuss the changes in our life after you've settled."

Anxiety robs me of my breath.

Dad asks what I want to do when we get home. Since it's late afternoon, I suggest we drop Loki at the house to give him a chance to explore his surroundings and grab a bite. Dad says it's a good idea, and when I ask Renn if he is hungry, he tells me he is always hungry, which I guess makes sense when you are six two and surf all day.

As soon as we get home—which, thank God, is *not* a brothel—I open Loki's carrier and fill him two bowls with water and food. I set a fresh litter tray in the laundry room, even though I'm pretty sure he is going to spend the first day or so hiding under the couch.

After I'm done, I look around me. The house looks almost identical to how I left it. *Almost.* But not quite. I don't know how to explain it, but it doesn't look so sad anymore. Mom's things are still here—paintings, pictures, and her favorite throw. But the place has been freshly painted, including one purple accent wall. There are a few paintings that weren't here before, and there are fresh flowers on the counter.

"Ready to roll?" Dad claps my shoulder. It is so awkward but so endearing that he is trying. I nod. We go back to the car. This time, I drive. It is important for me to get behind the wheel, especially after what happened to Dom. I could see myself swearing off driving due to trauma. I avoided my hometown for the same reason. I will never be able to take the BART again. There are just too many painful memories.

"Where to?" I ask.

"Cheesecake on Union Square?" Renn's eyes light up. "I could smash two of their bread baskets while I wait for my entrées."

"Too busy and touristy." I blow a raspberry at Renn, looking at the rearview mirror. For a moment, we're just normal teens fighting for the purpose of fighting.

"It's your call, Ever," Dad says, sitting beside me.

"Aw, but her choices always suck," Renn complains.

"How do you know?" Dad asks. "It's been years since she was here."

Aaand I want to throw up all over again.

Deciding to play it safe, I take us to a diner the entire family used to go to every Sunday. It's in Chinatown. It's called George's Greasy Spoon. From the outside, it is a train wreck of epic proportions. Nestled in a dilapidated four-story building, with people's laundry hanging over the sign, concealing most of it.

We step inside, and old George greets us at the door himself, even though the place is jam packed. I'm so taken aback I almost fall over my feet.

"Martin. Renn. Ever! Now that's a face I haven't seen in a while here." He hurries to show us to our table, asking me all about Boston— *Is it rainy? Is it beautiful? Is it as expensive as here?* It's like I never left. Like I am back in an old neighborhood. Despite feeling devastated on the inside, I feel the first green sprout of hope pushing through the ash inside me.

It's called hope, bitch. And it was always there. You just had to give it a little nudge, Pippa's voice laments in my head.

I'm still in a daze when George takes our order. Because I'm currently incapable of reading a menu without bursting into tears (thanks, Dom), I ask for my childhood Sunday staple—the hash brown sandwich. I'm not surprised when Renn and Dad order their favorites too. Renn goes for a double cheeseburger with crinkle-cut fries, and Dad asks for a big Cobb salad with extra bacon. In the same breath, Dad adds, "And the usual for the missus."

"She does like her pumpkin-spice pancakes." George doesn't write anything in his pad. He remembers everything by heart.

"You're ordering for *Mom*?" I cut my gaze to Dad, weirded out and oddly touched by the gesture.

He shrugs. "Every Sunday. It's a family tradition, remember?"

Yes. I remember us coming here every Sunday when she was alive. I didn't think they still did that.

"You and Renn still go here every week?" I hear the surprise in my voice. Also the hurt. I have no right to be offended. They've been here all along, begging me to join them.

"Yup." Renn takes a noisy slurp of his fountain soda.

"And what do you do with the pumpkin pancakes afterward?" I look between them, curious.

Renn sighs, his eyes dimming. "Look around you, Ev. It's San Francisco. There's always someone who'd be happy to receive a free hot meal."

Our food arrives quickly, hot and fresh, along with cornbread and yellow, thick butter that melts on your tongue. The butter transports me to memory lane. To Mom smearing it on the tip of my nose and making a face, causing me to laugh.

I'm surprised to find that I'm more exhilarated by the memory than hurt and pained by it.

The three of us eat and slide into easy conversation. I have a feeling my dad is anxious—almost starstruck—to see me here, in the flesh. I now understand that it is possible that I have mistaken his abrasiveness and lack of responsiveness as him being uninterested, when really, he is just deeply hurt by my absence.

I try to seem upbeat, even though it is draining. I guess I'm trying to prove myself to them. That I'm worthy of their love, even after what's happened.

Dad pays for the food, and we all drive back home. When we get inside, we notice Loki has already consecrated his new litter box with a fresh dump. He hasn't even bothered to cover it. It just sits there, in plain sight, waiting to be acknowledged.

"So this is how you're going to play, huh, punk?" Renn side-eyes my cat, then takes the stairs two at a time to his room. "Yo, Ever, if you want me to be on litter box duty, I'm telling you now—you're in charge of *all* my laundry."

"Like it smells better than Loki's poop!" I yell back to him, holding the banisters.

Dad asks me if I want to have a cup of tea with him on the patio. I say yes. I know what's coming. He is going to fill me in on the big secret they've been keeping from me. I help him prepare the tea, and we both take it to the backyard.

My parents' backyard is my favorite part of their house. It's all raised flower beds with lots of vegetables and fruit, and a greenhouse where Mom used to grow eggplants and lettuce and whatnot. The backyard is small, cramped, charming, and overlooks the Pacific Ocean. My heart thuds faster when I notice the garden looks great. I had no idea Dad had a green thumb.

We sit on two patio chairs and look at the ocean peeking through our brown fence.

Dad takes a deep breath. "You haven't been here for six years. A lot has changed. I know you've changed as a person. And . . . well, so did we."

I take a sip of my peppermint tea. So far, he is not telling me anything I don't know, but I have a feeling that's about to change soon.

"Yes," I say. "Trauma and tragedy change people. I wasn't expecting to come back and find you two in the same state I left you."

"Were you planning on coming back at all?" he asks.

"Of course."

"Then why did you leave?" he asks, instead of soldiering through with his mysterious news.

"Why?" I repeat dumbly. I've been focusing on Dom's death, and then the mess I've created with Joe, so much that I've hardly given some thought to the fact that my family would want answers. I bailed on them. They deserve an explanation.

I sit back in my chair. "I guess I couldn't bear the guilt. Every time I saw you and Renn, you looked wrecked. I knew I was the person who caused you all this heartache. And . . . well, I wanted to make it better for you. Every time you guys looked at me, I could see it in your eyes. That I'd caused this pain. I was embarrassed, and humiliated about what I'd done. I thought I was doing you a huge favor by removing myself from the situation."

"Embarrassed," he repeats. "You thought we were blaming you?"

"I knew you were." I shift, tucking my feet under my butt. "It was written plainly on yourselves."

He closes his eyes, shaking his head. "Yes. No. Maybe. I was very upset. I might've looked at you differently, but not because I thought you were guilty, only because I didn't know what to do with you and your brother, how to comfort you. I didn't realize at the time that you might notice. I didn't notice the change myself. I'm sorry."

"I should be the one apologizing, Dad. And I am. You just followed your heart. I mean, you weren't wrong. I caused it. All because of a stupid boy."

Dad takes a sip of his tea. "Was he, though?"

"Was he what?" I ask, confused.

"Stupid. Because when your mom talked to me about it, I remember her saying you were head over heels in love with him. That he was smart and artistic and that he made you laugh. That doesn't sound very stupid to me."

I swallow. "No," I say, finally. "He wasn't stupid at all. He was great." The best, really. "I met him in Salem afterward. Not intentionally, of course. A kismet of sorts."

My dad nods slowly, holding my gaze. "Seph, I assume."

"How did you know?" My eyes fill with tears. Just thinking about the Graves family makes me want to curl into a ball and cry. I'm also surprised he didn't say it was Dom. He was the one I was supposed to marry, after all.

Dad dips the tea bag into his mug in a soothing motion. "I saw the way you two were looking at each other when you talked at the church. Under that tree, when you thought no one could see you. The way you were the only thing that mattered to him, and he was the only person on earth to you. There was something very protective about the way he treated you. He reminded me of myself when your mother died. All I wanted to do was shield you and Renn from the world."

I'm caught red handed. Busted. But I feel oddly relieved to be able to talk about it with someone.

"Well, obviously, I can't keep in touch with Joe. That would be too messy."

"I think that's the issue, Everlynne. What you don't understand—what your generation doesn't understand, I think—is that things are naturally messy. They've always been messy. Perfect doesn't exist. Embarrassment and shame are a package deal. They're a part of life. You cannot remove these compartments from your existence. You have to meet your challenges head-on. When your mother died, she took a part of me with her to that grave. But losing you on top of that? Not being able to hug you, to talk to you, to cry on your shoulder and let you cry on mine? That made things unbearable. Some days, I wondered why I'd even gotten out of bed. But then I heard your brother snoring down the hallway and remembered. There's *always* someone to fight for."

I think about Dom's infidelities. Joe's harsh words before he kissed me the day Dom and I got engaged. I close my eyes. "It's hard to forgive people. Including yourself."

"I'll tell you what your mother always told me. It's a good lesson. 'Be thankful to those who helped you when you were down, and be thankful to those who didn't. The former are worth keeping, and the latter helped you realize it.'"

I break into tears for the millionth time this week, burying my face in my hands. Dad keeps talking.

"No. Shush. Don't feel bad. Even if you thought we were angry, you should've stayed. You should've fought for this family. Renn and I have been working on trying to get back to what we were for six years now, and we could've used the extra pair of hands."

I put my teacup aside and fling myself on him, crying into his chest. He wraps his arms around me tentatively. Frozen at first, and then, when he feels my body shaking against his, tighter. He drops his tea on the floor in the process. The cup breaks at our feet. He grabs the back of my head.

"Jesus, Ever. We thought we'd lost you forever."

"I thought I'd lost you forever," I say between sobs and hiccups. "I thought you hated me."

"I never hated you." Finally, his voice breaks. Finally, I can hear the emotion in it. "I only hated the situation, and wished your mother was alive, so she could tell me what to do to get you back."

It is so clear to me now that *this* was what I needed all this time. A hug from my dad. A confirmation that he still loves me despite everything. Salem was my cloak. I'd hidden from the world, because I thought it didn't want me.

He pulls away from me, clutching my arms. "Hey. I forgot to mention the best part."

"W-w-what part is that?" I sniffle and hiccup and generally look like a total mess.

"That the war Renn and I were fighting? We won. We are still a family. We laugh. We go places. We have vacations, and holidays, and dinners. We tell inside jokes. All we needed was for you to come back to us. And now that you have, everything will be okay."

For the first time in a long time, I believe in something good.

I believe in my family.

Wearing Dad's slippers, I clean up the broken china on the patio. I sweep the floor while he waters the flower beds. Every now and then, I look up to look at him. He is doing an awful job, drenching each bell pepper. I have no idea how he's kept the garden alive for so long.

I feel lighter after my conversation with him. But also tired from the long day and the flight. I don't know what I'm going to feel like tomorrow, but I know today is bearable, and that is a good start. The world did not end when I left Massachusetts. Dad and Renn did not change the locks and tell me to go away. And even though I am still guilt ridden about what I did to Joe—how I left things—I know he probably doesn't want to hear from me.

"Are you sure you know what you're doing?" I ask after a few minutes of watching Dad refilling the funnel for the fifteenth time. There is zero chance this is how he is sustaining this beautiful garden. There is also no way in hell he can handle the kind of water bill that comes with watering his plants this way.

Dad drops the empty funnel at his feet, moving a hand over his hair. He laughs. "I'm busted, aren't I?"

"I thought it was weird that the garden survived without Mom." I shrug. "Who's taking care of the garden, then? Lawrence?"

Lawrence had been our gardener since I was three. He and Mom used to spend a lot of time together, planting and trimming and laughing.

Dad shakes his head. "No. He had to retire three years ago. He had a knee surgery, and then his daughter needed him to watch the grandchildren while she was at work . . . it got too much for him."

Dad makes his way up the three stairs to the patio. I lean the broomstick against the wall, dusting my hands off. "Don't tell me *Renn* is keeping this garden alive?"

"Renn?" He lets out a high-pitched, nervous laugh. "I wouldn't put him in charge of dishwashing duties."

"Did you get a new gardener?" I frown, confused.

He shakes his head. "It felt wrong to let a stranger touch all the things Barbie had created."

"So who's in charge of it now?"

"Ever . . ." He puts his hands on my shoulder. "The thing I've been trying to tell you . . . the reason why I wanted you to come here for Thanksgiving last year, is because I'm seeing someone."

Silence engulfs us. I have no idea how I feel about what he's just told me. A part of me is angry. How dare he get over Mom? How dare he date? Is he having actual *sex* with another woman? What in the hell? This is wrong. This is Mom's house, with Mom's things. It feels deeply unjust that someone else is taking care of her garden. Of her *family*.

But then I also can't help but feel an acute sense of relief. Because he wasn't alone all this time. Because he did have a shoulder to cry on, even if it wasn't mine. Because it takes a lot of courage to move on from losing the love of your life. And because ultimately, I want him to be happy. *Mom* would want him to be happy.

It's also difficult for me to pass judgment on other people in my situation. I slept with Joe while still wearing Dom's engagement ring.

"Please say something." Dad actually cringes, taking a step back. "Anything."

"I . . . I don't know how I feel about this," I admit. "Does she sleep in Mom's bed?"

His face says it all. She does. She sleeps in Mom's bed. Okay. *Okay.* I take a deep breath. Count to ten in my head. Remind myself that perfect doesn't exist. That I, myself, slept with Joe and then bailed on him. That humans are deeply flawed creatures. That maybe what matters is that we are not malicious. That we don't *want* to hurt others. I know Dad did not move on because he wanted to hurt me.

"Are you happy with her?" I ask quietly.

He looks down at his shoes, thinking about it.

"I'm less unhappy when I'm with her," he says, finally. And this, of course, is exactly how I felt about Dom. The soothing notion that there was someone to take the pain away. Is Dad's girlfriend like Dom? Is his love for her guarded, comfortable, never coloring out of the lines? I don't dare ask him.

"Is she . . ." I'm trying to think of what I want to ask—pretty? Nice? Funny? Artistic? Eccentric? Mom-ish? Is she an entire bursting world? Complete with a northern English accent and a collection of Oasis and Smiths CDs?

Dad continues to stare like I'm holding the secrets of the universe in my palm and he really, *really* needs them to save the world right now.

"Complete the sentence," he asks firmly.

"I guess what I'm trying to ask is . . . will I like her?" I gulp.

A slow smile spreads across his face. "I think so. I think it is impossible not to like her. Renn *loves* her."

I'm sure he means this in a reassuring way, but all I feel is quiet rage that my brother has accepted someone else into our family without putting up a fight. Was she that forgettable?

"I'm happy," I say, finally. And then, in a louder voice: "I am. Very. Yes. Definitely."

It might not be the entire truth, but I will get there. I will rid myself of the weirdness and accept this. I must.

"Really? You don't think it's too soon?" His eyes light up.

"Well, that depends on when you met her," I answer truthfully.

"Eight months ago." He actually *blushes*. My dad, who is the least emotional person on planet earth.

"Yeah, I'm okay with that." I pick up the broomstick again and sweep, just to do something with my hands. "Tell me about her."

He tells me that her name is Donna. That she is his age. Widowed, with two kids, my age and a little older. That she actually used to be a professional tennis player before she became an instructor. And that Renn gets along really well both with her and with her sons, Dylan and Ashton.

I promise to meet her soon. He nods, looking sheepish.

"What?" I ask. But then it all clicks together. Dread falls over me. Oh, no. I really have been away for an eternity and a half.

"She is living here now, isn't she? That's why the house looks so pretty. Why there are fresh flowers on the kitchen counter and the garden is lush."

Dad looks apologetic. He wrings his fingers in his lap like a punished schoolgirl. "Things escalated quickly. She moved in this December. This was why I wanted to talk to you so urgently in November. I didn't want you to feel blindsided."

I deserve this. This feeling of being a guest in someone else's life, even though this someone is my dad.

"Just tell me one thing," I say.

He stares at me expectantly.

"Who makes better pancakes—Mom or her?"

"Oh, Donna does not make pancakes under this roof. That's the rule. We both decided it was better this way early on. Too many memories." He waves a hand in the air. "If we want pancakes, we go out."

I smile. "Then I think we're good here. I'm going upstairs to take a nap."

TWENTY-THREE

The answer to my question—how would I feel the next morning—presents itself the day after.

And the answer is: shitty. I feel shitty.

I am hyperaware of the fact that I have lost three of the people I cared most about—Mom, Dom, and now, possibly, *probably*, Joe. True, Joe is not dead, thank God, but with the kind of luck that's attached to people I care about, it is better to leave him be than to pursue any sort of connection with him.

Plus, it has to be said—even though I'm happy for Dad, I'm also destroyed by the idea that he is in love with another woman.

I spend the next two weeks holed up in my room. Silver lining: this time, I'm not as pathetic about it as the month that followed Dom's death.

No, I am now officially a high-functioning train wreck. I shower daily. I have to. Renn and Dad take turns banging on my bedroom door when I linger. I'm on cooking duty Tuesdays and Fridays. And they are always adamant I make healthy things. With lentils and vegetables. *Anything frozen from Costco doesn't count*, they say. The rest of the time, I'm in my bed. Reading, crying, processing.

I don't hear from Joe, and I shouldn't expect to. I slept with him, then moved to the other side of the country. *Again.* Only now he has to face the fact we both betrayed Dominic. Alone.

And yet I give myself some grace and allow myself to heal.

As I heal, I listen carefully to the telltale signs of happy life that rise from downstairs, seeping through the cracks of the floorboards. Donna comes to the house every day. Renn mentioned she is crashing at Dylan's place, to give me space, which I have to admit is a promising move on her part.

I haven't met her yet. I make sure I'm always in my room when she is here. But I hear her making Dad and Renn food whenever they deem mine inedible (which is always). I hear her whistle and sing old eighties songs (Duran Duran, Air Supply, Tina Turner) as she takes care of the garden. She always asks Renn if he needs something from the supermarket.

I can tell she is, at the very least, not Snow White's evil stepmom. I think these small doses of her that I consume without actually interacting with her are helping me come to terms with her presence in our lives. But I'm still worried that this is all for show. That she is putting on an act because she knows I'm listening.

There are other happy sounds. The sound of Renn and his friends laughing, playing video games, or chugging beer on the patio. The sound of Dad's cackling as he watches *The Office* reruns every day after work, even though he utters the iconic punch lines right along with Michael Scott. Loki conversing with whomever is downstairs, trying to coax them to throw him a piece of pastrami or two.

And at some point, two weeks after locking myself in my room, the idea of meeting people doesn't seem quite as hellish as it did before. The trigger is, as always, food.

It is a sunny Saturday. Donna, Dad, and Renn are downstairs, eating breakfast. The scent of fresh sourdough bread, butter, bacon, and beans wafts around the house, making my mouth water. Normally, I wait until everyone leaves before I eat the leftovers. But today, it doesn't feel like the end of the world to meet the woman Dad has fallen in love with if it means consuming greasy bacon and freshly squeezed orange juice.

I emerge from my room in my Cookie Monster onesie, determined to set any expectations for me low. The stairs creak as I descend them, and dread fills my gut when I think about all the looks I'm about to get.

But when I get to the landing, I see the three of them sitting around the dining table, talking animatedly. They don't see me at first. Or maybe they're giving me a few moments to collect myself. Donna is lean and red-headed—like Mom—with a narrow face and a gap in her front teeth. She is not as beautiful as the late Barbie Lawson, which is oddly and pettily comforting, but they both hold the same quality, of women who appear both genuinely nice and yet ooze not-to-be-messed-with vibes.

Dad is the first to notice me. He drops his fork on his plate, blinking, like he's seeing a ghost. I can tell he has no idea what to say. Donna follows his gaze to see what's made him freeze. Her face opens up when she sees me.

"Love that onesie," she says, popping a piece of bacon into her mouth casually. "Where'd you get it?"

You seem to be wanting a lot of things the Lawson women have for themselves, something inside me wants to snap. But then I remind myself I have to play nice, for Dad and Renn.

"My friend Nora bought it for me. Somewhere online, I don't know."

She stands up. She is wearing . . . a hot dog onesie? Could that be? With ketchup and mustard and everything. A smile tugs at my lips, but I bite it down quickly. I'm not Renn. I shall not betray Mom because of a simple onesie.

"Where'd you get yours?" I ask, not exactly coldly, but definitely not conversationally.

Dad and Renn exchange looks silently. They're smiling.

"Renn got it for me for Christmas. I think the store is called Rad and Bad."

"Is that so?" I turn to look at Renn pointedly, still standing up. "Weird that he managed to get you something cool, 'cause I've been getting kitty calendars and scented bath bombs from him for the last four years."

And I didn't even have a bath in my Salem apartment.

Renn points at me with his fork, which is full of scrambled eggs and bacon. "That's because I only put in effort with people I'm tight with, and you were MIA."

"We used to be tight," I say, but I don't feel the overwhelming sadness that comes every time I think about how much has changed in the last half decade. Instead, I am hopeful that we can maybe fix this.

"Right. And now you have to work your way back into my good graces." Renn downs an entire glass of orange juice before slamming it on the table. "You can start by massaging my feet every night."

Donna uses her foot to push the chair opposite hers.

"Have a seat, Ever. There's a plate for you on the table. The sourdough is still fresh."

"Did you make it?" I scrunch my nose, not making a move.

She rolls her eyes. "Do I look like I have all the time in the world?"

I sit down. I wolf an unholy amount of food, washing it down with orange juice. I don't talk much. Donna, Renn, and Dad converse between themselves. Every once in a while, they ask me what I think about what they're saying, but I don't feel under any kind of pressure to jump into the conversation. They don't bombard me with questions. More than anything, I'm blindsided by how much these three look and feel like a family unit. It is so painfully obvious I'm the odd one out. Donna calls Renn "Ruin," and Renn calls her "Danny." She and Dad volunteer at the local community center together. It is clear to me that by coming here, I've stepped into something that's already whole and functioning. So despite not being completely okay with it, and still feeling weirded out by the fact that there is a whole-ass stranger living in my childhood house full-time now, I tell Donna that she doesn't have to stay at Dylan's house on my account and can move back in.

"Don't stay away on my account. As you can tell, I'm mostly in my room." I shrug, playing it off.

Donna smiles. "We're all kind of counting on seeing more of you out of the room."

"Ah, she is trying to fix me already." I send Dad a venomous smile. "What a catch."

"Bitter much?" Renn kicks me under the table. "Seriously, what's wrong with you? She's being nice."

"Ever, this is uncalled for," Dad says flatly. I wait for Donna to do the whole fairy godmother thing and be *Oh, please, no, I understand.* Instead, she arches an eyebrow in my direction and says, "You know, only one person is going to lose if you quit on your life and stay in your room for eternity. And that person sure ain't gonna be me."

You just got verbally bitch-slapped, Pippa laughs in my head. *And it was epic. Kodak moment, dude.*

I rub at my face, feeling exhausted all of a sudden.

"Sorry. Sorry for being . . ." Unbearable. Rude. Disgusting. Shall I go on? "Difficult."

"You just lost your fiancé," Donna says mildly. "And believe it or not, as someone who has been there, you are not doing as bad as you think you are."

"I have no point of reference. I bailed fast when Dad lost Mom, so I couldn't see his full destruction," I mumble, pushing the leftovers on my plate around.

"I was a wreck. Losing the love of your life is the hardest thing you have to go through," Dad says. "But the good news is . . . you *go* through it."

He called Mom the *love of his life.* In front of Donna. And she still hasn't stuck a fork in his arm. This makes me feel like a huge rock has rolled off my heart.

"Such a fun topic." Renn claps with a smile. "But I vote we should change it. How are you feeling, Ev?"

I give it some genuine thought.

"Better . . . I think."

I mean it. It still hurts. I still think about Dom all the time, but I no longer feel like I have no control over my emotions. Like I have no idea what condition I am going to wake up in tomorrow. The anger I had toward him is almost all gone. It's now been replaced with quiet acceptance that Dom was far from the perfect guy I thought he was, and that is okay. That I will never get my closure with him, will never be able to ask him what went through his head when he did what he did—and that's okay too.

"Better or good?" Renn asks.

"Better." I drag a piece of bread in butter before popping it into my mouth. "And maybe a *little* good, now that simple carbs are involved."

"Good enough to come surfing with us? The guys and I are gonna catch some waves in about half an hour. The ocean will be flat, perfect for bad surfers like you."

I flip him the finger. He laughs.

"They've been wanting to say hi." Renn shrugs.

"You know I'm going to be a buzzkill."

"Not sure how to tell you this . . ." Renn pretends to take a deep breath. "But you've *always* been a buzzkill. Now you just have a valid reason to be."

I throw a piece of bread at him. He catches it in his mouth and chews.

"See what I have to deal with?" I ask Donna, jerking my thumb in Renn's direction.

She grins. "He tried to engage me in a fart war the other day. I think this is his version of showing affection."

And that's when I can't help it. I burst out laughing. That is such a Renn thing to do.

255

"You're disgusting!" I push Renn's shoulder.

"And you're stalling. So? You coming, or do you have a hot date with a Marilyn Manson album and your pillow?"

I love Renn's friends. Growing up, they used to tail Pippa and me pathetically, vying for crumbs of our attention. We were older, wiser, and we did not smell like goats and socks. Which, naturally, gave us the shine of rock stars.

"I'm sure Ever could use a little time to relax," Dad says sternly. "Not that there is anything wrong with your pot-smoking, wave-catching, job-avoiding friends."

Actually, hearing him list all the reasons why Renn is friends with screwups reminds me of how much I used to enjoy hanging out with them. Renn's crew are the least judgmental people I've ever met. They'd probably be chill if I decided to perform a satanic ceremony midsurf. And, yes, there is a chance I will burst out crying spontaneously—I've been doing that a lot lately—but I don't think it would freak them out. Besides, I could use the opportunity to stretch my limbs. See if I really am bad at surfing after years of not doing it.

"I'll go surfing." I surprise both Renn and myself by saying this.

Renn hides his smile with a can of soda he pops open. "Damn, Dad. Nice work."

"Can I borrow one of your surfboards?" I ask.

"No need. I kept your old one in pristine condition." Renn winks.

My heart races in my chest. "You did?"

He nods. "That's what good siblings do. Of course, you wouldn't know anything about that."

"This is going to work out perfectly. While you are out, I can move some of my things back here," Donna says. "Your dad and I can grill a few things for dinner. How does that sound?"

It sounds perfect.

No, not perfect, I remind myself. Perfect doesn't exist.

It sounds *just* right.

We go to Ocean Beach, Renn's favorite spot. The waves can get up to fifteen feet high in the winter, and the winds are moody. It's not SoCal flawless. The water moving in and out from under the Golden Gate Bridge shifts the sandbars, and sometimes it's foggy as shit. But Renn says that there is something boring and obvious about surfing the perfect Malibu waves, and I tend to agree.

Renn drives his red Wrangler, both of our surfboards secured on the roof rack. The windows are rolled down. His red-blond curls dance across his forehead. The brine and salt and the mouthwatering scents of morning pastries anchor me back to our childhood. I think about Joe. What's he doing right now? Who is he with? Sometimes I'm tempted to text him. But then I remember how much I've hurt him and think better of it.

"Are you seeing anyone right now?" I ask Renn. It is high time I take interest in my baby brother's love life. Especially since he is not a baby anymore. Last time we spoke on the phone, he was in bed with someone who sounded way older.

"I'm seeing lots of people," he says, evading the question.

"So you don't have a girlfriend?"

He scratches his jaw, "A girlfriend? No."

"But there must be someone," I insist. "You're being a smart-ass right now. If the answer was simple, you would've just said no."

Renn rolls his eyes. "There is someone. But it's not serious."

"Why isn't it serious?"

"That's a question you should ask her husband."

"Oh, Renn." I gasp. I'm no prude, but this is pretty shocking. Renn sleeping with a married woman. Before he is even of drinking age. He is a good kid, with a good head on his shoulders. Why would he put himself in such a toxic situation?

"See, this is why I didn't want to tell you." He takes a turn into the parking lot by the beach. "I knew you would jump to conclusions with Olympic leaps. It's not as bad as it sounds."

"Explain it to me, then." I fold my arms over my chest.

"She doesn't nag or demand things from me. She's not needy and doesn't want me to go on double dates with her boring friends. She's . . . more mature."

"What's more mature?" I ask. "Chronologically speaking. Give me an age."

"Thirty—"

"Thirty!"

". . . two."

"Renn!" I slap his arm.

He laughs. "Don't *Renn* me, sis. Her husband's cheating on her. He started it first! He is some financial-analyst big shot whatever. Always away. Screws his assistant on the reg."

"How'd you meet her?"

"She came in for surfing lessons last summer. Her therapist had told her that picking up a hobby in nature would do her good, since she is not ready to confront her husband about it. The way I see it, if he is not faithful—why should she be?"

"No. The way you should see it is—why should *you* put yourself in the middle of this explosive cluster?"

"I'm not in any cluster." He kicks the Jeep into park, then shoves his door open. "It's just harmless fun."

"Harm*ful*," I counter. "For everyone involved. You included."

Renn *tsks*. "We're here."

He hands me my surfboard and takes his, then turns his back on me. I gather the conversation is over for now. I pin it and make a note to get back to it when he least expects it. We proceed with our wetsuits to shore, where we meet Renn's friends—Ryland, Tim, and Clayton.

They're all holding their surfboards, ready to tackle the waves. They all look *huge* in comparison to the last time I saw them.

"Holy shit, dude, you got hot!" Clayton exclaims as he shoulder-bumps me.

"Hey! Shut your trap. I'm right here." Renn pushes him with a scowl.

"Yeah, Ever. You look great. Tragedy really agrees with you." Tim snickers.

Renn punches his arm. Hard. "Cut it out, dipshit."

Ryland sighs. "Excuse them. They don't know how to human properly."

I wave him off. "I don't take offense."

"No, but seriously, sorry about your fiancé." Clayton makes a face.

I wonder how these guys would react if they knew what Dom had done. If they knew the whole story.

I smile. "Actually, I'm starting to feel better."

"Good, it'll help when you get your ass wiped by us," Clayton says helpfully. "I'm sure you're a little rusty."

"I'll wipe the floor with y'all," I say cheerfully. "But if shit talk makes you feel better, have at it."

Clayton elbows Renn. "Why'd you say she was depressed? She seems like her usual smart-ass self to me."

They're not treating me with kid gloves, and I like it.

A minute later, we all charge into the waves. Our feet slap the wet sand as we gain momentum. We're cutting through the air. I'm a newly hatched baby turtle, rushing to the ocean to increase my chance of surviving a predator. My lungs open. My limbs loosen. Muscle memory reminds me who I was, who I am, who I'm meant to be. My body hits the cold water, and suddenly, I am sobered up. I'm clearheaded.

I'm *alive*.

A roar escapes from my mouth. Euphoria rushes over me. The simple, intense joy of being alive, and healthy and well, in this endless ocean, in one of the best cities in the world, robs me of my breath.

You're home now, Mom whispers somewhere inside me. *Relax. Smile. Enjoy this.*

I slide my body across the surfboard. I snap my eyes shut. The boys are shouting back and forth next to me.

"Don't steal my wave, asshole."

"Your ass is so out of shape."

"Hey, man, is your sister okay?"

In this moment in time, I am more than okay. I actually believe that it *will* be okay. That I will overcome the loss of Mom, and the loss of Dom.

But that maybe I don't have to lose other people who are still here on this earth. Maybe I'm not so horrible and cursed.

That's how I make the decision that it is time to apologize to Joe.

◆ ◆ ◆

On our drive back home, Renn pops open two cans of LaCroix and hands me one. We're both damp and shivering, even though we are not cold. Adrenaline zings through my veins. My body needed this reminder that it is still functioning. Capable.

Renn doesn't say anything. I know he doesn't want to reopen the subject of his not-girlfriend, but I can't stop myself. I clear my throat before I tell him what I haven't told anyone other than Joe. Not even Nora.

"Dom . . . he had a girlfriend."

"What?" Renn snorts out. "Like, you stole him from someone else?"

I shake my head. "He was two-timing us. I didn't know about her. They were together for three years."

"The bastard," Renn spits out, thunderous. "How'd you find out?"

"At the hospital, when I rushed to see how he was doing. She was there too."

"That's some bullshit!" he says. I'm glad he is mad. Because I'm about to turn the situation around on him in half a second.

"What would you have done if he'd made it? Would you have stuck with him?" Renn asks.

I've asked myself that question a million times in the past few weeks. The answer was always different. "No, I don't think I would have. I mean, I'd have stuck around to take care of him, to nurse him back to health. But not as his girlfriend."

"Well, you're more charitable than I am, that's for sure. How could you mourn him after this bullshit?" Renn raises his voice. "That's *fucked*."

"Just because he turned out to be a questionable person doesn't mean I should be one." I twist the engagement ring on my finger. Yes, I'm still wearing it. No, I have no idea why. "But now, see why I don't want that for you?"

Renn groans, then closes his eyes once we reach a red traffic light. "It's not the same."

"I don't want you in this situation. I don't want this on your conscience, or on your karma. This could come back to bite you when you least expect it."

"It's really casual. We're all about the fun."

"Have fun with single women. I'll be your first cheerleader. I promise."

"Single women want more."

"Not all of them," I point out. "You know, you *are* resistible to some people. Not many, but some."

Finally, Renn throws his arms in the air. "Fine. Fine. I'll break it off. God, you suck. Go back to Salem."

"I think I'm going to stick around for a while."

Renn turns to me and grins. "Actually, I'm *really* glad to hear that. You know who else is going to be happy to know that?"

I turn to look at him.

"Pippa."

◆　◆　◆

Later that night, after Dad and Donna have served us an actual feast and cracked open a bottle of wine, I'm in my room again.

Loki is in my lap. He is starting to get used to it here. He certainly enjoys having a safe backyard, where he can work on his tan and collect gifts for us in the form of dead mice and hummingbirds.

I decide there is no point in postponing the inevitable. I owe Joe an apology. But calling seems so . . . inconsiderate. Almost penetrating. What if he doesn't want to hear my voice after everything that happened?

I decide to write him a chain of text messages. That'll give him time to digest, collect himself, and decide what to write back. If anything at all.

Ever: I just wanted to send you a sign of life, since I've been notoriously bad about doing that throughout our history. I'm okay. I'm in San Francisco. I'm with Dad and Renn, and Dad's girlfriend, Donna, who owns a hot dog onesie, which should tell you everything you need to know about her as a person.

Ever: How are you doing? Are you still working at the dock? How are Gemma and Brad? Are you holding up?

Ever: Okay. I lied. I didn't want to tell you how I was doing. It is selfish of me to assume that you still care. What

I wanted to say is that I'm sorry. So terribly sorry. I know having sex wasn't in your plans. I know you regret it. I know you will have to live with what we did for the rest of your life. And I apologize for putting you in that position. It's all on me. I seduced you (if you can call it that). I asked to drink. I made sure we were both sufficiently drunk.

Ever: I'm just really sorry. Miss you.

I let out a breath and wait.

I stare at the screen for a minute. Then ten more. Then twenty. And then an hour. At some point, I fall asleep, dropping the phone on my face. I'm so exhausted I don't even have it in me to pick it up.

Sunday morning, I have one measly message waiting. Three words, and yet each of them weighs a ton.

Joe: I forgive you.

TWENTY-FOUR

On Monday, I open up the text messages from Pippa. I'm about to text her, then think better of it and call her. Unlike with Joe, I know Pippa has been waiting for me to pick up the phone and call. She deserves groveling and a good dose of squirming from yours truly. She's waited long enough.

She answers on the fourth ring, yawning into my ear. "Lawson. It was so obvious that whenever you decided to call, it'd be when I have a day off and can sleep in."

"Sorry." I glance at my watch—it's nine forty-five—as I'm pacing my tiny childhood room. "I can call again later. Or wait until you call me. Whatever works."

"Christ on a crutch," she snorts out. "*So* high strung. At least that didn't change. What's up?"

I'm stumbling all over myself trying to find the right words. I also suspect I'm crying again. I can't help it. She is not giving me crap. She is not asking me where I've been the last six years. She is not making it difficult or awkward or awful.

I take a deep breath and try to sound as casual as she does.

"I'm in San Francisco."

"Well, duh," she yawns.

"You knew?" I ask, surprised.

"Renn told me."

"You two talk?" I try to conceal my shock with a fake cough.

Pippa laughs harder. "Good to know you're still doing that thing where you cough when you get nervous."

"I'm not nervous," I lie.

"Really? So why don't you take your fingernails out of your mouth, missy?"

I realize I've been munching on them and do just that, then wipe my hand over my shirt. I'm amazed I have made it this far without talking to Pippa. She is the closest thing to Mom I have. She knows every piece of me. Even the bad ones. *Especially* those.

"We try to catch up once a month for coffee, Renn and me," she explains.

"Neither of you drink coffee," I say flatly.

"I said coffee? I meant beer."

"He is not twenty-one yet."

"That's not what his fake ID says." She laughs.

My mood is instantly lifted, even though Joe brushed me off and basically told me to go screw myself in his last message, though not in so many words.

I forgive you is code for *Don't worry about me. Just stay on your side of the continent and leave me the heck alone.*

It goes against what I want to do, but I have to respect his wishes.

There's a brief silence between Pippa and me before she sighs. "Fine. You can take me out for drinks and lunch."

I laugh. "Thank you. Where do you want to go? Your choice."

But I already know. We have a spot. It is the best restaurant in all of San Francisco.

"Wayfare Tavern. And I'm ordering cocktails. A *lot* of cocktails. Watch me blow up that bill."

"Go ham. When?" I ask.

"Noon. Don't be late."

She hangs up.

I stagger out of my room. It's a Monday, and Renn is at college and Dad is at work. Donna is sitting in the kitchen, reading the paper and listening to the radio like it's the nineties or something. She laughs at something the radio host says. She is pretty endearing, in a you-are-still-not-my-mom sort of way.

She glances beyond the rim of her reading glasses and smiles. "Hello, Ever. Would you like me to fix you a cup of coffee? Maybe an omelet?"

I shake my head and grab a seat in front of her. She puts her newspaper down and sits back. "You look . . . *thoughtful*."

"I have a lot on my mind," I say, still unsure how I feel about her. My heart desperately wants to reject her, but every other part of me realizes that she is being very nice and supportive, and that no part of her has to be. I'm not a surly teenager. I'm on the cusp of twenty-five.

She taps the table between us. "Unload some of it here. I'm a good listener."

I nibble on the side of my thumbnail, deciding that confiding in her is better than confiding in no one.

"I just called my best friend, whom I disappeared on six years ago. I'm seeing her at noon. At our favorite restaurant. I don't even know what she looks like these days. I don't know what she does for a living. If she's married."

"Good. You'll have a lot to catch up on, so there won't be any awkward silence." Donna raises her coffee cup in a salute motion.

"She really tried to stay in touch. What if I disappoint her? What if she realizes that I'm not all that? What if *she* decides to stop hanging out with me?"

Donna smiles. "That is highly unlikely, but if that happens—you'll survive it. Just like you've survived everything else life has thrown at you so far."

It is a surprisingly good answer. Honest but still uplifting.

"Now, how about we go to Westfield and buy you a few outfits to choose from, so when you see her, you'll look like a knockout?" Donna wiggles her shoulders.

"What's wrong with how I look?" I ask, feigning innocence. I look like a mess. I'm wearing one of Renn's shirts and torn yoga pants.

She doesn't take the bait and doesn't rush to apologize. "You look like you haven't gotten out of bed in nearly two months. Which, for the record, is exactly what's happened. Let's go."

"No thanks. You're not my real mom." I roll my eyes, joking.

"I don't aim to be. I have my own children, and they keep me *very* busy. Come on now." She stands up and carries the coffee mug to the sink.

"Can I come in my onesie?" I turn to look at her.

"Only if I can come in mine." Donna rinses the coffee mug with a shrug.

"Is this a dare?" My eyebrows hit my forehead.

Donna gives me an innocent look. "I raised two boys. You don't want to play this game with me. I will go there. In a heartbeat."

"If you wear your onesie to Westfield, coffee's on me," I say.

"If *you* wear your onesie to Westfield, shopping's on me," she retorts. After a pause, she adds, "Three-hundred-dollar limit, though. The place is expensive."

We shake on it. We both change into our onesies.

I race her to the car.

I win.

❖　❖　❖

One shopping trip and a makeover later, Pippa is sitting in front of me at the restaurant. It is surreal. She is even more stunning than I remembered. She is wearing a sage summer dress. Her hair cascades all the way down her ass. She doesn't have an engagement ring, but she does have a genuine Gucci bag, which was a lifelong ambition of hers.

"You look flawless," I choke out.

"You look like a stranger, you asshole." She squeezes my hand and orders us two cocktails. I'm guessing she is taking the BART and doesn't have to drive. I Ubered it here, but I think I'm going to walk home. It doesn't seem like she has plans for stopping at two or three drinks, and a girl has to save *some* money. Getting on the subway is not an option.

Pippa tells me that she is a web designer for a secondhand designer apparel site, which explains the Gucci bag. She lives with her boyfriend, Quinn, in Haight-Ashbury. When I congratulate her, she tells me that previously, she's also lived with Bryan, Jason, and Dan, so maybe I shouldn't be too excited.

"Is it not serious, then?" I ask, amused.

"It's as serious as it can be this time of the year. I believe I have . . . twelve, maybe fifteen soulmates. So far I've only met seven, though." Pippa giggles. "I knew Quinn was one of them when I brought him here and we both ordered the shellfish tower and champagne. I looked at him and thought: This man cannot sustain this lifestyle without getting rich. I'd better stick around."

"Is he?" I laugh. "Rich, I mean."

"He's on his way there." She sounds sure.

"What does he do?"

The food arrives. Pippa digs into her organic fried chicken, and I take a tentative bite of my burger. "He owns a nightclub in the Tenderloin."

"Aren't you worried? He is constantly around semidrunk, beautiful women."

She waves a hand at me. "I know he'd never cheat on me. I trust him with our relationship. Hell, I even trust him with my Netflix password!"

Shaking my head, I say, "You can never know these things. Trust me, I speak from experience."

She gives me a pitying look. "I'm sorry you've experienced infidelity, Ever, but that only means you didn't know the person you were with. If you do—if you truly see past the onion layers, if you touch the core—you always know. Don't tell me it's not the truth. Because you and I both know that when you left Spain, and that Joe guy stayed there, you didn't for one second think he'd cheat on you."

I'm pathetically close to breaking down and crying. She's hit a chord, and now my freshest, rawest wound is wide open and bleeding.

She is right. Maybe the problem was that I never truly peeled all the layers of Dom's onion. Because I *did* know Joe would never do this to me. I only assumed Dom wouldn't. Dom was always a bit of a mystery to me—What'd he see in me? What made us work?—while with Joe, it just felt right.

"Maybe you're right," I mumble.

"There's no *maybe* about it. I'm always right."

I reach for a french fry. Pippa grabs my hand and tugs it. "Hold up. You're *engaged*? Bitch, details. All of them. Right now!"

Maybe Renn doesn't tell her everything in their talks.

I tell her about Dom. How we met. How he died. How it was yet again my fault. About the stupid tampons. About the guilt that doesn't let go. And everything in between. About Joe, and how we are each other's muses, but we're not in touch, because we can't trust ourselves to keep our pants on when we're together, and also because I low-key don't want him to die, and everyone I love dies. Pippa's face changes expressions about twenty times a minute when I relay my last five months to her.

Once she is all caught up, she signals the waiter to get us more cocktails and some shots for good measure. "All of this happened and you didn't pick up the phone to consult your main squeeze? What the heck did I ever do to you?"

"About that . . ."

Gulping, I tell her the truth. That I was ashamed to give her a call. Embarrassed. That I disappeared because she'd asked too many questions. And also that she had offered me love and support I didn't feel I deserved.

"Salem was a punishment for me. All I wanted was to slip under the radar and merely exist. I worked. I ate. I showered. And I repeated. This whole time, I thought I was only punishing myself. I didn't realize I was punishing everyone who cared about me too. I'm sorry. So sorry, Pip. I feel like I need to spend the next decade apologizing to people for the way I've behaved."

Pippa pouts, checking her fingernails. "A decade? No. A month's worth of groveling should be sufficient. And drinks are on you. Anyway, you're not completely to blame. When I heard what happened with your mom, I had no idea how to behave, what to say to you. I felt totally unequipped. I thought if I bombarded you with questions and text messages, you would see that I cared. I didn't think how it might feel to be in your shoes. That should've been my first thought."

"We were both so young," I say.

Pippa takes my hand in hers from across the table. The waiter brings us two fresh cocktails. "You're still young, Ev. And I'm sorry you lost Dom, I really am, but you still have a lot to live for."

Tears roll down both our faces.

"Aw, bitch." Pippa wipes the corner of her eyes quickly. "You're ruining my makeup."

I laugh. "Ever since Christmas, when I first found out Joe and Dom were related, all I've wanted to do was pick up the phone and tell you. I knew you'd tell me what to do. How to make it right."

"You should've. I'd have been all over this situation. That's some *Days of Our Lives* shit."

Laughter escapes through my tears again. "What would you have said to me?"

"I would've told you the truth. That Joe is your forever. *For Ever*, if you would." She smiles. "Dom was a placeholder. Therefore, you were *his* placeholder. You should've fought for Joe. You should've gone after your heart, not your fears."

"He doesn't want anything to do with me anymore." I suck in a ragged breath.

"Have you tried talking to him?"

I nod. "He was curt at best, put off at worst."

"He might come around."

"He might not."

"Time dulls even the sharpest pain."

She is right, of course.

She is right, and now I think about the kind of life we would have had, had I called Pippa the day after Christmas and told her everything.

The only reason Dom wanted me, I suspect, is *because* I was so different from Sarah. I was the exact opposite of her. I was in no danger of going anywhere, of doing anything big. I was his comfort zone, and he was mine. The very thing that gave me reassurance and security in our relationship, how safe we were for each other, turned out to be our downfall.

I'd have broken things off with Dom. He'd have stayed with Sarah.

He wouldn't have gone to get me tampons that day.

He would have been safe.

Somewhere, in a parallel universe, Dom and Sarah and Joe and I go on double dates. We spend holidays together. We love who we're supposed to love.

"I know why you're here." Pippa sucks on her straw. "You're wrong. It wasn't your fault. Our destinies are prewritten. You didn't write Dom's and Barbie's stories."

I wish I could believe that. But I can't.

Winter slowly bleeds into spring. I no longer stay holed up in my room, even though I reserve the right to occasionally treat myself to spurts of self-pity.

At first, I leave the room because Donna gives me responsibilities around the house. Laundry duty, grocery shopping, taking care of the garden. When I protest and tell her all I do is work, she nicknames me Cinderella.

"I guess that makes you the vile stepmother." I blow her a raspberry one day as I'm folding Dad's seriously old and tattered underwear.

"You think?" Donna's eyes widen comically. "That's great. Good side characters are always boring."

Dad tells me I should think about my next step. I'm in my midtwenties and currently live rent-free, doing chores like a preteen. But the idea of going out there and finding out who I really am is still paralyzing to me.

Any person I become will be a person who is a virtual stranger to my mom, and becoming that person would be, in a way, truly and finally letting go of her.

This, by the way, is something I share with my new therapist, Lina, whom I see twice a week. Because: issues.

I see Pippa at least once a week. I hang out with Renn and his friends whenever they're around. I call Nora for weekly catch-ups. She now lives with Colt. They are planning their wedding, and the other day, she asked if I'd attend.

"Are you kidding me? I need to sign a fat check after everything I put you through. Of course I'll be there," I answer.

When I ask her if she keeps in touch with Joe, she says, "Nope. He hasn't really taken any of my calls. Colt tried too. I doubt he wants to hear from any of us, Ev. But I *did* see him the other day, down the street."

"When? Where? Who with?" I demand.

There is an uncomfortable silence on the other side of the line before she says, "I shouldn't . . ."

"Tell me, Nora," I all but bark at her.

She sighs. "I saw him by the Walgreens. With a woman. A brunette. He had his arm around her shoulder."

It hurts so much that I spend the rest of my day clutching my chest to keep my heart from spilling out. Joe is trying to move on. Why shouldn't he? We can't be together. I was with his brother. Plus, I hurt him the last time we were together. Then, finally, I left. *Again.*

For my twenty-fifth birthday, my family throws me a Halloween-themed bash, even though it's June. Donna invites Dylan and Ashton, whom I've met numerous times at this point. Renn gifts me a Malibu surfboard. Handcrafted and designed in goth themes, "Because you suck and need a beginner's surfboard, and because I love you enough to be honest with you about it."

It is the first personalized gift he's given me in six years, and I am so touched I don't give him smack for his sass.

Donna gets me a full hardcover collection of Jane Austen's classics.

Dad gets me two tickets to see a band I stopped listening to at age sixteen, but at least he tried.

I wait for a message from Joe all day. When one doesn't arrive, I decide to message him. I can't help myself. I miss him so much. It doesn't seem to get any better either. Like the memory of Dom, or even Mom.

And it's not just about me. I'm also worried about him. Yes, he is self-sufficient—has been his entire life—but he has just lost his brother, and I didn't make matters much better.

Ever: It's my twenty-fifth birthday today. How do you deal with celebrations after Dom?

When he doesn't answer, I send another text, knowing that I'm teetering on the line of unhinged.

Ever: Sometimes I think about you so much I can't sleep at night. Please tell me you're okay.

He answers after a beat. **I'm OK. Happy Birthday, E.**

My heart beats so fast I feel like I'm about to throw up. He answered. It's not much, but it's workable.

He is also hugging brunettes all over Salem and wants nothing to do with you or your friends, I remind myself smartly.

Ever: Are you writing?

Joe: You know the answer to that question.

Ever: Are you feeling better?

Joe: See last answer.

Ever: When's your birthday? You never told me.

He is going to turn twenty-six soon. I remember he is almost exactly a year older.

Joe: August 10th.

Ever: What can I get for you?

Joe: A fucking spine for yourself?

Unbelievably, I'm encouraged by what I see, not horrified by the dig.

Ever: I don't think a spine would help. I figured you wanted nothing to do with me, considering what we've been through.

Joe: Your logic works in mysterious ways. What Dom wanted and didn't want doesn't matter now. He is not here, so we can't hurt him.

Joe: I told you. I warned you. Don't break my heart again. You did.

I start typing **You are not in love with me, you were, and I went away precisely BECAUSE I'm still in love with you.** But it's too clingy, too honest, so I delete it. Then I write, **Some heartbreak it is. You are already parading other women all over town.** But then I delete that one, too, on the grounds that I don't want to sound like a stalker. Finally, I settle for generic.

Ever: Well, I'm always here if you need me.

I wait for another snarky comment, but all I get is a generic thumbs-up emoji.

That's the last I hear from him for a while.

During the first week of August, I walk past the gates of a small cemetery in Half Moon Bay.

San Francisco banned burials on its grounds in 1900, on the basis that the city is dense as all hell. In what must be one of the most dazzling cases of irony known to mankind, the city of San Francisco deemed burials to be health hazards. Let that sink in for a moment.

Thus, we bury our loved ones around the city, not inside it.

Barbara "Barbie" Lawson loved Half Moon Bay. A town in the Bay Area that still maintains its wild coastal beauty. It is essentially a string of beaches bracketed by cliffs. Dad chose to bury her there because he thought she'd enjoy the view.

I go alone. It's a weekday. Dad's at work, and Renn's at school taking summer classes. Even if they were available, I need to do this by myself.

I couldn't bring myself to attend Mom's funeral. I was too busy hurling my phone off a cliff and hating myself to pay her last respects. Also, I couldn't deal with the stares of everyone who would be attending. They all knew how she died.

So here I am now.

It takes me twenty-five minutes to find her grave. Partly because I'm so nervous, but mostly because cemeteries are like that. Difficult to navigate. Her grave is a generic one. A single upright granite headstone with a matching vase. I lift a batch of flowers I brought along with me and tuck them into her vase.

"Hey, Mom. Sorry it took me a minute. Or . . . you know, six years."

The silence is to be expected, but it still hurts. I don't sit down. I don't make myself comfortable.

"I know it's been a long time, and I know I wasn't here for your funeral . . . and yes, I know I was terrible to Renn and Dad. And Pippa too. I know all those things. So don't think I don't. It's just that . . ." I blink at her grave, thinking, *It's been so long*, but also *I remember her like it was yesterday*.

In my head, I can hear her say, *It's all right, darling. Just talk. I'm listening.*

I take a deep breath.

"It's just that I needed a few moments to collect myself after what happened. And see, those moments turned into a few years. I just wanted to thank you for saving me. For being the best mom a girl could have. I'm so sorry my guilt stood in the way of doing the right thing. I promise you, it's over now. I'll be good to everyone who is still alive and I love. Everyone."

And I mean it. *Everyone.*

The grave looks back at me. I still think Mom's death could have been prevented, but I no longer think I should pay for it with my own life by merely existing. There is no point. I know Mom would not draw any pleasure from knowing I am miserable. I know she would have wanted me to go to Berkeley. To be with Joe. To pursue my dream. The one that had made me so self-conscious and her so proud.

More than anything, I know that Mom would have wanted me to design her gravestone. She always joked about it while she was alive, obviously thinking it would happen in many, many decades.

It is not too late now.

"I can't make up for what happened. I wish I could. I wish I would have put my phone aside that day. Paid more attention to you. But since I can't go back to change the past, I'm going to do the one thing I know for a fact you'd have wanted me to do. Do you think Dad and Renn would mind?"

The grave is completely silent, of course, which is fine. The alternative would be terrifying. I know Dad and Renn would support this. So I sit in front of my mother's grave, take out a sketchbook and a pencil, and start sketching.

When I get back home, I call Gemma Graves. She is surprised but happy to hear from me. I ask how she and Brad are doing.

Be good to those who are still alive. I made a promise. I am going to keep it.

"It's hard to answer that question," she says. "Some days it is bearable. Some days it is not. The one thing both days have in common is that we can't control them."

I tell her that I've been meaning to catch up for a while now, and I apologize for not calling earlier. "I'm trying to get better at keeping in touch," I explain.

"Baby steps are the best steps. We learn a lot from them," comes her reply, sure and sunny, just like Gemma herself.

We chat for ten minutes. I play with the engagement ring that has *still* been on my finger the entire time. It soothes me and reminds me that Dom was here not all that long ago.

Gemma tells me about a beautiful tribute Dominic's middle school paid to him before they went on summer break. Apparently, he sponsored a kid there and paid for the kid's lunch for both semesters, and he also volunteered to give the kids a quick first aid course. We both cry, but it's a cleansing cry. It's a he-was-such-a-good-human cry.

And he was. Not all the time, no. And not to everyone. But he was.

Please don't call me perfect, he asked me on the Cape. No one's perfect.

I ask her if she could give me Joe's email. I explain that I don't want to burden him, but I want to show him something. She gives it to me and sighs. "Dom's always been so sweet and loving. Seph is so prickly . . . but that only makes me love him harder, you know?"

Yes, lady, I'm tempted to answer. *Actually, I do know.* Every bone in my body knows.

I promise to visit her and Brad once I'm back in Massachusetts, and we hang up.

I scan my initial sketch for my mother's grave and send it to Joe, along with the playlist I've been listening to while working on it. All Brit bands I think he would appreciate.

> Dear Joe,
>   I think it's time we invite our muses back. Don't you think?
>   —E.

The answer to my question is, apparently, no. Joe never bothers to reply. Not even when I find a place to DoorDash him toad-in-the-hole for his birthday, which I think he would appreciate, as a fellow Anglophile.

The next day, I send him another email. This time with old-school sketches I did long ago. The ones Dad sent me in the box all those months ago. The box I now know was meant to prompt me to come back home, not taunt me about my sins.

I add a few quotes I think would speak to him. Quotes about creativity and the muse. By William S. Burroughs, Stephen King, and Maya Angelou. This time, I don't write him anything more.

I'm not counting on him to get back in touch because he misses me. We've both shown admirable self-restraint in that department before. I'm counting on him to do so because he wants his creative mojo back.

After the third email I send him, I start feeling like a con man trying to convince him that I'm an African prince whose family got tragically killed in a helicopter accident and *needs* him to give me his bank account details so I can transfer all my millions into it, but I keep pushing through.

I don't hear from Joe on the third day, or the fourth one. I keep sending him tidbits of what I'm doing, things I'm working on. Music. Lyrics. Sketches. It's like pulling teeth. It is possible that he doesn't check his email very often. Or that my emails go straight to spam. It feels like flooring the accelerator when the car's in neutral. But it's better than not doing anything at all, and I can't stop thinking about what I promised Mom. I have to get better about how I treat the people I love who are still here.

And then, one day, two weeks after Joe's birthday, I log in to my email and find a new message from him. His name is in bold. **Joseph Graves.** My fingers quiver. So much hinges on his answer.

Please stop bothering me before I file a restraining order against you is a possibility.

But also, *Okay, let's play. Want to hold each other accountable? I'll write a little every day, you'll sketch.*

When I open his email, I find neither.

There is no text at all. Just a Word document attachment. With words. Four thousand three hundred and two of them, to be specific.

I open the file and gulp the words down like a parched man who has found water in the desert. Joe picked up where he left off in his manuscript. His character, a Holden Caulfield of sorts, is still on the road, trying to find the meaning of life in New Orleans. Although in the last chapter, he decides to move to Raleigh to get away from the drugs. I love it. It's raw. It's dark. It reminds me of the stuff I grew up on.

I write him an email back. It's one word.

From: Ever Lawson
To: Joseph Graves

More.

This time, it takes him less than five minutes to reply. Has he been waiting all this time for me to read it? What if I hadn't seen it right away? Adrenaline is running through my veins.

From: Joseph Graves
To: Ever Lawson

Do you think it's too Kerouac?

From: Ever Lawson
To: Joseph Graves

I think all authors use their literary hero's voice until they find their own. Keep going.

From: Joseph Graves
To: Ever Lawson

This is purely about work, Ever. I don't want to get together. Every time we do, you leave.

He is right. He is right and it kills me. He is right and I deserve this. He is right, and I don't want him to be right, because I know, deep down, it was always Joe.

From: Ever Lawson
To: Joseph Graves

I understand.

From: Joseph Graves
To: Ever Lawson

Know how I spent my birthday?

From: Ever Lawson
To: Joseph Graves

?

From: Joseph Graves
To: Ever Lawson

A threesome. They were great. I didn't think about
you. Not for a minute.

I swallow down a scream. I want to tear the walls down. To break
everything within reach. I want to stumble out to the street, a crazed
woman, grab a rando, and fuck him in an alleyway as payback. But I
can't. Because *he* had to watch me run off to a romantic Puerto Rican
vacation with his brother. Because I still wear Dom's engagement ring.

From: Ever Lawson
To: Joseph Graves

Glad to hear you've been enjoying yourself.

From: Joseph Graves
To: Ever Lawson

Your sketch is great. Keep sending me stuff.

From: Ever Lawson
To: Joseph Graves

Yeah. You, too.

TWENTY-FIVE

Weeks pass.

Joe and I slip into a routine. We email back and forth. I sketch. He writes. I critique. He offers helpful suggestions. We keep it strictly professional. Almost like coworkers. We don't mention Dom. We don't mention *us*.

We're playing it safe. Avoiding anything explosive. By the end of September, he's written no fewer than sixty thousand words in his book, *Winds of Freedom*, and I have a finished sketch of Mom's gravestone and a few other drafts for my portfolio.

In the evening, I email Joe that I'm going to ask Dad if we can update Mom's gravestone.

> Obviously, I don't want to disturb her. I figured out
> a way to install the new one on top of the old one.
> The dimensions should work. What do you think?

He doesn't reply back.

Instead, he *calls*.

It throws me off kilter to see his name on my phone screen. This is a breach of our unspoken agreement, and I don't know what to make of it. We've been so careful these past few weeks. We've veered away from anything that could reignite our feelings toward each other, even though on my part, those feelings have always been there. Excitement floods me. I don't realize how desperate I've been to hear his voice until I swipe the screen and notice that I'm shaking.

"You think it's a bad idea." I try to keep my voice even.

"No," he says, sounding out of breath and just as excited as I am. My heart melts into a pool in the pit of my stomach. "It's a rad-ass idea, and we both know that. I'm about to finish my book, and I have you to thank for that. It's time I do something for you. Remember when I saved you?"

"Of course I remember." I perch on my windowsill, overlooking the street. Loki jumps in my lap on cue, always happy to use me as a piece of furniture. I remember that night so well; it's still painted in my memory in vivid strokes. "You said I owed you one, and you always collect your debt." I let out an embarrassed chuckle. I have no business remembering things he told me seven years ago. "Well, consider mine paid, now that you're about to finish your book thanks to my determination. Or neediness, depending on how you look at it."

"Don't get ahead of yourself. Your debt was not paid in full." His voice is low and menacing all of a sudden.

"What do you mean?" I clutch my phone so hard that it's about to break.

"I saved your ass. You're not getting out of it by brainstorming with me. I help your muse just as much as you help mine."

"What else do you want?"

You, I want him to hit back at me. *I want you.*

"You still need to get on the BART," he says, in reality. Because he doesn't want me anymore. He said himself that it's over.

"Excuse me?"

"You're excused. All the same, this is the final thing on your to-do list before I consider you debt-free."

There's a brief silence, which I use to collect my jumbled thoughts.

"I think I need to find a job and an apartment first," I say cautiously.

"Nah, that would be out of order." I can practically envision him waving a dismissive hand at me. "Go to the same station where it happened. Get on that train. Face your demons."

"Joe," I say quietly, "you know I can't."

"Yes, you can. You went to her grave. How is that different?"

"I watched her *die* there," I hiss out, feeling my neck crawling with heat. Why is he doing this? It is so unnecessarily cruel. "It was pretty graphic too."

"You cannot swear off subways. You cannot never go underground again."

"Says who?" I drawl. "I've been doing that for seven years. Most cities don't even have an underground train system. Why does it matter?"

"It matters because you're letting fear win. Don't you see a pattern here? Fear was the reason why you stayed with Dom. Fear was the reason you bailed on me both times. Fear is why you don't get on a subway."

"Fear can win. It's not a competition."

"Ever," he says stoically. "You asked me what I wanted for my birthday."

"Yeah." I press my forehead against the cool glass of my window, closing my eyes. "I was kind of hoping you'd want . . . socks?"

He lets out a gruff laugh. God, it is horrible to be in love with your dead fiancé's brother. The absolute worst. It is especially tragic when you know what it feels like to kiss him, to make love to him, to be the center of his world, even if for one night.

"Keep the socks. I want you to get on that train."

"But Joe, it will be so horrible for me."

"You'll survive it. And live to tell the tale."

We are both quiet for a moment. I'm trying to think of more excuses I could use not to do it.

"I would want pictures when you do it. As proof." He is getting ahead of himself. I wonder if it's because he knows I'd cut off my right arm if it means pleasing him.

"Gee, dude. Where's the trust?"

"At the bottom of the Pacific Ocean, along with your old cell?" he suggests cordially. *Touché.* "We don't have the best track record."

I stroke Loki in my lap. "I bailed on you twice. There won't be a third time."

I hear him lighting himself a cigarette. "Color me skeptical and extremely fucking exasperated, love."

Love. Just the word on his tongue makes me shiver. But of course, it is a casual endearment, not a declaration.

Yes, I want to make Joe proud, but it's not just that. He is right. As long as I'm afraid of the subway, as long as I opt to walk instead of catch a train because I'm too scared to face this memory that I so violently shoved into a drawer in my brain, I cannot be completely free to build a life for myself.

True, I create. I leave the room. I see people. But I still haven't chosen a path. A direction. I still haven't decided what I'm going to do with my life. If I go back to Salem or stay here. Hell, I'm still paying half the rent for that god-awful pigsty. All because I'm too afraid of making a decision. I didn't want to slam the door on Salem. But my savings have been dwindling rapidly, and I can't keep doing that anymore.

"All right. I'll do it."

"When?" he shoots out.

"You want specifics?"

"Always."

"This Wednesday. At noon. It shouldn't be too crowded," I hear myself say.

"Take a picture of you with a Montgomery Street sign in the background."

"Yeah, yeah. I feel like I should ask you for something equally as unpleasant just to even the score," I grunt, pushing off the window. Loki jumps off my lap in a classic I-wanted-to-get-up-before-you-did cat move.

"You can, and should. I'm always at your service."

"Not always," I point out, remembering all the weeks he's spent ignoring me.

"No," he says thoughtfully after a beat. "Sometimes I manage to pull myself together and deny you. But not often. Have a good night, Ev."

"Wait!" I cry out.

He stays on the line but doesn't say anything. I know I'm going to ruin things, but I can't help myself. I can never help myself with this man.

"Did you really have a threesome?"

There's a stretch of silence before he answers: "Yes."

All this time, I've naturally assumed he said this to hurt me. Not so. Maybe Joe *has* moved on. I know he tried to fight it hard when Dom was in the picture.

"Is that all?" he asks.

"Yeah," I choke out.

He hangs up.

I put my phone down, grab a pillow from my childhood bed, and scream into it. When I'm done, I pad downstairs. I feel empty. Like if I jog, my internal organs would rattle in my body like pennies.

Dad and Donna are sitting on the patio. The sliding door is open. They're drinking iced tea and planning a last-minute vacation. Mexico, they think. Shorter flight time than Hawaii, and not as expensive.

"Plus," I hear Dad say at the tail end of their conversation, "if Ever needs us, we can get here faster."

And my mangled, put-together heart breaks all over again.

I clear my throat to announce my arrival.

"She's behind me, isn't she?" Dad flinches.

Donna turns her head, flashing me an easy smile. "Yes."

"Am I in trouble?" He turns to me.

I shake my head, advancing toward them. "No, but *I* should be for all the crap I've put you through."

"I do sometimes wish I could ground you. It was a power I didn't enjoy wielding quite as often as I should've back in the day." Dad strokes his chin thoughtfully.

"I was a great kid." I nudge his shoulder, then bend down to kiss his cheek.

"True. And unfortunately, parents and children don't play on even ground. You can get away with a lot more than I do."

I grab a seat in front of them. Donna must see the trepidation written on my face, because she stands up and stretches. "I think I'm going to try those new bath bombs Dylan got me. Have a good evening, you two."

It's just Dad and me now, and even though I imagined I would get cold feet, I find that I can meet his stare head-on. This is the moment of truth.

"There's something I've been working on these past two months. It was partly for self-healing, to get over what happened with Mom. But also a tribute to her, since she believed in what I did."

He offers me a small nod.

"I made a sketch for a new headstone for her. I know she already has one. I know I wasn't there to choose the existing one, and that's on me. But I thought maybe . . . if you'd let me . . . ."

Dad sits back, lacing his fingers together, tapping his lips. "If I'd let you . . . ?"

He is not going to go easy on me. For some reason, this feels really good. He doesn't treat me like delicate china anymore. That means I've grown stronger, right?

"I was wondering if you'd let me replace it. I'll take care of everything. I'll hire an artist. I'll pay for it. And I'll put it on top of the existing one, so nothing would be removed or disturbed."

"Do you think she'd have wanted this?" he asks cautiously. He doesn't take it lightly. After all, it is his late wife we are talking about. And they were crazy about one another.

"Yes." I chip away at my nail polish. "She always thought my designing headstones was awesome. She used to show my sketches off to clients and curators. I think she'd have appreciated the tribute. No." I frown. "I don't think. I *know*. She told me she'd want me to do this for her when she passed away."

Still, he is not giving me what I want. I think maybe I've found Dad's red limit. His deceased wife.

He appears deep in thought. "I'll need to see it first. Renn would want to approve too."

"That's not a problem," I say evenly. "I'll show you. And I'll be open to suggestions."

He offers me a curt nod. "That all?"

"Yes."

He stands up. Claps a hand on my shoulder. "I'm proud of you, Ever. You are turning out to be much stronger than I thought you were. Definitely your mother's daughter."

◆ ◆ ◆

It is Wednesday, at eleven forty-five in the morning, and I want to go home.

I'm standing at the mouth of the Montgomery Street Station, by the stairway leading down to the trains.

This is a mistake. I can't go back down there. A part of me—the one that clearly needs to be institutionalized—fears that I will walk right into the same gory scene I left behind all those years ago. The blood. The screams. The police tape. The train that stared back at me, daring me to do something.

I stumble to a nearby trash can and puke out my breakfast. I wipe my forehead, which is lined with cool sweat. A couple bypasses me. The woman narrows her eyes at me. I can hear her say, "She doesn't *look* like a homeless person, but I guess there are so many of them now it's hard to tell."

I'm too disoriented to care what people think about me. I'm shivering. I can't do this. I *have* to do this.

I check my watch. It's eleven fifty-three. Time doesn't have any significance to me. Nothing stops me from getting into the train station right this moment. Or at twelve thirty, for that matter. But I don't want to go off script here. Every minor change is a threat.

Pacing back and forth, I think about yesterday at dinner, when I showed Dad, Renn, and Donna my headstone sketch. They seemed to like it. This morning, I made some phone calls and asked around about sculptors who work with granite. It's going to put a real dent in my savings, but it's going to be worth it.

Eleven fifty-nine, and it is time to face the music.

I clutch the banister as I make my way down the stairs. The thick throng of people shoulder past me, unaware of and uninterested in my heartache. As soon as I'm inside, I lean against a column. I draw a deep breath full of sweat, piss, and steel brake dust.

I am here.

I am underground.

Just a couple of feet away from where it happened.

This is the place that made me who I am. My breaking point. This, right here, is why I carry all the guilt. All the self-loathing. This inherent sense of disbelief. That nothing is going to be okay. That things won't really get better. That time doesn't heal. It just makes you feel like you're stuck in a loop.

This is the place where I took a life.

Well, one of them. I'm responsible for Dom's loss of life too.

I'm nauseous again, but luckily, I've already emptied my stomach and have nothing left to vomit. The platform is teeming with people. The electronic sign above my head tells me the next train arrives in two minutes.

I take out my phone, angle it up from my chest area to catch both my face and the Montgomery Street sign behind me, and snap a picture for Joe. I'm as pale as a ghost and look physically unwell. Not exactly how I'd like Joe to see me, but at least he won't be able to smell the puke stench coming from my mouth.

I peer into the rails. They look so normal. So unassuming. Just a bunch of hot-rolled steel. There are no bloodstains, no human remains, no big **SOMEONE DIED HERE** sign. My tragedy has been dutifully erased. It only lives in my head now. The shriek of the approaching train pierces my ears. I hug the column, closing my eyes. The memory slams into me all at once, with forceful momentum. It is the first time I allow myself to fully remember. To go back and relive that scene.

Darling, take my hand. Take it.

I can't, Mom. It hurts. My ankle hurts so bad.

Please. Let me help you. I can hear the train coming.

Then being hurled back to safety. Flung across the platform. Just to look around me and notice she wasn't there.

I'm sobbing by the time the train arrives. My shoulders shake and my knees are bent. People are looking. The train stops in front of me. The doors slide open. I can't do this. I can't get inside. I turn around, toward the stairs, toward the world above. I'm going home. I can't do this.

"Ever." I hear a voice.

I look up, wiping my tears.

And there, in front of me, on the train in front of me, stands Joe. With his worn-out Levi's. With tousled dark curls that frame my favorite face in the entire world. With a cigarette tucked behind one ear. Beautiful and handsome and *alive*. He offers me his hand.

"What are you doing h-here?" I stammer.

"You won't find out unless you get on this train right about, let's see . . ." He twists his wrist to check an invisible watch. *"Now."*

I jump on the train a second before the doors slide shut. I fall into his open arms. He holds me up and tucks me under his armpit, like a protective older brother. He gazes down at me. "Hello, stranger."

"You came here to watch me get on a BART?"

He rolls his eyes. "Don't act like there's anything good on TV these days. It's not that big a deal."

"You do have a point." I decide to downplay the whole thing, to spare him any embarrassment.

I curl my fingers over his shirt, holding on to him. The train starts moving. We're safe inside it. I don't think about what happened last time I was here, and that is huge.

"I figured I can finish the book in a week if I lock myself up in a hotel room and write all day. I took some time off work."

"Actual time off work?" I arch an eyebrow. "Holy moly, but I thought writing is not a real grown-up thing people do?"

He bites down a grin, hitching a shoulder up. "Call me Peter Pan."

"You should be in the hotel, working." I keep talking to distract myself from the fact I am *on* a train right now. And it's moving fast, approaching another station, where someone could be under the tracks. I'm hyperaware of each breath coming in and out of my body.

"Because I need new experiences to write about, and as far as this one goes, it's a pretty damn memorable one."

I take a deep breath. "My breath might smell of vomit."

"Sweetheart." He tucks a lock of my hair behind my ear. "Nothing smells as bad as you did the night we went to the junkyard."

I swat his chest and laugh. He kisses the top of my (clean and shampooed) head. "Missed you, kiddo."

Missed me as what? A friend? A muse? A future sister-in-law? The love of his life? I have no idea where I stand with him, and I don't want to disrupt the fragile peace we have.

I bury my face in his chest. Inhale his scent. God, I missed him. He smells exactly like he did all those years ago. Ocean spray, male, and darkness. The undercurrent of sweetness. *The boy I love.*

"I can show you around," I murmur into his shirt. "You know . . . for research."

"All right." He gives me a slow, teasing smile full of promise. "For research."

TWENTY-SIX

It takes me a few minutes to gather myself and think about where I want to take Joe. I decide against the wharf. Joe works at the docks. The sight of an ocean, no matter how broad and blue, is anyone else's equivalent of a laptop screen or a calendar. It's his *job*. I would take him to a museum or the Golden Gate Bridge, but not only has he already been to the tourist attractions, but it is also about the way he and I do things. We always take the path less traveled.

And so, I decide our first stop is going to be my house.

"You're making me meet the *parents*?" He shoves his hands into his front pockets, taking in my street through hooded eyes. "This is the worst date I've ever not been on."

The reminder that it isn't, and never will be, a date stings. The truth is, I have no idea what we are right now. Friends? Brothers-in-arms? Grievers? Acquaintances? He is obviously over me—he had a threesome. Maybe one of the women he had it with is his girlfriend. Add to that the fact that after the last time we had sex, he didn't want to hear from me . . .

We're walking shoulder to shoulder. Well, more like my shoulder to his waist, he is so tall.

"You're not meeting anyone. Stay here." I shove him away from the little gate leading to my entrance.

I unlock my door, then slam it before he can peek inside. I rush to collect a six-pack of beer that belongs to Renn—he is going to kill me when he finds out—and some snacks from the pantry. I shove everything into one of Donna's reusable supermarket bags. When I get out, Joe is exactly where I left him. He is even wearing the same bored-with-your-shit expression. My heart thuds.

"I can see the six-pack from here." He points at the bag with the hand that holds a cigarette. "Are you pegging me for a cheap date?"

"As you said, it is not a date. And I need a car for where I want to take you." I round Dad's emergencies-only ancient Buick, which is parked on the street. I shove my version of picnic food into the trunk.

There's a Dom-shaped cloud above our heads, but neither of us acknowledges it. I think we're both asking ourselves the same questions—what would he have thought about this scene if he were alive? Would he hate that we're together, even as friends? Is what we're doing wrong? Bad? Immoral? Should we even care?

Joe cares either way. He cares, because in some sense, he will always be his big brother's shoulder to lean on. The strong one. The one who gave up things so that Dom could have them.

Joe flicks his half-smoked cigarette sideways. "I know what you're thinking. There's nothing wrong with what we're doing right now."

My gaze swings to him, and I bet my eyes are full of shock. "I just don't want you to regret this."

I slide into the driver's seat. He takes the passenger seat and buckles up. "I'm never going to regret you."

"How are you handling things?" I ask, clearing my throat.

"Some days are better than others. But the bad days are getting to be few and far between. I go to therapy, because . . . well, why the fuck not? All the cool kids are doing it now. And I live my life the way I think Dom would have wanted me to. I think that's the best we can do under the circumstances. Not let death dictate life for the living. What about you?"

I signal out of my parking spot and slide into traffic. "Yeah. I try to live my life the way Mom wanted me to. Or at least, I'm getting there. I still think about Dom all the time, but it no longer feels like someone is stabbing my lungs every time I try to breathe." I feel a little guilty admitting that. "Are you in touch with Sarah at all?"

Joe's lips press together into a hard line. He looks out the window. "Kind of. She is dating a new guy. Rich. A medical consultant. Who the hell can blame her? It's not like Dom was faithful. She doesn't have to play the devoted-girlfriend role. She gets a free pass."

Unsure if this rule applies only to Sarah or to me, I simply *hmm*. *And what about me?* I want to scream.

We arrive at Twin Peaks about thirty minutes later. The pair of uninhabited hills almost a thousand feet high offer the best view of San Francisco. I hurl the reusable supermarket bag out of the trunk and plop it between us on the car's trunk, popping open one beer for him and one for me. San Francisco spreads in front of us like a calendar girl. A mixture of medium-size skyscrapers nestled between sleepy neighborhoods, all built on hilly, uneven streets.

Joe clinks his beer with mine. "To being a little less fucked up than we were at the beginning of the year."

"And to helping our therapists finance their Hamptons time-shares."

We both take a pull of our beers.

"Why'd you choose this spot?" Joe asks, looking around us.

"The Twin Peaks are the only hills in San Francisco that have not been built over. I thought you'd get a kick out of being somewhere completely uninhabited."

"I've always been partial to people." He smirks.

"They're also a little dirty, like your mind. The Spaniards referred to the Twin Peaks lovingly as Los Pechos de la Chola. The Breasts of the Indian Maiden, if you will."

"So I'm basically sitting on a massive pair of tits." Joe nods, processing. He then lifts his beer again. "I'll drink to that."

"You'll drink to pretty much anything, won't you?" I tease.

He laughs. "I like my beer, but I've been watching my alcohol count recently. I don't want this to become a problem, now that I'm officially grieving a relative."

Joe tells me he is in San Francisco for exactly one week, and that he really does intend on writing all day, every day, but that we can meet during the evenings. I do the math in my head. That's seven dates with a man I am helplessly in love with and who is determined not to be with me. Only a fool would agree to this kind of arrangement. But unlike Joe, I don't count my alcohol units per week. I'm a drug addict on the loose, looking for her next hit. So I take the bait.

"Sure, I'll show you around if you behave."

"I never behave." He makes an adorable face.

"That's always been a problem." I smile at him, feeling warm all over. His gaze on me is like a weighted blanket, I swear.

"So what else is new with you?" he asks.

I hitch a shoulder up, cracking open my second beer. It's not that I want to get drunk again. It's that I want to ensure we don't leave here in the next few hours. Joe won't make me get behind the wheel buzzed. "I feel like I'm on the verge of something. I just don't know what that something is."

But I'm starting to realize what I want to do with my life.

"You're getting better. Stronger. I like that."

"What about you?" I jerk my chin toward him.

"I work, I eat, I write, repeat." He takes a pull of his beer.

"Are you dating anyone?" The question rolls out of my mouth before I can stop it. This is the problem with Joe. He makes my mouth and my brain disconnect from one another whenever he is around.

He smiles a closemouthed smile, then mimics zipping his lips shut and throwing the key off the mountain. He enjoys my squirming.

I snort out a nervous laugh. "It's whatever, Joe. I honestly don't care. I'm the one who keeps on leaving, remember?"

This is untrue, and also self-deprecating, but it's how I sometimes feel.

"I understand why you stopped answering me after Spain. And I understand why you left Salem too." Joe puts a hand on my shoulder. "I'm just at a place where I cannot have my heart broken again, no matter the reason."

That's when everything gets heavy and dark and wrong. I regret asking him about other women. I never get the answer that I want. And worst of all, I can't even blame him. He shouldn't be expected to wait around until I pull my head out of my ass.

"To your question." He rubs at my arm with an easy smile. "I'm not seeing anyone."

"Some would argue you saw plenty of the women you had a three-some with." Cool, cool, cool. I'm the obsessed rejected stalker now. What a terrific look.

He waves me off. "That was a high school pal who came to Salem for a visit. She called, and we went out for drinks. It was right around my birthday, and she wanted to celebrate. One thing led to another."

"That's just one woman, though. How did it become a threesome?" I refuse to let the subject go. I hope the CIA is recruiting soon. I could use a job.

"The bartender." He smiles apologetically.

"You should stop smoking." I change the subject.

"Why?" He takes out the soft Lucky Strike pack and tucks a ciga-rette in the corner of his mouth, just to spite me.

"Cancer."

"If I die, it's on me."

"What a selfish thing to say." I scowl. "If you die, you leave every-one else to cope and grieve. Your parents have been through enough."

"Maybe, after I finish the book."

"That's a week away." My voice brightens.

He chuckles. "*After* revisions."

"That could take years!"

"Yup. I can work with that timeline."

We talk for hours after that. About books, music, films we've recently watched. About the correspondence he's had with two literary agents who are interested in *Winds of Freedom*.

"One of them *did* say I should treat this as a working title only." Joe frowns. "Said it sounds like someone let one rip and is now feeling the relief."

I cackle. "I can never unhear what you just told me. You cannot use *Winds of Freedom*, buddy."

He elbows my ribs. "Instead of criticizing, help me."

"*Lost in New Orleans?*" I ask.

"Generic," he *tsks*.

"*Big Little Easy?*" I try again.

"Ever." His eyes widen. "Wow. That is *terrible*."

"At least mine doesn't sound like an ass burp."

"You're really poetic. Anyone ever told you that?"

"I think you did, once. And that was *after* we had sex."

We both laugh.

After the alcohol has seeped out of my system, I drive him to a boutique hotel in the Tenderloin. I tell him it's a rough neighborhood and that he should be mindful of that.

"They should be wary of me. I'm a Bostonian." He puffs his chest in an exaggerated way that makes me laugh.

"Just watch out, tough guy."

He kisses my cheek before leaving. I watch him go, then wait a few more minutes as I ogle the hotel door, waiting for him to . . . what? Realize he forgot to profess his undying love for me and jog back to my car?

Yes. I'm that much of a mess.

But since Joe isn't, the door doesn't open, and he doesn't come back and tell me we should be together.

On my way back home, I call Pippa and relay everything that happened today. Finally, I don't have to summon her into my memory. Talking to her regularly again soothes me.

"So he makes a huge romantic gesture but still wants you to know he is fucking other people?" she muses. I can hear her munching on baby carrots, her favorite snack. "Sounds to me like he's in deep denial. Now, who does that remind me of . . ." She taps her fingernail over a hard surface on the other line. "Oh, right. *You.*"

"Denial about what?" I bark. I'm about as friendly as a pet rock right now. Pippa is on the receiving end of my residual emotional carnage. That must mean we are back to being BFFs. You only dump your emotional mess on people you are close with.

"Your feelings toward Joe."

"I'm not in denial. I know damn well I'm in love with the bastard!" I punch the steering wheel, accidentally beeping at the car in front of me. The driver jerks forward automatically before realizing the light is still red. *Oops.*

Pippa laughs, delighted. "I just wanted you to hear yourself say that. Now all you need is to tell him."

"I don't think it's reciprocated." I worry my lower lip.

"I don't think it's your place to determine," she shoots back cheerfully.

"Anyway, what does it matter? I don't have the guts to be with him."

What would his parents think? What would the world think? The brother and the fiancée, finding comfort in each other's arms. This is not the truth, of course. But people never want the truth. Only the juiciest, most easily digestible narrative offered to them.

"Ah, living gutless. It worked so well for you before, didn't it?" Pippa teases. "There's no way around it, Ever. If you want to be happy— you have to take chances. You have to open yourself up to getting hurt."

"I'm scared to make a choice." My voice cracks as I round the car into my neighborhood.

"You know what's scarier?" she asks. "Not making one at all."

Joe and I stay true to our promise to focus on work during the weekdays.

He doesn't leave his hotel room. He writes nonstop. I find an artist to make Mom's gravestone and start doing research on universities in both California and Massachusetts. I bookmark them online and send them to Dad and Donna.

I spend my evenings with Joe. We go to watch a live band, we eat seafood, and we catch a movie. There's an underlying weirdness between us, but neither of us points that out. He treats me like I'm his baby sister. I treat him like he is a surly tourist. The week zips by fast. Too fast. A part of me grieves my last night with Joe. Another part of me is relieved. I'm tired of waiting for the clock to hit seven every day. Tired of counting back the hours, and the minutes, and the seconds until I see him. I'm exhausted. Of loving him in secret. Of pretending like I'm okay with what we are. With what we're not.

And it hits me, on my way to Joe's hotel. What am I doing? I have no business applying to schools in Massachusetts. If I stay in touch with him, he is going to detonate whatever is left of my heart into millions of microscopic pieces.

It is Joe's last evening. Tomorrow morning, he boards a plane back to Boston. We've both decided we'll order room service and stay in. When I arrive at his room, the food is already there, covered by silver cloches. Joe looks extra handsome. He's clean shaven, his hair still damp from the shower.

The place is a huge mess, just like his apartment. I like it. The chaos. How he thrives in it. I drop my backpack on his unmade bed and park my hands on my waist. "The room's never going to recover from your visit. You have a talent for ruining everything you touch."

"Same could be said about you," he deadpans. "Have a seat."

He cracks a bottle of wine open, then pours both of us glasses.

"Wine?" I feel my eyebrows rising. "Who are you, and what did you do to Joe?"

"I'm his evil twin, and he is currently tied up and gagged in the basement," he answers without missing a beat.

"Oh, well." I shrug. "What doesn't kill you . . ."

He laughs. "Figured we're not eighteen anymore. Might as well act our age."

"Let's not. Normal is so boring," I reply.

He hands me one of the glasses. It's a white wine. It smells fruity and oaky. I try the whole swirling and sniffing it thing but start cackling halfway through. So does Joe. Our eyes meet.

"Normal is boring," he muses. "You're right. Let's never be pretentious old fucks."

I nod. "You've got yourself a deal."

"Are we sure about getting drunk together?" I ask, taking a seat in front of the small table for two. I'm only joking. If this week has proved anything, it is that he doesn't have a lick of interest in me. Which is fine. Great. I don't *want* him to. Every time Joe and I reunite, the world around us shatters. And if he is not an option anymore . . . well, at least I won't hate myself quite as much for not acting on my feelings toward him.

He is still standing up. He is looking around the room, like there's something he wants to show me but doesn't know how to broach the subject.

"Ever?" he asks.

"That's my name."

"I finished the book."

"You . . . what?"

He crouches down to my eye level. His eyes are twinkling.

"It's done. I wrote *The End*. I even used a different font, to be fancy and shit."

"Not Times New Roman, I hope," I say, which is a dumb thing to say, but also so *us*. Dom never would have gotten it. But Joe does.

He grins. "Cambria."

I shoot up and fling my arms over him, squeaking. Wine sloshes over his shirt. We both ignore it. This is the best news. This book has been in the making for seven years. He finished it in a few short weeks. I cannot even begin to imagine what he must feel like. Even if it doesn't get published. Even if it sits on his shelf to collect dust. *He still did it.*

But then I know exactly what it feels like. Because I designed Mom's gravestone. I have finally created.

Joe pats my lower back, in a that's-enough gesture. I disconnect from him, feeling self-conscious all of a sudden. Touching wasn't a part of the deal. Not since he came here to San Francisco.

"It's just a first draft." His hands linger around my waist, but he doesn't hold me. "I'll have to spend the next few weeks polishing it."

"Doesn't matter. Now you have something to polish. I'm really proud of you."

"I couldn't have done it without you."

I know he means it, and it makes the occasion so much sweeter.

We both take a seat in front of the table again. Joe ordered us burgers and fries. My Forever Food. That's the crazy thing about us. I don't have to tell him what I like. He knows, because we love the same things. The same music, the same food, the same books. Maybe it makes sense that we keep finding our way toward one another. We're practically the same person.

"Have you decided whether you're going to stay here or come back to Salem?" He takes a juicy bite of his burger.

"No." I shift in my seat uncomfortably. "But the more I think about it, the more I realize maybe it's best if I stay here. I don't really have much going on there, and even if I move back to Massachusetts, it would be to go to college, which won't be in Salem."

"You have Nora," Joe points out, stabbing his french fry in an ocean of ketchup and mayo. "And you have me."

I smile sadly. "No offense, but I'm not moving across the country to hear about your random hookups and your day loading and unloading crates at the docks."

"Don't act like you can stay away from all those dock stories. And I'll keep my hookups to myself," he retorts, offering me a naughty smile. "I'll behave."

"Behaving is not in your nature—you said so yourself." I shake my head. "Besides, that would only make me feel more pathetic."

"Pathetic?" He frowns. "Why?"

Because I'm in love with you, but I'm too scared to be with you. Too scared to even tell you. This is the same thing as when I was eighteen all over again. Only now I've lost so much; I can't even begin to imagine what it would feel like to lose you too.

I push my food aside. I shouldn't be here. This understanding slams into me all at once. I shouldn't be keeping in touch with Joe. I'm in love with him, and we can't be together.

I stand up. "This was a mistake."

"What?" He pushes up to his feet, knocking his chair down behind him. "What are you talking about?"

"I can't do this anymore, Joe. I can't pretend that I'm your friend. It hurts too much. I like you." *I love you.* "And I know we can't be together. I respect that. Honestly, I don't even know if it's right for us. To be a couple after everything that went down. But I know if I keep in touch, it's going to keep hurting, and I will never get over you. I will never move on. I will never have a husband, and children, and a white picket fence, and an ever after. Right now, you hold my happiness in your hand. I have to turn my back on this happiness and find another."

I start making my way to the door, whirling midway to grab my backpack. I need to be out of here. I can't breathe. Joe grabs my wrist, tugging me back. I whip my head around. "Let me go."

"Can't," he hisses. His lips are barely moving. He looks strained. The struggle is plastered all over his face. This is the first time during his entire trip to San Francisco he hasn't looked relaxed and amused. This is the first time I can feel the intensity that used to zing between us every time we were in the same room. The anger. The fire. The desperation in our touch. We both tried to douse it. It didn't work.

"Why?" I bark out.

He rakes his fingers through his hair, looking down, looking *distraught*. "Because . . ."

"Because?"

"Oh, fuck it." He tosses his arms in the air. "Because I'm in love with you, Ever Lawson. I don't *like* you. I love you. Never stopped loving you. Not for one nanosecond."

My heart stammers to a stop. My mouth goes dry. He *what?*

Joe lets go of me. He starts pacing the room, a caged tiger new to captivity. He rolls his shoulders, breaking free of imaginary bonds. He looks like he wants to rip his skin off his body. Like he is allergic to this new, uncharted feeling.

"You think I enjoy being your friend?" he spits out. "It's torture! But I don't know what else to do. You're not ready for a relationship, and even if you were, I have no idea what something like that might look like. You don't even know what state you want to live in, for fuck's sake. You haven't even removed the goddamn engagement ring he gave you. Every time I see it, I'm reminded of your choice. Spoiler alert: it wasn't me."

"You weren't even an option the second time around." I'm surprised by my own words. "We both chose him to protect me."

"Yes." He breathes out. "We did. He always came first. But I burned for you every single day, Ever."

His eyes drop to the ring. I instinctively wrap my fingers around it. The ring is a souvenir from when Dom was alive, and that he loved me. That no matter what he did to me—how badly it ended—he still taught me how to live. Like a baby taking her first steps, I wobbled my way into life, and no matter how much I resent him for the way he behaved, I cannot forget how good he was to me.

"He *cheated* on you," Joe snarls. "And I had to sit there and watch you fall in love with him, knowing he was screwing another woman behind your back."

"Stop." I grab the hem of his shirt, trying to tug him to me. He shakes me off. "Stop talking, Joe."

He turns around, maintaining a safe distance from me. "Did you ever think why he stayed with you? It was why he did all things—his fear of loss. This is how screwed-up Dom was. He feared being alone more than he did being with the wrong person."

"Joe," I warn. "Joe, stop."

"Don't think that I can't live without you, Ever. I can. I just don't want to."

"Bullshit!" I cry out.

"Honest-to-God truth," he slams back.

"So why did you cut off all contact with me?" My eyes fill with tears. It was so hard to spend months of my life not speaking to him.

Joe closes his eyes, pinching the bridge of his nose.

"Because I didn't want to be your coping mechanism. Your rebound. Your designated mistake after going through something traumatic. The reason why I was so pissed with you when you left after we had sex wasn't because I had an issue with what we did to Dom. In a way, I think we'd have done him a favor. Dom was in love with Sarah. So much so he didn't have the balls to break up with her and move on. The only reason he stayed with you was because you were his plan B. It was sickening to watch both of you making a terrible choice and not being able to step in and stop you. And then he died, and through all the pain, and the guilt of being alive, of surviving, of not being able to stop it somehow, the only sliver of light was that you were both spared from having a terrible marriage. After we slept together, I felt used by you. A consolation prize. Like you screwed me just to prove a point to yourself. That you still could."

I shake my head. "I slept with you because I'd thought about you every night, ever since Christmas," I say, choking out the words. "Because I love you. God, Joe, I love you so much."

Joe's shoulders sag with relief. He shakes his head. There's still an invisible barrier between us. I'm glad it's there, humming, reminding us not to get close.

"Okay. Good. This is good. So you love me and I love you. Case closed. Move back to Massachusetts, and we'll pick up where we left off in Spain. It doesn't have to be complicated," he says.

Rubbing at my forehead, I look around the room. "What'll people think?"

"That we look cute together?" he drawls coolly.

"No one will accept us as a couple." I get flustered. "I wish things were easier. If only Dom had known that I was your Everlynne—"

"Actually, I thought about that," Joe says, cutting me off. "On the plane on my way here. I'm pretty sure he knew."

"Knew? What do you mean?"

He takes my hand and pulls me to the edge of the bed. We plop down. His eyes are sharp and alert. Maybe even a little manic.

"Dom had the memory of an elephant. Mom always joked about it. He remembered *everything*," Joe says. "Birthdays, historical dates, random people we went to school with. And I talked about you a *lot*."

"You're saying he knew who I was when we met and decided to pursue me anyway? To spite you?" Suspicion drips from my voice. Dom wasn't a saint by any stretch of the imagination, but he wasn't purposefully malicious either.

Joe shakes his head. "No. Not to spite me. I think he realized *after* the fact that you are Everlynne. *My* Everlynne. He put two and two together shortly after we met Christmas Eve."

"What makes you think that?"

"Small things that happened after Christmas. When I said I should have brunch with you and get to know you, he told me he'd tag along so you wouldn't feel ambushed. He hardly ever spoke about you around me, when before he would go on and on about you. I think the engagement was a way to make it a done deal. Dom usually wasn't one to rush into things."

I process everything that he is saying. Now that I think about it, Joe is right. Dom did seem a little off about things after we got back from his parents' after Christmas. And the proposal did come as a surprise.

Oh my God. Did Dom find out?

"But . . . why?" I whisper, feeling deflated and beaten. This makes no sense. None at all. "Why would he do this to us?"

"Because his fear of losing out was greater than his need to do the right thing—same reason why he dated both you and Sarah." He stands up and walks over to the window. "And because I think he tried to tell himself he was doing us both a favor. He'd seen how consumed I was by you for years. He'd always said I was crazy for not trying to move on. Every girlfriend, every date, I compared to you. And they all fell short. He wanted me to have a fresh start. I know this much. And Dom always thought he knew better than everyone else."

Joe works his jaw back and forth, staring onto the street pensively.

"For Chrissake, Dom!" Joe picks up the switchboard phone on the nightstand beside him, unplugs it, and hurls it across the room. It explodes into three pieces on the wall, landing on the floor. I start crying. I've never been so hurt by someone, and I can't even face Dom. I can't tell him he is a dirtbag and an asshole and a cheat. He would be the worst thing that happened to me if he hadn't brought Joe back into my life.

I'm lying in the bed, burying my face in my arms, weeping now. Joe's raspy voice floats somewhere above my head.

"I thought you two were close. That you got along." My voice is muffled as my lips move over the hard industrial linen of the hotel bed.

"We were all of those things. But ultimately, it didn't matter. Even though Dom was the golden child—the overachiever, the prom king—I had something he never had. I was the healthy one. I was the one my parents didn't have to worry about. I took my health for granted. I *smoked* in front of him. I drank excessively. We loved each other to death. We had the kind of closeness that only happens when you know you can lose someone. We went camping together and went to games together and became neighbors and hung out at least a few times a week. But ultimately, he still thought he deserved you more than I did. In his eyes, he'd paid his dues. He walked around with an inner clock that was always ticking, reminding him his time on this earth was limited."

The bed dips, and I know Joe is next to me. It doesn't feel as immoral as it would have a second ago. Screw Dom. Screw him all to hell. All this time I felt guilty about him, when I should've felt glee at kissing his brother on the day he proposed.

"You're too good a guy," I sigh, rubbing at my face.

"Why do you say that?" he asks gently.

"Because you stepped aside. Reluctantly, but you did."

"Turns out good guys *do* finish last." Joe tucks a lock of hair behind my ear, shaking his head. He looks wrecked. I hate what this is doing to him. "I should've just done it."

"Should've done what?" I put my hand over his so he can't pull it away from my cheek.

"Should've just walked to you and kissed the shit out of you the day before Christmas. It was my knee-jerk reaction when I saw your face again. I chose to act civilized. In retrospect—fuck civilization."

A chuckle escapes me. I press my forehead against his and close my eyes. Our fingers lace together. He ignores the big diamond on my engagement finger. For the first time in months I do too.

"Come with me to Boston," he croaks.

Something warm swooshes in my stomach. I want to. I really do. But that's what scares me. Joe is right. I am terrified of loving him. He means so much to me; the idea of trying and failing with him is . . . paralyzing to me.

"It's not a good idea," I say.

"Why?"

"Because I still haven't figured out what I want to do with my life. My family expects some firm resolutions from me. They want to know what I'm going to do. I can't just up and leave again."

Dad is going to kill me if I pull another Ever circa 2015. Where I just left for Boston and never looked back.

"Just for a few days." He brackets my face, kissing my lips softly. Sweetly. A faint brush of a touch. My whole body breaks in shivers. It remembers. It remembers Spain, and it remembers Joe's hallway. There's a memory album of all the times we touched tucked deep inside me.

I pull away from him. "We can't have sex."

"It's not sex." He kisses my nose. "It's not even in the same *neighborhood* as sex." His lips brush my collarbone. "Sex has nothing to do with it. Just come with me for a few days. Please."

"Okay, let me talk to my dad. I'll join you tomorrow or the next day."

"No time." He grabs my hand between us and tugs me to his body. I let myself enjoy his warmth. His hardness. "Tomorrow morning. Let's go grab your suitcase. You don't even have to bring your purse. My treat."

I kiss the side of his neck. "All right, Bill Gates. That's enough. I need to head back home. Dad and Donna are going to Mexico tomorrow."

"We're really not going to have sex, are we?" Joe's face falls. His hand is pressed on the small of my back. His erection is digging into my stomach. I'm turned on. I *want* to have sex. But I feel like we've both made huge progress, and I just want to know we're not acting on instinct here because of what we just found out about Dom.

"Not even a little."

"Ever." He buries his head in my shoulder, laughing. "You're killing me."

"Okay, let's make a deal that a Graves family member can *never* say that to me, not even jokingly." I rub his back.

It makes him laugh harder. "We're dark."

"That's why we're drawn to each other."

"But the wine sucks." He pulls away, making a disgusted face.

"The wine blows!" I laugh. "I bet Damon Albarn drinks fine wine. We're Oasis. Cheap lager and crisps all the way."

"Vinegar crisps."

"I can do you one grosser." I gag. "Prawn cocktail crisps."

He is staring at me now, the way he used to, in Spain. Openly and without embarrassment. "This week was the first one in years where I've been genuinely happy."

I smile. "Me too."

"Do you feel guilty?" he asks.

"A little," I admit. "You?"

"Nope."

I don't tell him what I'm thinking. That we both just found out Dom tried to ruin our lives . . . but that we still forgive him.

Because the wound is closed, and it's time to move on.

TWENTY-SEVEN

I tell Dad and Donna that I have things to sort out in Salem.

It's not a lie per se. I *do* have things to do in Salem.

I need to notify my landlord that Nora and I are breaking the lease. To officially move out of the pigsty also known as my apartment and remove the remainder of the furniture I left there, and I also need to give the Graveses the engagement ring back.

I don't mention that I'm going to spend time with Joe. I don't have to. They know he's been in San Francisco this whole last week and can connect the dots themselves.

"Just don't let the time there cloud your judgment." Dad is standing at the door, holding his suitcase handle, looking worried. This is his way of saying, *Please don't turn your back on us again for dick.* I hear him loud and clear.

"What he means to say is, don't feel pressured to make a decision one way or the other." Donna plays the good cop, giving Dad a playful shove. "We're happy you're choosing to go back to school, no matter where you'll be."

Renn bumps his shoulder against mine, ambling toward the door. "'Kay. 'Nuff talking. Dad, Donna, go away. I'll drive Ever to SFO. Have fun. Buy us gifts. Expensive ones. Goodbye."

He slams the door in their faces.

"Rude!" Dad points out from the other side of the door, and we laugh.

Renn turns to me, all business. "You all packed, sis?"

I nod, patting the duffel bag that I'm holding. Dad and Donna's flight leaves from Oakland International Airport, so we couldn't ride together.

"Finally. I'll have the house to myself. Thank you, Big Guy." Renn winks and points at the ceiling.

"You think having the house to yourself required divine intervention?" I raise an eyebrow.

Renn sighs. "It's been really bad, Ev. These people have, like, no life at all. They're always around."

"There's a solution for that," I point out.

"Already thought about it." Renn shakes his head. "I love them too much to kill them and make it look like a suicide pact."

I laugh. "I mean rent an apartment, you jackass."

"Excuse me?" Renn coughs, feigning shock. "This is San Francisco. I can't even rent a storage locker."

On the car ride to the airport, I ask, "Did you break up with that older chick?"

"I did, actually."

"How'd she take it?"

"Too well for my fragile little ego." He moves a toothpick around his mouth. "I think it was her wake-up call. She told me, 'Oh my God, my boy toy is dumping me. I really did hit rock bottom.'"

"She sounds like a smart cookie," I say, with all honesty. "Way too smart to be wasting time with your barely legal ass."

He chuckles. "She decided to confront her husband as a result. They had a big blowup, and now they're trying to work on their marriage. She quit her surfing lessons because her husband wasn't comfortable with her being taught by a guy who knows what it feels like to put his dick into every hole in her body."

"Surely, you could have told me this story without the last gross TMI bit."

"Totally," Renn agrees. "But where would be the fun in that? Good news is, the husband agreed to let go of the secretary he was screwing. In another universe this secretary and I hook up. I wonder if she is hot." He frowns.

"Maybe. But in this universe, you'll stick to girls your age. You know." I side-eye him. "When I lived in Salem, I used to worry that your never-ending stream of girlfriends was due to mommy issues stemming from losing Mom when you were super young."

"And what do you think now, Freud?" Renn spits the toothpick out the window, smirking.

"Now I just think you're an immature tool bag."

"See? It was a great idea to reconnect." He faux punches me on the arm. "Now you know that I'm a fuckboy, and I know that you are still a gloomy chick who overthinks everything and has the taste buds of a five-year-old."

We grin at each other as the car slows into a traffic jam leading to the airport.

"But seriously." Renn scratches at his stubble. "What do you think you're going to do after Mom's new gravestone is done?"

"Study," I say with finality. Because this is the one thing I *have* made up my mind about. I don't know where I want to live, but I want to study arts and media. I want to pursue my dreams.

"Duh. But where?" he asks.

"Don't know yet."

On one hand, California is where my family is. I have a human net to catch me here, if things go bad. On the other, I love Massachusetts. New England feels like my place. It also offers an array of really great art programs. New England is also where Joe is. Where the drug I crave the most is.

Renn pulls in front of the terminal. He doesn't have to get out of the car. I only have a duffel bag. I'll be back in just a couple of days.

"Take care of Loki." I wiggle a finger in his face.

"That bastard thinks so highly of himself; he needs to take care of me!"

"Take care of each other, then." I give him a quick peck on the cheek.

"Try not to get engaged in the few days you're spending there!" Renn calls to my back as I jog toward the revolving door. *"Again."*

I flip him the bird and disappear inside the airport.

My first stop after I land at Logan Airport is Gemma and Brad's home.

It makes sense to visit them first, because it is the part I dread the most and I'd like to get it out of the way. I splurge on a taxi ride to their house. I texted Gemma from the plane and asked if it was a good time to meet.

Gemma: It is always a good time to see you, Lynne! Of course. Come on over.

When the cab stops in front of their house, I'm bursting with trepidation. I've met the Graveses a few times after Dom passed away, but we always had a buffer. Sarah, Joe, Dad, Renn, Nora, and Colt. They were all here to take over when the conversation became stilted. Now I need to face Gemma and Brad on my own.

I tip the driver and waddle out of the back seat, holding my duffel bag close to my chest. I knock on their door twice and foolishly pray they don't open. Gemma contributes to my irrational hope by taking her time before flinging it open. But then she is here, thinner than I remembered. Her skin wraps around her bones like a spiderweb, and she looks tired, but she is still smiling.

"Lynne! Hello. You look well, my dear."

She draws me into a hug. I fall into her arms and surprise myself by not sobbing. I think I'm fresh out of tears and grief. I'm also relieved to say goodbye to Dom's engagement ring. Yes, I loved him. And maybe he loved me. But that ring didn't mean what it was supposed to mean. To either of us.

"Coming through. Coming through."

Brad maneuvers his way to the door, and that's when I notice their entrance is full of boxes. He reaches to hug me, and I squeeze him with a smile. Brad giving hugs is a new and welcome development. I wonder if he is a little less stoic, now that he's been reminded of the fragility of our existence.

"What's going on? Are you moving?" I step inside, following Gemma to the kitchen.

She waves her hand. "No, no. Joe brought over things from Dominic's apartment. I still need to unpack them."

"I'd love to help," I offer sincerely. It's going to suck, but not as hard as it would for Gemma and Brad to do it all by themselves.

"Nonsense." She flicks the kettle on as soon as we get to the kitchen. "It gives us something to do. And . . . you know, it's good to reminisce."

Her eyes shine with tears, but she doesn't let them fall. I reach over across the breakfast nook she is leaning against and hold her hand. "I know," I say.

"Joe tells me you helped him in San Francisco. He was so happy to write again. That's really kind of you." She wipes her eyes quickly.

Brad walks into the kitchen and silently tucks tea bags into mugs.

"Oh, he was a lifesaver for me too," I say. I also mean that literally.

Gemma looks like she is about to say something more but then shakes her head, as if ridding herself of an unpleasant thought.

"I made some lemon custard cookies." She pushes off the breakfast nook, opens a Tupperware, and arranges the cookies onto a decorative plate. "You take your tea with one sugar, correct?"

I nod as I sit at the breakfast nook. Gemma and Brad both approach me with the tea and cookies, nervous smiles on their faces. I take one cookie and start munching it, surprised that I can taste it. I haven't been able to taste things since Dom died.

"We wanted to apologize again," Gemma says, "for the whole ordeal with Sarah. How humiliating it must have been to both of you. I can only imagine how much more complex it made an already impossible situation."

"It's all right," I say, and I mean it. This past week, I've felt the pain brush past me, as opposed to going through me. It's like getting pushed by a stranger while hurrying to catch a train. Not like being run over by one.

"It's not," Brad says, toying with the cookie on his plate but not eating it. "But there's nothing we can do about it, unfortunately."

"Really, it doesn't matter now," I say. Then, remembering why I'm here, I hurry to remove the engagement ring from my finger. I slide it across the breakfast nook.

"Here. I want you to have it."

"Nonsense, Lynne. He gave it to you," Gemma says, but her eyes sparkle when they land on the ring. Another thing her son left behind.

"It's Ever," I correct her. It's good to claim my name— my identity—back. "And even though I'll always cherish the day Dom asked me to marry him, I need to move on. And the truth is, I think it belongs to you more than it belongs to me. It's a love song to you. He wanted to make you happy."

Gemma looks down, then starts crying. I notice it's not the same dark, hopeless sobs that tore from her body all those months ago. It's a cleansing, grateful cry. She smiles and pats my shoulder before brushing her tears away.

"Thank you, my dear. I appreciate it."

"You should try it on."

She hesitates for only a moment before going for it. It sits perfectly on her bony middle finger. She admires it, tilting her hand here and there, watching the diamond catching the last of the afternoon sunrays slipping through the big bay windows.

"It's really beautiful," she says.

"It looks right at home on your finger."

She looks up. "Are you truly doing okay?"

Nodding, I realize that I am. Things are still far from ideal, but I'm not unhappy anymore.

Gemma rubs at her cheek distractedly. I can tell something is eating at her, but she doesn't know how to approach the subject. She shoots Brad a look. He jerks his chin once, the movement barely there, to tell her to go ahead. What the hell is happening?

"Ly . . . *Ever*," she corrects, her skin flushing slightly. "I have an unusual request."

"Unusual is my expertise. Fire away."

"Can you come with me to the attic for a second? There's something I want to show you."

I follow her up the stairs to the second floor and watch as she pops open the hatch for the attic. She pulls the ladder down, and we both climb inside. It's the first time I've been in an attic. The place is surprisingly broad and unsurprisingly woody. It smells of dust and naphthalene. It is full to the brim with crates and boxes. They are all labeled. I drink it all in. The right-hand side of the attic is full of stuff with the name *Dominic* labeled on each box, and the left-hand side belongs to Seph.

I find it ironic that even the brothers' possessions look like they're having a standoff. And here I am, again, standing in the middle, between the two of them.

"Your sons sure have a lot of stuff." I try to crack the tense mood with a joke. It immediately falls flat between us. Gemma shoots me an uncertain look. Whatever she brought me here for, it is making her anxious.

I swallow hard. "Gemma? Why am I here?"

She slants her head toward the pile of Seph boxes. I follow her footsteps. She grabs a shoebox sitting atop a big cardboard box and holds it away from her body, as if it could bite her.

"I've been doing a lot of tidying up recently. Especially in the attic. It was a combination of things. I needed something to take my mind off Dominic and was also inspired by how Seph found my first-date dress in our old attic. I wanted to see what treasures I could find that would lead me to memories of Dominic."

I wait for her to continue. I'm not sure what she is holding, but since it has Joe's name on it, I can safely assume it has nothing to do with me. We didn't exchange anything in Spain. Other than bodily fluids and phone numbers, and those don't count.

Gemma smiles sadly. "Dominic was always such a sweet child. With a strong moral compass and a lot of compassion toward others. He always treated wounded animals in our backyard and was the first to approach a new kid who moved into our neighborhood. This somewhat changed after he was diagnosed with cancer. He became understandably angry. And then he beat the cancer and went back to being the Dominic we loved and adored. Then he thought he had cancer again, when he was in his early twenties."

I remember Dom telling me about it. I remember being horrified for him. I remember all of it like it was yesterday.

"Yes?" I ask her quietly, to encourage her to keep talking.

She opens the shoebox—finally—and takes out something that looks like a piece of paper. "Last week, when Seph was in San Francisco to complete his book, I started going through his things, because I was done with Dominic's side of the attic. I came across this."

She hands me a small piece of paper. Only it's not a paper. It's a photo. The Polaroid photo Joe took of me on the beach in Spain. My mouth drops open. My breath is stuck inside my throat, like a bone. My lips are puffy and my hair is a mess, and I look at the camera—at *him*—with so much emotion it makes me choke. The love I have for him is raw. The intimacy is palpable. I can *feel* this photo imprinting itself onto my DNA.

He kept it. All these years. He didn't throw it away. Didn't burn it in a small, controlled fire like I thought he would.

"The interesting thing about this photo," Gemma starts, "is that in the backdrop, you can see *Neptuno de Melenara*, the famous statue, so I knew it was taken in the Canary Islands, and by Seph. But the photo . . ." She sucks in a breath. "It looked familiar, and I realized why. I'd already seen it, on Christmas Day. Dom was holding it after he'd gone up to the attic to get his sports gear."

I shake my head, tears spilling on my cheek. "I had no idea, Gemma, I swear. I had no idea they were brothers before Christmas. And Dom didn't either. He must've found out then."

"I figured as much." She wraps her fingers around my arms, jerking me to her in a hug. "Listen now, Ever. You have to listen to me." She pulls away, holding my cheeks in her hands. We blink at each other. "Life's too short. Way too short. If you love Seph . . . if Seph loves you . . ."

She doesn't complete the sentence. She can't. Anything she says would be a betrayal to one of her sons. She is torn. Me, not so much. I no longer feel an obligation toward Dominic. I just don't know if Joe and I are each other's fate. Every time we come together, something terrible happens. I don't want any more casualties in this game of cat and mouse we play. Our love seems to be the bloodied, thorny kind. Something occurs to me, then.

"Gemma . . ."

"Yes?"

"Remember the wooden boat I got Dom?" I'm sure she does. She helped me pack his bedroom after he passed away.

Gemma nods, frowning at me. "What about it?"

"Where is it?"

She presses her lips together, her eyes downcast. Like she shouldn't tell. "Joe took it," she says, finally.

"Thank you, Gemma."

"No, thank you. For loving both my sons . . . and, although during different periods of time, making both of them happy."

The journey to Salem is a blur. When I arrive at my old apartment, Joe is waiting for me outside, sleeves rolled up to his shoulders. Flattened cardboard boxes are tucked under his arm. My heart hiccups as my eyes take in his beautiful face. I can't look at him and not think about the fact that he kept the photo. That he has endured so much from Dom, from his family, from *me*.

"You didn't have to come." I get out of the cab and give him a hug.

"Nothing beats moving your ass out of this shithole." He lifts my left hand and examines it. He notices the change right away, which means it's the first thing he looks at every time he sees me. He holds my left hand and turns it here and there. "No ring."

I lean my forehead against his shoulder. "No ring."

There is expectation in the air. I guess this is my time to say something profound. But I don't have anything to say. I'm not sure where my mind is at right now.

"Are you going to be looking at colleges while you're here?" he asks, his tone guarded this time. We've both been hurt so much.

"Actually, I'm only here for a couple days."

"Huh." He rubs at his chin. "I see."

I'm considering Tufts, Northeastern, and Boston University.

My heart tells me to tell him that the only reason I haven't decided yet is that I am scared. So, so scared to finally have him. To *lose* him.

My heart tells me to drop to my knees and beg him to help me make a decision. What would be right? What would be the least painful? If only someone could tell me that if we were together tomorrow, no one else would lose their life. No one else would suffer.

But my heart is not in charge anymore. I can't get a word out of my mouth. I can't even begin to think what to say.

"Right." Joe steps back, whipping his head around to look at the entrance door. "Shall we?"

We both walk inside. The place looks familiar and yet strange. Nora has moved all her things out at this point—the fact that she still pays half the rent is insane to me. It's just my stuff and the cursed sofa we got at the flea market together.

"I'll tackle the bedroom; you can pack the kitchen. Everything goes to charity. Other than expired food. That goes to the trash." I clap my hands together.

"No offense, Ev, but the place stinks."

"None taken." I smile. "And that makes sense. No one's been here in months."

Eight months, to be exact. Has it really been almost a year since Dom passed away?

Joe hooks his phone to his Bluetooth. The Smiths blast through the speakers.

"Morrissey!" I raise my fist in the air.

"I'd tattoo his name on my ass if he asked me. True story." Joe is already deep inside the kitchen, tossing things into a huge black garbage bag.

It is pathetic, how few things I have. Joe and I take three hours to have everything tucked away in boxes, labeled, and ready to be handed off to the nearest Salvation Army branch. We're sweaty and panting as we stand in an empty living room, save for that damn couch.

"When did you say your friend is going to pick it up?" I jolt my chin to the couch.

"Dale?" Joe glances at the time on his phone. "We still have about two hours. He works at the docks with me. Gets off at six."

Folding my arms over my chest, I look at the couch. "I used to get so mad at Nora and Colt whenever they had sex on this thing. I felt sexually harassed. Is that weird?"

Joe chuckles. "Depends. Were you *on* the couch while they were porking?"

"Aw, no."

"In that case, no harassment. Jealousy, maybe."

"You're a vile man, Joseph Graves."

"And you love it, Everlynne Lawson."

We both glance at each other, smirking. I'm the first to break the invisible barrier between us. I reach with my pinkie to touch his. It's just a brush, but it does the trick. Goose bumps roll over my skin. His cheeks pink.

"Thanks for being there for me," I whisper.

He smiles but doesn't say anything. His pinkie laces with mine. I suck in a breath. We stand like this, barely touching, the music coming from the Bluetooth bouncing against the empty walls. "This Charming Man." Such an underrated song. Joe clenches his pinkie through mine and tugs me to him. I let out a gasp, my body colliding with his. His mouth is on mine. His hands are in my hair. We are kissing like two crazed people in the middle of the empty living room, panting and moaning. He wraps his hands around me, backs me to the couch, and gives me a shove until I fall on top of it.

"What are you doing?" I ask, reaching for his belt.

"Making sure Dale gets a couch with an interesting life story."

TWENTY-EIGHT

Dale shows up for the couch. He looks about seven years old. Okay, more like seventeen. Still a baby, though. He and Joe do the bro hug and elaborate handshake.

"Where've you been, man?" Dale asks.

Joe hands him a cigarette, then ruffles his hair. "Took a little trip to Cali."

"What'd you lose there?" Dale frowns.

Joe jerks his thumb toward me. "This smart-ass. Dale, this is Ever. Ever, this is Dale."

We shake hands. I smile. It is surprisingly easy to smile after feeling Joe's weight against mine. Dale asks, "Is Ever your real name?"

"No. I just really like to be asked about it a thousand times."

Dale and Joe both laugh. I've got my sass back. This is huge. I haven't sassed in a long time.

Dale sniffs the air. "Is it just me or does the couch smell funky?"

Joe and I both conceal our chuckles with coughs. When Dale notices, he smacks Joe. "Gross, man. No way am I paying for it now."

"You weren't going to pay for it anyway." Joe slaps two twenties into his friend's hand. "Go buy that cute baby of yours something nice and tell her it's from Uncle Joey."

Dale the baby has a baby?

Dale rolls his eyes. "She's four months old. The only things she loves are bright colors and my girlfriend's tits. Which, honestly, are both awesome."

We drive back to Joe's apartment afterward. I tell him he is great for looking after Dale. His concern for the guy shines through.

"He's a good kid. A responsible one too. I like it when people show up and own up to their shit."

"High moral ground wasn't always a part of your charm." I grin. "Remember when you found a loophole for my condom problem in Spain?"

"My real solution might've made you slap me silly. I wanted in that hypothetical condom real bad."

"That makes two of us."

"Really?" He smirks. "You wanted into that condom too?"

We both laugh.

"I feel like we're in a limbo," he tells me as we slide past familiar scenery I never really paid attention to before. I lived on autopilot, waiting for life to begin when it was already happening.

"We *are* kind of in a limbo," I admit.

"Whose fault is that?"

Mine. It is all on me. And because of that, I keep silent. Unlike Dale, I don't own up or show up where Joe is concerned. I've only started doing it with my family. Baby steps, right?

Joe's nostrils flare. "I think I may be a rat."

"Excuse me?" I whip my head to look at him.

"A rat. I think I am one."

"Sorry, but you're going to have to elaborate here."

"In the 1950s, a guy named Curt Richter did a series of experiments on rats. It showed the resilience and power of hope. Basically, he threw rats into bucketsful of water and watched them drown. A group of them, he let die. Some took minutes. Some took days. But others, he offered help and support. Just when he felt that the rats were about to give up and give in, he would pull them up, giving them hope, before throwing them back into the bucket. He discovered that his hypothesis was right. Given a glimmer of hope, the rats decided to fight. They swam, mustering whatever energy was left in them to try to survive. I feel like I'm a rat. You show me a sliver of hope, and I jump at it. But I'm done jumping."

I watch him silently, unsure of what to say.

"I'm not going to wait for you forever." He speeds ahead, bypassing three cars in front of us. "At some point, I'm just going to drown."

"I know."

We order Chinese and eat it on the couch, our feet up on the coffee table. We play Jenga, and he wins. Twice. We have sex on his kitchen counter, on his couch, and in the shower. We talk about the best horror flicks ever made, and we're in complete agreement that *Get Out*, despite being fairly new, is the creepiest we've ever seen. Then we watch it together, just to make sure we don't want to change our minds. We don't.

When we go to bed, I wrinkle my nose and ask, "How many women have you . . . ahm, entertained in your bedroom?"

He looks upward, pretending to start counting them with his fingers. *One . . . two . . . three . . .*

"About thirty-five," he deadpans. "Some were entertained more than others, but almost all tried to buy a ticket for the next show."

"Manwhore." I gag.

"I prefer *sexually liberated individual*." He yanks me to him, planting a kiss on my lips. "Don't pout. Sex is a great distraction. It's a bulletproof way to forget about your worries."

"What are you so worried about?" I play with the elastic of his sweatpants. He's not wearing a shirt. We both kind of gave up on the idea of clothes in his apartment. They serve no purpose, seeing as we have sex on an hourly basis.

"*You,*" he says, clapping his hand over mine and stopping me from lowering his sweatpants. "This whole thing tastes like goodbye, and I don't like it."

I lick my lips. "I haven't made up my mind yet. I'm still looking at colleges in Boston."

"What's stopping you from moving back here?"

"What's stopping you from moving to San Francisco?" I counter.

"Nothing," he says matter-of-factly, surprising me. "San Francisco has docks, so I'll have a day job. It has publishing houses. It has you. But no one's invited me. That's my holdup."

This is my in. My chance to tell him that I want him by my side. But the fear is paralyzing. I'm scared of what our cursed relationship might result in. What if he dies too? I won't be able to survive. I won't. And now that Mom is dead, and Dom is dead, I just don't want to lose him. I'm irrationally scared something'll happen to Joe. Maybe because I know he is my only shot at happiness, I can't afford anything happening to him. Ever. Even if—illogically—giving him up means I'll never be happy.

And perhaps it is the happiness itself that scares me. The idea that I could laugh again, regularly, every day. That I would smile. That I would forget the dark past I've left behind.

This is the moment of truth, and in that moment of truth, I find that there's a part of me that's still a coward. That still wants to run and hide in an existence full of loneliness and Netflix and a cat who may very well hate me. A comforting, flatlined life where nothing dies but nothing really grows either.

"All right." I run a finger over his torso, mustering a fake smile. "I'll think about what to write on the invitation." I cup his erection. It's swollen and full in my hand. But when I try to kiss his neck, he withdraws with a cold smile.

"You do that, Ever. I'll give you some time to write it down."

He wrestles a tee onto his body, grabs his keys, and leaves.

I don't know when Joe comes back, but it is sometime in the middle of the night. When he walks inside, the room smells like it has been drenched in whiskey and cigarettes. He falls next to me on the mattress and starts snoring. I lie there, immobile and awake, my heart thudding wildly.

I want to invite him to San Francisco.

I want to be with him.

It is stupid, not to mention unreasonable, to be dismantled by something as crazy as thinking we're cursed. So irrational I cannot even articulate it to him without sounding like an idiot.

I toss and turn the entire night. My flight back to San Francisco is tonight, and I still don't know what I'm going to do. Joe expects an answer about where we stand.

Morning washes over the sky. I stand up and walk to the window, looking outside. Joe's bedroom faces the back of a market. The scents of the catch of the day, herbs, spices, and cooking rise up from the street.

I turn back around and advance toward the bed. I press my palm against his cheek. He is beautiful, warm, and alive. My heart clenches at the sight of him. It's always been like this. I never could resist the magic in Joseph Graves. And it occurs to me, depressingly, that really, I have nothing to offer to this guy. He is talented, gorgeous, and completely fantastic. He is fully baked, with his own personality, and traits, and ideas, and wishes. Me, I can barely figure out what I want to do with my life. I will only slow him down. And he would let me. Because that is the kind of guy Joe is.

I am doing him a disservice by sleeping with him, by messing with what he has left of his late brother—the precious memories they share together.

And even if I could overcome all my insecurities—which, let's admit it, is a stretch—I'm still left with one uncomfortable fact: I think something bad will happen if we become a couple.

The universe has rejected the idea of *us* over and over again. Who am I to defy it?

Quietly, and with a heavy heart, I grab my duffel bag and start gathering my things. I stop only to glance at the wooden boat he took from Dom. I know Joe didn't take it because he missed those summer vacations. He took it because of me. And the thought of breaking his heart for the second time makes my stomach turn.

When I'm done, I pick up a pen and a notepad in his kitchen and write him a message.

> Dear Joe,
>
> I'm sorry I was the bucket of water in our relationship. I'm sorry you were the rat. Most of all, I'm sorry I went with Pippa to that beach party all those years ago. Because that resulted in so much heartache for everyone we know, and two lost lives.
>
> I love you, which is why I'm leaving you.
>
> Yours, even from afar,
>
> Ever.

I close the door behind me. I take the stairs down. Waiting for the elevator seems so mundane, so trivial after what I've just done. I cut the cord. I made a decision. And I feel like shit about it.

Once I'm outside, I take an Uber to the Starbucks down the street. I need to put some distance between Joe and me. The entire journey there, I'm shaking. I'm nauseous. I want to stop a stranger walking down the street and tell them what I just did.

I walk into Starbucks and order a venti pumpkin-spice latte. I don't even like pumpkin spice. The Uber arrives and takes me to Colt's. The driver gives me a funny look through the rearview mirror and asks if everything is okay.

"Yes," I say. "Fine. Why?"

"Because you're crying . . . ?"

I touch my face. I *am* crying.

"Sorry." I wipe my eyes quickly.

When I get to Colt's, I buzz the doorbell to his swanky building. It's seven in the morning. He answers after the fourth buzz.

"Goddammit. I'm calling the police, punk."

"Hello to you too," I drawl. There's a pause on the other side. Even at my worst, I'm always down for some rough banter with Colt.

"Ever?" he asks in disbelief.

"Who else is going to show up at your door a crying mess before the birds are up?"

He buzzes me in. No questions asked. I take the elevator up and knock on his door with my duffel bag and swollen eyes. He flings the door open and takes me in. He is wearing flannel pajamas and a frown.

"Nor's still asleep. Come on in." He jerks his head. I follow him inside. He flicks the coffee machine on. Oh, shoot. I never even bothered to take the damn latte from Starbucks. I'm such a mess.

Colt takes one good look at me and realizes what I'm thinking. "I'd better wake up Nor. Wait here."

He hustles to the bedroom. In the meantime, I look around, marveling at Nora's new life. It's a beautiful apartment, complete with stainless steel appliances, custom cabinetry, and a sundeck. It is as far away from our shithole as humanly possible. And she gave all of this up for the longest time just because I was around.

Nora appears in the hallway, rubbing at her eyes. "Hey, babe! I thought we had a ten o'clock brunch date."

I suck in a breath. "I broke up with Joe."

"Oh, honey!"

The waterworks start again, and Colt, who's just come back from the bedroom, winces and says, "This is my cue to go grab some breakfast. You wait here, ladies."

He goes downstairs in his flannel pants and a hoodie, all to avoid the cry-fest.

Nora gathers me into her arms and kisses my temple. "I didn't even know you guys were together. Why did you do that? You're crazy about the asshole."

"He's better off without me."

"What a foolish thing to say."

I pull away. "No, Nora, I mean it. Our relationship is cursed. Every time we get together, something happens. Mom. Dom. And what if something happens to him? I'll never be able to live with myself."

She stares at me, aghast. "You've got to be kidding me. That's nonsense and a half."

Because I don't want to be a party pooper, and because really, there is nothing more to say, I force a smile and tell her, "I love this place."

Her face lights up immediately. "Right? Isn't it awesome?" She looks around, too, trying to see it from my eyes.

"Yes. When's the wedding?"

"April. Cherry blossom season. We're going big, baby."

"How can I help?" I ask, because frankly, that's what you're supposed to do when a good friend of yours tells you they're getting married in a few months.

"Well, actually, we were thinking of doing something a little special for the invitations, and I know you have a talent for sketches and such . . ." She smiles, color rising in her cheeks.

I'm momentarily speechless before gaining back my eloquence and saying, "Oh my God, yeah. Of course. It'll be my pleasure. My honor!" I correct myself.

She claps excitedly. "Thank you."

"That will be five hundred bucks for the design."

Her smile drops. I snort out a laugh and push her. She pushes me back. "Asshole."

The door flings open, and Colt walks inside with a paper bag full of something fried and greasy by the smell of it. "Ladies, I'm home."

He stops when he sees us holding each other's hands. We look giddy and excited. He turns to Nora, perplexed. "How did you do that?"

"How did I do what?" she asks.

"Make her happy and . . . I don't know, not crying anymore?"

I laugh. "She hired my services as an artist. I'm making your wedding invitations. Are you scared?"

"Only if you're going to put skulls and graves on them." He makes a face. Then, when he gets nothing from me, he says, "Please don't put any skulls and graves on them."

"There goes my creative freedom." I sigh.

"What's the damage?" He turns to ask her.

"This one's on the house," I say. "Least I can do after all the money Nor spent on rent."

I burn the entire day with Nora and Colt, and they drive me to the airport when it's time for my flight. Spending time with them was the best thing I could do, because it distracted me from Joe. But now that I'm at the airport, checking in, I look at my phone and realize that Joe hasn't called. He hasn't texted either. But everyone else in my life has.

Dad: Renn will wait at the airport to pick you up. Call me when you land.

Donna: I hope it went well. Let us know if you need anything.

Renn: Tell the pilot not to be late. It's pizza and poker night at Clayton's.

I answer all three of them and walk around the terminal. I haven't gone through security yet. Something stops me. I know exactly what that something is. Joe.

Some part of me still expects the coin to flip on our fate again. I pray for one perfect movie moment where Joe chases me at the airport and professes his love for me. When I close my eyes, I can almost see him. Running frantically, catching me in his arms, going down to one knee . . .

You're not a burden, Ever. And I don't care that you don't know what to do with your life yet. I love you just the way you are. We are not cursed. We'll make it work, you hear me?

But this is not a movie, and it doesn't happen. Nor should it. My own hypocrisy is not lost on me. From the get-go, from our time in Spain, Joe was the one to save me, to take care of me, to court me, to never give up on me. He was the one who wanted to work together. Create together. He was the one to come to San Francisco. In some ways, I became a bit of a rat too. Addicted to my next fix. To being desired and assured that he was still here, chasing me, loving me, fighting for me.

Joe deserves better. He deserves someone who is willing to fight for him, because he is worth fighting for. More than anything, he deserves a girl who wouldn't let something like a crippling, illogical fear of being a curse get in her way.

And that girl is not me.

Because I fully believe I am cursed.

It's when I go through security that I start to realize the magnitude of my mistake. Of leaving the way I have. Without talking it through. *Again.*

I pull out my phone and type him a message.

Ever: I think I made a terrible mistake.

One minute passes. Then two. Then twenty. He doesn't answer. His words from yesterday hit me somewhere deep.

At some point, I'm just going to drown.

Maybe the final casualty in our affair is Joe's hope.

"Ma'am? Do you mind putting your phone in the bin?"

The request snaps me out of it. I remove my shoes and go through the scanner. Collect my things. I make my way to my gate in a daze. When I reach it, I take a seat and stare at my phone. I start typing again. I can't help myself.

Ever: Spoiler alert: I'm about to sound like a world-class wuss.

Ever: I thought you would come chase me at the airport.

Ever: You know? Like in the movies?

Ever: They're always the best part in chick flicks. Casablanca. The Graduate. When Harry Met Sally. Almost Famous.

Ever: (Yes. I'm listing them chronologically because I know you will appreciate it).

Ever: (And yes, I know I left out Love Actually. I wasn't sure if you'd watched it. There are still so many things I don't know about you).

Ever: I just needed an assurance that our relationship is not cursed.

Ever: Because the truth is, I feel so unequipped to be with you. And I'm terrified something bad would happen if we get together again. That seems to be the pattern.

Ever: I'm done now. You are welcome for this pile of crap-tastic spamming.

Ever: Actually, I have one more thing to say—I'm really sorry. For everything.

By the time I board the plane, he still hasn't answered.

TWENTY-NINE

If I had to describe the flight back to San Francisco in one word, I would probably choose *excruciating*. If I had to choose two—*fucking excruciating*. Out of all the right decisions I have made this year, including, but not limited to, moving back to San Francisco, reconnecting with Dad and Renn, deciding to go back to school, giving the engagement ring back to Gemma—the one decision that mattered the most is the one I screwed up.

"Ten minutes to landing," the captain announces. Numbness washes all over me. The finality of my decision hits me with full force.

No more Joe. He said he was done chasing and fighting. He meant it.

"It's true." I press my forehead to the cool window, closing my eyes. "I have made a terrible mistake."

"You think?" The guy sitting beside me belches. "To me it looks like you made the right choice, opting out of that sketchy airplane food. I'm starting to regret that tuna sandwich."

I turn to look at him. He looks to be around fifty. Balding, with a suit and an easy smile. "Yikes. Did it have any mayo in it?"

"Fraid so."

"Expect a challenging forty-eight hours."

He nods in agreement. "That's my regret. What's yours? Why did you make a terrible mistake?"

"I broke up with the love of my life because of my insecurities. It's not the first time I've walked away from him. I feel like this is the straw that broke the camel's back. Rather, this is the point where the rat has been drowned." Joe's analogy pops into my head.

The guy *tsks*: "Rodents are a toughie."

"This one especially." I sink into my seat, getting more and more anxious by the minute.

"Do you love this rat?"

"Yes."

"Do you think this rat loves you back?"

Not anymore, considering my behavior these last seven years.

"I hope so."

"Only one way to find out if it really drowned, then. Take it from a divorce lawyer who has seen enough almosts in his lifetime. There is one bulletproof plan to finding out if your beau wants you or not."

"Well?" I ask expectantly.

"Ask him."

"But . . . but . . ." I can't believe the words are about to come out of my mouth. "I'm cursed, you see? My mom died trying to save me from getting hit by a train. And then my fiancé died buying tampons for me, even though I didn't even *need* tampons. Sorry, sorry." I wave my hands around, flustered. "TMI. Point is, anyone who gets close to me suffers."

"Anyone?" The man raises his eyebrows, clearly skeptical. "I should think there are more people around you than just the two of them. What about your dad? Your siblings? Your friends? *Their* friends?"

"Well—"

"Your coworkers? Extended family? What about your high school boyfriend? And the one that came after him? What about this plane? It's about to land safely, isn't it? I don't know, missy. Seems to me like you've attributed to yourself superpowers you can't really back up."

He is right. For every Mom and Dom, there are Dad and Donna and Joe and Renn living their best lives. Who am I to deem myself a dark, awful curse?

And maybe there was a dark, awful curse, but it wasn't necessarily what happened to Mom and Dom. Maybe the curse is the way I view everything. Through dark-tinted glasses of doom and gloom. Maybe the curse is the way I view the world. My fear of happiness.

What happened to Mom was horrible, yes. But it was an accident. And Dom had been living on the edge for a very long time, with or without me.

And look at everything else. I thought Dad and Renn hated me for years, when they actually longed for a relationship with me. I thought Dom was a good idea. That I didn't deserve Joe.

"Well?" The man beside me belches again. "Are you going to ask this rat if he likes you, or what?"

"Yes," I hear myself say. "I will. Immediately."

The penny drops with a *clink* just as the wheels of the plane hit SFO's tarmac.

California has my soul, but Massachusetts has my heart.

And I can no longer ignore my heart's desires.

I understand Joe. He is tired. Tired of chasing me. Tired of taking chances on me. Tired of hopping on planes for me. For the first time, the fact that he is letting me go sinks in. *Really* sinks in. And along with it an epiphany—I cannot live without him.

He once said he can live without me. He just doesn't want to. But I cannot go through life without seeing him. Without kissing him. Without hearing his thoughts about the most mundane things that happen to us in the world.

I got it all wrong. He was not the one who was supposed to chase me through the airport. It was me who was supposed to go after him.

We're not cursed. This is not the way I should be looking at it at all. On the contrary. Despite everything that happened, we always found our way to one another. If anything, we're a miracle. We *should* be together. How many people in this world get a second, third, and fourth chance?

The universe is not keeping us apart. It is bringing us together. Again, and again, and a-god-damn-gain.

I have to go to him.

I *have* to tell him how I feel.

No, he already knows how I feel. I have to tell him he is out of the limbo. That the rat has been pulled from the bucketful of water and thrown to safety.

I've made a choice.

I choose him.

The doors to the airplane open, and people trickle into the airplane sleeve. I push through the busy line of travelers on the plane. Shoving past passengers trying to get to their overhead baggage.

"Coming through. No time. Please get out of the way."

Normally, the epiphany happens *before* you get on a plane. Sometimes it's right on the plane, if you're going for super original. But not once have I seen a movie or a show where the dumbass heroine actually makes it to her destination, leaves the airplane, then walks right back to the American Airlines stand.

Yes, here I am, slapping the counter, breathless and sweaty. "I need a one-way ticket to Logan Airport. The earliest you've got. There's no time to waste."

The woman behind the counter obviously begs to differ. She looks up from her blanket of fake eyelashes, quirks a well-drawn eyebrow, and leisurely types something as she gazes at her screen. She seems deliberately slow. Is this how murderers are born? By telling people something is urgent and then watching said people slugging along?

"You said Logan International Airport?"

"Hmm."

Hmm? What kind of answer is that?

I try to appeal to her heart. "Please. It's urgent. I have to get there fast."

"And I have to get out of my tights, ma'am," she says impatiently. "We all have things to do. Please be patient."

It takes her a couple of more minutes—*of course* her computer chooses this exact moment to choke to death—before announcing, "There's a flight leaving out tomorrow morning. Six o'clock."

"No, no." I shake my head, frantic. "I need something sooner."

"You're out of luck. I have nothing for you."

"Please," I choke out. I'm not above begging. "I really don't want to turn around and leave this airport. I have to go back."

She rolls her eyes, then types something into her keyboard. She nods at the screen, like it is talking to her. "There's a flight boarding in forty minutes. But I only have one seat left."

"Yes! I'll take it! I'm one person!"

". . . it's business class. Twenty-five hundred dollars."

"Oh." I falter before squaring my shoulders. "Yes. I'll take it."

No big deal. It's just a month's worth of work for me. On a job I don't currently hold. I hand the ticket agent my credit card and pray to God the payment isn't declined. I hold my breath as she waits for the confirmation to go through. Then sag in relief when the ticket starts printing.

She hands it to me, still stoic. "Better make a run for it, or your plane will leave without you."

I run like my ass is on fire. Until I get to security, where I cut the line and explain my situation, frantic and blabbering, to people who protest. Then I run to the gate. Then I run *into* the plane. And what do you know, I'm on another five-hour flight to Boston.

Only this time, I don't stew on all the things I've done wrong. I think about ways to make them right.

Also, can we talk about how tragic it is that the first and probably last time I'm in business class, I'm too distracted to even take in my surroundings?

I bring my family up to speed in a chat group I create. Consisting of Donna, Renn, Dad, and myself.

Ever: I'm on a plane back to Boston.

Renn: Why? Did you forget your charger there?

Renn: J/k. WTF?

Dad: I second your brother's (less than eloquent) question.

Ever: I need to do something.

Donna: Could you please be a little less cryptic?

Ever: I need to win Joe back.

Donna: We are proud of you! (and slightly worried . . .)

Dad: Let us know when you land.

Renn: Young love is such a drag. No wonder I want nothing to do with it.

◆ ◆ ◆

It's early morning by the time I land at Logan International Airport. Weak rays of sunshine pierce through the clouds, making them look like fluffy pincushions. I feel like I haven't slept in years. My muscles hurt. My heart beats dully. Still, I've never been as ready to do something in my life.

I make my way to the taxi lane. Somewhere over the last twenty-four hours, I've lost my duffel bag, and I don't even care. I have my wallet with me, and that's all I need. Once I slide inside, I give the woman Joe's address. It's five in the morning, and I think I just might catch him before he goes to work if the driver goes over the speed limit.

"Salem, huh? That's some ride," she says.

"I'll double your pay if you floor it," I tell her from the back seat, yet again channeling my inner Bill Gates. I'm feeling ballsy with my bank account today.

The middle-aged lady eyes me curiously across her shoulder. "Tell you what. How 'bout I don't get us both killed, and you take a long, deep breath?"

"That's fair," I mumble. Meg Ryan would've charmed her into agreeing, but whatever.

Traffic from the airport is painfully slow. Then we get into Salem, and there is construction work on the main road. I get to Joe's apartment building half an hour later than I hoped to. I hit the buzzer, but no one answers. I'm pretty sure he doesn't want to see me anyway. Unfortunately for him, he doesn't have a choice.

I pull out my phone and call Gemma, well aware that it is way too early for social calls. She answers on the fourth ring but sounds wide awake.

"Hi, Ever, is everything okay?"

She sounds completely unaware of my drama with Joe. Figures. He isn't big on sharing.

"Yes. I mean, no. I don't know yet." I shake my head. "I was hoping to reach Joe, but I'm trying him at his apartment and he's not answering."

"Well, he's most likely at work by this hour. He starts very early," Gemma says reasonably. "Why don't you try him there?"

"Okay. Yeah. I should." There's an awkward pause before I ask, "Where does he work on the docks, exactly?"

She gives me the address at Pickering Wharf Marina, and I write it down on the back of my hand before calling an Uber.

It's yet another journey, but this one is quick and relatively painless. I spend the ride trying to flatten my hair into submission and get rid of the sleep from around my eyes.

Then finally—*finally*—I'm there. I hop out of the Uber and run toward a cluster of trucks and cargo containers. There are people around wearing orange hard hats and matching safety vests.

"Joseph!" I call out to a few of the men there, completely out of breath. "I'm looking for Joseph Graves. Or just Seph. Or just Joe."

They lift their eyes from the clipboard one of them holds and scan me. They must think I'm crazy. They're not completely off base.

"You want Joe?" one of them asks.

"Yes," I say. "God, yes. Wanting him is an understatement." But maybe I should save this declaration for the man I came here for, and not this random person. The guy lifts one eyebrow, obviously reassessing if he should disclose his colleague's whereabouts. For the first time in my life, I feel unabashedly myself. Free and unhinged.

"Who's asking?"

"His late brother's fiancé." I pause. "Oh! And his ex-girlfriend." I stop and frown. "Hopefully, his current girlfriend too. If things go right for me."

One of the men turns to the other two. "I knew he liked eccentric, but this is laying it on thick."

They laugh. I don't care. I just want to find him.

Finally, the guy with the clipboard tilts his chin toward the water. "See the forklift over there?"

"Yeah."

"He's inside. Good luck catching his attention. He listens to rock music on full blast."

I jog there with a huge smile on my face, because it is such a Joe thing to do. Listen to angry music while lifting heavy shit. I catch a glimpse of the yellow forklift before I see Joe. The closer I get, the more he comes into view. He looks miserable, his frown deep, his lips flat. He's never been more beautiful in his life. He's on the dock, in front of a ship, unloading giant crates. I'm about to approach him when a woman steps between the forklift and me.

"Excuse me, this is private property."

"I understand, but see this guy behind you?" I point over her shoulder. "He is the love of my life, and I need to tell him that."

I am bursting with excitement, expecting her to *Aww* and *Why didn't you say that?* To get out of my way. Can someone please finally grant me one perfect movie moment?

"Who, Joe?" She throws a look at the forklift, popping her gum. "Well, you can tell him that from where you're standing. No trespassing, ma'am. We're unloading expensive things here."

"Seriously?" I growl. "I'm not going to steal anything."

"And I wasn't going to eat an entire sleeve of RITZ Crackers yesterday. But then I did. Fickle is human nature. Stay here and call him."

When I see there is no reasoning with her, I resort to acting fully insane. I guess I deserve it, after everything I've put Joe through.

I cup my mouth and go at it.

"Joe! Joseph!"

He doesn't hear me. He has massive headphones on.

"Joe! Hey! Over here! Joe! Joe!"

I start jogging in a line parallel with the direction the forklift takes. He continues about his day, oblivious. Lifting crates with the forklift. Putting them somewhere else. Then again. And again.

"Joe! Hey! Hey!"

I'm aware of the dozens of pairs of eyes looking at me in amusement. Every longshoreman around who isn't Joe has caught up on the fact that I am trying to grab his attention. I continue jogging in the same line as Joe, my eyes on him, until I collide with a huge crate and fall on the ground.

"Aww."

That, of all things, gets his attention. Maybe it was the thud I made as I hit the metal crate. Joe pushes one headphone down and turns his head. He squints, then frowns. I don't think he is too happy to see me. My heart sinks.

"Ever?" he asks coldly.

"Joe!" I moan.

I'm still lying flat on the ground. Joe turns off the forklift but doesn't make a move toward me. I have a feeling he still suspects I came here just to tell him in another creative way that we can never be together. I get up and dust myself off, ignoring our growing audience and the embarrassment I must be causing him.

"Joe, I came back." I open my arms in the air, smiling like an idiot.

"I can see that." His expression is grim.

"Can we talk?"

He raises an eyebrow. "Are you not going to run off on me in the middle of our chat? It seems to be your expertise."

"Burn." The woman who gave me trouble laughs.

I shake my head, knowing I deserve all of this and more. "I promise not to run away unless you try to kill me, which . . . honestly? I wouldn't blame you for doing. Even then, I'd give you a head start."

"The bad news is you're not out of the doghouse. But my interest is piqued." He hops off the forklift, knotting his arms over his chest.

He sounds cold. Distant. Gone. I can't blame him. I have been an absolute nightmare to love. And he loved me anyway.

"I bought a first-class ticket here." I chuckle awkwardly, covering my face with my hands.

"All right." He quirks a brow. "Brownie points for determination. *Why?*"

"Why!" I laugh to myself, frantic, and desperate, and so far gone for him. "Because I love you. Because I don't want to lose you again. Not ever again. I read about that Curt Richter experiment on my way here," I tell him. "And I know all about the rats. The wild rats fought for their survival. They were savages. They didn't give up. You're my rat, Joe. I want you to be my rat. I promise not to land you in deep water ever again. From now on we'll swim together."

I'm searching his face. All I care about is his reaction, not the massive public declaration I've just made. He blinks a few times, taking me in. He is still by the forklift. A good twenty feet away from me, at least.

"How is this time different from all the others?" he insists. "How do I know you won't walk away tomorrow? Or the day after? Or in a month? I can't do this anymore, Ever. I can't put my heart in your slippery hands."

"They're no longer slippery!" I half beg, throwing my arms upward. "I swear. Sturdy as a surgeon's. My only hang-up wasn't about loving you—there was never any doubt in my mind that I loved you. It was about sparing you from the heartache of being with me. I thought I was cursed or something and didn't want you to . . . I don't know, I didn't want anything happening to you, I guess. Like Mom and Dom."

Every single person staring at us looks lost, entertained, and a little disturbed on Joe's behalf. Joe, himself, looks mostly exhausted.

"Ever, you've put me through hell."

"I know."

"And you chose my brother over me."

346

"No. No, I didn't. I never would have moved forward with the wedding; I can see that now. I *know* this in my bones, Joe. It was always you. Always."

"You've been flaky, indecisive, and torn about me from the get-go."

"Whoa." I lift my hands up in the air. "That part's not true. I've always loved you. I was just not always sure that love was enough to get over our obstacles. But I am now. I'm sure."

"One hundred percent?" he asks.

"One hundred and ten," I assure him.

There's a beat of silence. Clipboard Guy throws his hands in the air. "For Pete's sake, kiss her already. We have three more deliveries to unload before ten!"

With a rush of laughter, Joe runs toward me, and I run toward him—yes, trespassing—and we crash together, our lips finding one another. The kiss gets salty, fast. With my tears. With his tears. We laugh into it, our teeth knocking together. I haven't brushed my teeth in twenty-four hours, but I doubt he cares. Being awkward and a little gross around him seems to be the theme, and I'm embracing it.

"I'm sorry," I tell him. "I'm really sorry."

"For what?" He can't stop kissing me.

"All of it. I should've always chosen you. I should've never turned my back on you. Even when Mom died."

"Good thing I know how you can make it up to me." He picks me up by the backs of my thighs, laces my legs around his waist, and carries me away from the wharf.

Clipboard Guy is yelling after him that his shift has just started, but Joe and I both know that he is handing in his resignation before the day is over.

"How do I make it up to you?" I murmur into his mouth.

"Never leave again."

EPILOGUE

One year later.

"Don't be nervous." I press my cheek against Joe's back, embracing him from behind. He fumbles with the nicotine gum pack in his hand before popping two into his mouth.

"What the hell is *nervous*, anyway? The word sounds familiar. Alas . . ."

This is the biggest lie he's ever told me. The *only* one he may have told me in our lifetime. Because in a few short minutes, we are both going to leave this hotel room, take the elevator down to the Vine, a swanky restaurant in one of New York's most prestigious hotels, and celebrate his book release with an official dinner.

For Ever will be published tomorrow—Tuesday—and available in all major retailers. It has a new title, a gorgeous cover, and front-to-back superlatives from the biggest newspapers.

"Of course you're not." I turn him around, making him look me in the eye. "I'm just projecting."

"That you are." He kisses me softly as he collects my face in his big palms. He tastes of nicotine gum. "Shit. I hate not smoking."

"And I hate the idea of you dying on me from cancer." I tug at his tie playfully, biting on his lower lip. "So deal."

It was on the second anniversary of Dom's death that Joe decided to quit smoking to honor his brother's fight against cancer. It's been three months now, and Joe is still bitter about the whole thing.

I pick up the book sitting on the nightstand next to us. *For Ever* is literary fiction with a dash of mystery, a few twists and turns, and a lot of self-search. Joe changed the hero's name to Ever—*Everett*—but every time I think about the new title, I know that it was a nod to me. We helped each other create when birthing something new seemed as wild as learning how to fly.

I run my palm over the hardcover. It's blue and red, with the New Orleans landscape in the background. "I love everything about this book."

"Of course you do." Joe kisses my cheek, then takes the book and shoves it into a drawer. He is still embarrassed to call himself an author. "It is an elaborate love letter to you."

"It's about a guy who has one year to live, and he fucks the entire world in the process." I frown.

"Yeah, well." Joe waves a hand. "All the rest of it."

We go down in the elevators. A maître d' greets us at the front of the Vine. A black-and-gold room with elevator music and utensil-clicking sounds. Joe's fingers float over the small of my back, which is exposed through a backless black dress. The hostess shows us to a long table, where, already waiting, are Gemma, Brad, Dad, Donna, Renn, Sarah, her *husband*, Rich, Nora (happily married), Colt (obviously ditto), and Pippa, who brought along a brand-new boyfriend whose name I refuse to remember until he passes the three-week test.

There is also Joe's agent, Bianca, and a suit from his publishing house, who came with his wife and a monstrous stack of books for Joe to sign.

When they see my boyfriend, they all stand up and clap. Our table draws curious glances from other diners. I take Joe's hand and raise it in the air in triumph, because it is a huge win that he managed to get his book published. He has already signed another book deal with the same publisher.

The *New York Minute* called *For Ever* "evocative and wild." The *Flying Pen* said, "Joseph Graves is a master storyteller," and *Books Tribune* called the novel "exhilarating and unforgettable." Joe may be too humble to see himself as a successful author, but I, an (almost) objective observer, can tell he is already there.

"I still can't believe I'm sleeping with a literary god," I murmur into Joe's ear as we proceed to our place at the table. He is shaking hands with people and whispers back through a tightly woven smile, "I can't believe it either. Who are you cheating on me with?"

I laugh and yank him down to sit next to me, but he remains standing. I look up at him. He picks up a bottle of wine and pours a glass for me and a glass for him. Then he grabs his glass and clinks a fork over it.

"Is there a speech?" Brad asks, midbite into the complimentary baguette.

"There must be a speech." Gemma wrenches the rest of the bread from between her husband's fingers.

"Please tell me it's going to be short. I'm *starving*." Renn slumps in his seat. "My body's still on the Pacific time zone. I think I missed, like, two meals."

"Patience, kiddo." Joe points at Renn with his wineglass. "And there is no speech. Just a realization I would like to share with you a minute before this book comes out and I officially become a national embarrassment."

We all wait to hear what he has to say. *For Ever* is dedicated to Dominic. It was Joe's idea. Once the anger and disappointment had made their way through our systems, acceptance and forgiveness came next. Not that Dom had a chance to ask for any of those things. But see, forgiving people who hurt us is not about those people at all. It is about choosing to move on with our lives. Letting go of the grudges. Healing without depending on someone else's journey.

"Well, I'm not getting any younger," Pippa points out with a sweet fake smile, raising her cocktail in a toast. "Give us the deets, Joe."

Joe looks down at me and smiles. My heart expands in my chest. I'm so proud of us. Of the road less traveled we have both taken to get here. We still haven't reached our final destination, but wherever we go—we're going together.

He opens his mouth, his eyes zeroing in on mine.

"The past two decades have been a crazy ride from start to finish. A lot has happened. But one thing stayed through it all. It made it possible, even when things seemed *im*possible. And that thing is called hope. Hope made me realize something important. The one thing that makes a person rich is not their money, or their talent, or even their connections. It is their hope. Where there is hope, there is life. And where there is life, anything is possible. I owe my hope to one special person. She is here today, and I have a feeling she'll be here for a very long time. Which is good, because no one knows what tomorrow will bring. All I know is that tomorrow, life is going to change. Not only for me. *For Ever.*"

Joe and I live in San Francisco. I attend Berkeley. I study art and design and have an Etsy shop where I sell custom-made sketches. I've moved on from designing gravestones, although I do that, too, on commission. I also draw characters, caricatures (especially of rock stars), and more. I'm at no risk of getting rich from the gig, but it keeps my bank account from being completely empty. There is something incredibly empowering about making a living by doing what you love, so I focus on being grateful for that.

Joe has recently quit his job as a longshoreman. He now works from home. Which is great, because I study long hours, and someone needs to be there for Loki to stare at with deep disapproval. We live in a tiny studio apartment, but it is ours, and we love it.

One day, I get back to the apartment to find a Post-it Note on the fridge. It entails a simple instruction.

Drive to the cemetery to see your mom.

It is written in Joe's handwriting. Which is great, because I'm still listening to true-crime podcasts, and I'm still worried someone is going to murder me in a totally unexpected way.

I take my keys, kiss the top of Loki's head, and drive to Half Moon Bay. It's Friday night, and traffic is a mess. I put Duran Duran's "Save a Prayer" on the stereo, because it was Mom's favorite song and (still) arguably the best song in the world. Ever since I moved back to San Francisco, I have visited her every couple of months. We have great conversations. One sided but great nonetheless.

I resist the urge to call Joe on my way there. Knowing him, he wouldn't pick up anyway. That's the drawback of having an acerbic, mostly detached boyfriend. I know I am the love of his life . . . but I also know that he is a stubborn son of a gun.

When I get to the cemetery, I find that the parking lot is even emptier than usual. After grabbing a parking spot, I get out of the car and start making my way to Mom's grave. I look left and right as I cross the street. I'm so confused. Everything looks the same. Joe is nowhere in sight.

I stop by my mother's tombstone and scan the new design I made by myself. It is incredibly detailed. It is the shape of her arm—the arm that cradled me, that wiped my tears off, that pulled me to safety when I fell onto the rails—and it is tattooed to its last inch, just like Mom's arm in real life. The design is so unique, so comprehensive. Dad says he gets asked about it *all* the time.

"Hey, Mom." I perch on a patch of grass by her grave. "Any idea where Joe is?"

Even when she doesn't answer, I can feel her presence. I shake my head, rolling my eyes. "No, we didn't have a fight. He asked me to come here. What the heck?"

I pull out my phone to call him. I'm swiping the screen when I hear a voice behind me.

"Your turn."

I whip my head around. Joe is standing there, among the graves. The most beautiful Graves I have ever seen. In a peacoat and with tousled hair.

"My turn?" I swivel to him fully. There is not enough air, not enough oxygen for me to fully function.

"To save me."

"How?" I want to know. I think I *might* know, but I want to hear it.

His face breaks into a heartbreaking smile of the Joe Graves variety. "Be my forever, Ever. Be my wife. The mother of my children. The person I file joint taxes with. I want it all. The good and the bad. The boring and the interesting. And the in between, which we will determine ourselves."

I know what he is asking, even if he doesn't go down on one knee.

Even when he doesn't produce a ring.

Even when we are both as still as the gravestones we are surrounded by.

In another world, in another universe, we'd have been married. Maybe even with a kid. In another universe, maybe Mom would still be with us. Maybe tonight, we'd be having dinner while she babysat our child. And then there's *another* world. One where Joe and I went our separate ways. One where Joe is asking someone else to marry him right about now—maybe Presley—and I'm sitting in my room, rearranging my album collection and still hating my life.

There are so many versions to reality. All of them dictated by the slightest decision. But right now, I know I made the right one.

I reach my arm between us, opening my palm. Guiding him to safety.

"Come with me," I say, paying him back for all those years when he saved me from drowning. "There's another chapter in our story I want to write."

ACKNOWLEDGMENTS

This book was terrifying to write, but I'm happy I wrote it nonetheless, because it threw me out of my comfort zone. Change is a scary place, but it is the only place where you can grow, especially as an artist. I'm incredibly grateful for the support and the encouragement from the following people who helped me in this journey:

Tijuana Turner, Vanessa Villegas, and Ratula Roy, for reading and rereading this book over and over again. Yamina Kirky, Marta Bor, Sarah Plocher, Pang Theo, Jan Cassie—you ladies are my ride or die. Special thanks to Parker and Ava, who chanted YES, YOU CAN every time I thought I couldn't. There's a slight chance you were right.

Huge thanks to my agent, Kimberly Brower, at Brower Literary, and Tijuana Turner and Jill Glass for being PR superstars. A lot of thanks go to Caroline Teagle Johnson and to the amazing editorial team at Montlake, who are an absolute delight to work with, including Anh Schluep, Lindsey Faber, Cheryl Weisman, Bill Siever, and Elyse Lyon.

Most of all, and as always, I would like to thank my readers. In an ever-changing world, there is one constant I will never take for granted—you. Thank you for taking a chance on my books. I appreciate it from the bottom of my heart.

L.J. Shen

PREVIEW: TURN THE PAGE FOR A SNEAK PEEK OF *PLAYING WITH FIRE*: A ROMANTIC STAND-ALONE

PROLOGUE

GRACE

The only thing to remain completely untarnished after the fire was my late momma's flame ring.

It was a cheap-looking ring. The type you get in a plastic egg when you shove a dollar into a machine at the mall. Grandma Savvy said Momma always wanted me to have it.

Fire symbolized beauty, fury, and rebirth, she explained. Too bad in my case, it symbolized nothing but my demise.

Grams told me bedtime stories about phoenixes rising from their own ashes. She said that was what Momma wanted for herself—to rise above her circumstances and prevail.

My momma wanted to die and start over.

She only got one out of the two.

But me? I got both.

◆　◆　◆

November 17th, 2017
Sixteen years old

The first time I woke up in a hospital bed, I'd asked the nurse to help me put the ring back on my finger. I brought the ring to my lips and mouthed a wish, like Grandmomma had taught me.

I didn't wish for the insurance money to kick in quickly, or to end world poverty.

I asked for my beauty back.

I passed out shortly after, exhausted by my sheer existence. Asleep, I caught specks of conversations as visitors flooded my room.

". . . prettiest girl in Sheridan. Elegant little nose. Pert lips. Blonde, blue-eyed. Crying shame, Heather."

"Might as well been a model."

"Poor thing doesn't know what she's wakin' up to."

"She ain't in Kansas no more."

I treaded out of the induced coma slowly, not sure what was waiting for me on the other side. It felt like swimming against crushed glass. Even the slightest movement ached. Visitors—classmates, my best friend Karlie, and boyfriend Tucker—came and went, patting, cooing, and gasping while my eyes were closed.

Oblivious to my consciousness, I heard them crying, shrieking, stuttering.

My old life—school plays, cheer practice, and stealing hasty kisses with Tucker under the bleachers—felt untouchable, unreal. A sweetly cruel spell I'd been under that evaporated.

I didn't want to face reality, so I didn't open my eyes, even when I could. Until the very last minute.

Until Tucker walked into my hospital room and slipped a letter between my limp fingers resting on the sheet.

"Sorry," he croaked. It was the first time I'd heard him frazzled, insecure. "I can't do this anymore, and I don't know when you'll wake up. It's not fair to me. I'm too young for . . ." He trailed off, and his chair scraped the floor as he shot up to his feet. "I'm just sorry, okay?"

I wanted to tell him to stop.

To confess I was awake.

Alive.

Well.

Sort of.

That I was buying time, because I didn't want to deal with the new me.

In the end I kept my eyes closed and heard him leave.

Minutes after the door clicked shut, I opened my eyes and let myself cry.

◆ ◆ ◆

The day after Tucker broke up with me in a letter, I decided to face the music.

A nurse skulked into my room like a mouse, her movements hurried and efficient. She eyed me with a mixture of wariness and curiosity, like I was a monster shackled to the bedrails. By the promptness in which she appeared, I gathered they'd been waiting for me to open my eyes.

"Good mornin', Grace. We've been waitin' for you. Sleep well?"

I tried to nod, regretting the ambitious movement immediately. My head swam. It felt swollen and feverish. My face was fully wrapped and bandaged, something I'd noticed the first time I came to. There were tiny gaps in the bandages for my nostrils, eyes, and mouth. I probably looked like a mummy.

"Why, I'll take that little nod as a yes! Are you hungry by any chance? We'd love to take the tube out and feed you. I can send someone over to get you some real food. I believe we're servin' beef patties with rice and banana cake. Would you like that, hon?"

Determined to rise from my own ashes, I mustered all the physical and mental strength I possessed to answer, "That'd be real nice, ma'am."

361

"It'll be here right quick. And I've got more good news for ya. Today is *the* day. Doctor Sheffield is finally gonna take them bandages off!" She tried to inject false enthusiasm into her words.

I flipped the ring on my thumb absentmindedly. I wasn't anywhere near ready to see the new me. Nonetheless, it was time. I was conscious, lucid, and had to face the music.

The nurse filled out her chart and dashed out. An hour later, Dr. Sheffield and Grams came in. Grams looked like hell. Gaunt, wrinkled, and sleep-deprived, even in her Sunday dress. I knew she'd been living in a hotel since the fire and was in a full-blown war with our insurance company. I hated that she'd been going through this alone. Normally, I was the one doing the talking whenever we needed to get things done.

Grams took my hand in hers and pressed it to her chest. Her heart was beating wildly against her ribcage.

"Whatever happens"—she wiped her tears with leathery, shaky fingers—"I'm here for you. You hear that, Gracie-Mae?"

Her fingers froze on my ring.

"You put it back." Her mouth fell open.

I nodded. I was afraid if I opened my mouth, I'd start crying.

"Why?"

"Rebirth," I answered simply. I hadn't died like Momma, but I *did* need to rise from my own ashes.

Dr. Sheffield cleared his throat, standing between us.

"Ready?" He flashed me an apologetic smile.

I gave him a thumbs-up.

Here's to the beginning of the rest of my life . . .

He removed the bandages slowly. Methodically. His breath fanned across my face, smelling of coffee and bacon and mint and that clinical, hospital scent of plastic gloves and sanitizers. His expression did not betray his feelings, though I doubted he had any. To him, I was just another patient.

He didn't offer me any words of encouragement as I watched the long, cream ribbon twirling before my eyes, becoming longer. Dr.

Sheffield removed my hopes and dreams along with the fabric. I felt my breath fading with each twist of his hand.

I tried to swallow down the lump of tears in my throat, my eyes drifting to Grandmomma, searching for comfort. She was by my side, holding my hand with her back ramrod straight, her chin up.

I searched for clues in her expression.

As the bandages curled into a pile on the floor, her face warped in horror, pain, and pity. By the time parts of my face were exposed, she looked like she wanted to shrivel into herself and vanish. I wanted to do the same. Tears prickled my eyes. I fought them out of instinct, telling myself it didn't matter. Beauty was a seasonal friend; it always walked away from you eventually—and never returned when you truly needed it.

"Say somethin'." My voice was thick, low, unbearably raw. "Please, Grandmomma. Tell me."

I'd enjoyed the perks of my looks since I was born. Sheridan High was all about Grace Shaw. Modeling scouts stopped Grams and me when we visited Austin. I was the most prominent actress in school plays and a member of the cheer team. It had been obvious, if not expected, that the splendor of my looks would pave a path for me. With hair rich and gold as the Tuscan sun, a pert nose, and luscious lips, I knew my looks were my one-way ticket out of this town.

"Her mother wasn't worth spit, but luckily Grace inherited her beauty," I once heard Mrs. Phillips telling Mrs. Contreras at the grocery store. *"Let's just hope she fares better than the little hussy."*

Grams looked away. Was it really that bad? The bandages were completely gone now. Dr. Sheffield tilted his head back, inspecting my face.

"I would like to preface this by saying you are a very lucky girl, Miss Shaw. What you went through two weeks ago . . . many people would have died. In fact, I am amazed you are still with us."

Two weeks? I'd been in this bed for fourteen days?

I stared at him blankly, not knowing what he was looking at.

"The infected areas are still raw. Keep in mind that as your skin heals, it will become less agitated, and there's an array of possibilities we can explore down the line in terms of plastic surgery, so please do not be disheartened. Now, would you like to look at your face?"

I gave him half a nod. I needed to get it over with. See what I was dealing with.

He stood up and walked over to the other side of the room, plucking a small mirror from a cabinet, while my grandmomma collapsed on top of my chest, her shoulders quaking with a sob that ripped through her scrawny body. Her clammy hand gripped mine like a vise.

"What am I to do, Gracie-Mae? Oh my lord."

For the first time since I was born, a rush of anger flooded me. It was my tragedy, my life. My *face*. *I* needed to be consoled. Not her.

With each step Dr. Sheffield took, my heart sank a little lower. By the time he reached my bed, it was somewhere at my feet, pounding dully.

He handed me the mirror.

I put it up to my face, closed my eyes, counted to three, then let my eyelids flutter open.

I didn't gasp.

I didn't cry.

In fact, I didn't make a sound.

I simply stared back at the person in front of me—a stranger I didn't know and, frankly, would probably never befriend—watching as fate laughed in my face.

Here was the ugly, uncomfortable truth: my mother died of an overdose when I was three.

She didn't have the rebirth she'd longed for. She never did rise from her own ashes.

And, looking at my new face, I knew with certainty that neither would I.

WEST

November 17th, 2017
Seventeen years old

The best opportunity to kill myself presented itself four months after my seventeenth birthday.

It was pitch-black. A thin layer of ice coated the road. I was driving back from my Aunt Carrie's, sucking on a green candy cane. Aunt Carrie sent my parents food, groceries, and prayers on a weekly basis. It felt crap to admit it, but both my folks couldn't drag themselves out of bed—with or without her religious praying.

Pine trees lined the winding road to our farm, rolling over a steep hill that made the engine groan with effort.

I knew it would look like the perfect accident.

No one would assume any differently.

Just a terrible coincidence, so close to the other tragedy that had struck the St. Claire household.

I could practically envision the headline tomorrow morning in the local newspaper.

Boy, 17, hits deer on Willow Pass Road. Dies immediately.

The deer was standing right there, in the middle of the road, idly staring at my vehicle as I approached at an escalating speed.

I didn't flash my headlights. I didn't pump the brakes.

The deer continued staring as I floored it, my knuckles white as I choked the steering wheel.

The car zipped through the ice so fast it shook from the speed, skidding forward. I could no longer control it. The wheel was not in sync with the tires.

Come on, come on, come on.

I squeezed my eyes shut and let it happen, my teeth slamming together.

The car began to cough, slowing down, even as I pressed my foot harder onto the gas pedal. I popped my eyes open.

No.

The car was decelerating, each inch it ate slower than the previous one.

No, no, no, no, no.

The pickup died three feet away from the deer, coming to a full stop.

The dumb animal finally decided to blink and amble away from the road, its hooves snapping against the ice with gentle *clicks*.

Stupid fucking deer.

Stupid fucking car.

Stupid fucking me, for not hurling myself out of the goddamn pickup when I still had the chance, right off the cliff.

It was quiet for a few minutes. Just me and the deceased pickup and my beating heart, before a scream tore from my throat.

"Fuckkkkkk!"

I punched the steering wheel. Once, twice . . . three times before my knuckles started bleeding. I braced my foot over the console and ripped the steering wheel out of the pickup, dumping it on the passenger seat and raking my fingers down my face.

My lungs burned and my blood dripped all over the seats as I tore everything inside the pickup. I ripped the radio from its hub, throwing it out the window. I smashed the windshield with my foot. Broke the glove compartment. I wrecked the pickup like the deer couldn't.

And yet, I was still alive.

My heart was still beating.

My phone rang, its cheerful tune taunting me.

It rang again and again and fucking again.

I tore it from my pocket and checked who it was. A miracle? A heavenly intervention? An unlikely savior who actually gave a fuck? Who could it be?

Scam Likely

Of course.

No one gave half a fuck, even when they said they did. I boomeranged my cell into the woods then got out of the vehicle and started my ten-mile walk back to my parents' farm.

Truly fucking hoping I'd bump into a bear and let it finish the goddamn job.

ABOUT THE AUTHOR

L.J. Shen is a *Wall Street Journal, USA Today, Washington Post,* and number one Amazon bestselling author of contemporary, new adult, and young adult romance. Her books have been sold in twenty different countries, and she hopes to visit all of them.

She lives in Florida with her husband, rowdy sons, and rowdier pets and enjoys good wine, bad reality TV shows, and reading to her heart's content. Connect with her on her website at www.authorljshen.com or on Instagram (@authorljshen), or join her Facebook group at http://goo.gl/QZJ0NC. Sign up for her newsletter at https://bit.ly/3LhsIrb, and text SHEN to 313131 to get new release alerts (United States only).